I BLEW IT GOOD THIS TIME, A REAL PRODUCTION NUMBER. NOW THEY BOTH KNOW I'M HERE.

The kitchen is cluttered. The morning's dishes are still in the sink. Three cardboard boxes stand on the floor, each half full of wrapped dishes and utensils . . .

So that's it. They're moving.

There's a miasma of oppression and apprehension all through the apartment. Alice's mouth is tighter, her eyes frightened. Lowen comes out into the living room, reluctant and dutiful. Furtively he tests the air as if to feel me in it.

Alice is really shook; takes a cigarette from Lowen's pack and smokes it in quick, inexpert puffs. "You say you can feel her?"

"Yes."

"Where?"

"Somewhere close. Always close to me."

Alice stubs out the cigarette. "And we sure know it's *she*, don't we? . . . I'm *scared*, Lowen. How long have you known?"

"Almost from the start."

"And you never told me."

"Look, Al, I can't tell you how I know, but I don't think she means any harm."

Alice gulps down her sherry and fills the glass. "The—hell—she—doesn't."

—Parke Godwin
from "The Fire When It Comes"

Books by Terry Carr

The Best Science Fiction of the Year #10
The Best Science Fiction of the Year #11
Fantasy Annual III
Fantasy Annual IV
Fantasy Annual V

Published by TIMESCAPE BOOKS

FANTASY ANNUAL V

TERRY CARR, EDITOR

A TIMESCAPE BOOK
PUBLISHED BY POCKET BOOKS NEW YORK

Another *Original* publication of TIMESCAPE BOOKS

A Timescape Book published by
POCKET BOOKS, a Simon & Schuster division of
GULF & WESTERN CORPORATION
1230 Avenue of the Americas, New York, N.Y. 10020

ISBN: 0-671-45436-6

First Timescape Books printing November, 1982

10 9 8 7 6 5 4 3 2 1

POCKET and colophon are registered trademarks
of Simon & Schuster.

Use of the trademark TIMESCAPE is by exclusive license
from Gregory Benford, the trademark owner.

Printed in the U.S.A.

CREDITS

Contents

INTRODUCTION

Fantasy Annual IS, AS ITS TITLE SUGGESTS, A compilation of the best new tales of the fantastic published during the previous year.

Most of these stories will be completely new to you, unless you assiduously read every fantasy magazine that appears—and every science fiction magazine, too. Even if you do, you'll find stories here that have been published in such unusual sources as *High Times,* or only in book form.

Four of the tales in the present book were nominated for the Nebula Award, with Michael Bishop's "The Quickening" winning that award as Best Novelette of the Year. No doubt several of these stories will also be nominated for and may win other awards, too, such as the Hugo Award and the World Fantasy Award.

All types and moods of fantasy are eligible for this book: frightening stories, whimsical ones, tales of adventure and magic. You'll never quite know what's coming next—and that's the point of good fantasy, I think.

—TERRY CARR
April 1982

Let's start with a ghost story . . . but by no means an ordinary one. This tale of a young married couple who move into an apartment haunted by the ghost of an actress who never managed to live her life properly has its share of weird, but it's also about love and the meaning of life itself.

Parke Godwin, author of *Firelord* and co-author (with Marvin Kaye) of *The Masters of Solitude* and *Wintermind,* began writing ten years ago with a suspense novel and then a historical novel, subsequently moving into the fantasy genre with the above novels plus shorter stories published in *Fantasy and Science Fiction, Amazing, Galileo, The Twilight Zone,* and *Gallery.* Further fantasy novels are forthcoming from Berkley and Bantam Books. He says "The Fire When It Comes" began life in late 1973 as a full-length novel that got bogged down. "Only the central character, Gayla, refused to die and moaned periodically, 'Write me . . . write me,' until I just had to resurrect her. I never think of Gayla as a story but a person, very real and alive. I've known dozens like her in show business—beautiful, committed and doomed."

THE FIRE WHEN IT COMES

Parke Godwin

For Betty H.—wherever.

GOT TO WAKE UP SOON.

I've been sick a long time, I mean really sick. Hard to remember why or how long, but it feels like that time I had a hundred-and-three fever for a week. Sleep wasn't rest but endless, meaningless movement, and I'd wake up to change my sweaty night dress for a clean one which would be soaked by sunup.

But this boring, weary dream has gone on for ages. I'm walking up and down the apartment trying to find the door. The furniture isn't mine. People come and go, replaced by others with even tackier sofas in colors loud enough to keep them awake, and I flutter around and past them on my own silly route as if I'd lost an earring and had to find it before I could get on with life. None of it's very real, murky as *cinéma vérité* shot in a broom closet. I have to strain to recognize the apartment, and the sound track just mumbles. No feeling at all.

Just that it's gone on so long.

All right, enough of this. Lying around sick and fragile is romantic as hell, but I have to get it together, drop the needle on the world again and let it play. I'm—

Hell, I am out of it, can't even remember my name, but there's a twinge of pain in trying. Never mind, start with simple things. Move your hand, spider your fingers out from under the covers. Rub your face, open your eyes.

That hasn't worked the last thousand times. I can't wake up, and in a minute the stupid dream will start again with a new cast and no script, and I'll be loping up and down

after that earring or the lost door. Hell, yes. Here it comes.
Again.

No. It's different this time. I'd almost swear I was awake,
standing near the balcony door with the whole long view of
my apartment stretching out before me: living room, pull-
man kitchen, the bedroom, bathroom like an afterthought
in the rear. For the first time, it's clear daylight and the
apartment is bare. Sounds are painfully sharp. The door
screams open and shuts like thunder.

A boy and a girl.

She's twenty-two at the outside, he's not much older. He
looks sweet, happy and maybe a little scared. Nice face,
the kind of sensitive expression you look at twice. The girl's
mouth is firmer. Small and blonde and compact. I know
that expression, tentative only for a moment before she
begins to measure my apartment for possibilities, making
it hers.

"Really a lot of room," she says. "I could do things with
this place if we had the money."

My God, they're so *loud*. The boy drifts toward me
while he bangs cupboard doors, checks out the bathroom,
flushes the toilet.

"The john works. No plumbing problems."

"Al, come here. Look, a balcony."

"Wow, Lowen, is that for real?"

Of course it's real, love. Open the door, take a look and
then get the hell out of my dreams.

"Let's look, Al." He invites the girl with one hand and
opens the balcony door. He's in love with her and doesn't
quite know how to handle it all yet. They wander out onto
my tiny balcony and look down at 77th Street and out over
the river where a garbage scow is gliding upstream. It's a
lovely day. Jesus, how long since I've seen the sun? Kids
are romping in the playground across Riverside Drive.
Lowen and Al stand close together. When he pulls her to
him, her hand slips up over his shoulder. The gold ring
looks new.

"Can we afford it, Lowen?"

"We can if you want it."

"If? I never wanted anything so much in my life."

They hold each other and talk money as if it were a
novelty, mentioning a rent way over what I pay. The frig-
ging landlord would love to hang that price tag on this
place. Lowen points to the drainpipe collar bedded in a

patch of cement, monument to my epic battle with that
bastard to clear the drain and anchor it so every rain didn't
turn my balcony into a small lake. Lowen's pointing to
letters scratched in the cement.

"GAYLA."

That's right, that's me. I remember now.

They look through the apartment again, excited now that
they think they want it. Yes, if they're careful with their
budget, if they get that cash wedding present from Aunt
Somebody, they can work it. I feel very odd; something is
funny here. They're too real. The dream is about them now.

Hey, wait a minute, you two.

The door bangs shut after them.

Hey, wait!

I run out onto the balcony and call to them in the street,
and for the first time in this fever dream, I'm conscious of
arms and legs that I still can't feel, and a fear growing out
of a clearing memory.

Hey, hello. It's me, Gayla Damon.

Lowen turns and tilts his head as if he heard me, or
perhaps for one more look at where he's going to live with
Al-short-for-Alice. I can't tell from his smile, but I lean to
it like a fire in winter, out over the low stone parapet—and
then, oh Christ, I remember. For one terrible, sufficient
flash, the memory flicks a light switch.

If I could cry or be sick, I'd do that. If I screamed loud
enough to crack the asphalt on West End Avenue, nobody
would hear. But I let it out anyway, and my scream fills
the world as Lowen and Al stroll away toward Riverside
Drive.

As if they could actually see me hunched over the balcony edge, head shaking back and forth in despair. They
could will their real bodies to stop, real eyes lift again to a
real, vacant balcony.

Because they're real. I'm not. Not sick or dreaming, just
not.

You died, Gayla baby. You're dead.

The last couple of days have been bad. Panic, running
back and forth, scared to death or life, I don't know which,
trying to find a way out without knowing where to go or
why. I know I died; God, am I sure of that, but not how or
how to get out.

There's no fucking door! Lowen and Al sail in and out

unloading their junk, but when I try to find the door, it's Not, like me. I'm stuck here. I guess that's what frightens all of us because you can't imagine Not. I never bought the MGM version of heaven. For me, being dead was simply not being, zero, zilch, something you can't imagine. The closest you can come is when a dentist knocks you out with Pentothal or how you felt two years before you were born.

No. I don't end, you say. Not me, not the center of the universe. And yet it's happened and I'm stuck with it, no way out, trying to hack the whole thing at once, skittering back and forth from the bedroom to the living room, through the kitchen with its new cream paint, crawling like cigarette smoke in the drapes, beating my nothing-fists against the wall sometimes, collapsing out of habit and exhaustion into a chair or bed I can't feel under me, wearing myself out with the only sensation left, exhaustion and terror.

I'm not dead. I can't be dead, because if I am, why am I still here. Let me out!

To go where, honey?

There's a kind of time again. Al's pinned up a Japanese art calendar in the kitchen, very posh. This month it's a samurai warrior drawing his sword; either that or playing with himself. I can't see it that well, but the date is much too clear. 1981. No wonder the rent's gone up. Seven years since I—

No, that word is a downer. Exited is better. Just how is still a big fat blank wrapped in confusion. All I remember is my name and a few silly details about the apartment. No past, no memory to splice the little snippets of film that flash by too swiftly to catch. Not that it matters, but where's my body? Was I buried or burned, scattered or canned in memoriam in some mausoleum? Was there a husband, a lover? What kind of life did I have?

When I think hard, there's the phantom pain of someone gone, someone who hurt me. That memory is vaguely connected with another of crying into the phone, very drunk. I can't quite remember, just how it made me feel. Got to organize and think. I've worn myself out running scared, and still no answers. The only clear thought is an odd little thing; there must have been a lot of life in me to be kept so close to it.

Don't ask me about death. The rules are all new. I might be the first of the breed. It's still me, but unable to breathe or sleep or get hungry. Just energy that can still run down from overuse, and when that happens, Lowen and Al grow faint.

Everything we do takes energy. A step, a breath, lifting an arm. Because it takes so little, we never notice until we're sick with something like a raging case of flu. That's when we're reminded of the accounting department. Take a step and pant. Take another and stop to rest. Try to walk faster and feel your body straining to function on a fraction of its usual energy. That's all there is to me now, energy, and not much of that. I have to conserve, just float here by Al's painfully correct window drapes and think.

Does anyone know I'm here. I mean, Anyone?

A few more days. Al and Lowen are all moved in. Al's decor works very hard at being House Beautiful, an almost militant graciousness. Style with clenched teeth. And all her china matches; hell yes, it would. But let's face it: whatever's happening to me is because of them. When they're close, I get a hint of solid objects around me, as if I could reach out and touch tables and chairs or Lowen, but touching life costs me energy. The degree of nearness determines how much of my pitiful little charge is spent. Like being alive in a way. Living costs. I learned that somewhere.

Just got the hell scared out of me. Al has a mirror in the bedroom, a big antique affair. Sometimes when she brushes her hair, I stand behind her, aching out of habit to get that brush into my own mop. Tonight as I watched, I saw myself behind her.

I actually jumped with fright, but Al just went on pumping away with the brush while I peered over her head at Gayla Damon. Thirty-three—I remember that now—and beginning to look it. Thank God that won't bother me any more. Yes, I was tall. Brownish-black hair not too well cut. Thin face, strong chin, eyes large and expressive. They were my best feature, they broadcast every feeling I ever had. Lines starting around my mouth. Not a hard mouth but beginning to turn down around the edges, a little tired. Hardness would have helped, I guess. Some of Natalie Bond's brass balls.

Nattie Bond: a name, another memory.

No, it's gone, but there was a kind of pain with it. I

stared at the mirror. Cruddy old black sweater and jeans: was I wearing them? You'd think I could check out in something better. Hey, brown eyes, how did they do you for the curtain call? Touch of pancake, I hope. You always looked dead without it. Oh, shit . . .

A little crying helps. Even dry it's something.

I watch Lowen more and more, turning to him as a flower follows the sun, beginning to learn why I respond to him. Lowen's a listener and a watcher. He can be animated when he's feeling good or way down if he's not. Tired, depressed or angry, his brown eyes go almost black. Not terribly aggressive, but he does sense and respond to the life going on around him.

He likes the apartment and being quiet in it. He smokes, too, not much but enough to bother Al. They've worked out a compromise: anywhere but the bedroom. So, sometimes, I get a surprise visit in the living room when Lowen wakes up and wants a smoke. He sits for a few minutes in the dark, cigarette a bright arc from his mouth to the ashtray. I can't tell, but sometimes it seems he's listening to pure silence. He turns his head this way and that—toward me sometimes—and I feel weird; like he was sifting the molecules of silence, sensing a weight in them. Sometimes in the evening when he and Al are fixing dinner, Lowen will raise his head in that listening way.

It's a long shot hope, but I wonder if he can feel *me*.

Why has he brought me back to time and space and caring? All these years there's been only blurred shadows and voices faint as a radio in the next room. Real light and sound and thought came only when he walked in. When Lowen's near, I perk up and glow; when he leaves, I fade to drift, disinterested, by the balcony door.

Lowen Sheppard: twenty-four at most, gentle, unconsciously graceful, awkward only when he tries to be more mature than he is. Don't work at it, lover, it'll come. Soft, straight brown hair that he forgets to cut until Al reminds him, which is often. She's great on detail, lives by it. Faces this apartment like a cage of lions to be tamed, a little scared of it all. Perhaps it's the best she ever had.

Lowen seems used to this much or maybe better. Mister nice guy, not my type at all, and yet I'm bound to him by a kind of fascination, bound without being able to touch his hair or speak to him. And it's no use wondering why, I'm learning that, too. Like that old Bergman flick where death comes to collect Max Von Sydow. Max says, "Tell me what eternity is like." And Death says, "Who knows? I just work here."

Don't call us. We'll call you.

Well, dammit, *someone* is going to know I'm here. If I can think, I can do, and I'm not going to sit here forever just around the corner from life. Lowen and Al are my world now, the only script left to work with. I'm a part of their lives like a wart on the thigh, somewhere between God and a voyeur.

Wait, a memory just . . . no. Gone too quick again.

If I could touch Lowen somehow. Let him know.

Lowen and Al are settled in, place for everything and everything in its place, and Al daring it to get out of line. Lowen works full time, and Al must do some part-time gig. She goes out in the early afternoon. The lights dim then. Just as well; I don't like what she's done with my apartment. Everything shrieks its price at you, but somehow Al's not comfortable with it. Maybe she never will be. That mouth is awful tight. She wanted to keep plastic covers over the sofa and chairs, the kind that go *crunkle* when you sit on them and make you feel like you're living in a commercial. But Lowen put his foot down on that.

"But Al, they're to use, not just to look at."

"I know, but they're so nice and new."

"Look, I wear a rubber when we make love. I don't need them on the furniture."

She actually blushed. "Really, Lowen."

Son of a—she makes him—? Do guys still wear those things? Whatever happened to the sexual revolution?

It's indicative of their upbringing the way each eats, too. Al sits erect at the table and does the full choreography with her knife and fork, as if disapproving mama was watching her all the time. Cut the meat, lay the knife down, cross the fork to her right hand, spear, chew, swallow, and the whole thing over again. Left hand demurely in her lap.

Lowen leans slightly into his plate, what-the-hell elbows on the table. More often than not, he uses the fork in his left hand, placing things on it with his knife. The way he handles them both, he's definitely lived in England or Europe. Not born there, though. The fall of his speech has a hint of softness and mid-South nasal. Virginia or Maryland. Baltimore, maybe.

Perhaps it's just plain jealousy that puts me off Alice. She's alive. She can reach out and touch, hold, kiss what I can only look at. She's the strength in this marriage, the one who'll make it work. Lowen's softer, easier, with that careless assurance that comes from never having to worry about the rent or good clothes. He's been given to; Al's had to grab and fight. Now he's got a job and trying to cut it on his own for the first time. That's scary, but Al helps. She does a pretty fair job of supporting Lowen without letting him notice it too much.

She has her problems, but Lowen comes first. She gets home just before him, zips out to get fresh flowers for the table. A quick shower and a spritz of perfume, another swift agony at the mirror. And then Lowen is home and sitting down to dinner, telling her about the day. And Al listens, not so much to the words but the easy, charming sound, the quality she loves in him, as if she could learn it for herself. She's from New York, probably the Bronx. I remember the accent somehow. Petite and pretty, but she doesn't believe it no matter how much attention Lowen gives her. Spends a lot of time at the mirror when he's gone, not admiring but wondering. What does she really look like? What type is she, what kind of image does she, should she, project, and can she do it? Lipstick: this shade or that? So she fiddles and narrows her eyes, scrutinizing the goods, hopes for the advertised magic of Maybelline and ends up pretty much the same: more attractive than she thinks, not liking what she sees.

Except she doesn't see. She's carried it around all her life, too busy, too nervous and insecure to know what she's got. Stripped down for a bath, Al looks like she never had a pimple or a pound of fat in her life, but I swear she'll find something wrong, something not to like.

Don't slop that goo on your face, girl. You're great already. God, I only wish I had your skin. The crap I had to put on and take off every night, playing parts like—

Parts like . . .

My God, I remember!

I was an actress. That's what I remember in quick flashes of hard light. The pictures whiz by like fast cars, but they're slowing down: stage sets, snatches of dialogue, dim faces in the front rows. Bill Wrenn giving me a piece of business to work out. Fragments of me like a painting on shattered glass. I grope for the pieces, fitting them together one by one.

Bill Wrenn: there's a warm feeling when I think of him, a trusting. Where did I meet him? Yes, it's coming back.

Bill directed that first season at Lexington Rep. Gentle and patient with a weariness that no longer expected any goodies from life, he always reminded me of a harried sheepdog with too many sheep to hustle. Forty years old, two marriages and struck out both times, not about to fall hard again.

But he did for me. I made it easy for him. We were out of the same mold, Bill and I. He sensed my insecurity as a woman and found ways to make it work for me on-stage, found parts in me I'd never dream of playing. With most men, my whole thing began in bed and usually ended there. Bill and I didn't hurry; there was a love first. We enjoyed and respected each other's work, and theater was a church for us. We'd rehash each performance, sometimes staying up all night to put an extra smidge of polish on business or timing, to get a better laugh, to make something good just a hair better. We started with a love of something beyond us that grew toward each other, so that bed, when it came, was natural and easy as it was gorgeous.

I made him love me, my one genuine conquest. We even talked about getting married—carefully skirting around a lot of if's. I seem to remember him asking me one night in Lexington. I *think* he asked then; there's a thick haze of vodka and grass over that night. Did I say yes? Not likely; by that time the old habits were setting in.

It was too good with Bill. That's not funny. Perfection, happiness, these are frightening things. Very few of us can live with them. After a while, I began to resent Bill. I mean, who the hell was he to take up so much of my life? I began to pick at him, finding things not to like, irritating habits like the nervous way he cleared his throat or dug in his ear when he was thinking out some stage problem; the way he picked his feet in bed and usually left the bathroom a mess. Just bitchiness. I even over-reacted when he gave me notes after a performance. All bullshit and panic; just looking for a way out. How dare you love me, Bill Wrenn? Who asked you? Where did I get that way, where did it begin?

When Nick Charreau came into the company, he was tailor-made for me.

He was alone onstage the first time I saw him, a new cast replacement going through his blocking with the stage manager. Everything his predecessor did, Nick adjusted to show himself in a better light. He wasn't a better actor, but so completely, insolently sure of himself that he could pull off anything and make it look good, even a bad choice. Totally self-centered: if there were critics in the house, Nick lit up like a sign, otherwise it was just another working night in the sticks.

Nick was a lot better-looking than Bill and eighteen years younger. Even-featured with a sharp, cool, detached expression. Eyes that looked right through you. He could tell me things wrong with myself that would earn Bill Wrenn a reaming out, but I took it from Nick. He didn't get close or involved all the way down. Perhaps that's why I chose him, out of cowardice. He wouldn't ever ask me to be a person.

When he finished the blocking session, I came down to lean on the stage apron. "You play that far back, you'll upstage everyone else in the scene."

"It's my scene. I'm beautifully lit up there." Nick's smile was friendly with just the right soupçon of cockiness. A little above us all, just enough to tickle my own self-doubt and make me want to take him on. I can handle you, mister. You're not so tough.

But he was. There was always part of Nick I couldn't reach or satisfy. I started out challenged, piqued, to cut him down to size in bed and ended up happy if he'd just smile at me.

Looking over Al's shoulder in the mirror, I know it's not what we're born but what we're made into. The game is called Hurt me, I haven't suffered enough. I needed a son of a bitch like Nick. You don't think I'd go around deserving someone like Bill, do you?

Call that weird, Alice? You're the same song, different verse. You have that wary, born-owing-money look yourself. You handle it better than I did—you knew a good man when you saw one—but you still feel like a loser.

The fights with Bill grew large, bitter and frequent. He knew what was happening and it hurt him. And one night we split.

"When will you grow up, Gayla?"

"Bill, don't make it harder than it has to be. Just wish me luck."

Dogged, tired, plopping fresh ice cubes into his drink. "I care about you. About you, Gayla. That makes it hard. Nick's twenty-two and about an inch deep. He'll split in six months and you'll be out in the cold. When will you learn, Gay? It's not a game, it's not a great big candy store. It's people."

"I'm sorry, Bill."

"Honey," he sighed, "you sure are."

I still hovered, somehow needing his blessing. "Please? Wish me luck."

Bill raised his glass, not looking up. "Sure, Gay. With Nick you'll need it."

"What's that mean?"

"Nothing, forget it."

"No, you don't just say things like that."

"Sorry, I'm all out of graciousness."

"What did you mean I'll need it."

Bill paused to take a swallow of his drink. "Come on, Gay. You're not blind."

"Other women? So what."

"Other anybody."

"Oh boy, you're—"

"Nick swings both ways."

"That's a lie!"

"He'd screw a light socket if it helped him to a part."

That was the nastiest thing Bill ever said about anyone. I felt angry and at the same time gratified that he made it easier to walk out mad. "Goodbye, Bill."

And then he looked up at me, showing what was hidden before. Bill Wrenn was crying. Crying for me, the only person in this fucking world who ever did. All the pain, anger, loss, welling up in those sad sheepdog eyes. I could have put my arms around him and stayed . . . no, wait, the picture's changing. I'm here in the apartment. *Get him out of here, Nick*—

No, it goes too fast or I will it to go. I can't, won't remember that yet because it hurts too much, and like a child I reach, cry out for the one thing I could always trust.

Bill-l-l—

Not a scream, just the memory of sound.

Lowen looks up from his book, puzzled. "Al? You call me?"

No answer. It's late, she's asleep.

Once more Lowen seems to listen, feeling the air and the silence, separating its texture with his senses. Searching. Then he goes back to his book, but doesn't really try to read.

He heard me. He heard *me*. I can reach him.

Sooner or later he'll know I'm here. Bust my hump or break my heart, I'll do it. Somehow. I've got to live, baby. Even dead it's all I know how to do.

I've hit a new low, watched Lowen and Al make love. At first I avoided it, but gradually the prospect drew me as hunger draws you to a kitchen; hunger no longer a poignant memory but sharp need that grows with my strength.

I've never watched lovemaking before. Porn, yes, but that's for laughs, a nowhere fantasy. One of the character men in Lexington had a library of films we used to dig sometimes after a show, hooting at their ineptitude. They could make you laugh or even horny now and then, but none of them ever dealt with reality. Porn removes you from the act, puts it at a safe distance.

Real sex is awkward, banal and somehow very touching to watch. It's all the things we are and want: involvement, commitment, warmth, passion, clumsiness, generosity or selfishness, giving and receiving or holding back, all stained with the colors of openness or fear, lovely—and very vulnerable. All that, and yet the words are inadequate; you can't get any of that from watching. Like the man said, you had to be there.

Rogers and Astaire these two are not. It's all pretty straight missionary and more of an express than a local. Lowen does certain things and Al tries a few herself, sort of at arm's length and without much freedom. I don't think Lowen's had much experience, and Al, though she needs sex, probably learned somewhere that she oughtn't like it all that much. She's the new generation; she's heard it's her right and prerogative, but the no-no was bred in early, so she compromises by not enjoying it, by making it uphill for both of them. She inhibits Lowen without meaning to. He has to wait so long for her to relax and then work so hard to get her going. And of course at the best moment, like an insurance commercial in the middle of a cavalry charge, he has to stop and put on that stupid rubber.

I wonder if Al's Catholic, she never heard of a diaphragm? Or maybe it's money. That's not so far out. Maybe she's uptight about getting pregnant because she remembers how it was to grow up poor. Maybe it's a lot of things adding up to tense ambivalence, wondering why the bells don't ring and the earth shake like she read in *Cosmopolitan*. I seem to remember that trip.

She doesn't give herself much time to relish it afterward, either. Kiss-kiss-bang-bang, then zip with the Kleenex and pit-pat into the shower as if someone might catch them. Maybe that's the way it was before they married, a habit that set before either of them realized it.

But I've touched Lowen. God, yes, for one galvanized split second I felt his body against me. I paid for it, but it had to be.

It was after they made love and Al did her sprint from bed through the shower and into her nightie-cocoon. Lowen went into the bathroom then. I heard the shower running and drifted in after him.

His body looked marvelous; smooth light olive against Al's blue flower-patterned bath curtains, the soap lather standing out sharp white against the last of his summer tan. Not too muscular; supple like Nick. It'll be a while before he has to worry about weight.

Lowen soaped and rinsed, and I enjoyed the shape of his chest and shoulders when he raised his arms over his head.

You're beautiful, Mr. Sheppard.

I had to do it then. I moved in and kissed him, *felt* his chest, stomach, the bulge of his cock against the memory of my pelvis. Only a second, a moment when I had to hold him.

The sensation that shivered through me was like a sudden electric shock. I pulled back, frightened and hurt, hovering in the shower curtain. Lowen jerked, grabbing for the towel rack, taut, scared as myself. Then, slowly, the fear faded and I saw that listening, probing attitude in the lift of his head before the instinctive fear returned. Lowen snapped the water off, stumbled out of the tub and just sat down on the john, dripping and shaking. He sat there for minutes, watching the water drying on his skin, runnelling down the sides of the tub. Once he put a hand to his lips. They moved, forming a word I couldn't hear.

You felt me, damn you. You know I'm here. If I could just talk to you.

But the exhaustion and pain ebbed me. We slumped at opposite ends of the small bathroom, Lowen staring through me, not hearing the sob, the agony of the pictures that flashed into life. Touching him, I remember. After the shock of life comes the memory, filling me out by one more jagged fragment, measuring me in pain.

Al, Al, frowning at your mirror, wondering what magic you lack—I should have your problem. The guys probably lined up around the block when you were in school. Not for Gayla Damon; hell, that wasn't even my real name, not for a long, hard time. First there was big, fat Gail Danowski from the Bronx like you, and at seventeen what your men prayed for and likely never got, I couldn't give away.

Why do I have to remember that? Please, I tried so hard to get away from it. My father who worked for the city as a sandhog, my dumpy mother with her permanent look of washed-out disgust, both of them fresh off the boat in 1938. My sister Sasha who got married at seventeen to get away from them. Big change: all Zosh did after that was have kids for that beer-drinking slob husband of hers. Jesus, Charlie disgusted me. Sunday afternoons he'd come over and watch football with my father, swill beer and stuff potato chips. Every once in a while he'd let out a huge belch, then sigh and pat his pot gut like he was so goddam pleased with himself. For years, while Zosh's teeth went and her skin faded to chalk delivering five kids.

And me growing up in the middle of it, waiting for the big event of the day in the south Bronx, the Good Humor truck out on the street.

"Mommy, mommy, the goojoomer's here! C'n I have a dime for the goojoomer?"

"Y'fadda din leave me no money."

Urgent jingling from the Good Humor, ready to leave and take excitement with it. "Mommy!"

"Geddouda here. I ain't got no dime, now shaddup."

I used to think about that a lot: a lousy dime. So little and so much to a kid. Go to hell, Momma. Not for the dime, but for a whole beauty you never had and never missed. You weren't going to keep me from it.

It wasn't much better in high school. I was embarrassed to undress for gym because of the holes in my underwear. And the stains sometimes because I had to use Momma's kotex and she didn't care if she ran out. I could have used tampax; virgin or not, I was a big, healthy ox like her and

Zosh. I could have conceived an army. When Momma found the tampax I bought, she slapped me halfway across the room.

"What's this, hah? *Hah?* I ain't got enough trouble, you started already? You sneakin around, you little bitch?"

No such luck, Momma. They didn't want me. The closest I got to boys was talking about them. Sitting in a coffee shop over the debris of my cheap, starchy lunch, the table a garbage dump of bread crusts, spilled sugar and straw wrappers, shredding food bits and paper ends like our envious gossip dissected the girls we knew and the boys we wanted to know.

I never had any sense about men or myself. That happens when you're five foot seven in high school and still growing. A sequoia in a daisy bed, lumpy and lumbering, addicted to food, my refuge when I lost the courage for school dances. I fled home to the ice box and stayed there, eating myself out of my clothes, smearing my acne with pHisoHex, or huddled for hours in a movie, seeing it twice over to pretend I was Hepburn or Bacall, slim, brittle and clever. Or Judith Anderson tearing hell out of *Medea*. I read the play and practiced the lines at my mirror with stiff approximations of her gestures.

But it was *A Streetcar Named Desire* that changed my life. I hardly spoke for days after seeing it. The play stabbed me deep and sparked something that was going to be. I bought more plays and devoured them. Fewer trips to the movies now and more downtown to Broadway and the village. Live theater, not unreeling on a spool, but happening the moment I saw it.

I was still a lump, still a hundred and fifty pounds of un-lusted-after virgin bohunk, and nobody was going to star Gail Danowski in anything but lunch. I walked alone with my dreams while the hungers grew.

You can go a little mad with loneliness, past caring. Virginity? I couldn't give it away, Momma; so I threw it away. No big Zanuck production, just a boy and a party I can't picture too clearly. We were drinking and wrestling, and I thought: all right, why not? Just once I'm gonna grab a little happiness even if it's just getting laid, what am I saving it for? But I had to get drunk before he fumbled at me. If there was pain or pleasure, I barely felt them, only knew that at last I tasted life where it sprang from the fountain. A meager cup, the cut version, the boy pulling at his clothes afterward, distant, disgusted.

"Shit, whyn't you tell me, Gail?"

Tell you what, lover? That I was a virgin, that by accident you were the first? Is that a guilt trip? Whatever I lost, don't mourn it. Cry for the other things we lose in parked cars and motel beds because we're too drunk or there's too much guilt or fear for beauty. It was the beauty I missed. Be first any time, score up a hundred stiff, clumsy girls, say the silly words, break a hundred promises, brag about it afterwards. But leave something of yourself, something of beauty. Only that and you part with a blessing.

He didn't.

The next morning, hung over and miserable, I looked at that frazzled thing in the mirror, had clean through and down to rock bottom, and knew from here on out I'd have to be me or just another Zosh. That day I started to build Gayla Damon.

I graduated an inch taller and thirty pounds lighter, did hard one-week stock as an apprentice. Seventeen hours a day of walk-ons, painting scenery, fencing and dance classes. Diction: practicing for hours with a cork between my teeth—

"Baby, the word is dance. DAAnce, hear the A? Not de-e-ance. Open your mouth and *use* it when you speak."

—Letting my hair grow and moving down to Manhattan, always running away from that lump in the mirror. I never outran her. She was always there, worrying out of my eyes at a thousand auditions, patting my stomach and thighs, searching a hundred dressing room mirrors, plastering pancake on imagined blemishes, grabbing any man's hand because it was there. The years just went, hurrying by like strangers on a street, trailing bits of memory like broken china from a dusty box: buses, planes, snatches of rehearsal, stock, repertory, old reviews.

Miss Damon's talent is raw but unmistakable. When she's right, she *is* theater, vivid, filled with primordial energy that can burn or chill. If she can learn to control . . . she was superbly cast as . . .

—A self-driven horse record-time sprinting from nowhere to noplace. Life? I lived it from eight to eleven o'clock every night and two matinees a week. For three hours each night, I loved, hated, sang, sorrowed enough for three lifetimes. Good houses, bad houses, they all got the best of me because my work had a love behind it. The rest was only filler and who cared? Season after season of repertory, a dozen cities, a dozen summer towns barely glimpsed from opening night to closing, a blur of men and a lot of beds, flush or broke, it didn't matter.

Zosh caught a show once when I was playing in Westchester. Poor Zosh: pasty and fat as Momma by then, busting out of her dresses and her teeth shot. She came hesitantly into my dressing room, wondering if someone might throw her out. The first stage play she ever saw. She didn't know really what to make of it.

"Oh, it was great and all. You look good, Gail. God, you really got some figure now, what size you wear? I never knew about plays. You know me'n school, I always got my girl friend to write my reports."

She barely sipped the scotch I poured her. "Charlie never buys nothin but beer." I wanted to take her out for a good dinner, but no, she had a sitter at home and it was expensive, and Charlie would yell if she came home too late when he was out bowling.

"Let the dumb fuck yell. You're entitled once in a while."

"Hey, you really gettin a mouth on you, Gail."

"Speaking of that, doesn't Charlie ever look at yours? Doesn't he know you need a dentist?"

"Well, you know how it is. The kids take it out of you."

I gave Zosh a hundred dollars to get her teeth fixed. She wrote that she spent it on the house and kids. *There was the gas bill and Christmas. You cant complain theres nobody on the other end of the phone. Ha-ha. My friends all want to know when your on TV.*

Are you still around, Zosh? Not that it matters. They buried you years ago. No one was going to do that to me.

And then suddenly I was thirsty, that big, scary number. Working harder, running harder without knowing where, doing the where-did-it-all-go bit now and then (while the lights caught her best, most expressive angle). Where are you now, Bill? You must be pushing fifty. Still a great lay, I hope. Did you find someone like me or just the opposite. I wouldn't blame you.

And how about you, Nick?

He'll split in six months. You'll be out in the cold.

When Bill said that, I remember thinking: hell, he's right. I'm thirty-two and after that comes thirty-three. Fourteen years, seven dollars in the bank, and where the hell am I?

But I was hung up on Nick's eyes and Nick's body and trying to please him. Perhaps there were other, unspoken things that have nothing to do with loving or sex. You get used very early to not liking yourself. You know you're a fraud, someday they'll all know. The Lump hiding inside your dieted figure and with-it clothes knows you haven't changed, no matter what. The Lump doesn't want to like you. How can she tolerate anyone who does? No, she'll sniff out someone who'll keep her in her lowly place.

Crimes and insanities. Hurting Bill was a very countable sin, but I knew what I needed. So it was Nick, not Bill, who moved in here with me.

And where are you this dark night, Nick? Did you make the big time? I hope so. You're almost thirty now. That's getting on for what you had to sell. Your kind of act has a short run.

My mind wanders like that when Lowen's not around.

Energy builds again, the lights fade up. I drift out onto the balcony, feeling that weight of depression it always brings. My sense of color is dimmed because the kids are asleep. Seventy-seventh Street is a still shot in black and white. Not a soul, not even a late cab whispering up Riverside Drive.

Hey, look! There's a meteor, a falling star. Make a wish: be happy, Bill Wrenn.

And listen! A clock tower. Even with Lowen asleep, I can hear it. Two—three—four o'clock. Definitely, I'm getting stronger. More and more I can feel and sometimes see my legs when I walk, less like floating in a current. I move back through the apartment to hover over Lowen as he sleeps. Wanting. Wondering.

After all this time, why should it be Lowen who wakes me? He felt me in that shower, and we both wonder how, why? Nothing's clear but that I can touch life again with him. If that's wrong, I didn't write the script. Name any form of life you want. A cold germ is just a bug trying to make a living in the only way it knows, in a place it doesn't understand, and it only takes a little out of the place trying. That's me, that's all of us. I'll take what I need to

live. If there's air to breathe, don't tell me I can't. That's
academic.

Al sleeps tiny and still beside Lowen, hardly a bump
under the covers. It must be wonderful to sleep like that.
I could never stay out more than two hours at a time. No,
wait: here she comes up out of it with a sigh and turnover
that barely whispers the covers. She slides out of bed and
pit-pats to the bathroom. Bladder the size of an acorn, up
three times a night like I was.

When the john flushes, Lowen stirs and mumbles, flops
over and sinks again. The bathroom door creaks, Al slips
back in beside him. She doesn't settle down yet, but rests
on one elbow, a momentary vigil over Lowen, a secret
protecting. I'll bet he doesn't know she watches him like
that. Then she slides under the covers very close, one arm
over him, fingers spread lightly on his skin where his
pajama top is unbuttoned.

To lie beside Lowen like that, to touch him simply by
willing it. If that were my hand resting on his skin. What
wouldn't I give for that?

The idea is sudden and frightening. Why not?

If I could get inside Al, stretch out my arm through hers,
wear it like a glove; just for a moment move one real
finger over Lowen's skin. It couldn't hurt her, and I need
it so.

I wait for Al to fall asleep, scared of the whole notion.
It could hurt. It hurt to touch Lowen before. Maybe it's
against some natural law. They're flesh, I'm a memory.
Lots of maybe's but I have to try. Slow and scared, I drift
down over Al and will what shape there is to me into the
attitude of her body. There's no shock when I touch her,
but a definite sensation like dipping into swift-running
water. So weird, I pull away and have to build up my
nerve to try again, settling like a sinking ship as the current
of Al's healthy young life surges and tingles around me,
and her chest rises and falls like a warm blanket over cozy
sleep. My breasts nestle into hers, my arm stretching slowly
to fill out the slim contour of her shoulder, elbow, wrist.
It's hard and slow, like half-frozen syrup oozing through a
hose. My fingers struggle one by one into hers.

So tired. Got to rest.

But I feel life, I *feel* it, humming and bubbling all
around me. Jesus, I must have sounded like a steel mill

inside, the way I drove myself. The power, such a wonder. Why did I waste so much time feeling miserable?

The electric clock glows at 5:03. More minutes pass while each finger tests itself in Al's, and then I try to move one on Lowen's skin.

The shock curdles me. I cringe away from it, shriveling back up Al's arm, all of me a shaky little ball in her middle. Just as in the shower, I felt skin against skin, even the tiny moisture of pores, but it drains me as if I've run five miles.

Rest and try again. Slow, so slow, so hard, but my fingers creep forward into Al's again. Same thing: the instant I let myself feel with Al's flesh, there's a bright shock and energy drains. If that's not enough, those delicate fingers weigh ten pounds each. I push, poop out, rest, try again, the hardest battle of my life, let alone death, and all in dogged silence broken only by their breathing and the muted whir of the clock.

6:32. The dark bedroom grays up to morning. I can see Lowen's face clearly now: very young, crumpled with sleep. He can't hear my soundless, exhausted panting like the heartbeat of a hummingbird.

6:48. Twelve minutes before the clock beeps the beginning of their day, one finger, one slender thread binding me to Lowen . . . moves. Again. I go dizzy with the sensation but hang on, pouring the last of my strength into one huge effort. The small hand flexes all five fingers like a crab, sliding over the sparse hair of Lowen's chest. A flashframe of Bill, of Nick, and a thrill of victory.

Hi, baby. I made it.

Then Al stirs, moves *don't, please, wait!* and flips over on her other side, unconcerned as a pancake. I let go, used up, drifting out to nowhere again, barely conscious of space or objects, too burned out even to feel frustrated after all that work.

But I did it. I know the way now. I'll be back.

Night after night I kept at it, fitting to Al's body, learning how to move her fingers without burning myself out. Stronger and surer, until I could move the whole hand and then the arm, and even if Lowen pressed the hand to his mouth or nestled his cheek against it, I could hold on.

And then I blew it, the story of my life. Klutz-woman strikes again. I tried to get in when they were making love. I said before they're not too dexterous in bed. Al gets uptight from the start, and I can see her lying there, eyes tight shut over Lowen's shoulder, hoping he'll come soon and get it over with. Not always; sometimes she wants it as much as him, but the old hangups are always there. She holds back, so he holds back. It's usually one-sided and finished soon.

But that evening everything seemed perfect. They had a light supper, several drinks rather than the usual one, and Lowen didn't spare the vodka. They just naturally segued to the bedroom, not rushed or nervous, undressing each other slowly, enjoyably, melting into each other's arms. Al brought in a candle from the supper table. Nice touch: Nick and I used to do that. They lie there caressing each other, murmuring drowsily. Lowen looks gorgeous in the soft glow, Al like a little Dresden doll. And me—poor, pathetic afterthought—watching it all and yearning.

Jesus, Al, act like you're alive. That's a man. Take hold of him.

Damn, it was too much. The hell with consequences. I draped myself over Al with the ease of practice, stretched my arms and legs along hers. Foolhardy, yes, but at last *my* arms went around Lowen, smoothing, then clawing down his back.

Love me, baby. Love all of me.

My mouth opened hungrily under his, licking his lips and then nipping at them. I writhed Al's slim body under his, pushed her hands to explore him from shoulders to thighs. I never had much trouble in bed. If the guy had anything going and didn't run through it like a fire drill, I could come half a dozen times, little ones and big ones, before he got there.

With Lowen it was like all the best orgasms I ever had. The moment before you start to go, you want to hold back, prolong it, but you can't. I was dependent on Al's chemistry now. Her body was strangely stiff as I hauled her over on top of Lowen. Something new for her. She went taut, resisting it.

"Lowen, wait."

He can't wait, though I'm the only one who sees the irony and the lie. Lowen is coming, I certainly want to, but Al is out of it. I want to *scream* at her, though I should have guessed it long before this. She always times her cries with his, as if they came together.

But it's a lie. She's faking it. She's learned that much.

My God, you're alive, the greatest gift anyone ever got. Does a past tense like me have to show you how?

With a strength like life itself, I churned her up and down on Lowen, hard, burning myself out to tear Al's careful controls from her emotions. She moaned, fighting me, afraid.

"Lowen, stop. Please stop."

You don't fake tonight, kid.

"Stop!"

No way. Go ... *go!*

Lowen gripped her spasmodically, and I felt his hips tremble under mine/hers. He couldn't hold back any longer. With the last ounce of my will, I bent Al's body down over his, mouth to mouth.

"Now, Lowen. Now!"

Not Al's voice but mine, the first time I've heard it in seven years. Deeper, throatier than Al's. In the middle of coming, an alien bewilderment flooded Lowen's expression. Al stiffened like she was shot. With a cry of bleak terror, she tore herself loose and leaped clear off the bed, clawing for the lamp switch, big-eyed and terrified in the hard light.

"Oh, God. Oh, Jesus, what's happening?"

Confused, a little out of it himself now, Lowen sat up to stare back at her. "Al, what's the matter?"

She shuddered. "It's not me."

"What?"

"It's not *me.*" She snatched up her bathrobe like the last haven in the world. Lowen reached for her instinctively, comforting.

"It's all right, honey, it's—"

"No. It's like something hot inside me."

He went on soothing her, but he knew. I could see that in his eyes as he pulled Al down beside him. He knew: the last thing I saw, because the lights were going down for me, their last spill playing over memory-fragments before fading. A confused montage: Nick putting on his jacket, me fumbling for the phone, then pulling at the balcony door, and the darkness and the silence then were like dying again.

I've had some hangovers in my time, mornings of agony after a messy, screaming drunk. Coming back to queasy consciousness while the night's party repeats in your mind like a stupid film loop, and you wonder, in a foggy way, if you really spilled that drink on somebody, and—oh no— you couldn't have said *that* to him, and if you're going to be sick right then or later.

Then the smog clears and you remember. Yeah. You spilled it and did it and you sure as hell said it, and the five best bloody marys in the world won't help.

I blew it good this time, a real production number. Now they both know I'm here.

December 23. I know the date because Al's carefully crossed the days off her calendar where she never bothered before. I've been turned off for days. Almost Christmas, but you'd never know it around here. No holly, no tree, just a few cards opened and dropped on the little teakwood desk where they keep their bills. When Lowen brushes one aside, I can see a thin line of dust. Al hasn't been cleaning.

The kitchen is cluttered. The morning's dishes are still in the sink. Three cardboard boxes stand on the floor, each half full of wrapped dishes and utensils.

So that's it. They're moving. A moment of panic: where do I go from here, them? All right, it was my fault, but . . . don't go, Lowen. I'm not wild about this script myself, but don't ask me to turn out the lights and die again. Because I won't.

There's a miasma of oppression and apprehension all through the apartment. Al's mouth is tighter, her eyes frightened. Lowen comes out into the living room, reluctant and dutiful. Furtively he tests the air as if to feel me in it. He sits down in his usual chair. 3:13 by the miniature grandfather clock on the book case. The lights and sound come up slowly with Lowen's nearness. He's home early this afternoon.

Al brings out the Waterford sherry set and puts it on the coffee table. She sits down, waiting with Lowen. The whole scene reminds me of actors taking places before the curtain rises, Al poised tensely on the sofa, revolving her sherry glass in white fingers, Lowen distant, into his own thoughts. The sound is still lousy.

". . . feel silly," Lowen ventures. ". . . all this way . . . time off from . . . just to . . ."

"No! . . . live here like this, not with . . ." Al is really shook; takes a cigarette from Lowen's pack on the coffee table and smokes it in quick, inexpert puffs. "You say you can feel her?"

Lowen nods, unhappy. He doesn't like any of this. "I loved this place from the first day."

"Lowen, answer me. Please."

"Yes."

"Where?"

"Somewhere close. Always close to me."

Al stubs out the cigarette. "And we sure know it's *she*, don't we?"

"Al—"

"Oh, hell! I loved this place too, but this is crazy. I'm *scared*, Lowen. How long have you known?"

"Almost from the start."

"And you never told me."

"Why?" Lowen looks up at her. "I'm not a medium; nothing like this ever happened before. It was weird at first, but then I began to feel that she was just *here*—"

"What!"

"—and part of things like the walls. I didn't even know it was a woman at first."

"Until that time in the shower," Al finishes for him. "Bitch."

Thanks a lot, kid. At least I know what to do with him.

"Look, Al, I can't tell you how I know, but I don't think she means any harm."

Al gulps down her sherry and fills the glass. "The—hell —she—doesn't. I'm not into church any more. Even if I were, I wouldn't go running for the holy water every time a floor creaked, but don't tell me she doesn't mean anything, Lowen. You know what I'm talking about." Her hands dry-wash each other jerkily. "I mean that night, the way we made love. I—always wanted to make love to you like that. That . . . free."

The best you ever had, love.

Al gets up and paces, nervous. "All right, I've got these goddam problems. You get taught certain things are wrong. If it's not for babies, it's wrong. It's wrong to use contraceptives, but we can't afford a baby, and—I don't know, Lowen. The world is crazy. But that night, it wasn't me. Not even my voice."

"No, it wasn't."

"All right." Her voice quavers a little as she sits back down. "I loved this place too. But even if I'd been screwing since I was six, I couldn't live with that."

Lowen must be way down, depressed, because my energy

is wavering with his, and sound fades in and out. There's a muffled knock at the door. Lowen opens it to a bald little man like a wizened guru in a heavy, fur-collared overcoat.

Wait, I know this guy. It's that little weasel, Hirajian, from Riverside Realty. He rented me this place. Hirajian settles himself in a chair, briefcase on his knee, declining the sherry Al offers. He doesn't look too happy about being here, but the self-satisfied little bastard doesn't miss Al's legs which make mine look bush league in retrospect.

I can't catch everything but Hirajian's puzzled by something Al's saying. No problem about the lease, he allows, apartments rent in two days now, but she's apparently thrown him a curve.

Al now: ". . . not exactly our wish, but . . ."

"Unusual request . . . never anything . . ."

Now Al is flat and clear: "Did you find out?"

Hirajian opens his briefcase and brings out a sheet of paper while I strain at his through-the-wall mumble.

"Don't know why . . . however, the tenants . . . before you . . ." He runs through a string of names until I make the connection. The tenants who came after me, all those damned extras who wandered through my dreams before Lowen.

Lowen stops him suddenly. He's not as depressed as Al; there's an eagerness in the question. "Did anyone die here?"

"Die?"

"It's very important?" Al says.

Hirajian looks like an undertaker's assistant now, all professional solemnity and reluctance. "As a matter of fact, yes. I was getting to that. In 1974, a Miss Danowski."

Lowen's head snaps up. "First name?"

"Gail."

"Anyone named Gayla? Someone cut the name Gayla in the cement on the balcony."

"That was the Danowski woman. Gayla Damon was her stage name. She was an actress. I remember because she put that name on the lease and had to do it again with her legal signature."

"Gayla."

"You knew her, Mr. Sheppard?"

"Gayla Damon. I should, it's awfully familiar, but—"

"Single?" Al asks. "What sort of person was she?"

Hirajian cracks his prim little smile like a housewife

leaning over a back fence to gossip. "Yes and no, you know show people. Her boyfriend moved in with her. I know it's the fashion nowadays, but *we,*" evidently Riverside and God, "don't approve of it."

There's enough energy to laugh, and I wish you could hear me, you little second-string satyr. You made a pass when you showed me this place. I remember: I was wearing that new tan suit from Bergdorf's, and I couldn't split fast enough. But it was the best place yet for the money, so I took it.

Damn it, how did I die? What happened? Don't fade out, weasel. Project, let me hear you.

Al sets down her sherry glass. "We just can't stay here. It's impossible."

Don't go, Lowen. You're all I have, all there is. I won't touch Al, I promise never again. But don't go.

Of course there were promises, Nick. There's always a promise. No one has to spell it out.

I said that once. I'm starting to remember.

While Hirajian patters on, Lowen's lost in some thought. There's something in his eyes I've never seen before. A concern, a caring.

"You mean he didn't come back even when he heard Gayla was dead?"

I love the way he says my name. Like a song, new strength.

"No end of legal trouble," Hirajian clucks. "We couldn't locate him or any family at first. A Mister . . . yes, a Mister Wrenn came and made all the arrangements. An old boyfriend, I suppose."

You did that for me, Bill? You came back and helped me out. Boy, what I had and threw away. Sand through my fingers.

"Gayla. Gayla Damon." I grow stronger as Lowen repeats my name, stronger yet as he rises and takes a step toward the balcony door. I could touch him, but I don't dare now. "Yes. Just the name I forgot. It's hard to believe, but it's the only thing I can believe."

Such a queer, tender look. Al reads it too. "What, Lowen?"

He strides quickly away to the bedroom, and the lights dim a little. Then he's back with a folded paper, so deep in some thought that Al just stares at him and Hirajian is completely lost.

"The things we learn about life," Lowen says. "An English professor of mine said once that life is too random for art; that's why art is structured. Mr. Hirajian, you said no one else ever complained of disturbances in this apartment. I'm not a medium, can't even predict the weather. But I'm beginning to understand a little of this."

Will you tell me, for Christ's sake?

He hands the paper to Al. It looks like an old theater program. "You see, Mister Hirajian, she's still here."

He has to say it again, delicately as possible. Hirajian pooh-pooh's the whole notion. "Oh really, now, you can't be sure of something like that."

"We know," Al says in a hard voice. "We haven't told you everything. She, it, something's here, and it's destructive."

"No, I don't think so." Lowen nods to the program. I can't see it too well. "Eagle Lake Playhouse, 1974. I saw her work."

You couldn't have. You were only—

"She played Gwendolyn in *Becket*. That's her autograph by her name."

Where the hell is Eagle Lake? Wait a minute. Wait—a—minute. I'm remembering.

"My father was taking me back to school. I spent my whole life in boarding schools all the way through college. Dad thought for our last night together, he'd take me to an uplifting play and save himself making conversation. My parents were very efficient that way.

"Gayla only had one scene, but she was so open, so completely translucent that I couldn't take my eyes off her."

I did play Eagle Lake, and there's a faint memory of some double-breasted country club type coming back for an autograph for his kid.

"I still remember, she had a line that went: 'My lord cares for nothing in this world, does he?' She turned to Becket then, and you could see a *line* in that turn, a power that reached the other actor and came out to the audience. The other actors were good, but Gayla lit up the stage with something—unbearably human."

Damn right, love. I was gangbusters in that role. And you saw me? I could almost believe in God now, though He hasn't called lately.

"I was sixteen, and I thought I was the only one in the

world who could be so lonely. She showed me we're all alike in that. All our feelings touch. Next day I hitchhiked all the way back to the theater from school. . . ." Lowen trails off, looking at Al and the apartment. "And this was her place. She wasn't very old. How did she die?"

"Depressing," Hirajian admits. "Very ugly and depressing, but then suicide always is."

What!

"But as regards your moving out just because——"

The hell I did, no fucking *way*, mister. No. No. NO! I won't listen to any more. Don't believe him, Lowen.

Lowen's on his feet, head tilted in that listening attitude. Al puts down her glass, pale and tense. "What is it?"

"She's here now. She's angry."

"How do you know?"

"Don't ask me how, damn it. I know. She's here."

No, Lowen. On the worst, weakest day of my life, I couldn't do that. Listen. Hear me. Please.

Then Al's up, frightened and desperate. "Go away, whoever you are. For the love of God, go away."

I barely hear her, flinging myself away from them out onto the balcony, silent mouth screaming at the frustration and stupid injustice of it. A lie, a lie, and Lowen is leaving, sending me back to nothing and darkness. But the strength is growing, born of rage and terror. Lowen. Lowen. Lowen. Hear me. I didn't. *Hear me.*

"Lowen, don't!"

I hear Al's voice, then the sudden, sharp sound of the balcony door wrenching open. And as I turn to Lowen, the whole uncut film starts to roll. And, oh Jesus, I remember.

Eagle Lake. That's where it ended, Lowen. Not here, no matter what they tell you. That's where all the years, parts, buses, beds, the whole game came to an end. When I found that none of it worked any more. Maybe I was growing up a little at last, looking for the *me* in all of it.

Funny: I wasn't even going to audition for stock that summer. Bill called me to do a couple of roles at Eagle Lake, and Nick urged me to go. It was a good season, closing with *A Streetcar Named Desire*. The owner, Ermise Stour, jobbed in Natalie Bond for Blanche DuBois, and I was to be her understudy. Nattie's name wasn't smash movie box office any more, but still big enough for stock and star-package houses. She'd be Erm's insurance to make up whatever they lost on the rest of the season.

Erm, you tough old bag. You were going to sell that broken down theater after every season. I'll bet you're still there, chain smoking over a bottle of Chivas and babying that ratty poodle.

Ermise lived in a rambling ex-hotel with a huge fireplace in the lounge. We had all our opening night parties there with a big blaze going because Eagle Lake never warmed up or dried out even in August.

At the opening party for *Becket,* all of us were too keyed up to get drunk, running on adrenalin from the show, slopping drinks and stuffing sandwiches, fending off the local reviewers, horny boy scouts with a course in journalism.

Dinner? No thanks. I've got a horrible week coming up, and it's all I can do to shower and fall into bed. Bill, let's get *out* of here. Thanks, you're a jewel, I needed a refill. Gimme your sweater. Jesus, doesn't it ever get warm in this place? You could age beef in our dressing room.

Nick was down for a few days the week before. Bill rather pointedly made himself scarce. He was still in love with me. That must have hurt, working with me day after day, keeping it inside, and I didn't help matters by dragging Nick everywhere like a prize bull: hey, look what I got! Smart girl, Gayla. With a year's study, you could be an idiot.

But Nick was gone, and we'd managed to get *Becket* open despite failing energy, colds, frayed nerves and lousy weather. It was good just to stand with Bill against the porch railing, watching moths bat themselves silly against the overhead light. Bill was always guarded when we were alone now. I kept it light and friendly, asked about his preparations for *Streetcar.* He sighed with an Old Testament flavor of doom.

"Don't ask. Erm had to cut the set budget, first read-through is tomorrow morning, and Nattie's plane won't get in until one. I'm going to be up all night and I'll still only be about five pages ahead of you people on blocking."

"Why's she late?"

"Who the hell knows? Business with her agent or something. You'll have to read in for her."

Good. One more precious rehearsal on my Blanche, one more time to read those beautiful words and perhaps find

one more color in them before Natalie Bond froze it all in
star glitter. That was all I had to look forward to now. The
fatigue, the wet summer, lousy houses, all of it accumulated to a desolation I couldn't shrug off. I had a small part
in *Streetcar*, but understudying Natalie Bond meant watching her do my role, never to touch the magic myself.
Maybe her plane could crash—just a little—but even then,
what? Somehow even the thought of Nick depressed me.
Back in New York he'd get in to see the right agents where
I couldn't, landing commercials, lining up this, grabbing
that, always smarter at business than me.

That night before the party I sat on my bed, staring
glumly at the yellow-green wallpaper and my battered Sam-
sonite luggage, and thought: *I'm tired of you. Something's
gone. There's gotta be more than this.* And I curled up in
my old gray bathrobe, wallowing in self-pity. Nick, you
want to get married? Bring me the towel and wash my
back? Baby me a little when I feel rotten, like now? There's
a big empty place in me wants to be pregnant with more
than a part. Tired, negative, I knew Nick would never
marry me. I was kidding myself.

So it was good to have Bill there on the porch for a
minute. I leaned against him and he put an arm around
me. We should have gone to bed and let it be beautiful one
more time. It would have been the last.

"Tired, Gay?"

"I want to go home."

Except I never in my whole life found where it was.

Natalie Bond came and conquered. She knew her lines
pretty well going in and crammed the rest with me in her
room or the restaurant down our street. No one recognized
her at first with her hair done just the right shade of
fading dishwater blonde for Blanche, most of her thin face
hidden behind a huge pair of prescription sunglasses. She
was nearsighted to blindness; some of her intensity on film
must have come from trying to feel out the blocking by
braille. But a pro she was. She soaked up Bill's direction,
drove herself and us, and I saw the ruthless energy that
made Nattie a star.

I saw other things, too. Nattie hadn't been on a live
stage for a lot of years. She missed values left and right in
Blanche, and didn't have time to pick them up on a two-
week stock schedule. Film is a director's medium. He can
put your attention where he wants with the camera. Stage

work takes a whole different set of muscles, and hers were flabby, unused to sustaining an action or mood for two and a half hours.

But for the first time that season, we were nearly sold out at the box office. Erm was impressed. Bill wasn't.

"They're coming to see a star. She could fart her way through Blanche and they'll still say she's wonderful."

Maybe, but life wasn't all skittles for Nattie. She had two children in expensive schools and got endless phone calls from her manager in California about taxes.

"I gotta work, honey," she told me over black coffee and dry toast. "The wolf's got my ass in his chops already."

She meant it. Another phone call, and that same afternoon between lunch and rehearsal call, Nattie Bond was gone, and I was sitting in Ermise's living room again while Erm swore back and forth across the worn carpet, waving her drink like a weapon, and Bill tried to look bereaved. He always wanted me for Blanche. He had me now.

"Fucked me from the word go." Ermise sprayed ashes over the rug and her poodle. "She knew this when she signed and never said a goddam word."

The facts filtered through my rosy haze. Natalie's agent had a picture deal on the coast so close to signing that it was worth it to let Ermise sue. They'd just buy up her contract—if she could be in Los Angeles tomorrow.

Ermise hurled her cigarette into the trash-filled fireplace, gulped the last of her drink and turned a mental page. Nattie was one problem, the show another. "You ready to go, Gayla?"

"In my sleep, love."

I was already readjusting the role to the Blanche in my ear and not as sorry for the box office as Erm. Screw 'em all, they were going to see ten times the Blanche Nattie Bond could give them on the best day she ever worked.

"Bill wants me to give you a raise," Ermise said. "Wish I could, Gay, but things are tight."

I pulled the worn script out of my jeans, grinning like a fool back at Bill who couldn't hide his glee any more. "Just pay on time, Erm. Keep out of my hair and don't clutter up my stage. Bill, let's go to work."

From my first rehearsal, the play convulsed and became a different animal. The whole cast had to shift gears for me, but no longer suffused by Nattie's hard light they began to find themselves and glimmer with life. I ate and slept with the script while Blanche came sure and clear. Hell, I'd been rehearsing her for fourteen years. It wasn't hard to identify with the hunger for love half appeased in bed-hopping and sexual junk food and what that does to a woman. The blurred, darkening picture of a girl waiting in her best dress to go to the dance of life with someone who never came.

Play Blanche? Hell, I *was* Blanche. And Stella with her stupid hots for Stanley, Roxane on her silly balcony, loving the wrong guy in the dark for the wrong reasons. I was Ophelia, fucked up and used and never knowing why or how; Alice falling on her butt through the Looking Glass, hunting for a crown on the eighth row that some son of a bitch sawed clean off the board. Man, I was *all* of them, the whole reamed-out world looking up at God and wondering where it all went with nothing to show. I paid my dues.

Then, just as it seemed to be coming together, it went flat, deader than I am now. But out of that death came a beautiful, risky answer.

Blanche DuBois is a bitch of a role and demands a powerhouse actress. That's the problem. Like the aura that surrounds Hamlet, the role accumulates a lot of star-shtick and something very subtle can get lost. I determined to strip away the layers of gloss and find what was there to begin with.

"The part's a trap, Bill. All those fluttery, curlicued lines reach out and beg you to *act* them. And you wind up with dazzle again, a concert performance."

"Cadenzas," he agreed with me. "The old Williams poetry."

"Right! Cadenzas, scales. No, by God! I've played the deep South. There's a smothered quality to those women that gets lost that way. The script describes her as a moth. Moths don't dazzle. They don't glitter."

"Remember that night on the porch," Bill said thoughtfully. "They don't glitter, but they do need the light."

And that was it. Blanche aspired to the things she painted with foolish words. A dream of glitter seen by a nearsighted person by a failing candle. The lines are ornate, but just possibly Blanche is not quite as intelligent as she's been played.

A long artistic chance, but they're the only ones worth

taking. If you don't have the guts to be wrong, take up accounting.

So my Blanche emerged a very pathetic woman, a little grotesque as such women are, not only desperate for love but logical in her hopes for Mitch. For all of Belle Reeve and the inbred magnolias, she's not that far above him. Bill gave me my head, knowing that by finding my own Blanche, even being wrong for a while, I'd find the play's as well. On my terms and with my own reality.

I had three lovely labor-pained days of seeing her come alive. On the third day, I was sitting in a corner of the stage with coffee and a sandwich, digging at the script while the others lunched. When Sally Kent walked in, I snapped at her.

"Where's the rest? It's two o'clock. Let's go."

"They want you over at the office, Gay."

"What the hell for? I don't have time. Where's Bill?"

"At the office," Sally admitted reluctantly. "Natalie Bond is here. She's back in the show."

The kiss of death. Even as I shook my head, no, Erm wouldn't do this to me, I knew she would.

Ermise hunched in a chair by the fireplace, bitter with what she had to do, trying not to antagonize Bill any further. He poised on the sofa, seething like a malevolent cat.

"Nattie will do the show after all," Ermise said. "I have to put her back in, Gay."

I couldn't speak at first; sick, quivering on my feet with that horrible end-of-the-rope hollowness in my stomach. No place to go from here. No place . . .

"When we pulled her name off the advertising, we lost more than a third of our reservations." Erm snorted. "I don't like it. I don't like *her* right now, but she's the only thing'll keep my theater open."

Bill's comment cut with the hard edge of disgust. "You know what this does to the cast, don't you? They've re-adjusted once. Now they have to do it again and open in two days. They were coming beautifully, they were an ensemble with Gayla. Now they're the tail end of a star vehicle."

Bill knew it was already lost, but he was doing this for me.

Ermise shook her head. "Gay, honey, I can't afford it, but I'm gonna raise you retroactive to the first week of your contract." Her hands fluttered in an uncharacteristically helpless gesture. "I owe you that. And you'll go back in as Eunice. But next season—"

I found my voice. It was strange, old. "Don't do this to me. This role, it's mine, I earned it. She'll ruin it."

"Don't look at me," Bill snapped to Ermise. "She's right."

Ermise went defensive. "I don't care who's right. You're all for Gay. Fine, but I can't run a theater that way. Lucky to break even as it is. Nattie's back, she plays and that's the end of it. Gay's contract reads 'as cast'. She's Eunice. What else can I say?"

I showed her what else. I ripped the *Streetcar* script in four parts and threw them in the fireplace. "You can say goodbye, Ermise. Then you can take your raise and shove it." I was already lurching toward the door, voice breaking. "Then you can put someone in my roles, because I'm leaving."

I meant it. Without Blanche, there was no reason to stay another minute. Finished. Done.

Except for Natalie Bond. I found her in her hotel room, already dressed for rehearsal and running over the script.

"Come on in, Gayla. Drink?"

"No."

She read my tension as I crouched with my back against the door. "All right, hon. Get it off your chest."

"I will."

I told the bitch what I felt and what I thought and didn't leave anything out. It was quite a speech for no rehearsal, beginning with my teens when I first knew I had to play Blanche, and the years and hard work that made me worthy of it. There wasn't a rep company in the east I hadn't worked, or a major role from Rosalind to Saint Joan I hadn't played. To walk out on the show like she did was pure shit. To crawl back was worse.

"Right," said Nattie. She faced me all through it, let me get it all out. I was crying when I finished. I sank down on a chair, grabbing for one of her Kleenex.

"Now do you want a drink?"

"Yes, what the hell."

She wasn't all rat, Nattie. She could have put me down with the star routine, but she fixed me a stiff gin and soda without a word. I remember her fixing that drink: thick glasses and no make up, gristly thin. She had endless trouble with her uterus, infection after painful infection and a work schedule that never allowed her to heal properly. A hysterectomy ended the whole thing. Nattie's face was thinner than mine, all the softness gone, mouth and cheeks drawn tight. No matter how sincere, the smile couldn't unclench.

And this, I thought, is what I want to be? Help me, Nick. Take me home. There's gotta be a home somewhere, a little rest.

"Know what we're like?" Nattie mused. "A little fish swimming away from a big, hungry fish who's just about to be eaten by a bigger fish. That's us, honey. And that's me in the middle."

She screwed Ermise but someone shafted her too. The picture deal was a big fat fake. The producer wanted someone a little bigger and hustled Nattie very plausibly to scare the lady into reaching for a pen.

"I'm broke, Gayla. I owe forty thousand in back taxes, my house is on a second mortgage and my kids' tuition is overdue. Those kids are all I have. I don't know where the hell to go from here, but Ermise needs me and I sure as hell need the job."

While I huddled over my drink, unable to speak, Nattie scribbled something on a memo pad.

"You're too good to waste, you're not commercial, and you'll probably die broke. But I saw your rehearsal this morning."

I looked up at her in weepy surprise. The smile wasn't quite so hard just then.

"If I can do it half that well, Gay. Half."

She shoved the paper into my hand. "That's my agent in New York. He's with William Morris. If he can't get you work, no one can. I'll call him myself." She glanced at her dressing table clock. "Time, gotta run."

Nattie divined the finality in my shoulders as I sagged toward the door. "You going to play Eunice?"

"No. I'm leaving."

Pinning her hair, she shot me a swift, unsmiling appraisal through the mirror. "Good for you. You got a man in New York?"

"Yeah."

"Get married," she mumbled through a mouthful of pins.

"It's not worth it." As the door closed, she raised her voice.
"But call my agent."

My bags were packed, but I hadn't bothered to change
clothes. That's why my permanent costume, I suppose.
Who knew then I'd get very tired of black. Bill insisted on
driving me to the airport. When he came for me, I must
have looked pathetic, curled up on the bed in one more
temporary, damp summer room just waiting to eject me.
No love lost; I got damned sick of yellow-green wallpaper.

Bill sat on the edge of the bed. "Ready, love?"

I didn't move or answer. Done, finished. Bill put aside
the old hurt and lay down beside me, bringing me into his
arms. I guess something in him had to open in spite of his
defenses. He opened my heart gently as a baby's hand
clutched around something that might harm it, letting me
cry the last of it out against his shoulder. The light faded
in the room while we lay together.

We kissed goodbye like lovers at the departure gate. Bill
was too much a part of me for anything less. Maybe he
knew better than I how little was waiting for me.

"Be good, Gay."

"You too." I fiddled with his collar. "Don't forget to
take your vitamins, you need them. Call me when you get
back."

He hugged me one last time. "Why don't you marry me
some time?"

For a lot of reasons, Bill. Because I was a fool and
something of a coward. The stunting begins in the seed
when we learn not to like ourselves. The sad thing about
life is that we usually get what we really want. Let it be.

Funny, though: that was my first and last proposal, and
I kissed him goodbye, walked out of his life and four hours
later I was dead.

There was time on the plane to get some of it together.
Natalie was a star, at the top where I wanted to be, and
look at her: most of the woman cut out of her, flogged to
work not by ambition but need. Driven and used. She reminded me of a legless circus freak propelling herself on
huge, overdeveloped arms, the rest of her a pitiful afterthought cared for by an expensive gynecologist. I thought:
at least when I get home there'll be Nick. Don't call him
from the airport, let it be a surprise. We'll get some coffee

and coldcuts from Zabar's, make love and talk half · the
night. I needed to talk, to see us plain.

Get married, Nattie said. It isn't worth it.

Maybe not the way I chased it for fourteen years. I'd
call her agent, keep working, but more New York jobs with
time left over to be with Nick, to sit on my balcony and
just breathe or read. To make a few friends outside of
theater. To see a doctor and find out how tough I really
am, and if everything in the baby box is working right, so
that maybe—

Like she said, so maybe get married and have kids while
I can. A little commitment, Nick, a little tomorrow. If the
word sounds strange, I just learned it. Give me this, Nick.
I need it.

The light was on in our living room as I hauled my suitcase out of the cab and started up. Hell, I won't even buzz,
just turn the key in the lock and reach for him.

I did that.

There was—yes, I remember—one blessed moment of
breathing the good, safe air of my own living room as I set
down the luggage. I heard a faint stirring from the bedroom. Good, I've surprised him. If Nick was just waking
from a nap, we'd have that much more time to touch each
other.

"It's me, baby."

I crossed to the bedroom door, groping inside for the
light switch. "I'm home."

I didn't need the switch. There was enough light to see
them frozen on the torn-up bed. The other one was older,
a little flabby. He muttered something to Nick. I stood
there, absurd myself, and choked: "Excuse me."

Then, as if someone punched me in the stomach, I stumbled to the bathroom, pushed the door shut and fell back
against it.

"Get him out of here, Nick!"

The last word strangled off as I doubled over the john
and vomited all the horrible day out of me, with two hours
left to live, retching and sobbing, not wanting to hear
whatever was said beyond the door. After a short time, the
front door closed. I washed my face, dried it with the stiff,
clumsy movements of exhaustion, and got out to the living
room somehow, past the bed where Nick was smoking a
cigarette, the sheet pulled up over his lean thighs.

I remember pouring a drink. That was foolish on an

empty stomach, the worst thing I could have done. I sat on the sofa, waiting.

"Nick." The silence from the bedroom was the only thing I could feel in my shock. "Nick, please come out. I want to talk to you."

I heard him rustle into his clothes. In a moment Nick came out, bleak and sullen.

"Why are you back so early?"

"No, they—" My reactions were still disjointed, coming out of shock, but the anger was building. "They put Nattie Bond back in the show. I walked out."

That seemed to concern him more than anything else. "You just walked out? They'll get Equity on you."

The delayed reaction exploded. *"Fuck* Equity! Never mind about Equity, what are *we* gonna do?"

"What do you mean?" he asked calmly.

"Oh, man, are you for real?" I pointed at the door. "What was that?"

"That may be a Broadway job." He turned away into the kitchen. "Now get off my back."

"The hell I—"

"Hey look, Gayla. I haven't made any promises to you. You wanted me to move in. Okay, I moved in. We've had it good."

I began to shake. "Promises? Of course there were promises. There's always a promise, nobody has to spell it out. I could have gone to bed with Bill Wrenn plenty of times this summer, but I didn't."

He only shrugged. "So whose fault is that? Not mine."

"You bastard!" I threw my glass at him. He ducked, the thing went a mile wide, then Nick was sopping up whiskey and bits of glass while I shook myself apart on the couch, teeth chattering so hard I had to clamp my mouth tight shut. It was all hitting me at once, and I couldn't handle half of it. Nick finished cleaning up without a word, but I could see even then the tight line of his mouth and the angry droop of his eyelids. He had guts of a kind, Nick. He could face anything because it didn't matter. All the important things were outside, to be reached for. Inside I think he was dead.

"The meanest thing Bill ever said to me," I stuttered. "When I left him for you, h-he said you played both sides of the fence. And I c-called him a goddam liar. I couldn't believe he'd be small enough to—Nick, I'm falling apart.

They took my show, and I came home to you because I don't know what to do."

Nick came over, sat down and held me in his arms. "I'm not, Gayla."

"Not what?"

"What Bill said."

"Then w-what was this?"

He didn't answer, just kissed me. I clung to Nick like a lost child.

Why do we always try to rewrite what's happened? Even now I see myself pointing to the door and kissing him off with a real Bette Davis sizzler for a curtain. Bullshit. I needed Nick. The accounting department was already toting up the cost of what I wanted and saying: *I'll change him. It's worth it.*

I only cried wearily in his arms while Nick soothed and stroked me. "I'm not that," he said again. "Just that so many guys are hung up on role-playing and all that shit. Oh, it's been said about me."

I twisted in his lap to look at him. "Nick, why did you come to me?"

The question gave him more trouble than it should. "I like you. You're the greatest girl I ever met."

Something didn't add up. Nothing ever bugged Nick before; he could always handle it, but he was finding this hard.

"That's not enough," I persisted. "Not tonight."

Nick disengaged himself with a bored sigh. "Look, I have to go out."

"Go out? Now?" I couldn't believe he'd leave me like this. "Why?"

He walked away toward the bedroom. I felt the anger grow cold with something I'd never faced before, answers to questions that gnawed at the back of my mind from our first night. "Why, Nick? Is it him? Did that fat queer tell you to come over after you ditched the hag?"

Nick turned on me, lowering. "I don't like that word."

"Queer."

"I said—"

"Queer!"

"All right." He kicked viciously at the bedroom door with all the force he wanted to spend stopping my mouth. "It's a fact in this business. That's why I get in places you don't. It's a business, cut and dried, not an *aht fawm* like you're always preaching."

"Come off it, Nick." I stood up, ready for him now and wanting the fight. "That casting couch bit went out with Harlow. Is that how you get jobs? That and the cheap, scene-stealing tricks you use when you know and I know I played you against the fucking wall in Lexington, you hypocritical son of a bitch."

Nick threw up a warning hand. "Hey, wait just one damn minute, Bernhardt. I never said I was or ever could be as good as you. But I'll tell you one thing." Nick opened the closet and snaked his jacket off a hanger. "I'll be around and working when nobody remembers you, because I know the business. You've been around fourteen years and still don't know the score. You won't make rounds, you don't want to be bothered waiting for an agent to see you. You're a goddam *ahtist*. You won't wait in New York for something to develop, hell no. You'll take any show going out to Noplaceville, and who the hell ever sees you but some jerkoff writing for a newspaper no one reads. Integrity? Bullshit, lady. You are *afraid* of New York, afraid to take a chance on it."

Nick subsided a little. "That guy who was here, he produces. He's got a big voice where it counts." Again he looked away with that odd, inconsistent embarrassment. "He didn't want to sleep with me, really. He's basically straight."

That was too absurd for anger. "Basically?"

"He only wanted a little affection."

"And you, Nick? Which way do you go basically? I mean was it his idea or yours?"

That was the first totally vulnerable moment I ever saw in Nick. He turned away, leaning against the sink. I could barely hear him. "I don't know. It's never made much difference. So what's the harm? I don't lose anything, and I may gain."

He started for the door, but I stopped him. "Nick, I need you. What's happened to me today, I'm almost sick. Please don't do this to me."

"Do what? Look." He held me a moment without warmth or conviction. "I'll only be gone a little while. We'll talk tomorrow, okay?"

"Don't go, Nick."

He straightened his collar carefully with a sidelong

glance at the mirror. "We can't talk when you're like this. There's no point."

I dogged him desperately, needing something to hang onto. "Please don't go. I'm sorry for what I said. Nick, we can work it out, but don't leave me alone."

"I have to." His hand was already on the door, cutting me off like a thread hanging from his sleeve.

"Why!" It ripped up out of the bottom, out of the anger without which we never love or possess anything. "Because that fat faggot with his job means more than I do, right? How low do you crawl to make a buck in this business? Or is it all business? Jesus, you make me sick."

Nick couldn't be insulted. Even at the end, he didn't have that to spare me. Just a look from those cool blue eyes I tried so hard to please, telling me he was a winner in a game he knew, and I just didn't make it.

"It's your apartment. I'll move."

"Nick, don't go."

The door closed.

What did I do then? I should remember, they were the last minutes of my life. The door closed. I heard Nick thumping down the carpeted stairs, and thank God for cold comfort I didn't run after him. I poured a straight shot and finished it in one pull.

A hollow, eye-of-the-storm calm settled on me and then a depression so heavy it was a physical pain. I wandered through the apartment drinking too much and too fast, talking to Nick, to Bill, to Nattie, until I collapsed, clumsy, hiccuping drunk on the floor with half an hour to live.

Another drink. Get blind, drunk enough to reach . . . something, to blot out the Lump. Yeah, she's still with you, the goddam little loser. Don't you ever learn, loser? No, she won't ever learn. Yesterday did this day's madness prepare. What play was that and who cares?

I tried to think but nothing came together. My life was a scattered tinkertoy, all joints and pieces without meaning or order. A sum of apples and oranges: parts played, meals eaten, clothes worn, he said and I said, old tickets, old programs, newspaper reviews yellowed and fragile as Blanche's love letters. Apples and oranges. Where did I leave anything of myself, who did I love, what did I have? No one. Nothing.

Only Bill Wrenn.

"Christ, Bill, help me!"

I clawed for the phone with the room spinning and managed to call the theater. One of the girl apprentices answered. I struggled to make myself understood with a thickening tongue. "Yeah, Bill Wrenn, 'simportant. Gayla Damon. Yeah, hi, honey. He's not? Goddammit, he's *gotta* be. I *need* him. When'll he be back? Yeah . . . yeah. Tell'm call Gayla, please. Please. Yeah, trouble. Real trouble. I need him."

That's how it happened. I dropped the phone in the general vicinity of the hook and staggered to the pitching sink to make one more huge, suicidal drink, crying and laughing, part drunk, part hysteria. But Bill was going to bail me out like he always had, and, boy, ol' Gay had learned her lesson. I was a fool to leave him. He loved me. Bill loved me and I was afraid of that. Afraid to be loved. How dumb can you get?

"How dumb?" I raged mushily at the Lump in the mirror. "You with the great, soulful eyes. You never knew shit, baby."

I was sweating. The wool sweater oppressed my clammy skin. Some sober molecule said take it off, but no. It's cooler out on my balcony. I will go out on my beautiful, nighted balcony and present my case to the yet unknowing world.

I half fell through the door. The balcony had a low railing, lower than I judged as I stumbled and heaved my drunken weight behind the hand flung out to steady myself and—

Fell. No more time.

That's it, finished. Now I've remembered. It was that sudden, painless, meaningless. No fade out, no end title music resolving the conflict themes, only torn film fluttering past the projector light, leaving a white screen.

There's a few answers anyway. I could get a lump in my throat, if I had one, thinking how Bill came and checked me out. God, let's hope they kept me covered. I must have looked awful. Poor Bill; maybe I gave you such a rotten time because I knew you could take it and still hang in. That's one of the faces of love, Mister Wrenn.

But I'd never have guessed about Lowen. Just imagine: he saw me that long ago and remembered all these years because I showed him he wasn't alone. I still can't add it up. Apples and oranges.

Unless, just maybe ...

"Lowen!"

The sound track again, the needle dropped on time. The balcony door thunders open and slams shut. Al calls again, but Lowen ignores her, leaning against the door, holding it closed.

"Gayla?"

His eyes move searchingly over the balcony in the darkening winter afternoon. From my name etched in the cement, around the railing, Lowen's whole concentrated being probes the gray light and air, full of purpose and need.

"Gayla, I know you're here."

As he says my name, sound and vision and my own strength treble. I turn to him, wondering if through the sheer power of his need he can see me yet.

Lowen, can you hear me?

"I think I know what this means."

I stretch out my hand, open up, let it touch his face, and as I tingle and hurt with it, Lowen turns his cheek into the caress.

"Yes, I feel you close."

Talk to me, Lowen.

"Isn't it strange, Gayla?"

Not strange at all, not us.

"When I saw you that night, I wanted to reach out and touch you, but I was just too shy. Couldn't even ask for my own autograph."

Why not? I could have used a little touching.

"But I hitched all the way from school next day just to catch a glimpse of you. Hid in the back of the theater and watched you rehearse."

That was Blanche. You saw that?

"It was the same thing all over again. You had something that reached out and showed me how we're all alike. I never saw a lonelier person than you on that stage. Or more beautiful. I cried."

You saw Blanche. She did have a beauty.

"Oh, Gayla, the letters I wrote you and never sent. Forgive me. I forgot the name but not the lesson. If you can hear me: you were the first woman I ever loved, and you taught me right. It's a giving."

I hear Al's urgent knock on the other side of the door. "Lowen, what is it? Are you all right?"

He turns his head and smiles. God, he's beautiful. "Fine, Al. She loves this place, Gayla. Don't drive her away."

I won't, but don't go. Not now when I'm beginning to understand so much.

He shakes his head. "This is our first house. We're new, all kinds of problems. Parents, religion, everything."

Can you *hear* me?

"We were never loved by anyone before, either of us. That's new, too. You pray for it—"

Like a fire.

"—like a fire to warm yourself."

You do hear me.

"But it's scary. What do you do with the fire when it comes?" Lowen's hands reach out, pleading. "Don't take this away from her. Don't hurt my Al. You're stronger than us. You can manage."

I stretch my hand to touch his. With all my will, I press the answer through the contact.

Promise, Lowen.

"Don't make me shut you out. I don't know if I could. Go away and keep our secret? Take a big piece of love with you?"

Yes. Just that I was reaching for something, like you, and I had it all the time. So do you, Lowen. You're a—

I feel again as I did when the star fell across the sky, joyful and new and big as all creation without needing a reason, as Lowen's real fingers close around the memory of mine.

You're a *mensche*, love. Like me.

Lowen murmurs: "I feel your hand. I don't care what anyone says. Your kind of woman doesn't kill herself. I'll never believe it."

Bet on it. And thank you.

So it was a hell of a lot more than apples and oranges. It was a giving, a love. Hear that, Bill? Nattie? What I called life was just the love, the giving, like kisses on the wind, thrown to the audience, to my work, to the casual men, to whom it may concern. I was a giver, and if the little takers like Nick couldn't dig that, tough. That's the way it went down. All the miserable, self-cheating years, something heard a music and went on singing. If Nattie could do it half as well. If she was half as alive as me, she meant. I loved all my life, because they're the same thing. Man, I was beautiful.

That's the part of you that woke me, Lowen. You're green, but you won't go through life like a tourist. You're going to get hurt and do some hurting yourself, but maybe someday . . .

That's it, Lowen. That's the plot. You said it: we all touch, and the touching continues us. All those nights, throwing all of myself at life, and who's to say I did it alone? So when you're full up with life, maybe you'll wake like me to spill it over into some poor, scared guy or girl. You're full of life like me, Lowen. It's a beautiful, rare gift.

It's dark enough now to see stars and the fingernail sliver of moon. A lovely moment for Lowen and me, like a night with Bill a moment before we made love for the first time. Lowen and I holding hands in the evening. Understanding. His eyes move slowly from my hand up toward my face.

"Gayla, I can see you."

Can you, honest?

"Very clear. You're wearing a sweater and jeans. And you're smiling."

Am I ever!

"And very beautiful."

Bet your ass, love. I feel great, like I finally got it together.

One last painful, lovely current of life as Lowen squeezes my hand. "Goodbye, Gayla."

So long, love.

Lowen yanks open the door. "Al, Mister Hirajian? Come on out. It's a lovely evening."

Alice peeks out to see Lowen leaning over the railing, enjoying the river and the early stars. His chest swells; he's laughing and he looks marvelous, inviting Al into his arms the way he did on their first day here. She comes unsurely to nestle in beside him, one arm around his waist. "Who were you talking to?"

"She's gone, Al. You've got nothing to be afraid of. Except being afraid."

"Lowen, I'm not going to—"

"This is our house, and nobody's going to take it away from us." He turns Al to him and kisses her. "Nobody wants to, that's a promise. So don't run away from it or yourself."

She shivers a little, still uncertain. "Do you really think we can stay. I can't—"

"Hey, love." Lowen leans into her, cocky and charming

but meaning it. "Don't tell a *mensche* what you can't. Hey, Hirajian."

When the little prune pokes his head out the door, Lowen sweeps his arm out over the river and the whole lit-up west side. "Sorry for all the trouble, but we've changed our minds. I mean, look at it! Who could give up a balcony with a view like this?"

He's the last thing I see before the lights change: Lowen holding Al and grinning out at the world. I thought the lights were dimming, but it's something else, another cue coming up. The lights cross-fade up, up, more pink and amber, until—my God, it's gorgeous!

I'm not dead, not gone. I feel more alive than ever. I'm Gail and Gayla and Lowen and Bill and Al and all of them magnified, heightened, fully realized, flowing together like bright, silver streams into—

Will you look at that *set*. Fantastic. Who's on the lights?

So that's what You look like. Ri-i-ght. I'm with it now, and I love You too. Give me a follow-spot, Baby.

I'm on.

Most of us have known people of great potential whom we liked and perhaps even loved,
but whose lives went downhill into tragedy.
When they asked for help, years after drifting
away from us, were we too busy with our own
lives to answer? Here's an eerie story of one
such person and how she caused people to remember her.

George R. R. Martin has won both Hugo and
Nebula Awards for stories such as "A Song for
Lya" and "Sandkings," each of which became
title stories of collections of his shorter work.
His novels include *Dying of the Light* and *Wind-
haven,* the latter written in collaboration with
Lisa Tuttle.

REMEMBERING MELODY

George R. R. Martin

TED WAS SHAVING WHEN THE DOORBELL sounded. It startled him so badly that he cut himself. His condominium was on the thirty-second floor, and Jack the doorman generally gave him advance warning of any prospective visitors. This had to be someone from the building, then. Except that Ted didn't know anyone in the building, at least not beyond the trade-smiles-in-the-elevator level.

"Coming," he shouted. Scowling, he snatched up a towel and wiped the lather from his face, then dabbed at his cut with a tissue. "Shit," he said loudly to his face in the mirror. He had to be in court this afternoon. If this was another Jehovah's Witness like the one who'd gotten past Jack last month, they were going to be in for a very rough time indeed.

The buzzer buzzed again. "Coming, dammit," Ted yelled. He made a final dab at the blood on his neck, then threw the tissue into the wastebasket and strode across the sunken living room to the door. He peered through the eyehole carefully before he opened. "Oh, hell," he muttered. Before she could buzz again, Ted slid off the chain and threw open the door.

"Hello, Melody," he said.

She smiled wanly. "Hi, Ted," she replied. She had an old suitcase in her hand, a battered cloth bag with a hideous red-and-black plaid pattern, its broken handle replaced by a length of rope. The last time Ted had seen her, three years before, she'd looked terrible. Now she looked worse. Her clothes—shorts and a tie-dyed T-shirt—were wrinkled

50

and dirty, and emphasized how gaunt she'd become. Her ribs showed through plainly; her legs were pipestems. Her long stringy blond hair hadn't been washed recently, and her face was red and puffy, as if she'd been crying. That was no surprise. Melody was always crying about one thing or another.

"Aren't you going to ask me in, Ted?"

Ted grimaced. He certainly didn't *want* to ask her in. He knew from past experience how difficult it was to get her out again. But he couldn't just leave her standing in the hall with her suitcase in hand. After all, he thought sourly, she was an old and dear friend. "Oh, sure," he said. He gestured. "Come on in."

He took her bag from her and set it by the door, then led her into the kitchen and put on some water to boil. "You look as though you could use a cup of coffee," he said, trying to keep his voice friendly.

Melody smiled again. "Don't you remember, Ted? I don't drink coffee. It's no good for you, Ted. I used to tell you that. Don't you remember?" She got up from the kitchen table and began rummaging through his cupboards. "Do you have any hot chocolate?" she asked. "I like hot chocolate."

"I don't drink hot chocolate," he said. "Just a lot of coffee."

"You shouldn't," she said. "It's no good for you."

"Yeah," he said. "Do you want juice? I've got juice."

Melody nodded. "Fine."

He poured her a glass of orange juice and led her back to the table, then spooned some Maxim into a mug while he waited for his kettle to whistle. "So," he asked, "what brings you to Chicago?"

Melody began to cry. Ted leaned back against the stove and watched her. She was a very noisy crier, and she produced an amazing amount of tears for someone who cried so often. She didn't look up until the water began to boil. Ted poured some into his cup and stirred in a teaspoon of sugar. Her face was redder and puffier than ever. Her eyes fixed on him accusingly. "Things have been real bad," she said. "I need help, Ted. I don't have anyplace to live. I thought maybe I could stay with you awhile. Things have been real bad."

"I'm sorry to hear that, Melody," Ted replied, sipping at his coffee thoughtfully. "You can stay here for a few days, if you want. But no longer. I'm not in the market for a roommate." She always made him feel like such a bastard, but it was better to be firm with her right from the start.

Melody began to cry again when he mentioned roommates. "You used to say I was a *good* roommate," she whined. "We used to have fun, don't you remember? You were my friend."

Ted set down his coffee mug and looked at the kitchen clock. "I don't have time to talk about old times right now," he said. "I was shaving when you rang. I've got to get to the office." He frowned. "Drink your juice and make yourself at home. I've got to get dressed." He turned abruptly and left her weeping at the kitchen table.

Back in the bathroom, Ted finished shaving and tended to his cut more properly, his mind full of Melody. Already he could tell that this was going to be difficult. He felt sorry for her—she was messed up and miserably unhappy, with no one to turn to—but he wasn't going to let her inflict all her troubles on him. Not this time. She'd done it too many times before.

In his bedroom, Ted stared pensively into the closet for a long time before selecting the gray suit. He knotted his tie carefully in the mirror, scowling at his cut. Then he checked his briefcase to make sure all the papers on the Syndio case were in order, nodded, and walked back into the kitchen.

Melody was at the stove, making pancakes. She turned and smiled at him happily when he entered. "You remember my pancakes, Ted?" she asked. "You used to love it when I made pancakes, especially blueberry pancakes, you remember? You didn't have any blueberries, though, so I'm just making plain. Is that all right?"

"Jesus," Ted muttered. "Dammit, Melody, who said you should make *anything?* I told you I had to get to the office. I don't have time to eat with you. I'm late already. Anyway, I don't eat breakfast. I'm trying to lose weight."

Tears began to trickle from her eyes again. "But—but these are my special pancakes, Ted. What am I going to do with them? What am I going to *do?*"

"Eat them," Ted said. "You could use a few extra pounds. Jesus, you look terrible. You look like you haven't eaten for a month."

Melody's face screwed up and became ugly. "You bastard," she said. "You're supposed to be my *friend*."

Ted sighed. "Take it easy," he said. He glanced at his watch. "Look, I'm fifteen minutes late already. I've got to go. You eat your pancakes and get some sleep. I'll be back around six. We can have dinner together and talk, all right? Is that what you want?"

"That would be nice," she said, suddenly contrite. "That would be real nice."

"Tell Jill I want to see her in my office, right away," Ted snapped to the secretary when he arrived. "And get us some coffee, will you? I really need some coffee."

"Sure."

Jill arrived a few minutes after the coffee. She and Ted were associates in the same law firm. He motioned her to a seat and pushed a cup at her. "Sit down," he said. "Look, the date's off tonight. I've got problems."

"You look it," she said. "What's wrong?"

"An old friend showed up on my doorstep this morning."

Jill arched one elegant eyebrow. "So?" she said. "Reunions can be fun."

"Not with Melody they can't."

"Melody?" she said. "A pretty name. An old flame, Ted? What is it, unrequited love?"

"No," he said, "no, it wasn't like that."

"Tell me what it was like, then. You know I love the gory details."

"Melody and I were roommates back in college. Not just us—don't get the wrong idea. There were four of us. Me and a guy named Michael Englehart, Melody and another girl, Anne Kaye. The four of us shared a big run-down house for two years. We were—friends."

"Friends?" Jill looked skeptical.

Ted scowled at her. "Friends," he repeated. "Oh, hell, I slept with Melody a few times. With Anne, too. And both of them balled Michael a time or two. But when it happened, it was just kind of—kind of *friendly*, you know? Our love lives were mostly with outsiders. We used to tell each other our troubles, swap advice, cry on one another's shoulders. Hell, I know it sounds weird. It was 1970, though. I had hair down to my ass. Everything was weird." He sloshed the dregs of his coffee around in the cup and looked pensive. "They were good times, too. Special times. Sometimes I'm sorry they had to end. The four of us were close, really close. I loved those people."

"Watch out," Jill said, "I'll get jealous. My roommate and I cordially despised each other." She smiled. "So what happened?"

Ted shrugged. "The usual story," he said. "We graduated, drifted apart. I remember the last night in the old house. We smoked a ton of dope and got very silly. Swore eternal friendship. We weren't ever going to be strangers, no matter what happened, and if any of us ever needed help, well, the other three would always be there. We sealed the bargain with—well, kind of an orgy."

Jill smiled. "Touching," she said. "I never dreamed you had it in you."

"It didn't last, of course," Ted continued. "We tried, I'll give us that much. But things changed too much. I went on to law school, wound up here in Chicago. Michael got a job with a publishing house in New York City. He's an editor at Random House now, been married and divorced, two kids. We used to write. Now we trade Christmas cards. Anne's a teacher. She was down in Phoenix the last I heard, but that was four, five years ago. Her husband didn't like the rest of us much, the one time we had a reunion. I think Anne must have told him about the orgy."

"And your house guest?"

"Melody," he sighed. "She became a problem. In college, she was wonderful: gutsy, pretty, a real free spirit. But afterwards, she couldn't cut it. She tried to make it as a painter for a couple of years, but she wasn't good enough. Got nowhere. She went through a couple of relationships that turned sour, then married some guy about a week after she'd met him in a singles bar. That was terrible. He used to get drunk and beat her. She took about six months of it, and finally got a divorce. He still came around to beat her up for a year, until he finally got frightened off. After that, Melody got into drugs—bad. She spent some time in an asylum. When she got out, it was more of the same. She can't hold a job or stay away from drugs. Her relationships don't last more than a few weeks. She's let her body go to hell." He shook his head.

Jill pursed her lips. "Sounds like a lady who needs help," she said.

Ted flushed and grew angry. "You think I don't know

that? You think we haven't tried to help her? *Jesus!* When she was trying to be an artist, Michael got her a couple of cover assignments from the paperback house he was with. Not only did she blow the deadlines, but she got into a screaming match with the art director. Almost cost Michael his job. I flew to Cleveland and handled her divorce for her, gratis. Flew back a couple of months later and spent quite a while there trying to get the cops to give her protection against her ex-hubby. Anne took her in when she had no place to live, got her into a drug rehabilitation program. In return, Melody tried to seduce her boyfriend— said she wanted to *share* him, like they'd done in the old days. All of us have lent her money. She's never paid back any of it. And we've listened to her troubles, God but we've listened to her troubles. There was a period a few years ago when she'd phone every week, usually collect, with some new sad story. She cried over the phone a lot. If *Queen for a Day* was still on TV, Melody would be a natural!"

"I'm beginning to see why you're not thrilled by her visit," Jill said dryly. "What are you going to do?"

"I don't know," Ted replied. "I shouldn't have let her in. The last few times she's called, I just hung up on her, and that seemed to work pretty well. Felt guilty about it at first, but that passed. This morning, though, she looked so pathetic that I didn't know how to send her away. I suppose eventually I'll have to get brutal and go through a scene. Nothing else works. She'll make a lot of accusations, remind me of what good friends we were and the promises we made, threaten to kill herself. Fun times ahead."

"Can I help?" Jill asked.

"Pick up my pieces afterwards," Ted said. "It's always nice to have someone around afterwards to tell you that you're not a son-of-a-bitch even though you just kicked an old dear friend out into the gutter."

He was terrible in court that afternoon. His thoughts were full of Melody, and the strategies that most occupied him concerned how to get rid of her most painlessly, instead of the case at hand. Melody had danced flamenco on his psyche too many times before; Ted wasn't going to let her leech off him this time, nor leave him an emotional wreck.

When he got back to his condo with a bag of Chinese food under his arm—he'd decided he didn't want to take her out to a restaurant—Melody was sitting nude in the middle of his conversation pit, giggling and sniffing some white powder. She looked up at Ted happily when he entered. "Here," she said. "I scored some coke."

"Jesus," he swore. He dropped the Chinese food and his briefcase, and strode furiously across the carpet. "I don't *believe* you," he roared. "I'm a *lawyer,* for Chrissakes. Do you want to get me disbarred?"

Melody had the coke in a little paper square and was sniffing it from a rolled-up dollar bill. Ted snatched it all away from her, and she began to cry. He went to the bathroom and flushed it down the toilet, dollar bill and all. Except it wasn't a dollar bill, he saw as it was sucked out of sight. It was a twenty. That made him even angrier. When he returned to the living room, Melody was still crying.

"Stop that," he said. "I don't want to hear it. And put some clothes on." Another suspicion came to him. "Where did you get the money for that stuff?" he demanded. "Huh, *where?*"

Melody whimpered. "I sold some stuff," she said in a timid voice. "I didn't think you'd mind. It was good coke." She shied away from him and threw an arm across her face, as if Ted was going to hit her.

Ted didn't need to ask whose stuff she'd sold. He knew; she'd pulled the same trick on Michael years before, or so he'd heard. He sighed. "Get dressed," he repeated wearily. "I brought Chinese food." Later he could check what was missing and phone the insurance company.

"Chinese food is no good for you," Melody said. "It's full of monosodium glutamate. Gives you headaches, Ted." But she got to her feet obediently, if a bit unsteadily, went off towards the bathroom, and came back a few minutes later wearing a halter top and a pair of ratty cutoffs. Nothing else, Ted guessed. A couple of years ago she must have decided that underwear was no good for you.

Ignoring her comment about monosodium glutamate, Ted found some plates and served up the Chinese food in his dining nook. Melody ate it meekly enough, drowning everything in soy sauce. Every few minutes she giggled at some private joke, then grew very serious again and resumed eating. When she broke open her fortune cookie, a wide smile lit her face. "Look, Ted," she said happily, passing the little slip of paper across to him.

He read it. OLD FRIENDS ARE THE BEST

FRIENDS, it said. "Oh, shit," he muttered. He didn't even open his own. Melody wanted to know why. "You ought to read it, Ted," she told him. "It's bad luck if you don't read your fortune cookie."

"I don't want to read it," he said. "I'm going to change out of this suit." He rose. "Don't do anything."

But when he came back, she'd put an album on the stereo. At least she hadn't sold that, he thought gratefully.

"Do you want me to dance for you?" she asked. "Remember how I used to dance for you and Michael? Real sexy. . . . You used to tell me how good I danced. I could of been a dancer if I'd wanted." She did a few dance steps in the middle of his living room, stumbled, and almost fell. It was grotesque.

"Sit down, Melody," Ted said, as sternly as he could manage. "We have to talk."

She sat down.

"Don't cry," he said before he started. "You understand that? I don't want you to cry. We can't talk if you're going to cry every time I say anything. You start crying and this conversation is over."

Melody nodded. "I won't cry, Ted," she said. "I feel much better now than this morning. I'm with you now. You make me feel better."

"You're *not* with me, Melody. Stop that."

Her eyes filled up with tears. "You're my friend, Ted. You and Michael and Anne, you're the special ones."

He sighed. "What's wrong, Melody? Why are you here?"

"I lost my job, Ted," she said.

"The waitress job?" he asked. The last time he'd seen her, three years ago, she'd been waiting tables in a bar in Kansas City.

Melody blinked at him, confused. "Waitress?" she said. "No, Ted. That was before. That was in Kansas City. Don't you remember?"

"I remember very well," he said. "What job was it you lost?"

"It was a shitty job," Melody said. "A factory job. It was in Iowa. In Des Moines. Des Moines is a shitty place. I didn't come to work, so they fired me. I was strung out, you know? I needed a couple days off. I would have come back to work. But they fired me." She looked close to tears again. "I haven't had a good job in a long time, Ted. I was an art major. You remember? You and Michael and Anne used to have my drawings hung up in your rooms. You still have my drawings, Ted?"

"Yes," he lied. "Sure. Somewhere." He'd gotten rid of them years ago. They reminded him too much of Melody, and that was too painful.

"Anyway, when I lost my job, Johnny said I wasn't bringing in any money. Johnny was the guy I lived with. He said he wasn't gonna support me, that I had to get some job, but I couldn't. I *tried*, Ted, but I couldn't. So Johnny talked to some man, and he got me this job in a massage parlor, you know. And he took me down there, but it was crummy. I didn't want to work in no massage parlor, Ted. I used to be an art major."

"I remember, Melody," Ted said. She seemed to expect him to say something.

Melody nodded. "So I didn't take it, and Johnny threw me out. I had no place to go, you know. And I thought of you, and Anne, and Michael. Remember the last night? We all said that if anyone ever needed help . . ."

"I remember, Melody," Ted said. "Not as often as you do, but I remember. You don't ever let any of us forget it, do you? But let it pass. What do you want this time?" His tone was flat and cold.

"You're a lawyer, Ted," she said.

"Yes."

"So, I thought—" Her long, thin fingers plucked nervously at her face. "I thought maybe you could get me a job. I could be a secretary, maybe. In your office. We could be together again, every day, like it used to be. Or maybe—" She brightened visibly. "—maybe I could be one of those people who draw pictures in the courtroom. You know. Like of Patty Hearst and people like that. On TV. I'd be good at that."

"Those artists work for the TV stations," Ted said patiently. "And there are no openings in my office. I'm sorry, Melody. I can't get you a job."

Melody took that surprisingly well. "All right, Ted," she said. "I can find a job, I guess. I'll get one all by myself. Only—only let me live here, okay? We can be roommates again."

"Oh, Jesus," Ted said. He sat back and crossed his arms. "No," he said flatly.

Melody took her hand away from her face and stared at him imploringly. "Please, Ted," she whispered. "Please."

"No," he said. The word hung there, chill and final.

"You're my *friend*, Ted," she said. "You *promised*."

"You can stay here a week," he said. "No longer. I have my own life, Melody. I have my own problems. I'm tired of dealing with yours. We all are. You're nothing but problems. In college, you were fun. You're not fun any longer. I've helped you and helped you and helped you. How goddam much do you want out of me?" He was getting angrier as he talked. "Things change, Melody," he said brutally. "People change. You can't hold me forever to some dumb promise I made when I was stoned out of my mind back in college. I'm not responsible for your life. Tough up, dammit. Pull yourself together. I can't do it for you, and I'm sick of all your shit. I don't even like to see you anymore, Melody, you know that?"

She whimpered. "Don't say that, Ted. We're friends. You're special. As long as I have you and Michael and Anne, I'll never be alone, don't you see?"

"You *are* alone," he said. Melody infuriated him.

"No, I'm not," she insisted. "I have my friends, my special friends. They'll help me. You're my *friend*, Ted."

"I used to be your friend," he replied.

She stared at him, her lip trembling, hurt beyond words. For a moment he thought that the dam was going to burst, that Melody was finally about to break down and begin one of her marathon crying jags. Instead, a change came over her face. She paled perceptibly, and her lips drew back slowly, and her expression settled into a terrible mask of anger. She was hideous when she was angry. "You bastard," she said.

Ted had been this route too. He got up from the couch and walked to his bar. "Don't start," he said, pouring himself a glass of Chivas Regal on the rocks. "The first thing you throw, you're out on your ass. Got that, Melody?"

"You scum," she repeated. "You were never my friend. None of you were. You lied to me, made me trust you, used me. Now you're all so high and mighty and I'm nothing, and you don't want to know me. You don't want to help me. You never wanted to help me."

"I did help you," Ted pointed out. "Several times. You owe me something close to two thousand dollars, I believe."

"Money," she said. "That's all you care about, you bastard."

Ted sipped at his scotch and frowned at her. "Go to hell," he said.

"I could, for all you care." Her face had gone white. "I cabled you, two years ago. I cabled all three of you. I needed you, you promised that you'd come if I needed you, that you'd be there, you promised that and you made love to me and you were my friend, but I cabled you and you didn't come, you bastard, you didn't come, none of you came, none of you came." She was screaming.

Ted had forgotten about the telegram. But it came back to him in a rush. He'd read it over several times, and finally he'd picked up the phone and called Michael. Michael hadn't been in. So he'd reread the telegram one last time, then crumpled it up and flushed it down the toilet. One of the others could go to her this time, he remembered thinking. He had a big case, the Argrath Corporation patent suit, and he couldn't risk leaving it. But it had been a desperate telegram, and he'd been guilty about it for weeks, until he finally managed to put the whole thing out of his mind. "I was busy," he said, his tone half-angry and half-defensive. "I had more important things to do than come hold your hand through another crisis."

"It was *horrible*," Melody screamed. "I needed you and you left me all *alone*. I almost *killed* myself."

"But you didn't, did you?"

"I could have," she said, "I could have killed myself, and you wouldn't even of cared."

Threatening suicide was one of Melody's favorite tricks. Ted had been through it a hundred times before. This time he decided not to take it. "You could have killed yourself," he said calmly, "and we probably wouldn't have cared. I think you're right about that. You would have rotted for weeks before anyone found you, and we probably wouldn't even have heard about it for half a year. And when I did hear, finally, I guess it would have made me sad for an hour or two, remembering how things had been, but then I would have gotten drunk or phoned up my girlfriend or something, and pretty soon I'd have been out of it. And then I could have forgotten all about you."

"You would have been sorry," Melody said.

"No," Ted replied. He strolled back to the bar and freshened his drink. "No, you know, I don't think I would have been sorry. Not in the least. Not guilty, either. So you

might as well stop threatening to kill yourself, Melody, because it isn't going to work."

The anger drained out of her face, and she gave a little
whimper. "Please, Ted," she said. "Don't say such things.
Tell me you'd care. Tell me you'd remember me."

He scowled at her. "No," he said. It was harder when
she was pitiful, when she shrunk up all small and vulnerable and whimpered instead of accusing him. But he had to
end it once and for all, get rid of this curse on his life.

"I'll go away tomorrow," she said meekly. "I won't
bother you. But tell me you care, Ted. That you're my
friend. That you'll come to me. If I need you."

"I won't come to you, Melody," he said. "That's over.
And I don't want you coming here anymore, or phoning,
or sending telegrams, no matter what kind of trouble you're
in. You understand? Do you? I want you out of my life,
and when you're gone I'm going to forget you as quick as I
can, 'cause lady, you are one hell of a bad memory."

Melody cried out as if he had struck her. *"No!"* she said.
"No, don't say that, remember me, you *have* to. I'll leave
you alone, I promise I will, I'll never see you again. But
say you'll remember me." She stood up abruptly. "I'll go
right now," she said. "If you want me to, I'll go. But make
love to me first, Ted. Please. I want to give you something
to remember me by." She smiled a lascivious little smile
and began to struggle out of her halter top, and Ted felt
sick.

He set down his glass with a bang. "You're crazy," he
said. "You ought to get professional help, Melody. But I
can't give it to you, and I'm not going to put up with this
anymore. I'm going out for a walk. I'll be gone a couple of
hours. You be gone when I get back."

Ted started for the door. Melody stood looking at him,
her halter in her hand. Her breasts looked small and
shrunken, and the left one had a tattoo on it that he'd
never noticed before. There was nothing even vaguely desirable about her. She whimpered. "I just wanted to give
you something to remember me by," she said.

Ted slammed the door.

It was midnight when he returned, drunk and surly, resolved that if Melody was still there, he would call the

police and that would be the end of that. Jack was behind the desk, having just gone on duty. Ted stopped and gave him hell for having admitted Melody that morning, but the doorman denied it vehemently. "Wasn't nobody got in, Mr. Cirelli. I don't let in anyone without buzzing up, you ought to know that. I been here six years, and I never let in nobody without buzzing up." Ted reminded him forcefully about the Jehovah's Witness, and they ended up in a shouting match.

Finally Ted stormed away and took the elevator up to the thirty-second floor.

There was a drawing taped to his door.

He blinked at it furiously for a moment, then snatched it down. It was a cartoon, a caricature of Melody. Not the Melody he'd seen today, but the Melody he'd known in college: sharp, funny, pretty. When they'd been roommates, Melody had always illustrated her notes with little cartoons of herself. He was surprised that she could still draw this well. Beneath the face, she'd printed a message.

I LEFT YOU SOMETHING TO REMEMBER ME BY.

Ted scowled down at the cartoon, wondering whether he should keep it or not. His own hesitation made him angry. He crumpled the paper in his hand and fumbled for his keys. At least she's gone, he thought, and maybe for good. If she left the note, it meant that she'd gone. He was rid of her for another couple of years at least.

He went inside, tossed the crumpled ball of paper across the room towards a wastebasket, and smiled when it went in. "Two points," he said loudly to himself, drunk and self-satisfied. He went to the bar and began to mix himself a drink.

But something was wrong.

Ted stopped stirring his drink and listened. The water was running, he realized. She'd left the water running in the bathroom.

"Christ," he said, and then an awful thought hit him: maybe she hadn't gone after all. Maybe she was still in the bathroom, taking a shower or something, freaked out of her mind, crying, whatever. *"Melody!"* he shouted.

No answer. The water was running, all right. It couldn't be anything else. But she didn't answer.

"Melody, are you still here?" he yelled. "Answer, dammit!"

Silence.

He put down his drink and walked to the bathroom. The door was closed. Ted stood outside. The water was definitely running. "Melody," he said loudly, "are you in there? Melody?"

Nothing. Ted was beginning to be afraid.

He reached out and grasped the doorknob. It turned easily in his hand. The door hadn't been locked.

Inside, the bathroom was filled with steam. He could hardly see, but he made out that the shower curtain was drawn. The shower was running full blast, and judging from the amount of steam, it must be scalding. Ted stepped back and waited for the steam to dissipate. "Melody?" he said softly. There was no reply.

"Shit," he said. He tried not to be afraid. She only talked about it, he told himself; she'd never really do it. The ones who talk about it never do it, he'd read that somewhere. She was just doing this to frighten him.

He took two quick strides across the room and yanked back the shower curtain.

She was there, wreathed in steam, water streaming down her naked body. She wasn't stretched out in the tub at all; she was sitting up, crammed in sideways near the faucets, looking very small and pathetic. Her position seemed half-fetal. The needle spray had been directed down at her, at her hands. She'd opened her wrists with his razor blades and tried to hold them under the water, but it hadn't been enough; she'd slit the veins crosswise, and everybody knew the only way to do it was lengthwise. So she'd used the razor elsewhere, and now she had two mouths, and both of them were smiling at him, smiling. The shower had washed away most of the blood; there were no stains anywhere, but the second mouth below her chin was still red and dripping. Trickles oozed down her chest, over the flower tattooed on her breast, and the spray of the shower caught them and washed them away. Her hair hung down over her cheeks, limp and wet. She was smiling. She looked so happy. The steam was all around her. She'd been in there for hours, he thought. She was very clean.

Ted closed his eyes. It didn't make any difference. He still saw her. He would always see her.

He opened them again; Melody was still smiling. He

reached across her and turned off the shower, getting the sleeve of his shirt soaked in the process.

Numb, he fled back into the living room. God, he thought, God. I have to call someone, I have to report this, I can't deal with this. He decided to call the police. He lifted the phone, and hesitated with his finger poised over the buttons. The police won't help, he thought. He punched for Jill.

When he had finished telling her, it grew very silent on the other end of the phone. "My God," she said at last, "how awful. Can I do anything?"

"Come over," he said. "Right away." He found the drink he'd set down, took a hurried sip from it.

Jill hesitated. "Er—look, Ted, I'm not very good at dealing with corpses. Why don't you come over here? I don't want to—well, you know. I don't think I'll ever shower at your place again."

"Jill," he said, stricken. "I need someone right now." He laughed a frightened, uncertain laugh.

"Come over here," she urged.

"I can't just *leave* it there," he said.

"Well, don't," she said. "Call the police. They'll take it away. Come over afterwards."

Ted called the police.

"If this is your idea of a joke, it isn't funny," the patrolman said. His partner was scowling.

"Joke?" Ted said.

"There's nothing in your shower," the patrolman said. "I ought to take you down to the station house."

"Nothing in the shower?" Ted repeated, incredulous.

"Leave him alone, Sam," the partner said. "He's stinko, can't you tell?"

Ted rushed past them both into the bathroom.

The tub was empty. Empty. He knelt and felt the bottom of it. Dry. Perfectly dry. But his shirt sleeve was still damp. "No," he said. "No." He rushed back out to the living room. The two cops watched him with amusement. Her suitcase was gone from its place by the door. The dishes had all been run through the dishwasher—no way to tell if anyone had made pancakes or not. Ted turned the wastebasket upside down, spilling out the contents all over his couch. He began to scrabble through the papers.

"Go to bed and sleep it off, mister," the older cop said. "You'll feel better in the morning."

"C'mon," his partner said. They departed, leaving Ted still pawing through the papers. No cartoon. No cartoon. No cartoon.

Ted flung the empty wastebasket across the room. It caromed off the wall with a ringing metallic clang.

He took a cab to Jill's.

It was near dawn when he sat up in bed suddenly, his heart thumping, his mouth dry with fear.

Jill murmured sleepily. "Jill," he said, shaking her.

She blinked up at him. "What?" she said. "What time is it, Ted? What's wrong?" She sat up, pulling up the blanket to cover herself.

"Don't you hear it?"

"Hear what?" she asked.

He giggled. "Your shower is running."

That morning he shaved in the kitchen, even though there was no mirror. He cut himself twice. His bladder ached, but he would not go past the bathroom door, despite Jill's repeated assurances that the shower was not running. Dammit, he could *hear* it. He waited until he got to the office. There was no shower in the washroom there.

But Jill looked at him strangely.

At the office, Ted cleared off his desk, and tried to think. He was a lawyer. He had a good analytical mind. He tried to reason it out. He drank only coffee, lots of coffee.

No suitcase, he thought. Jack hadn't seen her. No corpse. No cartoon. No one had seen her. The shower was dry. No dishes. He'd been drinking. But not all day, only later, after dinner. Couldn't be the drinking. Couldn't be. No cartoon. He was the only one who'd seen her. No cartoon. I LEFT YOU SOMETHING TO REMEMBER ME BY. He'd crumpled up her cable and flushed her away. Two years ago. Nothing in the shower.

He picked up his phone. "Billie," he said, "get me a newspaper in Des Moines, Iowa. Any newspaper, I don't care."

When he finally got through, the woman who tended the morgue was reluctant to give him any information. But she softened when he told her he was a lawyer and needed the information for an important case.

The obituary was very short. Melody was identified only as a "massage parlor employee." She'd killed herself in her shower.

"Thank you," Ted said. He set down the receiver. For a long time he sat staring out of his window. He had a very good view; he could see the lake and the soaring tower of the Standard Oil building. He pondered what to do next. There was a thick knot of fear in his gut.

He could take the day off and go home. But the shower would be running at home, and sooner or later he would have to go in there.

He could go back to Jill's. If Jill would have him. She'd seemed awfully cool after last night. She'd recommended a shrink to him as they shared a cab to the office. She didn't understand. No one would understand . . . unless . . . He picked up the phone again, searching through his circular file. There was no card, no number; they'd drifted that far apart. He buzzed for Billie again. "Get me through to Random House in New York City," he said. "To Mr. Michael Englehart. He's an editor there."

But when he was finally connected, the voice on the other end of the line was strange and distant. "Mr. Cirelli? Were you a friend of Michael's? Or one of his authors?"

Ted's mouth was dry. "A friend," he said. "Isn't Michael in? I need to talk to him. It's . . . urgent."

"I'm afraid Michael's no longer with us," the voice said. "He had a nervous breakdown, less than a week ago."

"Is he . . . ?"

"He's alive. They took him to a hospital, I believe. Maybe I can find you the number."

"No," Ted said, "no, that's quite all right." He hung up.

Phoenix directory assistance had no listing for an Anne Kaye. Of course not, he thought. She was married now. He tried to remember her married name. It took him a long time. Something Polish, he thought. Finally it came to him.

He hadn't expected to find her at home. It was a school day, after all. But someone picked up the phone on the third ring. "Hello," he said. "Anne, is that you? This is Ted, in Chicago. Anne, I've got to talk to you. It's about Melody. Anne, I need help." He was breathless.

There was a giggle. "Anne isn't here right now, Ted," Melody said. "She's off at school, and then she's got to visit her husband. They're separated, you know. But she promised to come back by eight."

"Melody," he said.

"Of course, I don't know if I can believe her. You three were never very good about promises. But maybe she'll come back, Ted. I hope so.

"I want to leave her something to remember me by."

Children always become impatient to grow up and experience the pleasures of adulthood, and indeed they have much to look forward to . . . but if you were ten years old and you woke one day to find yourself twenty-six years older, would your experiences be all that you'd dreamed?

Thomas M. Disch's novels include *The Genocides, Camp Concentration, 334,* and *On Wings of Song,* which won the John W. Campbell Memorial Award; his short stories have been often reprinted, most notably in *Fundamental Disch.* He has also published several volumes of poetry, and a historical novel, *Neighboring Lives,* written in collaboration with Charles Naylor.

THE GROWN-UP

≋≋≋≋≋≋≋≋≋≋≋≋≋≋≋≋≋≋≋≋≋≋≋≋≋≋≋

Thomas M. Disch

ALWAYS WE AWAKE TO OUR METAMORPHOSED condition, to the awareness that the strange body in the bed is our own. Women awake and discover, after centuries of dreaming, that they are men. Worms awaken into birds and music bursts from their astonished throats. An elderly businessman awakes and knows himself to be a plane tree: His leaves reach for the light and swell with growth. Often the amazement is too much to bear, and our awakening is brief. We slip back into being the rudimentary creatures that we were. We become less, and sleep resumes its old sovereignty, until once more, without warning, we awaken.

So it was when Francis awoke, one morning in July. He had gone to bed a 10-year-old; he woke 26 years older. Even before his eyes were open the shock of the transformation had wiped out the particulars of his old identity. He was free, therefore, simply to glory in this enormous fulfillment: the mass of his arms, the breadth of his chest, his sheer immensity. He stood up. He stretched, and touched, with his fingertips, the plaster nubbles of the room's low ceiling. So big!

And there, in the mirror mounted to the closet door, was the proof of his transformation and its benediction. His, the mustache, the smile, the teeth. His, the legs and arms, the muscled neck, the . . . His mind, abashed, refused to name it, but it was his as well, with all the rest.

He thought: I must get dressed.

In clothes he was even more amazingly a grown-up. Tying a tie had proved to be beyond him, but there was, in the same drawer as his socks, a single clip-on bow, white polka-dots on maroon.

And in the closet, on a shelf, a straw hat.

He clattered down the fire stairs, 20 flights, each flight a full clockwise rotation through the four points of the compass, and arrived in the lobby giddy and out of breath, but still exultant, like a painter on the day of *vernissage*. Here he was, for all the world to see!

An older man than himself, in the most magnificent of uniforms, approached. His heart poised at the edge of panic, but the man in the uniform was (though curious) entirely deferential.

"Good morning, Mr. Kellerman. Isn't the elevator working? It was just a moment ago."

"Oh. Yes, right. The elevator." He smiled.

His name was Mr. Kellerman!

There were mirrors all over the lobby, and as he made his way before them, he couldn't keep from grinning. The name—*his* name—repeated itself inside his head like the tune of a solemn but still pretty spirited march.

The man in the uniform slipped round him and opened the plate-glass door.

"Thank you," he thought to say.

The scalloped edge of the building's blue marquee brushed his hat as he walked beneath it. Walking along, he could see *over* the tops of the cars parked on the street. What a difference it made, being tall! His muscles all worked so much harder. He felt like Frankenstein, giant hands swinging like counterweights to the crashing of his feet. He flexed his thick fingers. On the middle finger of his right hand was a ring, a square black chunk of something encased in gold. Smash, crash, smash, crash, he crossed the street, passing a woman being wheeled in a wheelchair by another younger woman. He tipped his hat to them and said, "Good morning, ladies." He was thrilled by the resonance of the voice that boomed from his chest.

A grown-up . . .

One by one, he thought of all the dirty words he knew, but didn't say them aloud, even in a whisper. He *could* have, though, any time he wanted to. He could be a dirty old bum, if that's what he wanted. Was it? he wondered. Probably not.

*   *   *

At first the neighborhood had been nothing but tall brick apartment buildings, but now he was on a block of small businesses. In front of one store was a bench with newspapers on it. He wondered if they'd make any sense to him. They never had, before.

He picked up a paper and took it inside the store, which also sold candy and cigarettes. He must have been a foot taller than the boy behind the counter.

"How much is this?" he asked, holding up the paper.

The boy bent his head sideways, conveying in some indefinable way a sense of unfriendliness. "Quarter."

He reached into his back pocket, where he had had the foresight to place that most essential item of the clothes that grown-ups wear, his billfold. It was stuffed full of money, more than he could imagine spending all at once. He took out a dollar bill, handed it to the boy behind the counter, and waited for his change. The boy rang the register, took out three quarters, and handed them to him. A shiver went up and down inside his body. He felt as though he'd done something irrevocably adult.

There was a café further down the block, called Lenox Café, where he sat down at a table next to the front window. While he waited for the waitress, he read the newspaper's headline: CARTER ARRIVES AND ESTABLISHES CONVENTION BASE. AIDES HAVE ALL PREPARATIONS READY FOR A FIRST-BALLOT NOMINATION WEDNESDAY.

He read on a while longer, but it was all the same sort of thing and made no more sense than it ever had. He wasn't stupid—he knew what the words meant—but he really couldn't see why grown-ups ever got interested in the things newspapers wrote about. So, in fact, he *wasn't* a grown-up, completely.

He was and he wasn't. It was strange, but he didn't find it upsetting. After all, lots of things are strange.

When the waitress came from the back of the café, she said, "Hello, Frank."

"Oh. Hello there."

"Hello there, Ramona," she insisted.

"What?"

"My name: Ramona. Remember?"

"Oh sure."

She smiled, in not a nice way. "What'll it be?"

"Uh." He knew he didn't like coffee. "How about a beer?"

"Schaeffer's. Miller's. Bud. Heineken."

"Heineken."

She raised an eyebrow, tightened and tilted the side of her mouth. "That be all?"

"Yes."

Now that he'd ordered, he realized he didn't want to stay in the café, where the waitress seemed to know him and he had to pretend to know her.

She flipped the pink order book closed and put it in the pocket of her apron. Under the apron she was wearing a very short and shimmery black dress with a white collar, and under the dress light stockings that made her legs look black and featureless. In some way he couldn't put his finger on she seemed all wrong. Yet there wasn't anything that unusual about her. She looked like almost any other waitress. And very strange.

In fact, *all* the grown-ups he could see on the sidewalk outside the restaurant looked strange. Uncomfortable and dazed, as though, like him, they were all having to *pretend* to be grown-ups and didn't enjoy it. Himself, he loved it. Loved *being* a grown-up, that is. The pretending wasn't especially fun. He hadn't considered that there might be people who knew him, knew his name and maybe more important things, like where he worked. Assuming that he already had some kind of job, the way he already had a name.

Mr. Kellerman. It seemed a reasonable enough name. Mr.—he looked inside the wallet again—Francis Kellerman. There it was, spelled out a dozen times: on his Master-Charge card, and on similar cards for different stores; on his Social Security card; on a card that said he was a member of something; and, yes, on a driver's license!

The waitress, Ramona, came back with a bottle of beer and a glass. She poured some of the beer into the glass and set it down in front of him.

"Thank you, Ramona," he said. "Here—" taking it from the billfold "—is a dollar."

She took the dollar and gave him a funny look. He decided he must have said the wrong thing.

"Keep the change," he suggested.

"Prick," she said flatly, and walked to the back of the café.

He tasted the beer, but he couldn't swallow any. He spit a mouthful of it back into the glass.

"Blaigh!" he said, loud enough for Ramona to hear, and left the restaurant, leaving the worthless newspaper behind. As soon as he was out of the door he got the giggles, and couldn't stop till he was halfway back to the apartment where Mr. Francis Kellerman lived.

When he got there, though, he couldn't get in. The big glass door was locked and there was no one in the lobby, so knocking wasn't any help. He knocked anyhow. No one came. If he'd had a set of keys . . . But (he looked in all his pockets) he didn't. He'd forgotten that grown-ups always use keys.

Finally a lady came along who lived in the building, and she let him in. This time he used the elevator. He'd forgotten the apartment number, but he knew where it was along the hall.

The door was open (the way he'd left it probably), which was good, and someone was inside, which wasn't. A bald man with sunglasses was putting things into a suitcase spread open on the unmade bed.

"Hey!" Francis said.

The man looked up. He was holding stereo headphones.

"Mister, you're in the wrong apartment." What had begun as a cautious rebuke ended up as out-and-out anger. The man was a burglar—he was robbing the apartment!

The man backed away toward the kitchen. The spiraling wire of the headphones followed, bobbling.

"Hey, you better get out of here. Right now!" His voice boomed incredibly. "Do you hear me—right *now!*"

The man dropped the headphones and ducked through the open door of the kitchen. Francis could hear him rummaging around in the silverware. Looking (Francis realized with alarm) for a knife.

He acted quickly. Fighting, after all, is still a natural accomplishment for most boys his age. He unplugged a floor lamp, upended it, and stood poised beside the kitchen door. When the man came out, armed with a butcher knife, Francis let him have it. The lamp base raised a large lump on the man's bald head, but he hadn't been cut or, fortunately, killed. Francis didn't know what he'd have done with a dead body, but this one, which was only unconscious, was no problem. He dragged it out to the stairwell (where there was a *second* suitcase, packed and ready to go) and left it, the body, on the landing. He brought the suitcase back to his apartment. Then, feeling vengeful and mischievous, he went back, undressed the burglar (even took his underpants), and threw all the clothes down the incinerator chute. Serves him right, he thought.

This time when he left the apartment he didn't forget to take his keys and to lock the door behind him.

"That son of a bitch," he said aloud, when he was alone in the elevator. "Trying to steal my things. *Son* of a bitch." But he was basically over feeling upset or angry or anything but tickled over the idea of the burglar waking up without his clothes. What would he think? What could he do?

Returning to the breezy freedom of the street, where he could go in any direction he wanted and where no one could tell him what to do or what not to, he began to realize how totally lucky he was, something that most of the other grown-ups around didn't seem to understand at all as clearly. He would go into stores and buy something, anything at all, just for the fun of spending his money. He bought flowers in a flower shop, and a book called *Reassessments*. He bought a bottle of perfume, an electric popcorn popper, another ring (for his left hand), a telephone that you could see the insides of, a $150 backgammon set (after the salesman had explained the basic rules), and 20 Marvel comic books. Which was about as much, even with a shopping bag, as he could easily lug around.

Then, as he was going past a church, it occurred to him that God must be behind the whole thing that was happening to him. It was a Catholic church. He didn't know if he was a Catholic, or what, but it seemed logical that his not knowing that was as much God's doing as his, so it ought not to matter if he prayed here rather than some other church. The important thing was to stay on God's good side.

There was no one else inside, so he went right up to the front and knelt down on one of the padded kneelers and started praying. First he thanked God for having made him a grown-up, then asked, with a good deal of feeling, not to be changed back. After that there didn't seem to be much else to say, since he didn't have friends or relatives to ask favors for, or enterprises to be concerned about. He did remember to ask to be forgiven for the dirty trick he'd played on the burglar, but he wondered if God would really have been angry with him for that, since, after all, he *was* a burglar. Before he left he unwrapped the flowers and put them in a vase on the altar. Beside the vase he placed the copy of *Reassessments*. Even though he wasn't sure that this was exactly the right offering, it seemed more appropriate than perfume or a popcorn popper or his other purchases (which were all things, moreover, that he'd like to have for himself). Anyhow, God would like the flowers. There were two dozen of them and they were the most expensive kind they'd had in the shop.

He was driving the car he'd rented at Hertz Rent a Car, a bright red '76 Dodge Charger, driving it slowly and carefully on the least busy streets he'd been able to find. Ten blocks on a one-way street going north then a right, and another right, and then ten blocks in the other direction. You only had to push the button marked Drive and steer. It was easy. Around and around, in and out of traffic. It was easy, but it wasn't as much fun as he'd thought it would be beforehand, so after only an hour of practice, he pulled up in front of an army surplus store into a space that didn't require a lot of complicated parking.

While he was locking the door, one of the girls who'd been leaning against the store window came over and asked him if he wanted to score.

"Hey, cowboy," she said, "you want to score?"

She'd called him cowboy, because of the hat and boots he was wearing, which he'd bought just after he'd come out of the church that afternoon.

"What?" he said.

She pushed her tangly red hair back from her eyes. "Do you want to fuck?"

He was so astonished he couldn't think what to say. But, really, why should he be surprised? He was a grown-up, and this was one of the most basic things that grown-ups did. So why not?

"Why not," he said.

"It's twenty bucks," she said. She was able to talk without quite closing her mouth entirely.

"Fine," he said.

Her mouth opened a little wider, and her tongue moved forward over her lower teeth, retracted, and came forward again. It seemed strange, but friendly even so.

"Where do we go?" he asked.

"You don't want to use the car?"

"Oh. Right." He unlocked the door, and they got in. "Now what?"

She told him where to drive, which was to a kind of parking lot beside the river. On two sides were broad brick buildings without windows. On the way here he'd gone through a red light and nearly run down a pedestrian. The girl had only laughed. She didn't seem at all concerned about his driving, which was reassuring.

When they were in the parking lot, she opened up his trousers and reached inside his underpants to take hold of his thing. He wondered if he wasn't supposed to be doing the same to her. He knew girls didn't have anything there but a crack. The idea was for the man to get his thing inside the woman's crack, and then to move around until some kind of juice squirted out. He started looking for buttons or a zipper on her shorts.

She wiggled around and in no time her shorts were on the floor of the car.

He bent forward so he could see where her crack was. She spread her legs helpfully. "You like that?" she asked.

"I guess so." Then, because that didn't seem adequate, or even polite, "Sure." But it lacked conviction.

She took hold of his thing again and started tugging at it. It felt quite satisfying, like scratching poison ivy, but somehow it didn't seem right that he should be making love to this girl who didn't know the first thing about him. She seemed so nice, and was trying so hard.

"I believe in being honest," he announced.

"Oh boy." She let go of his thing and pushed back her hair. "Here we go. What is it?"

"You probably won't believe this," he began tentatively, "but I think I should tell you anyhow. I've got a kind of . . . problem, I guess you'd say."

"Yeah? What's that?"

"I'm only ten years old."

"No kidding. Ten years old."

"I said you wouldn't believe it, but it's true. This morning when I woke up I had this grown-up body, but my head, inside, is only ten years old."

"I believe it."

"You do?" He couldn't tell from her tone of voice if that was true, but she seemed no less friendly than before. "It doesn't bother you?"

"Listen, cowboy, your age doesn't matter, not to me. What the hell—*I'm* ten too."

"You are? Really?"

"Sure. You could say we all are. In a way. You know?"

"No. I mean . . ."

"Look here, in my eyes." He looked in her eyes. "You see?"

"What am I supposed to be seeing?"

"Me, age ten."

"You don't *seem* any different, or . . . Oh."

"You saw."

"Maybe. But it wasn't . . . what I thought it would be."

"How's it different?"

"Sadder, I guess. If that's what you meant I should be seeing. I mean . . . I mean it isn't as though your age is *printed* there, like a driver's license."

"Have you *got* a driver's license?" she asked.

"Oh yeah. They wouldn't let me have this car till I showed it to them."

"Listen, cowboy, time flies. You want to do something, or don't you?"

"Sure." He braced his mind against the words, and said them: "I'd like to fuck you."

"Then come here."

He was already beside her, but she scrunched round into a different position and made him do the same.

"Comfortable?" she asked.

"Fine. Sure."

"Okay. Now just relax. Close your eyes. Now tell me, what does it feel like when I do this?"

"Warm," he said, after concentrating on the exact sensation. "But not right there. In my stomach, more."

"Then there's no problem. Just think about some little girl friend of yours and leave the driving to me. All right?"

"All right."

The feeling in his stomach started to spread everywhere in his body. There were little bubbles of color fizzing in the darkness of his head. They became faces, faces of women whose names he almost remembered. It started to hurt.

And then he could see the building where he would have to go to work tomorrow—a gigantic office building with gray glass walls. His back bent. His hands flexed in the air.

His left boot pressed into the accelerator. His right was up
on the seat of the car.

He could see his whole life, clear as day. There was his
desk, his telephone, a calendar that showed a single day at
a time. And his secretary, Miss Appleton. His back bent in
the other direction. There was a paper full of numbers,
stacks of papers, and he understood them with a persistent
clarity that was also a cloudy pain everywhere inside him,
a sorrow beyond the reach of his mind, which was now,
again, as the child within fell back into its long, long slum-
ber, the mind of a grown-up only.

He came.

Always we awake to our metamorphosed condition, to
the awareness that the strange body in the bed is our own.
Women awake and discover, after centuries of dreaming,
that they are men. Worms awaken into birds and music
bursts from their astonished throats. An elderly businessman awakes and knows himself to be a plane tree: His
leaves reach for the light and swell with growth. Often the
amazement is too much to bear, and our awakening is
brief. We slip back into being the rudimentary creatures
that we were. We become less, and sleep resumes its old
sovereignty.

This story has some science-fictional elements, since it's set in a London of the far future when the sun is dying; but as Bettine, the Lord Mayor's girl, is imprisoned in the Tower of London and visited by ghosts from past millennia, matters become very fantastic indeed. When Elizabeth I arrives to tell her of her final duty in life, things come to a dramatic head.

C. J. Cherryh is one of the most popular and respected authors of modern science fiction and fantasy. She won a Hugo Award in 1979 for her short story "Cassandra," and her novels include *Downbelow Station* and *The Pride of Chanur*. A sequel to *Downbelow Station* is currently in the works.

THE HAUNTED TOWER

C. J. Cherryh

THERE WERE GHOSTS IN OLD LONDON, THAT part of London outside the walls and along the river, or at least the townsfolk outside the walls believed in them: mostly they were attributed to the fringes of the city, and the unbelievers inside the walls insisted they were manifestations of sunstruck brains, of senses deceived by the radiations of the dying star and the fogs which tended to gather near the Thames. Ghosts were certainly unfashionable for a city management which prided itself on technology, which confined most of its bulk to a well-ordered cube (geometrically perfect except for the central arch which let the Thames flow through) in which most of the inhabitants lived precisely ordered lives. London had its own spaceport, maintained offices for important offworld companies, and it thrived on trade. It pointed at other cities in its vicinity as declined and degenerate, but held itself as an excellent and enlightened government: since the Restoration and the New Mayoralty, reason reigned in London, and traditions were cultivated only so far as they added to the comfort of the city and those who ruled it. If the governed of the city believed in ghosts and other intangibles, well enough; reliance on astrology and luck and ectoplasmic utterances made it less likely that the governed would seek to analyze the governors upstairs.

There were some individuals who analyzed the nature of things, and reached certain conclusions, and who made their attempts on power.

For them the Tower existed, a second cube some distance down the river, which had very old foundations and very old traditions. The use of it was an inspiration on the part of the New Mayoralty, which studied its records and found itself a way to dispose of unwanted opinion. The city was self-contained. So was the Tower. What disappeared into the Tower only rarely reappeared . . . and the river ran between, a private, unassailable highway for the damned, so that there was no untidy publicity.

Usually the voyagers were the fallen powerful, setting out from that dire river doorway of the city of London.

On this occasion one Bettine Maunfry came down the steps toward the rusty iron boat and the waters of old Thames. She had her baggage (three big boxes) brought along by the police, and though the police were grim, they did not insult her, because of who she had been, and might be again if the unseen stars favored her.

She boarded the boat in a state of shock, sat with her hands clenched in her lap and stared at something other than the police as they loaded her baggage aboard and finally closed the door of the cabin. This part of the city was an arch above the water, a darksome tunnel agleam with lights which seemed far too few; and she swallowed and clenched her hands the more tightly as the engines began to chug their way downriver toward the daylight which showed at the end.

They came finally into the wan light of the sun, colors which spread themselves amber and orange across the dirty glass of the cabin windows. The ancient ruins of old London appeared along the banks, upthrust monoliths and pillars and ruined bits of wall which no one ever had to look at but those born outside—as she had been, but she had tried to forget that.

In not so long a time there was a smooth modern wall on the left side, which was the wall of the Tower, and the boat ground and bumped its way to the landing.

Then she must get out again, and, being frightened and unsteady, she reached out her hand for the police to help her across the narrow ramp to the shore and the open gate of that wall. They helped her and passed her on to the soldier/warders, who brought her within the gates; she stood on stones which were among the most ancient things in all of ancient London, and the steel gates, which were not at all ancient, and very solid, gaped and hissed and snicked shut with ominous authority. The chief warder, a gray-haired man, led her beyond the gatehouse and into the interior of the Tower which, to her surprise, was not a building, but a wall, girding many buildings, many of them crumbling brick and very, very old-seeming. Guards followed with her baggage as she walked this strange, barren courtyard among the crumbling buildings.

"What are these stones?" she asked of the older man who led the way, proper and militarily slim. "What are they?"

But he would not answer her, as none of them spoke to her. They escorted her to the steps of a modern tower, which bestraddled ancient stones and made them a part of its structure, old brick with gleaming steel. The older man showed her through the gateway and up the steps, while the others followed after. It was a long climb—no lift, nothing of the sort; the lights were all shielded and the doors which they passed were all without handles.

Third level; the chief warder motioned her through a doorway just at the top of the stairs, which led to a hall ending in a closed door. She found the guards pushing her luggage past her into that short corridor, and when she did not move, the chief warder took her arm and put her through the archway, himself staying behind. "Wait," she cried, "wait," but no one waited and no one cared. The door shut. She wept, she beat at the closed door with her fists, she kicked the door and kicked it again for good measure, and finally she tried the door at the other end of the hall, pushed the only door switch she had, which let her into a grim, one-room apartment, part brick and part steel, a bed which did not look comfortable, thinly mattressed; a bathroom at least separate of the single room, a window, a wall console: she immediately and in panic pushed buttons there, but it was dead, quite dead. Tears streamed down her face and she wiped them with the back of her hand and snuffled because there was no one to see the inelegance.

She went to the window then and looked out, saw the courtyard and in it the guards who had brought her heading to the gates; and the gates opening on the river and closing again.

Fear came over her, dread that perhaps she was alone in this place and the stones and the machines might be all there was. She ran to the panel and punched buttons and pleaded, and there was nothing; then she grew anxious that the apartment door might close on its own. She scurried

out into the short hallway and dragged her three cases in
and sat down on the thin mattress and cried.

Tears ran out after a time; she had done a great deal of
crying and none of it had helped, so she sat with her hands
in her lap and hoped earnestly that the screen and the
phone would come on and it would be Richard, his honor
Richard Collier the mayor, to say he had frightened her
enough, and he had.

The screen did not come on. Finally she began to snuffle
again and wiped her eyes and realized that she was staying
at least . . . at least a little time. She gathered her clothes
out of the boxes and hung them; laid out her magazines and
her books and her knitting and sewing and her jewelry and
her cosmetics and all the things she had packed. . . . At
least they had let her pack. She went into the bath and sat
down and repaired her makeup, painting on a perfectly
insouciant face, and finding in this mundane act a little
comfort.

She was not the sort of person who was sent to the
Tower; she was only a girl, (though thirty) the Mayor's
girl. She was plain Bettine Maunfry. His Honor's wife
knew about her and had no resentments; it just could not
be that Marge had turned on her; she was not the first girl
His Honor had had, and not the only even at the moment.
Richard was jealous, that was all, angry when he had
found out there might be someone else, and he had power
and he was using it to frighten her. It had to be. Richard
had other girls and a wife, and there was no reason for
him to be jealous. He had no right to be jealous. But he
was; and he was vindictive. And because he was an important man, and she was no one, she was more frightened
now than she had ever been in her life.

The Tower was for dangerous criminals. But Richard
had been able to do this and get away with it, which she
would never have dreamed; it was all too cruel a joke. He
had some kind of power and the judges did what he
wanted; or he never even bothered to get a court involved.

The tears threatened again, and she sniffed and stared
without blinking at her reflected image until the tears dried.
Her face was her defense, her beauty her protection. She
had always known how to please others. She had worked
all her life at it. She had learned that this was power, from
the time she was a tiny girl, that she must let others have
control of things, but that she could play on them and get

them to do most things that she wanted. *I like people,* was the way she put it, in a dozen variants; all of which meant that as much as she hated technical things she liked to know all about different types of personalities; it sounded altruistic, and it also gave her power of the kind she wanted. Most of the time she even believed in the altruism . . . until a thing like this, until this dreadful grim joke. This time it had not worked, and none of this should be happening.

It would still work, if she could get face-to-face with Richard, and not Richard the Lord Mayor. She tested a deliberate and winning smile in the mirror, perfect teeth, a bewitching little twitch of a shoulder.

Downy lashes rimming blue eyes, a mouth which could pout and tremble and reflect emotions like the breathing of air over water, so fine, so responsive, to make a man like His Honor feel powerful . . . that was all very well: she knew how to do that. He *loved* her . . . after a possessive fashion; he had never said so, but she fed his middle-aged vanity, and that was what was hurt; that had to be it, that she had wounded him more than she had thought and he had done this, to show her he was powerful.

But he would have to come, and see how chastened she was and then he would feel sorry for what he had done, and they would make up and she would be back safe in the city again.

He would come.

She changed to her lounging gown, with a very deep neckline, and went back and combed her dark masses of hair just so, just perfect with the ruby gown with the deep plunge and the little bit of ruby glitter paler than the blood-red fabric. . . . He had given that to her. He would remember that evening when he saw her wearing it.

She waited. The silence here was deep, so, so deep. Somewhere in this great building there should be *someone* else. It was night outside the window now, and she looked out and could not bear to look out again, because it was only blackness, and reminded her she was alone. She wished that she could curtain it; she might have hung something over it, but that would make the place look shabby, and she lived by beauty. Survived by it. She sat down in the chair and turned on the light and read her magazines, articles on beauty and being desirable which now, while they had entertained her before, seemed shatteringly *important*.

Her horoscope was good; it said she should have luck in romance. She tried to take this for hopeful. She was a Pisces. Richard had given her this lovely charm which she wore about her neck; the fish had real diamond eyes. He laughed at her horoscopes, but she knew they were right.

They must be this time. *My little outsider,* he called her, because like most who believed in horoscopes, she came from outside; but she had overcome her origins. She had been a beautiful child, and because her father had worked Inside, she had gotten herself educated . . . was educated, absolutely, in all those things proper for a girl, nothing serious or studious, nothing of expertise unless it was in Working With People, because she knew that it was just not smart at all for a girl to be too obviously clever . . . modesty got a girl much further . . . that and the luck of being beautiful, which let her cry prettily. Her childish tantrums had gotten swift comfort and a chuck under the chin, while her brothers got spanked, and that was the first time she had learned about *that* kind of power, which she had always had. It was luck, and that was in the stars. And her magazines told her how to be even more pleasing and pleasant and that she succeeded in what she thought she did. That it worked was self-evident: a girl like her, from the outside, and a receptionist in His Honor the Mayor's office, and kept by him in style people Outside could not imagine. . . .

Only there were bad parts to it too, and being here was one, that she had never planned for—

A door opened somewhere below. Her heart jumped. She started to spring up and then thought that she should seem casual and then that she should not, that she should seem anxious and worried, which was why Richard had sent her here. Perhaps she should cry. Perhaps it was Richard. It *must* be Richard.

She put the magazine away and fretted with her hands, for once in her life not knowing what to do with them, but even this was a pretty gesture and she knew that it was.

The door opened. It was the military warden, with dinner.

"I can't eat," she said. It seemed upon the instant that intense depression was the ploy to use. She turned her face away, but he walked in and set it on the table.

"That's your business," he said, and started to leave.

"Wait." He stopped and she turned her best pleading look on him . . . an older man and the kind who could be intensely flattered by beauty . . . flattered, if she seemed vulnerable, and she put on that air. "Please. Is there any word . . . from Richard?"

"No," he said, distressingly impervious. "Don't expect any."

"Please. Please tell him that I want to talk to him."

"If he asks."

"Please. My phone doesn't work."

"Not supposed to. It doesn't work for all prisoners. Just those with privileges. You don't have any."

"*Tell* him I want to see him. Tell him. It's his message. Won't *he* decide whether he wants to hear it?"

That got through. She saw the mouth indecisive. The man closed the door; she heard the steps going away. She clutched her hands together, finding them shaking.

And she ignored the food, got out her magazine again and tried to read, but it hardly occupied her mind. She dared not sit on the bed and prop her knees up and read; or sit down to eat; it was too informal, too unlovely. She started to run her hand through her hair, but that would disarrange it. She fretted back and forth across the floor, back and forth, and finally she decided she could put on her negligee and if His Honor walked in on her that was to the better.

She took out not the bright orange one, but the white, lace-trimmed, transparent only here and there, innocent; innocence seemed precious at the moment. She went to the mirror in the bath, wiped off the lipstick and washed her face and did it all over again, in soft pinks and rosy blushes; she felt braver then. But when she came out again to go to bed, there was that black window, void and cold and without any curtain against the night. It was very lonely to sleep in this place. She could not bear to be alone.

And she had slept alone many a night until Tom had come into her life. Tom Ash was a clerk in the Mayor's office in just the next office over from hers; and he was sweet and kind . . . after all, she was beautiful, and still young, only thirty, and seven years she had given to Richard, who was not handsome, though he was attractive after the fashion of older, powerful men; but Tom was . . . Tom was handsome, and a good lover and all those things romances said she was due, and he loved her moreover. He had said so.

Richard did not know about him. Only suspected. Tom had got out the door before Richard arrived, and there was no way in the world Richard could know who it was; more to the point, Richard had asked who it was.

And if Richard had power to put her here despite all the laws he had power to put Tom here too, and maybe to do worse things.

She was not going to confess to Richard, that was all. She was not going to confess, or she would tell him some other name and let Richard try to figure it all out.

Richard had no proof of anything.

And besides, he did not own her.

Only she liked the good things and the pretty clothes and the nice apartment Tom could never give her. Even her jewelry . . . Richard could figure out a way to take that back. Could blacklist her so she could never find a job, so that she would end up outside the walls, exiled.

She was reading a romance about a woman who had gotten herself into a similar romantic triangle, and it was all too very much like her situation. She was almost afraid to find out how it ended. Light reading. She had always liked light reading, about real, *involved* people, but of a sudden it was much too dramatic and involved her.

But it had to have a happy ending; all such stories did, which was why she kept reading them, to assure herself that she would, and that beautiful women could go on being clever and having happy endings.

Whoever *wanted* tragedy?

She grew weary of reading, having lost the thread of it many times, and arranged the pillows, and having arranged herself as decorously as she could, pushed the light switch by the head of the bed and closed her eyes.

She did sleep a time, more exhausted than she had known, and came to herself with the distinct impression that there had been someone whispering nearby, two someones, in very light voices.

Children, of all things; children in the Tower.

She opened her eyes, gaped upon candlelight, and saw to her wonder two little boys against the brick wall, boys dressed in red and blue brocades, with pale faces, tousled hair and marvelous bright eyes.

"Oh," said one, "she's awake."

"Who are you?" she demanded.

"She's beautiful," said the other. "I wonder if she's nice."

She sat bolt upright, and they held each other as if *she* had frightened them . . . they could hardly be much more than twelve . . . and stared at her wide-eyed.

"Who *are* you?" she asked.

"I'm Edward," said one; "I'm Richard," said the other.

"And how did you get in here?"

Edward let go Richard's arm, pointed vaguely down. "We live here," said young Edward, and part of his hand seemed to go right through the wall.

Then she realized what they must be if they were not a dream, and the hair rose on the back of her neck and she drew the sheet up to cover her, for they *were* children, and she was little covered by the gown. They were quaint and somewhat wise-eyed children, in grown-up clothes which seemed old and dusty.

"How did you get here?" Richard echoed her own question. "Who sent you here? Are you Queen?"

"Richard Collier. The Lord Mayor."

"Ah," said Edward. "A Richard sent us here too. He's supposed to have murdered us both. But he didn't, you know."

She shook her head. She did not know. She never bothered with history. She kept clinging to the idea that they were a dream, some old school lesson come out of her subconscious, for while she believed in ghosts and horoscopes, her mind was reeling under the previous shocks.

"We always come first," said Edward. "I am a king, you know."

"First? What *are* you? What are you doing here?"

"Why, much the same as everyone else," young Edward laughed, and his eyes, while his face was that of a child, now seemed fearsomely old. "We live here, that's all. What's your name?"

"Bettine."

"Bettine? How strange a name. But most are strange now. And so few come here, after all. Do you think he will let you go?"

"Of course he'll let me go."

"Very few ever leave. And no one leaves . . . lately."

"You're dead," she cried. "Go away. Go away."

"We've been dead longer than you've been alive," said Richard.

"Longer than this London's stood here," said Edward. "I liked my London better. It was brighter. I shall always prefer it. Do you play cards?"

She sat and shivered, and Richard tugged at Edward's sleeve.

"I think we should go," said Richard. "I think she's about to be afraid."

"She's very pretty," said Edward. "But I don't think it's going to do her any good."

"It never does," said Richard.

"I go first," said Edward, "being King."

And he vanished, right through the wall; and Richard followed; and the candle glow went out, leaving dark.

Bettine sat still, and held the bedclothes about her, and finally reached for the light button, feverishly, madly, and blinked in the white glare that showed nothing wrong, nothing at all wrong. But there was a deathly chill in the air.

She had dreamed. This strange old place gave her nightmares. It had to be that. Tears ran from her eyes. She shivered and finally she got up and picked at her cold dinner because she wanted something to take her mind off the solitude. She would not look up at the window over the table, not while there was night outside.

She would have shadows beneath her eyes in the morning, and she would not be beautiful, and she had to be. At last she gathered the courage to go back to bed, and lay wrapped in her nightrobe and shivering, in the full light, which she refused to turn out.

She tried the phone again in the morning, and it still refused to work. She found everything saner with the daylight coming in through the window again and the room seemed warmer because of it. She bathed and washed her hair and dried it, brushing it meticulously. It had natural curl and she fashioned it in ringlets and tried it this way and that about her face.

Suddenly the door open on the short hallway closed; she sprang up and looked toward it in consternation, heard footsteps downstairs and dithered about in panic, finally flung on a dress and fluffed her hair and while she heard footsteps coming up the long stairs, leaned near the mirror in the bath and put on her makeup with swift, sure strokes, not the full job, which she had no time for, but at least the touch of definition to the eyes, the blush to lips and cheeks. . . .

It was Richard come to see her, come to ask if she had had enough, and she had, oh, she had. . . .

The far-side door opened. She ran to the door on her side, waited, hands clasped, anxious, meaning to appear anxious and contrite and everything and anything that he should want.

Then the outer door closed again; and hers opened. She rushed to meet her visitor.

There was only a breakfast tray, left on the floor, and the door closed, the footsteps receding.

"Come back!" she cried, wept, wailed.

The steps went on, down the stairs.

She stood there and cried a good long time; and then because she found nothing else to do, she gathered up the tray. She had to bend down to do it, which disarranged her hair and upset her and humiliated her even with no one to see it. She was angry and frightened and wanted to throw the tray and break all the things in sight; but that would make a terrible mess of food and she reckoned that she would have to live in it if she did that, or clean it up herself, so she spared herself such labor and carried it meekly back to the table. She was sick to her stomach, and there was the old food tray which was smelling by now, and the new one which brought new, heavy aromas. She considered them both with her stomach tight with fear and her throat so constricted with anger and frustration that she could not swallow her breaths, let alone the food.

She carried the old tray to the anteroom and set it on the floor, and suddenly, with inspiration, began to search through her belongings for paper . . . she *had* brought some, with the sewing kit, because she made patterns for her embroideries and for her knitting. She searched through the needles and the yarns and found it at the bottom, found the pen, sat down at the desk and chewed the pen's cap, trying to think.

"Richard," she wrote, not "Dearest Richard," which she thought might not be the right approach to an angry man. "I am frightened here. I must see you. Please. Bettine."

That was right, she thought. To be restrained, to be calm, and at the same time dissuade him from doing worse to frighten her. Pathos. That was the tone of it. She folded it up, and with a clever impulse, stitched thread through it to seal it, so that the jailer should not be getting curious without making it obvious. "To His Honor Richard Collier," she wrote on the outside, in the beautiful letters she had practiced making again and again. And then she took it and set it in the supper tray, out in the hall, so that it should leave with the dishes and whoever got it would have to think what to do with it. And throwing away a letter to the Mayor was not a wise thing to do.

She sniffed then, satisfied, and sat down and ate her breakfast, which did fill a little bit of the loneliness in her stomach, and made her feel guilty and miserable afterward, because she had eaten too much; she would get fat, that was what they wanted, feeding her all that and leaving her nothing to do but eat; she would soon be fat and unlovely if there was nothing to do here but eat and pace the floor.

And maybe she would be here a long time. That began to penetrate her with a force it had not until now. A second day in this place . . . and how many days; and she would run out of things to read and to do . . . she set the second tray in the hall too, to be rid of the smell of the food, and punched buttons trying to close the door from inside; the whole console was complicated, and she started punching buttons at random. There were controls she did not know; she punched buttons in different combinations and only succeeded in getting the lights out in a way in which she could not get them on again, not from any combination of buttons until finally she punched the one by the bed. That frightened her, that she might cut off the heating or lose the lighting entirely and be alone in the dark when the sun should go down. She stopped punching buttons, knowing nothing of what she was doing with them, although when she had been in school there had been a course in managing the computers . . . but that was something the other girls did, who had plain long faces and fastened their hair back and had flat bodies and thought of nothing but studying and working. She hated them. Hated the whole thing. Hated prisons that could be made of such things.

She picked up her knitting and thought of Tom, of his eyes, his body, his voice . . . he *loved* her; and Richard did not, perhaps, but used her because she was beautiful, and one had to put up with that. It brought things. Would buy her way out of here. Richard might be proud and angry and have his feelings hurt, but ultimately he would want his pride salved, and she could do that, abundantly, assuring him that she was contrite, which was all she had to do, ultimately.

It was Tom she daydreamed of, wondering where he was and if he was in the Tower too. Oh, surely, surely not; but the books she read seemed so frighteningly real, and dire things happened for jealousy. She began to think of Tom in that kind of trouble, while her hands plied the colored yarns, knitting click, click, click, measuring out the time, stitch by stitch and row by row. Women did such things and went on doing them while the sun died because in all of women's lives there were so many moments that would kill the mind if one thought about them, which would suck the heart and the life out of one, and engrave lines in the face and put gray in the hair if ever one let one's mind work; but there was in the rhythm and the fascination of the stitches a loss of thought, a void, a blank, that was only numbers and not even that, because the mind did not need to count, the fingers did, the length of a thread against the finger measured evenly as a ruler could divide it, the slight difference in tension sensed finely as a machine could sense, the exact *number* of stitches keeping pattern without really the need to count, but something inward and regular as the beat of a heart, as the slow passing of time which could be frozen in such acts, or speeded past.

So the day passed; and click, click, click the needles went, using up the yarn, when she did not read; and she wound more and knitted more, row upon row, not thinking.

There was no noon meal; the sun began to fade, and the room grew more chill. I shall have to ask for more yarn someday, she thought with surprising placidity, and realized what that thought implied and refused to think anymore. At last she heard the steps coming up to the door and this time she refused to spring up and expect it to be Richard. She went right on with her knitting, click, click, while the steps came up and opened the door and closed it again.

Then quite calmly she went out and retrieved the new. tray, saw with a little surge of hope that the message and the trays had gone. So, she thought; so, it will get to him; and she sat down and had her dinner, but not all of it. She took the tray out to the anteroom after, and went back and prepared herself for bed.

The light faded from the window, and the outside became black again; again she avoided looking toward it, because it so depressed her, and made the little room on the third level so lonely and so isolated.

And again she went to bed with the light on, because she was not willing to suffer more such illusions . . . they *were* illusions, and she put her mind from them all day long. She *believed* in supernatural things, but it had stopped being something which happened to someone else, and something which waited to happen to her, which was not shivery-entertaining, not in the least. It rather made her fear she was losing touch with things and losing control of her imagination, and she refused to have that happen.

She put on her white negligee again, reckoning that she just could be summoned out of bed by a phone call . . . after all, the message *could* be carried to His Honor Richard Collier direct. But it was more likely that it would go to his office instead, and that the call would come tomorrow, so she could relax just a bit and get some sleep, which she really needed. She was not actually afraid this second night, and so long as lights were on, there was no likelihood that she would have silly dreams about dead children.

Dead children. She shuddered, appalled that such a dream could have come out of her own imagination; it was not at all the kind of thing that a girl wanted to think about.

Tom . . . now *he* was worth thinking about.

She read her story; and the woman in the story had problems *not* direr than hers, which made her own seem worse and the story seem trivial; but it was going to be a happy ending. She was sure that it would, which would cheer her up.

Would they give her more books, she wondered, when these ran out? She thought that in the morning she would put another note on the tray and ask for books for herself; and maybe she should not, because that would admit to the jailer that she thought she was staying; and *that* would get to Richard too, who would ask how she was bearing up. She was sure that he would ask.

No. She would not ask for things to indicate a long stay here. They might give them to her, and she could not bear that.

Again she found she was losing the thread of the story, and she laid the book down against the side of the bed. She

tried to think of Tom and could not, losing the thread of
him too. She dreamed only the needles, back and forth, in
and out, click.

The light dimmed . . . to candlelight; she felt it dim
through her closed lids; and she cracked a lid very carefully, her muscles rigid and near to shivering. The dream
was back; she heard the children laughing together.

"Well," said Edward's voice, "hello, Bettine."

She looked; she had to, not knowing how near they were,
afraid they might touch her. They were standing against the
bricks again, both of them, solemn-faced like boys holding
some great joke confined for the briefest of moments.

"Of course we're back," said the boy Richard. "How are
you, lady Bettine?"

"Go away," she said; and then the least little part of her
heart said that she did not really want them to go. She
blinked and sat up, and there was a woman walking toward
her out of the wall, who became larger and larger as the
boys retreated. The newcomer was beautiful, in an ancient
mode, wearing a golden brocade gown. The visitor dipped
a curtsy to the boy king Edward, who bowed to her.
"Madam," the boy-king said; and "Majesty," said the
stranger, and turned curious eyes on *her*. "She is Bettine,"
said Edward. "Be polite, Bettine: Anne is one of the
queens."

"Queen Anne?" asked Bettine, wishing that she knew a
little more of the ancient Tower. If one was to be haunted,
it would be at least helpful to know by whom; but she had
paid very little attention to history—there was so much of
it.

"Boleyn," said the queen, and spread her skirts and sat
on the end of her bed, narrowly missing her feet, very
forthright for a dream. "And how are you, my dear?"

"Very well, thank you, Majesty."

The boys laughed. "She only half believes in us, but she
plays the game, doesn't she? They don't have queens now."

"How pretty she is," said the queen. "So was I."

"I'm not staying here," Bettine said. It seemed important
in this web of illusions to have that clear. "I don't really
believe in you entirely. I'm dreaming this anyway."

"You're not, my dear, but there, there, believe what you
like." The queen turned, looked back; the children had
gone, and another was coming through, a handsome man

in elegant brocade. "Robert Devereaux," said Anne. "Robert, her name is Bettine."

"Who is he?" Bettine asked. "Is he the king?"

The man named Robert laughed gently and swept a bow; "I might have been," he said. "But things went wrong."

"Earl of Essex," said Anne softly, and stood up and took his hand. "The boys said that there was someone who believed in us, all the same. How nice. It's been so long."

"You make me very nervous," she said. "If you were real I think you'd talk differently; something old. You're just like me."

Robert laughed. "But we aren't like the walls, Bettine. We do change. We listen and we learn and we watch all the passing time."

"Even the children," said Anne.

"You died here."

"Indeed we did. And the same way."

"Murdered?" she asked with a shiver.

Anne frowned. "Beheaded, my dear. Quite a few had a hand in arranging it. I was maneuvered, you see; and how should I know we were spied on?"

"You and Essex?"

"Ah, no," said Robert. "*We* weren't lovers, then."

"Only now," said Anne. "We met . . . posthumously on my part. And how are you here, my dear?"

"I'm the Mayor's girl," Bettine said. It was good to talk, to have even shadows to talk to. She sat forward, embracing her knees in her arms. Suddenly the tears began to flow, and she daubed at her eyes with the sheet, feeling a little silly to be talking to ectoplasms, which all the fashionable folk denied existed; and yet it helped. "We quarreled and he put me here."

"Oh dear," said Anne.

"Indeed," said Lord Essex, patting Anne's hand. "That's why the boys said we should come. It's very like us."

"You died for love?"

"Politics," said Anne. "So will you."

She shook her head furiously. This dream of hers was not in her control, and she tried to drag things her own way. "But it's a silly quarrel. And I won't die. They don't kill people here, they don't."

"They do," Anne whispered. "Just like they did."

"Well," said Essex, "not axes, any more. They're much neater than they were."

"Go away," Bettine cried. "Go away, go away, go away."

"You'd do well to talk with us," said Anne. "We could make you understand what you're really up against. And there's really so much you don't seem to see, Bettine."

"Don't think of love," said Essex. "It's not love, you know, that sends people here. It's only politics. I know that. And Anne does. Besides, you don't sound like someone in love, do you? You don't sound like someone in love, Bettine."

She shrugged and looked down, expecting that they would be gone when she looked up. "There *is* someone I love," she said in the faintest of whispers when she saw they were not gone.

Anne snorted delicately. "That's not worth much here. Eternity is long, Bettine. And there's love and love, Bettine." She wound insubstantial fingers with the earl's. "You mustn't think of it being love. That's not the reason you're here. Be wise, Bettine. These stones have seen a great deal come and go. So have we; and you don't have the face of one who loves."

"What do *you* know?" she cried. "You're nothing. I know *people*, believe me. And I know Richard."

"Good night, Bettine," Anne said.

"Good night," Essex said very softly and patiently, so that she did not seem to have ruffled either of them at all. And the children were back, who bowed with departing irony and faded. The lights brightened.

She flounced down among the bedclothes sulking at such depressing ideas and no small bit frightened, but not of the ghosts—of her situation. Of things they said. There was a chill in the air, and a whiff of dried old flowers and spices . . . the flowers, she thought, was Anne; and the spice must be Essex. Or maybe it was the children Edward and Richard. The apparitions did not threaten her; they only spoke her fears. That was what they really were, after all. Ectoplasms, indeed. She burrowed into the covers and punched out the lights, having dispensed with fear of ghosts; her eyes hurt and she was tired. She lay down with utter abandon, which she had really not done since she came, burrowed among the pillows and tried not to think or dream at all.

In the morning the phone came on and the screen lit up.

"Bettine," said Richard's voice, stern and angry.

She sprang up out of the covers, went blank for a moment and then assumed one of her bedroom looks, pushed her thick masses of hair looser on her head, stood up with a sinuous twist of her body and looked into the camera, moue'd into a worried frown, a tremble, a look near tears.

"Richard. Richard, I was so afraid. Please." Keep him feeling superior, keep him feeling great and powerful, which was what she was *for* in the world, after all, and how she lived. She came and stood before the camera, leaned there. "I want out of here, Richard. I don't understand this place." Naïveté always helped, helplessness; and it was, besides, truth. "The jailer was terrible." Jealousy, if she could provoke it. "Please, let me come back. I never meant to do anything wrong . . . what is it I've *done*, Richard?"

"Who was he?"

Her heart was beating very fast. Indignation now; set him off balance. "No one. I mean, it was just a small thing and he wasn't anyone in particular, and I never did anything like that before, Richard, but you left me alone and what's a girl to do, after all? Two weeks and you hadn't called me or talked to me—?"

"What's the *name*, Bettine? And where's the grade-fifty file? Where is it, Bettine?"

She was the one off balance. She put a shaking hand to her lips, blinked, shook her head in real disorganization. "I don't know anything about the file." This wasn't it, this wasn't what it was supposed to be about. "Honestly, Richard, I don't know. What file? Is *that* what this is? That you think I *stole* something? Richard, I never, I never stole anything."

"Someone got into the office. Someone who didn't belong there, Bettine; and you have the key, and I do, and that's a pretty limited range, isn't it? My office. My private office. Who did that, Bettine?"

"I don't know," she wailed, and pushed her hair aside— the pretty gestures were lifelong-learned and automatic. "Richard, I've gotten caught in something I don't understand at all, I don't understand, I don't, and I never let anyone in there." (But Tom had gotten in there; *he* could have, any time, since he was in the next office.) "Maybe the door . . . maybe I left it open and I shouldn't have, but, Richard, I don't even know what was in that file, I swear I don't."

"Who was in your apartment that night?"

"I—it wasn't connected to that, it wasn't, Richard, and I wish you'd understand that. It wasn't anything, but that I was lonely and it was a complete mistake, and now if I gave you somebody's name then it would get somebody in trouble who just never was involved; I mean, I might have been careless, Richard, I guess I was; I'm terribly sorry about the file, but I did leave the door open sometimes, and you were gone a lot. I mean . . . it was possible someone could have gotten in there, but you never told me there was any kind of trouble like that. . . ."

"The access numbers. You understand?"

"I don't. I never saw that file."

"Who was in your apartment?"

She remained silent, thinking of Tom, and her lip trembled. It went on trembling while Richard glared at her, because she could not make up her mind what she ought to do and what was safe. She could *handle* Richard. She was sure that she could.

And then he blinked out on her.

"Richard!" she screamed. She punched buttons in vain. The screen was dead. She paced the floor and wrung her hands and stared out the window.

She heard the guard coming, and her door closed and the outer door opened for the exchange of the tray. Then the door gave back again and she went out into the anteroom after it. She carried the tray back and set it on the table, finally went to the bath and looked at herself, at sleep-tangled hair and shadowed eyes and the stain of old cosmetic. She was appalled at the face she had shown to Richard, at what she had been surprised into showing him. She scrubbed her face at once and brushed her hair and put slippers on her bare feet, which were chilled to numbness on the tiles.

Then she ate her breakfast, sparingly, careful of her figure, and dressed and sat and sewed. The silence seemed twice as heavy as before. She hummed to herself and tried to fill the void. She sang—she had a beautiful voice, and she sang until she feared she would grow hoarse, while the pattern grew. She read some of the time, and, bored, she found a new way to do her hair; but then she thought after she had done it that if Richard should call back he might not like it, and it was important that he like the way she looked. She combed it back the old way, all the while mistrusting this instinct, this reliance on a look which had already failed.

So the day passed, and Richard did not call again.

They wanted Tom. There was the chance that if she did give Richard Tom's name it could be the right one, because it was all too obvious who *could* have gotten a file out of Richard's office, because there had been many times Richard had been gone and Tom had followed her about her duties, teasing her.

Safest not to ask and not to know. She was determined not to. She resented the thing that had happened—politics—politics. She hated politics.

Tom . . . was someone to love. Who loved her; and Richard had reasons which were Richard's, but it came down to two men being jealous. And Tom, being innocent, had no idea what he was up against . . . Tom could be hurt, but Richard would never hurt her; and while she did not tell Richard, she still had the power to perplex him. While he was perplexed he would do nothing.

She was not totally confident . . . of Tom's innocence, or of Richard's attitude. She was not accustomed to saying no. She was not accustomed to being put in difficult positions. Tom should not have asked it of her. He should have known. It was not fair what he did, whatever he had gotten himself involved in—some petty little record-juggling—to have put her in this position.

The pattern grew, delicate rows of stitches, complex designs which needed no thinking, only seeing, and she wept sometimes and wiped at her eyes while she worked.

Light faded from the window. Supper came and she ate, and this night she did not prepare for bed, but wrapped her night robe about her for warmth and sat in the chair and waited, lacking all fear, expecting the children, looking forward to them in a strangely keen longing, because they were at least company, and laughter was good to hear in this grim place. Even the laughter of murdered children.

There began to be a great stillness. And not the laughter of children this time, but the tread of heavier feet, the muffled clank of metal. A grim, shadowed face materialized in dimming light.

She stood up, alarmed, and warmed her chilling hands before her lips. "Edward," she cried aloud. "Edward, Richard . . . are you there?" But what was coming toward her was taller and bare of face and arm and leg, bronze elsewhere, and wearing a *sword,* of all things. She wanted the children; wanted Anne or Robert Devereaux, any of the others. This one . . . was different.

"Bettine," he said in a voice which echoed in far distances. "Bettine."

"I don't think I like you," she said.

The ghost stopped with a little clank of armor, kept fading in and out. He was young, even handsome in a foreign way. He took off his helmet and held it under his arm. "I'm Marc," he said. "Marcus Atilius Regulus. They said I should come. Could you see your way, Bettine, to prick your finger?"

"Why should I do that?"

"I am oldest," he said. "Well—almost, and of a different persuasion, and perhaps it is old-fashioned, but it would make our speaking easier."

She picked up her sewing needle and jabbed her cold finger, once and hard, and the blood welled up black in the dim light and fell onto the stones. She put the injured finger in her mouth, and stared quite bewildered, for the visitor was very much brighter, and seemed to draw a living breath.

"Ah," he said. "Thank you with all my heart, Bettine."

"I'm not sure at all I should have done that. I think you might be dangerous."

"Ah, no, Bettine."

"Were you a soldier, some kind of knight?"

"A soldier, yes; and a knight, but not the kind you think of. I think you mean of the kind born to this land. I came from Tiberside. I am Roman, Bettine. We laid some of the oldest stones just . . ." he lifted a braceletted arm, rather confusedly toward one of the steel walls. "But most of the old work is gone now. There are older levels; all the surly ones tend to gather down there. Even new ones, and some that never were civilized, really, or never quite accepted being dead, all of them—" he made a vague and deprecating gesture. "But we don't get many now, because there hasn't been anyone in here who could believe in us . . . in so very long . . . does the finger hurt?"

"No." She sucked at it and rubbed the moisture off and looked at him more closely. "I'm not sure *I* believe in you."

"You're not sure you don't, and that's enough."

"Why are you here? Where are the others?"

"Oh, they're back there."

"But why you? Why wouldn't they come? I expected the children."

"Oh. They're there. Nice boys."

"And why did *you* come? What has a soldier to do with me?"

"I—come for the dead. I'm the psychopomp."

"The what?"

"Psychopomp. Soul-guider. When you die."

"But I'm not going to die," she wailed, hugging her arms about her and looking without wanting to at the ancient sword he wore. "There's a mistake, that's all. I've been trying to explain to the others, but they don't understand. We're civilized. We don't go around killing people in here, whatever *used* to happen. . . ."

"Oh, they *do*, Bettine; but we don't get them, because they're very stubborn, and they believe in nothing, and they can't see us. Last month I lost one. I almost had him to see me, but at the last he just couldn't; and he slipped away and I'm not sure where. It looked hopelessly drear. I try with all of them. I'm glad you're not like them."

"But you're wrong. I'm not going to die."

He shrugged, and his dark eyes looked very sad.

"I can get out of here," she said, unnerved at his lack of belief in her. "If I have to, there's always a way. I can just tell them what they want to know and they'll let me go."

"Ah," he said.

"It's true."

His young face, so lean and serious, looked sadder still. "Oh Bettine."

"It *is* true; what do *you* know?"

"Why haven't you given them what they want before now?"

"Because. . . ." She made a gesture to explain and then shook her head. "Because I think I can get out of it without doing that."

"For pride? Or for honor?"

It sounded like something *he* should say, after all, all done up in ancient armor and carrying a sword. "You've been dead a long time," she said.

"Almost the longest of all. *Superbia*, we said. That's the wrong kind of pride; that's being puffed up and too important and not really seeing things right. And there's *exemplum*. That's a thing you do because the world needs it, like setting up something for people to look at, a little marker, to say Marcus Regulus stood here."

"And what if no one sees it? What good is it then, if I never get out of here? There's being brave and being stupid."

He shook his head very calmly. "An *exemplum* is an *exemplum* even if no one sees it. They're just markers, where someone was."

"Look outside, old ghost. The sun's going out and the world's dying."

"Still," he said, *"exempla* last . . . because there's nothing anyone can do to erase them."

"What, like old stones?"

"No. Just moments. Moments are the important thing. Not every moment, but more than some think."

"Well," she said, perplexed and bothered. "Well, that's all very well for men who go around fighting ancient wars, but I don't fight anyone. I don't like violence at all, and I'll do what I can for Tom but I'm not brave and there's a limit."

"Where, Bettine?"

"The next time Richard asks me, that's where. I want out of here."

He looked sad.

"Stop that," she snapped. "I suppose you think you're superior."

"No."

"I'm just a girl who has to live and they can take my job away and I can end up outside the walls starving, that's what could happen to me."

"Yes, sometimes *exempla* just aren't quick. Mine would have been. And I failed it."

"You're a soldier. I'm a woman."

"Don't you think about honor at all, Bettine?"

"You're out of date. I stopped being a virgin when I was thirteen."

"No. *Honor*, Bettine."

"I'll bet you were some kind of hero, weren't you, some old war hero?"

"Oh no, Bettine. I wasn't. I ran away. That's why I'm the psychopomp. Because the old Tower's a terrible place; and a good many of the dead do break down as they die. There were others who could have taken the job: the children come first, usually, just to get the prisoners used to the idea

of ghosts, but I come at the last . . . because I know what
it is to be afraid, and what it is to want to run. I'm an
Atilius Regulus, and there were heroes in my house, oh,
there was a great one . . . I could tell you the story. I will,
someday. But in the same family there was myself, and they
were never so noble after me. *Exemplum* had something to
do with it. I wish I could have left a better one. It came on
me so quickly . . . a moment; one lives all one's life to be
ready for moments when they come. I used to tell myself,
you know, that if mine had just—crept up slowly, then I
should have thought it out; I always did think. But I've
seen so much, so very much, and I know human beings,
and do you know . . . quick or slow in coming, it was what
I *was* that made the difference, thinking or not; and I just
wasn't then what I am now."

"Dead," she said vengefully.

He laughed silently. "And eons wiser." Then his face
went sober. "O Bettine, courage comes from being ready
whenever the moment comes, not with the mind . . . I
don't think anyone ever is. But what you *are* . . . can be
ready."

"What happened to you?"

"I was an officer, you understand. . . ." He gestured at
the armor he wore. "And when the Britons got over the
rampart . . . I ran, and took all my unit with me—I didn't
think what I was doing; *I* was getting clear. But a wise old
centurion met me coming his way and ran me through right
there. The men stopped running then and put the enemy
back over the wall, indeed they did. And a lot of men were
saved and discipline held. So I was an *exemplum,* after all;
even if I was someone else's. It hurt. I don't mean the
wound—those never do quite the way you think, I can tell
you that—but I mean really hurt, so that it was a long long
time before I came out in the open again—after the Tower
got to be a prison. After I saw so many lives pass here.
Then I decided I should come out. May I touch you?"

She drew back, bumped the chair, shivered. "That's not
how you . . . ?"

"O no. *I* don't take lives. May I touch you?"

She nodded mistrustingly, kept her eyes wide open as he
drifted nearer and a braceletted hand came toward her face,
beringed and masculine and only slightly transparent. It
was like a breath of cool wind, and his young face grew
wistful. Because she was beautiful, she thought, with a

little rush of pride, and he was young and very handsome and very long dead.

She wondered. . . .

"Warmth," he said, his face very near and his dark eyes very beautiful. "I had gone into my melancholy again . . . in all these last long centuries, that there was no more for me to do, no souls for me to meet, no special one who believed, no one at all. I thought it was all done. Are there more who still believe?"

"Yes," she said. And started, for there were Anne and Essex holding hands within the brickwork or behind it or somewhere; and other shadowy figures. The children were there, and a man who looked very wet, with a slight reek of alcohol, and more and more and more, shadows which went from brocades to metals to leather to furs and strange helmets.

"Go away," she cried at that flood, and fled back, overturning the tray and crowding into the corner. "Get out of here. I'm not going to die. I'm not brave and I'm not going to. Let someone else do the dying. I don't want to die."

They murmured softly and faded; and there came a touch at her cheek like a cool breeze.

"Go away!" she shrieked, and she was left with only the echoes. "I'm going mad," she said then to herself, and dropped into the chair and bowed her head into her hands. When she finally went to bed she sat fully dressed in the corner and kept the lights on.

Breakfast came, and she bathed and dressed, and read her book, which began to come to its empty and happy ending. She threw it aside, because her life was not coming out that way, and she kept thinking of Tom, and crying, not sobs, just a patient slow leaking of tears, which made her makeup run and kept her eyes swollen. She was not powerful. She had lost all illusion of that. She just wanted out of this alive, and to live and to forget it. She tried again to use the phone and she could not figure out the keyboard which she thought might give her access to someone, if she knew anything about such systems, and she did not.

For the first time she became convinced that she was in danger of dying here, and that instead, Tom was going to, and she would be in a way responsible. She was no one, no one against all the anger that swirled about her. She was quite, quite helpless; and not brave at all, and nothing in her life had ever prepared her to be. She thought back to days when she was a child, and in school, and all kinds of knowledge had been laid out in front of her. She had found it useless . . . which it was, to a ten-year-old girl who thought she had the world all neatly wrapped around her finger. Who thought at that age that she knew all the things that were important, that if she went on pleasing others that the world would always be all right.

Besides, the past was about dead people and she liked living ones; and learning about science was learning that the world was in the process of ending, and there was no cheer in that. She wanted to be Bettine Maunfry who had all that she would ever need. Never think, never think about days too far ahead, or things too far to either side, or understand things, which made it necessary to decide, and prepare.

Moments. She had never wanted to imagine such moments would come. There was no time she could have looked down the long currents of her life, which had *not* been so long after all, and when she could have predicted that Bettine Maunfry would have gotten herself into a situation like this. People were supposed to take care of her. There had always been someone to take care of her. That was what it was being female and beautiful and young. It was just not supposed to happen this way.

Tom, she thought. O Tom, now what do I do, what am I supposed to do?

But of course the doing was hers.

To him.

She had no idea what her horoscope or his was on this date, but she thought that it must be disaster, and she fingered the little fishes which she wore still in her décolletage for His Honor Richard Collier to see.

And she waited, to bend as she had learned to bend; only . . . she began to think with the versatility of the old Bettine . . . never give up an advantage. *Never.*

She went in and washed her face and put on her makeup again, and stopped her crying and repaired all the subtle damages of her tears.

She dressed in her handsomest dress and waited.

And toward sundown the call came.

"Bettine," His Honor said. "Have you thought better of it, Bettine?"

She came and faced the screen and stood there with her

lips quivering and her chin trembling because weakness worked for those who knew how to use it.

"I might," she said.

"There's no 'might' about it, Bettine," said Richard Collier, his broad face suffused with red. "Either you do or you don't."

"When you're here," she said, "when you come here and see me yourself, I'll tell you."

"Before I come."

"No," she said, letting the tremor become very visible. "I'm *afraid*, Richard; I'm afraid. If you'll come here and take me out of here yourself, I promise I'll tell you anything I know, which isn't much, but I'll tell you. I'll give you his name, but he's not involved with anything besides that he had a silly infatuation and I was lonely. But I won't tell anything if you don't come and get me out of here. This has gone far enough, Richard. I'm frightened. Bring me home."

He stared at her, frowning. "If I come over there and you change your mind, Bettine, you can forget any favors you think I owe you. I won't be played with. You understand me, girl?"

She nodded.

"All right," he said. "You'll tell me his name, and you'll be thinking up any other detail that might explain how he could have gotten to that office, and you do it tonight. I'm sure there's some sense in that pretty head, there's a girl. You just think about it, Bettine, and you think hard, and where you want to be. Home, with all the comforts . . . or where you are, which isn't comfortable at all, is it, Bettine?"

"No," she said, crying. She shook her head. "No. It's not comfortable, Richard."

"See you in the morning, Bettine. And you can pack, if you have the right name."

"Richard—" But he had winked out, and she leaned there against the wall shivering, with her hands made into fists and the feeling that she was very small indeed. She did not want to be in the Tower another night, did not want to face the ghosts, who would stare at her with sad eyes and talk to her about honor, about things that were not for Bettine Maunfry.

I'm sorry, she thought for them. I won't be staying and dying here after all.

But Tom would. That thought depressed her enormously. She felt somehow responsible, and that was a serious burden, more serious than anything she had ever gotten herself into except the time she had thought for ten days that she was pregnant. Maybe Tom would—lie to them; maybe Tom would try to tell them she was somehow to blame in something which was not her fault.

That frightened her. But Tom loved her. He truly did. Tom would not hurt her by anything he would say, being a man, and braver, and motivated by some vaguely different drives, which had to do with pride and being strong, qualities which she had avoided all her life.

She went through the day's routines, such of the day as was left, and packed all but her dress that Richard said matched her eyes. She put that one on, to sit up all the night, because she was determined that Richard should not surprise her looking other than beautiful, and it would be like him to try that mean trick. She would simply sleep sitting up and keep her skirts from wrinkling, all propped with pillows: that way she could both be beautiful and get some sleep.

And she kept the lights on because of the ghosts, who were going to feel cheated.

Had he really died that way, she wondered of the Roman, the young Roman, who talked about battles from forgotten ages. Had he really died that way or did he only make it up to make her listen to him? She thought about battles which might have been fought right where this building stood, all the many, many ages.

And the lights faded.

The children came, grave and sober, Edward and then Richard, who stood and stared with liquid, disapproving eyes.

"I'm sorry," she said shortly. "I'm going to be leaving."

The others then, Anne and Robert, Anne with her heart-shaped face and dark hair and lovely manners, Essex tall and elegant, neither looking at her quite the way she expected—not disapproving, more as if they had swallowed secrets. "It was politics after all," asked Anne, "wasn't it, Bettine?"

"Maybe it was," she said shortly, hating to be proved wrong. "But what's that to me? I'm still getting out of here."

"What if your lover accuses you?" asked Essex. "Loves do end."

"He won't," she said. "He wouldn't. He's not likely to."

"*Exemplum*," said a mournful voice. "O Bettine, is this yours?"

"Shut up," she told Marc. He was hardest to face, because his sad, dark gaze seemed to expect something special of her. She was instantly sorry to have been rude; he looked as if his heart was breaking. He wavered, and she saw him covered in dust, the armor split, and bloody, and tears washing down his face. She put her hands to her face, horrified.

"You've hurt him," said Anne. "We go back to the worst moment when we're hurt like that."

"O Marc," she said, "I'm sorry. I don't want to hurt you. But I want to be *alive,* you understand . . . can't you remember that? Wouldn't you have traded anything for that? And you had so much . . . when the sun was young and everything was new. O Marc, do you blame me?"

"There is only one question," he said, his eyes melting-sad. "It's your moment, Bettine. Your moment."

"Well, I'm not like you; I never was; never will be. What good is being right and dead? And what's right? Who's to know? It's all relative. Tom's not that wonderful, I'll have you to know. And neither's Richard. And a girl gets along the best she can."

A wind blew, and there was a stirring among the others, an intaken breath. Essex caught at Anne's slim form, and the children withdrew to Anne's skirts. "It's *her*," said young Edward. "*She's* come."

Only Marc refused the panic which took the others; bright again, he moved with military precision to one side, cast a look back through the impeding wall where a tiny figure advanced.

"She didn't die here," he said quietly. "But she has many ties to this place. She is one of the queens, Bettine, a great one. And very seldom does *she* come out."

"For me?"

"Because you are one of the last, perhaps."

She shook her head, looked again in bewilderment as Anne and Robert and young Richard bowed; and Edward inclined his head. Marc only touched his heart and stepped further aside. "Marc," Bettine protested, not wanting to lose him, the one she trusted.

"Well," said the visitor, a voice like the snap of ice. She seemed less woman than small monument, in a red and gold gown covered with embroideries and pearls, and ropes of pearls and pearls in crisp red hair; she had a pinched face out of which two eyes stared like living cinder. "Well?"

Bettine bowed like the others; she thought she ought. The Queen paced slowly, diverted herself for a look at Essex, and a slow nod at Anne. "Well."

"My daughter," said Anne. "The first Elizabeth."

"Indeed," said the Queen. "And Marc, good evening. Marc, how do you fare? And the young princes. Quite a stir, my dear, indeed quite a stir you've made. I have my spies; no need to reiterate."

"I'm not dying," she said. "You're all mistaken. I've told them I'm not dying. I'm going back to Richard."

The Queen looked at Essex, offered her hand. Essex kissed it, held it, smiled wryly. "Didn't you once say something of the kind?" asked the Queen.

"He did," said Anne. "It was, after all, your mistake, daughter."

"At the time," said Elizabeth. "But it was very stupid of you, Robert, to have relied on old lovers as messengers."

Essex shrugged, smiled again. "If not that year, the next. We were doomed to disagree."

"Of course," Elizabeth said. "There's love and there's power; and we all three wanted that, didn't we? And you . . ." Again that burning look turned on Bettine. "What sort are you? Not a holder. A seeker after power?"

"Neither one. I'm the Lord Mayor's girl and I'm going home."

"The Lord Mayor's girl." Elizabeth snorted. "The Lord Mayor's girl. I have spies, I tell you; all London's haunted. I've asked questions. The fellow gulled you, this Tom Ash. Ah, he himself's nothing; he works for others. He needs the numbers, that's all, for which he's paid. And with that list in others' hands your precious Lord Mayor's in dire trouble. Revolution, my dear, the fall of princes. Are you so blind? Your Lord Mayor's none so secure, tyrant that he is . . . if not this group of men, this year, then others, next. They'll have him; London town's never cared for despots, crowned or plain. Not even in its old age has it grown soft-witted. Just patient."

"I don't want to hear any of it. Tom loved me, that's all. Whatever he's involved in . . ."

Elizabeth laughed. "I was born to power. Was it accident? Ask my mother here what she paid. Ask Robert here what he paid to try for mine, and how I held it all the same . . .

no hard feelings, none. But do you think your Lord Mayor gained his by accident? You move in dark waters, with your eyes *shut*. You've wanted power all your life, and you thought there was an easy way. But you don't have it, because you don't understand what you want. If they gave you all of London on a platter, you'd see only the baubles. You'd look for some other hands to put the real power in; you're helpless. You've trained all your life to be, I'll warrant. I know the type. Bettine. What name is that? Abbreviated and diminished. *E-liz-a-beth* is our name, in fine round tones. You're tall; you try to seem otherwise. You dress to please everyone else; I pleased *Elizabeth*, and others copied me. If I was fond, it was that I liked men, but by all reason, I never handed my crown to one, no. However painful the decision . . . however many the self-serving ministers urging me this way and that, I did my own thinking; yes, Essex, even with you. Of course I'd hesitate, of course let the ministers urge me, of course I'd grieve—I'm not inhuman—but at the same time they could seem heartless and I merciful. And the deed got done, didn't it, Robert?"

"Indeed," he said.

"You were one of my favorites; much as you did, I always liked you; loved you, of course, but liked you, and there weren't as many of those. And you, Mother, another of the breed. But this modern bearer of my name—you have none of it, no backbone at all."

"I'm not in your class," Bettine said. "It's not fair."

"Whine and whimper. You're a born victim. I could make you a queen and you'd be a dead one in a fortnight."

"I just want to be comfortable and I want to be happy."

"Well, look at you."

"I will be again. I'm not going to be dead; I'm going to get out of this."

"Ah. You want, want, want; never look to see how things *are*. You spend all your life reacting to what others do. Ever thought about getting in the first stroke? No, of course not. I'm Elizabeth. You're just Bettine."

"I wasn't born with your advantages."

Elizabeth laughed. "I was a bastard . . . pardon me, Mother. And what were you? Why aren't *you* the Mayor? Ever wonder that?"

Bettine turned away, lips trembling.

"Look at me," said the Queen.

She did so, not wanting to. But the voice was commanding.

"Why did you?"

"What?"

"Look at me."

"You asked."

"Do you do everything people ask? You're everyone's victim, that's all. The Mayor's girl. You choose to be, no getting out of it. You *choose,* even by choosing not to choose. You'll go back and you'll give His Honor what he wants, and you'll go back to your apartment . . . maybe."

"What do you mean maybe?"

"Think, my girl, think. Girl you are; you've spent your whole majority trying to be nothing. I think you may achieve it."

"There's the Thames," said Essex.

"It's not what they take from you," said Anne, "it's what you give up."

"The water," said Edward, "is awfully cold, so I've heard."

"What do you know? You didn't have any life."

"But I did," said the boy, his eyes dancing. "I had my years . . . like you said, when the sun was very good."

"I had a pony," said Richard. "Boys don't, now."

"Be proud," said Elizabeth.

"I know something about you," Bettine said. "You got old and you had no family and no children, and I'm sure pride was cold comfort then."

Elizabeth smiled. "I hate to disillusion you, my dear, but I *was* happy. Ah, I shed a few tears, who doesn't in a lifetime? But I had exactly what I chose; and what I traded I knew I traded. I did precisely as I wanted. Not always the storybook I would have had it, but for all that, within my circumstances, precisely as I chose, for all my life to its end. I lived and I was curious; there was nothing I thought foreign to me. I saw more of the world in a glance than you've wondered about lifelong. I was ahead of my times, never caught by the outrageously unanticipated; but your whole life's an accident, isn't it, little Elizabeth?"

"Bettine," she said, setting her chin. "My *name* is Bettine."

"Good," laughed the Queen, slapping her skirted thigh. "Excellent. Go *on* thinking; and straighten your back, woman. Look at the eyes. Always look at the eyes."

The Queen vanished in a little thunderclap, and Essex swore and Anne patted his arm. "She was never comfortable," Anne said. "I would have brought her up with gentler manners."

"If I'd been your son—" said Essex.

"If," said Anne.

"They'll all be disturbed downstairs," said young Edward. "They *are,* when she comes through."

They faded . . . all but Marc.

"They don't change my mind," said Bettine. "The Queen was rude."

"No," said Marc. "Queens aren't. She's just what she is."

"Rude," she repeated, still smarting.

"Be what you are," said Marc, "I'll go. It's your moment."

"Marc?" She reached after him, forgetting. Touched nothing. She was alone then, and it was too quiet. She would have wanted Marc to stay. Marc understood fear.

Be what she was. She laughed sorrowfully, wiped at her eyes, and went to the bath to begin to be beautiful, looked at eyes which had puffed and which were habitually reddened from want of sleep. And from crying. She found herself crying now, and did not know why, except maybe at the sight of Bettine Maunfry as she was, little slim hands that had never done anything and a face which was all sex and a voice that no one would ever obey or take seriously . . . just for games, was Bettine. In all this great place which had held desperate criminals and fallen queens and heroes and lords, just Bettine, who was going to do the practical thing and turn in Tom who had never loved her, but only wanted something.

Tom's another, she thought with curiously clear insight, a *beautiful* person who was good at what he did, but it was not Tom who was going to be important, he was just smooth and good and all hollow, nothing behind the smiling white teeth and clear blue eyes. If you cracked him it would be like a china doll, nothing in the middle.

So with Bettine.

"I love you," he had protested. As far as she had known, no one had ever really loved Bettine Maunfry, though she had sold everything she had to keep people pleased and smiling at her all her life. She was not, in thinking about it, sure what she would do *if* someone loved her, or if she would know it if he did. She looked about at the magazines with the pictures of eyes and lips and the articles on how to sell one's soul.

Articles on love.

There's love and love, Anne had said.

Pleasing people. Pleasing everyone, so that they would please Bettine. Pretty children got rewards for crying and boys got spanked. While the world was pacified, it would not hurt Bettine.

Eyes and lips, primal and demetrean.

She made up carefully, did her hair, added the last items to her packing.

Except her handwork, which kept her sane. Click, click. Mindless sanity, rhythms and patterns. There was light from the window now. Probably breakfast would arrive soon, but she was not hungry.

And finally came the noise of the doors, and the steps ascending the tower.

Richard Collier came. He shut the door behind him and looked down at her frowning; and she stood up in front of the only window.

Look them in the eyes, the Queen had said. She looked at Richard that way, the Queen's way, and he evidently did not like it.

"The name," he said.

She came to him, her eyes filling with tears in spite of herself. "I don't want to tell you," she said. "It would hurt somebody; and if you trusted me you'd let me straighten it out. I can get your file back for you."

"You leave that to me," Richard said. "The name, girl, and no more—"

She had no idea why she did it. Certainly Richard's expression was one of surprise, as if he had calculated something completely wrong. There was blood on her, and the long needle buried between his ribs, and he slid down to lie on the floor screaming and rolling about, or trying to. It was a very soundproof room; and no one came. She stood and watched, quite numb in that part of her which ought to have been conscience; if anything feeling mild vindication.

"Bettine," she said quietly, and sat down and waited for him to die and for someone who had brought him to the tower to miss him. Whoever had the numbers was free to use them now; there would be a new order in the city; there would be a great number of changes. She reckoned that if she had ordered her life better she might have been better prepared, and perhaps in a position to escape. She was not. She had not planned. It's not the moments that can be planned, the Roman would say; it's the lives . . . that lead to them.

And did London's life . . . lead to Bettine Maunfry? She suspected herself of a profound thought. She was even proud of it. Richard's eyes stared blankly now. There had not been a great deal of pain. She had not wanted that, particularly, although she would not have shrunk from it. In a moment, there was not time to shrink.

There was power and there was love, and she had gotten through life with neither. She did not see what one had to do with the other; nothing, she decided, except in the sense that there really never had been a Bettine Maunfry, only a doll which responded to everyone else's impulses. And there had been nothing of her to love.

She would not unchoose what she had done; that was Elizabeth's test of happiness. She wondered if Richard would.

Probably not, when one got down to moments; but Richard had not been particularly smart in some things.

I wonder if I could have been Mayor, she thought. Somewhere I decided about that, and never knew I was deciding.

There was a noise on the stairs now. They were coming. She sat still, wondering if she should fight them too, but decided against it. She was not, after all, insane. It was politics. It had to do with the politics of His Honor the Mayor and of one Bettine, a girl, who had decided not to give a name.

They broke in, soldiers, who discovered the Mayor's body with great consternation. They laid hands on her and shouted questions.

"I killed him," she said. They waved rifles at her, accusing her of being part of the revolution.

"I led my own," she said.

They looked very uncertain then, and talked among themselves and made calls to the city. She sat guarded by rifles, and they carried the Mayor out, poor dead Richard. They talked about the murder and wondered that she could have had the strength to drive the needle so deep. Finally—incredibly—they questioned the jailer as to what kind of prisoner she was, as if they believed that she had been more than the records showed, the imprisoned leader of some cause, the center of the movement they had been hunting.

They talked about more guards. Eventually she had them, in great number, and by evening, all the Tower was ringed with soldiery, and heavy guns moved into position, great batteries of them in the inner court. Two days later she looked out the window and saw smoke where outer London was, and knew there was riot in the town.

The guards treated her with respect. Bettine Maunfry, they called her when they had to deal with her, not girl, and not Bettine. They called on her—of all things, to issue a taped call for a cease-fire.

But of her nightly companions . . . nothing. Perhaps they were shy, for at night a guard stood outside in the anteroom. Perhaps, after all, she was a little mad. She grieved for their absence, not for Richard and not for Tom, living in this limbo of tragic comedy. She watched the city burn and listened to the tread of soldiers in the court, and watched the gun crews from her single window. It was the time before supper, when they left her a little to herself—if a guard at the stairside door was privacy; they had closed off the anteroom as they usually did, preparing to deliver her dinner.

"Quite a turmoil you've created."

She turned from the window, stared at Marc in amazement. "But it's daytime."

"I *am* a little faded," he said, looking at his hand, and looked up again. "How are you, Bettine?"

"It's ridiculous, isn't it?" She gestured toward the courtyard and the guns. "They think I'm dangerous."

"But you are."

She thought about it, how frightened they were and what was going on in London. "They keep asking me for names. Today they threatened me. I'm not sure I'm *that* brave, Marc, I'm really not."

"But you don't know any."

"No," she said. "Of course I don't. So I'll be counted as brave, won't I?"

"The other side needs a martyr, and you're it, you know that."

"How does it go out there? Do the Queen's spies tell her?"

"Oh, it's violent, quite. If I were alive I'd be out there; it's a business for soldiers. The starships are hanging off just waiting. The old Mayor was dealing under the table in favoring a particular company, and the company that supported him had its offices wrecked . . . others just standing by waiting to move in and give support to the rebels, to outmaneuver their own rivals. The ripple goes on to stars you've never seen."

"That's amazing."

"You're not frightened."

"Of course I'm frightened."

"There was a time a day ago when you might have ended up in power; a mob headed this way to get you out, but the troops got them turned."

"Well it's probably good they didn't get to me. I'm afraid I wouldn't know what to do with London if they gave it to me. Elizabeth was right."

"But the real leaders of the revolution have come into the light now; they use your name as a cause. It's the spark they needed so long. Your name is their weapon."

She shrugged.

"They've a man inside the walls, Bettine . . . do you understand me?"

"No. I don't."

"I couldn't come before; it was still your moment . . . these last few days. None of us could interfere. It wouldn't be right. But I'm edging the mark . . . just a little. I always do. Do you understand me now, Bettine?"

"I'm going to die?"

"He's on his way. It's one of the revolutionaries . . . not the loyalists. The revolution needs a martyr; and they're afraid you *could* get out. They can't have their own movement taken away from their control by some mob. You'll die, yes. And they'll claim the soldiers killed you to stop a rescue. Either way, they win."

She looked toward the door, bit her lip. She heard a door open, heard steps ascending; a moment's scuffle.

"I'm here," Marc said.

"Don't you have to go away again? Isn't this . . . something I have to do?"

"Only if you wish."

The inner door opened. A wild-eyed man stood there, with a gun, which fired, right for her face. It *hurt*. It seemed too quick, too ill-timed; she was not ready, had not said all she wanted to say.

"There are things I wanted to do," she protested.

"There always are."

She had not known Marc was still there; the place was undefined and strange.

"Is it over? Marc, I wasn't through. I'd just figured things out."

He laughed and held out his hand. "Then you're ahead of most."

He was clear and solid to her eyes; it was the world which had hazed. She looked about her. There were voices, a busy hum of accumulated ages, time so heavy the world could scarcely bear it.

"I could have done better."

The hand stayed extended, as if it were important. She reached out hers, and his was warm.

"Till the sun dies," he said.

"Then what?" It was the first question.

He told her.

Herewith, a short, sharp story on a classic fantasy theme.

Roger Zelazny's novels include the Amber series, *Lord of Light, This Immortal, Damnation Alley,* and many others.

AND I ONLY AM ESCAPED TO TELL THEE

Roger Zelazny

IT WAS WITH THEM CONSTANTLY—THE BLACK patch directly overhead from whence proceeded the lightnings, the near-blinding downpour, the explosions like artillery fire.

Van Berkum staggered as the ship shifted again, almost dropping the carton he carried. The winds howled about him, tearing at his soaked garments; the water splashed and swirled around his ankles—retreating, returning, retreating. High waves crashed constantly against the ship. The eerie, green light of St. Elmo's fire danced along the spars.

Above the wind and over even the thunder, he heard the sudden shriek of a fellow seaman, random object of attention from one of their drifting demonic tormentors.

Trapped high in the rigging was a dead man, flensed of all flesh by the elements, his bony frame infected now by the moving green glow, right arm flapping as if waving—or beckoning.

Van Berkum crossed the deck to the new cargo site, began lashing his carton into place. How many times had they shifted these cartons, crates, and barrels about? He had lost count long ago. It seemed that every time the job was done a new move was immediately ordered.

He looked out over the railing. Whenever he was near, whenever the opportunity presented itself, he scanned the distant horizon, dim through the curtain of rain. And he hoped.

In this, he was different. Unlike any of the others, he had a hope—albeit a small one—for he had a plan.

A mighty peal of laughter shook the ship. Van Berkum shuddered. The captain stayed in his cabin almost constantly now, with a keg of rum. It was said that he was playing cards with the Devil. It sounded as if the Devil had just won another hand.

Pretending to inspect the cargo's fastenings, Van Berkum located his barrel again, mixed in with all the others. He could tell it by the small dab of blue paint. Unlike the others it was empty, and caulked on the inside.

Turning, he made his way across the deck again. Something huge and bat-winged flitted past him. He hunched his shoulders and hurried.

Four more loads, and each time a quick look into the distance. Then— Then . . . ?

Then!

He saw it. There was a ship off the port bow! He looked about frantically. There was no one near him. This was it. If he hurried. If he was not seen.

He approached his barrel, undid the fastenings, looked about again. Still no one nearby. The other vessel definitely appeared to be approaching. There was neither time nor means to calculate courses, judge winds or currents. There was only the gamble and the hope.

He took the former and held to the latter as he rolled the barrel to the railing, raised it, and cast it overboard. A moment later he followed it.

The water was icy, turbulent, dark. He was sucked downward. Frantically he clawed at it, striving to drag himself to the surface.

Finally there was a glimpse of light. He was buffeted by waves, tossed about, submerged a dozen times. Each time, he fought his way back to the top.

He was on the verge of giving up when the sea suddenly grew calm. The sounds of the storm softened. The day began to grow brighter about him. Treading water, he saw the vessel he had just quitted receding in the distance, carrying its private hell along with it. And there, off to his left, bobbed the barrel with the blue marking. He struck out after it.

When he finally reached it, he caught hold. He was able

to draw himself partly out of the water. He clung there and panted. He shivered. Although the sea was calmer here, it was still very cold.

When some of his strength returned, he raised his head, scanned the horizon.

There!

The vessel he had sighted was even nearer now. He raised an arm and waved it. He tore off his shirt and held it high, rippling in the wind like a banner.

He did this until his arm grew numb. When he looked again the ship was nearer still, though there was no indication that he had been sighted. From what appeared to be their relative movements, it seemed that he might well drift past it in a matter of minutes. He transferred the shirt to his other hand, began waving it again.

When next he looked, he saw that the vessel was changing course, coming toward him. Had he been stronger and less emotionally drained, he might have wept. As it was, he became almost immediately aware of a mighty fatigue and a great coldness. His eyes stung from the salt, yet they wanted to close. He had to keep looking at his numbed hands to be certain that they maintained their hold upon the barrel.

"Hurry!" he breathed. "Hurry . . ."

He was barely conscious when they took him into the lifeboat and wrapped him in blankets. By the time they came alongside the ship, he was asleep.

He slept the rest of that day and all that night, awakening only long enough to sip hot grog and broth. When he did try to speak, he was not understood.

It was not until the following afternoon that they brought in a seaman who spoke Dutch. He told the man his entire story, from the time he had signed aboard until the time he had jumped into the sea.

"Incredible!" the seaman observed, pausing after a long spell of translation for the officers. "Then that storm-tossed apparition we saw yesterday was really the *Flying Dutchman!* There truly *is* such a thing—and you, you are the only man to have escaped from it!"

Van Berkum smiled weakly, drained his mug, and set it aside, hands still shaking.

The seaman clapped him on the shoulder.

"Rest easy now, my friend. You are safe at last," he said, "free of the demon ship. You are aboard a vessel with a fine safety record and excellent officers and crew—and just a few days away from her port. Recover your strength and rid your mind of past afflictions. We welcome you aboard the *Marie Celeste*."

~~~~~~~~~~~~~~~~~~~~~~~~~~~~~~~~

A lot of people who move to New York City find it a confusing, hostile place to live—but very few of them discover that dinosaurs inhabit the city.

Tony Sarowitz, like many other sf and fantasy writers including Lisa Tuttle and J. Michael Reaves in this book, studied writing in the Clarion workshops. His stories have appeared in *New Dimensions*, *Galaxy*, *Isaac Asimov's SF Magazine*, and *Fantasy and Science Fiction*. The story below won the Transatlantic Review Award.

DINOSAURS ON BROADWAY

Tony Sarowitz

AFTER A MONTH IN NEW YORK, IT SEEMED TO
Sylvia that everything she did was part of a dream. She
looked across the desk at the interviewer, a Mrs. Vedicchio,
and stared at the beautiful white hair piled on her head like
whipped cream. "New York isn't Oregon," Mrs. Vedicchio
said, as if this was a point of subtle misunderstanding between them. Sylvia nodded. It was her third job interview
of the day, and she was thinking about her own hair, which
seemed limp and heavy to her, as if it were made of clay.
In a certain sense, it was; Clay was her name. Her name
was Sylvia Clay. "Perhaps if you had a master's," Mrs.
Vedicchio went on, "or a few local references. Adminis-
trative positions in parenting and early childhood are so
hard to find these days." Sylvia nodded again and smiled,
picturing herself eating Mrs. Vedicchio's white hair with a
spoon.

She thought about hair while she walked to the subway
station at 116th, and she made a list in her mind of a few
things, besides Oregon, that New York was not. It was not
warm in January, which was this month. It was not a gentle
fragrance carried on the wind. It was not the Triassic,
Jurassic, or Cretaceous period of the Mesozoic era (this
last item from a picture book about dinosaurs that she had
bought for Madeline a week ago). She stood on the subway platform and looked at her wristwatch, thinking about
how long she had before Maddy was due out of school.
She thought about Maddy and looked at the yellow eyes of
the approaching train and thought about the noise, which
was like the howl of a beast. She imagined that it was a

beast, an armored ankylosaur, its tough hide scraping along
the tunnel wall as it charged down the track. She closed her
eyes, and all her thoughts were pictures in her mind—subway trains, snowdrifts, white hair, dinosaurs, wildflowers.
Then the platform tilted sixty degrees and she fell onto the
tracks.

Mishaps seemed to be a way of life for Sylvia in New
York. There had been runaway buses, stray bullets flying
past her on the street. This, however, was her first time in
an ambulance. The noise of the siren was horrible. She sat
up and tried to explain that she was fine, nothing wrong
aside from a few scrapes and bruises, but the attendant
cooed at her, "No, no," and gently eased her down onto
the stretcher. The ambulance wailed on. At the hospital,
the admitting nurse insisted that she be examined, and
although Sylvia could remember rolling safely off the
tracks, she began to wonder if the train hadn't hit her after
all instead of gliding by her like a screeching black cloud.
She counted her fingers and toes in sudden panic. "I feel
ridiculous," she told the doctor, wide-eyed. "Is this a
symptom of something, shock, concussion, to feel so entirely absurd?"

She was sitting in a waiting area, sipping tea from a
Styrofoam cup when Richard arrived. He stood in front of
her, hands on his hips, coat still buttoned, scarf immacu-
lately tucked around his neck. "What's the bottom line,
Syl?" he said.

She tried to make a joke of it. "I can't get a job without
training. I was just trying to get on the right track." He
stared at her. "I'm fine," she said. "It was nothing, really.
In a minute I'm going to pick up Maddy. They shouldn't
have even called you. But I'm glad you're here. If you're
glad, that is. I hope you weren't in the middle of anything."

"As long as you're all right, healthwise," he said.
"Maddy and I would have a hell of a time coping if anything happened to you. You are all right, aren't you?"

"Yes, Dick." She was accustomed by now to this new
lingo of his, this bureaucratese. She told herself that it was
a superficial manner of speech, nothing more, as if he'd
adopted the accent and idiom of a foreign land. She stood
and put on her coat. "Wife-wise, I'm fine."

"Well." He clapped his hands in a businesslike manner.
"The office isn't expecting me back. We'll get Maddy, then
eat out somewhere, give you an evening to recoup." He

paused. "I mean, if it's all right with you. If I wouldn't be in the way."

"Of course not," she said, smiling. He nodded seriously and went to open the door.

Sylvia often felt small on the streets of New York. It had to do with the height of the buildings and the density of the crowds. She was a small woman to begin with, just two inches over five feet. In the midst of a crowd she felt lost.

She had fallen behind Dick on the sidewalk. His walk had changed since they'd moved, his strides had become short and brisk. Watching him from behind made her think of aftershave ads. She ran up to him and took his arm, and he turned to her, an utter stranger. She stepped back, confused, speechless. The man barely glanced at her before walking on, and for a moment, it seemed to her that any one of a dozen broad backs walking away from her on the street could be Dick's. Then she saw him. She took hold of his arm so tightly that he looked at her with surprise.

"What are you thinking?" he asked.

She shook her head. She was thinking nothing that she could put into words. As they walked down the street together, she pictured a brachiosaur submerged to its hips in the East River, neck outstretched, tenderly nipping at the greenery of a penthouse garden terrace.

Dick waited outside while Sylvia talked to Maddy's first-grade teacher. "I'm worried about Maddy," Sylvia said. "She's been so quiet the past month, since we moved."

Ms. Brown was an overweight black woman in her late fifties. She wore a cotton print dress—tiny yellow ducks on a field of green. "Never you mind, Miz Clay," she said with a wide grin. "Your little girl's just fine. Why, given the paradigms of normalcy accepted by modern pedagogic thought, she's moving right along toward optimal self-actualization. Next year we might think on the possibility of issuing a few proximity reinforcers during the morning module, but then she'll have a new facilitator. She won't be my dumpling any more."

This was something that Sylvia had thought a lot about, as much as she was able to think about anything, these days. "I just want to know if she's all right," she said. "I know something about children, what's healthy and what isn't. When we lived in Eugene, I organized parenting groups and childcare co-ops. I saw how Maddy acted with other kids. I know——"

"Oooeee," Ms. Brown exclaimed. "You sure were something, Miz Clay. You say this was Eugene?"

"Eugene, Oregon."

"Is that in the USA?" Laughing, she put her palm firmly between Sylvia's shoulder blades and propelled her toward the door. "Your little girl's settling down to her new school just fine. You don't worry, now. Hear? Come on over here, Maddy. Your momma's waiting on you."

Outside, Maddy ran for her father's arms. He lifted her high, then brought her down to eye level. "How's my pumpkin? How's my little girl?"

Maddy opened her mouth and pointed at her throat.

"Soon," he said. "We're eating Chinese food tonight. Yum. At a restaurant. How's that?"

She nodded emphatically, then gave him a quick hug and squirmed to be let down. They had always been close, father and daughter. Sylvia pulled her coat tighter and buttoned the collar. Snow had begun to fall.

They walked down 73rd Street. Maddy ran ahead and waited at the corner. "She was never this quiet back home. Back in Eugene," Sylvia said. "I'm worried about her."

"She's fine," Dick said. He covered his head with his newspaper as they came to the corner. Maddy motioned for him to bend over. She stroked his chin, then wiggled her stubby fingers. Dick laughed. "I've told you a thousand times. I shaved because we moved to New York. Men don't wear beards in New York." He took her hand and they started across the street.

"Wait for the green," Sylvia called, then started across herself. A cab roared through the intersection. It squealed its brakes and swerved, spraying the sidewalk with black slush, missing her by inches.

Late in the Cretaceous period, about 100 million years ago, the Arctic Ocean and the Gulf of Mexico were connected by a vast shallow sea dividing North America in two. "Look at this, Maddy," Sylvia called, holding the picture book open on her lap. There was a diagram showing east and west America split by a ribbon of water as if a great tongue had licked the continent from Corpus Christi to Tuktoyaktuk on the Mackenzie Bay. If Columbus had sailed 100 million years ago, if it was 100 million years ago now, they would have had to cross that ocean to reach New York. They would probably be speakers of separate language, visitors from a foreign land. "Maddy?"

She had fallen asleep on the rug by her dollhouse. "I'll get her," Sylvia said, although Dick had not moved from his chair. He looked embedded there, corporate tax forms piled high by his feet, on his lap, on the coffee table by his side. She pictured a paleontologist of the future working with pick and brush to extricate his fossilized remains from the easy chair, chipping with terrible patience at reams of petrified IRS returns, an impossible task, hopeless.

She put Madeline to bed, then returned to the sofa and sat with her feet tucked under her. The book was still open to the same page. She traced the diagram of the inland sea with her fingertip, then looked to the illustration on the facing page, an artist's rendering of the scene. Brontosaurs wallowed in the shallows, munching on the top leaves of giant palms. Crested pteranodons glided above the calm slate waters on leathery twelve-foot wings.

"I wish you wouldn't put so much of your time into reading that stuff, Syl," Dick said. "We need to take a forward-looking approach to our new life here. If plants and animals were what we wanted, we could have looked for a place in the suburbs, Scarsdale or White Plains or something."

"Sorry." She shut the book and put it by her side. It was, after all, only a child's picture book, and she was tired; it had been a long day. Her hands wanted to open the book again, and so she clasped them on her lap and watched Dick tap his pipe in the ashtray. She wished it was warm enough to open a window. She had enjoyed the smell of his tobacco in the house in Eugene, but it seemed cloying here in the apartment. She wondered if it had to do with the size of the rooms, or if it was some basic incompatibility of smoke with New York air, which had a flavor and density of its own.

"Why are we here?" she asked.

"Pardon? On this planet? In this room?"

"I don't know what I was thinking about." Her hand fluttered in the air. "I'm sorry. You're in the middle of something."

"No." He put aside the paper he'd been reading and looked at her. "We haven't been keeping proper track of our emotional inventory the past weeks, have we?" he asked. "How have you been getting along?"

"Okay, I guess. A little crazy. I can't seem to get my feet on the ground." The understatement of the era. The largest dinosaurs were reputed to have had two brains, one in their head and another at the base of their tails. Sylvia felt as if she had half a dozen or more, each in contention with the others, all shouting out of turn. She tilted her head back against the sofa cushions and closed her eyes.

"I suppose we have to expect a certain restructuring of our day-to-day experience here. Any luck with the job hunt?"

"No." She shook her head side to side without lifting it from the cushion. "No luck, no promises, no hope. No, no, no." She felt a shiver of giddy exhaustion.

"I hope you won't allow that incident in the subway to impact negatively on your attitude toward living here."

"It's not that. It's—" Her mind was empty. She opened her eyes and stared at the ceiling, the seams in the plaster visible through the new coat of white paint. Not a single word would come.

"Sometimes," he said, and something in his voice made her look at him, "sometimes you have to stop being yourself so much, so that you can be yourself *here*, yourself in New York. It's not the same, psychologically speaking."

"I love you no matter where we are," she said. She put her head back on the cushion and closed her eyes. She should go to bed, she thought, or she would drift to sleep right here. She heard him shuffling papers, getting back to work.

"You'll find a job," he said. "Expertise is always marketable. And over the long term, I think you'll find you like living in New York. It's an exciting place. Alive."

Sylvia smiled, nodded. She too thought of New York as alive at times, a huge sluggish animal of asphalt and stone, slowly but surely digesting them all. She wanted to tell Dick how correct he was.

"I wonder what I'd know about you," he said, "if I could read your mind."

"I wonder what I'd know about me," she murmured.

Sylvia woke in the dark. She felt Richard sitting up in the bed beside her. He cried out, a cry of loss rather than pain, a frightened, anguished sound. She sat up, held his arm firmly and put her other hand on the back of his neck. She called his name. He cried out again, more quietly this time, then fell limply back onto the bed. After a moment, he whispered, "Again?"

She nodded, then realized that it was too dark for him to see. "Yes." It was the third time in the last four nights.

"It's all right," he mumbled, turning on his side away from her. "Never mind." He shook off her hand, hugged his pillow to his stomach.

Sometimes she felt she knew him as well as she knew herself. Better. But sometimes she found herself watching him suspiciously, wondering if he was about to metamorphose into something entirely unexpected, imagining that she might wake up some morning beside a stone, or a bird, or a clipboard.

"Richard?" she called softly. Already he was asleep.

The weather report predicted a cold day. Sylvia laid Maddy's clothes out on the sofa—underwear, warm pants, turtleneck sweater—and went to cook breakfast. By the time the oatmeal was done, Maddy was dressed and playing on the living room floor with her Raggedy Ann doll. She flew the doll in figure-eights through the air, making buzzing engine noises and laughing. At the table, she propped it up by her plate while she ate.

"Going to be one cold day," Sylvia said, as if to herself. "Looks like snow." Maddy looked at her doll, the cloth face, the idiotic smile, and shook her head slowly, sadly. The doll, with Maddy's hand behind it, commiserated with a shake of its own.

Dick came out of the bedroom tucking in his shirt. He sat at the table, full of bluster and good cheer. "You have to prioritize your life," he said, banging the table with his fist. "Know what you want and take it." He reached over and pinched Maddy's cheek, and she giggled.

They left at the same time, Maddy and Dick. Sylvia put the dishes away and left a few minutes after. She didn't like being in the apartment alone. She felt uneasy there, despite the window gates and police lock. To her mind, protection implied the need for protection, which in turn implied danger. The locks and bars made her feel like a morsel, a nutmeat ripe within its shell.

She stopped at the coffee shop on the corner, as she

did every morning, and ordered a cup of tea. She held the cup in both hands, the heat in her palms, and looked into the tea. She saw shapes in the steam, animals rearing on their hind legs, strange birds in flight. She closed her eyes and felt herself rising with the steam, a bird soaring up on a column of warm air.

A man stood at the corner of 71st Street and Second Avenue. He was young, in his early twenties. He was dressed in ill-fitting clothes, and he wore no socks, although it was a very cold day. Above the black stubble on his cheeks, his skin was pale. "For God's sake!" he shouted at the passersby. "For God's sake!" Sylvia paused to watch him. Others looked away as they walked past. "What's the matter with everyone?" he yelled, rocking from one foot to the other, coming dangerously near the edge of his balance. "Why doesn't anybody help? What's going on here?" He began to cry.

"I'll help," Sylvia said. She stood a few steps away from him, afraid to come closer. "Do you need food? Money? Are you—What can I do?"

At each question he tried to speak, then shook his head. Sylvia felt embarrassed. She went over and shook his arm gently, shocked by how thin it felt through his sleeve. "Do you need a doctor? Just nod. There's a restaurant over here. Can I buy you lunch?" She felt like a supplicant, as if she was more helpless than he. He waved his hand as if to motion her away. She found a ten dollar bill in her purse and stuffed it in his pocket.

"Quick," he said. "How do you feel?"

"What?" She stepped back.

"Don't think. Dammit, you're losing it." He took a pen and a small dog-eared notebook from an inside pocket. "What was your feeling at the moment you gave me the money? How about guilt? Would you say you were feeling very guilty, fairly guilty, slightly guilty, or not at all—"

Sylvia grabbed the notebook from his hand and threw it into the street. It vanished under the flow of cars. She watched a few loose pages pinwheel down the street, then turned her back and started away. "Why did you do that?" he called plaintively behind her. "What the hell was that for?"

By the time she reached the next corner, he was yelling. "Just try to get your ten bucks back, bitch."

It was 10:15; her appointment for an interview at the city's Agency for Child Development was for 11. She stopped at her bank, handed the teller her check and ID. He stared at her Oregon driver's license. "We've only been here a month," she explained. He looked from the picture on her license to her face, then back at the license. "Am I still me?" she asked, smiling. He pushed the money toward her across the counter. He looked at her as if he could see the wall behind her, as if she wasn't there.

She left the bank at 11:05. At first she assumed that her watch had somehow leapt ahead an extra half hour. She tapped the crystal face with her finger, then went back inside the bank. The clock on the wall and her watch agreed perfectly—11:05, now 11:06. It was impossible. She knew that she had been in the bank for perhaps ten minutes, fifteen at the most. She stood there looking from one timepiece to the other, trying to reconcile her memory with the uncompromising hour.

Outside, she walked slowly down Second Avenue, trying to think. She went past a pay phone, glanced at her watch. She was already ten minutes late. There was no excuse that she could think of, nothing for her to say. The ACD office was in the City Hall building on Church Street at the southern tip of Manhattan, a twenty-minute ride by cab. She began to walk more quickly, as if she could cover the ninety-four blocks on foot, as if she could arrive ten minutes before she started. She didn't notice the yellow rope lying across the sidewalk between 66th and 67th, barely saw the workman standing in the street, or heard the faint sound of the cable snapping five floors above. Still, all these signals came together somewhere in her mind, and she stopped short just as the piano fell.

It was a Steinway grand with a beautiful ebony finish. It fell five stories in a second and a half, smashing to the ground with a demented, tortured chord, a lunatic twang. For a moment, the air seemed full of flying wood and wire, and then everything was still, and Sylvia was standing there, untouched, with wreckage strewn all around.

The workman had fallen in the street. Now he pushed himself to his feet and staggered over to her, clutching his shoulder. He sat on the collapsed piano frame, lowering himself gingerly onto it as if it was a delicate and valuable heirloom.

"Are you all right?" Sylvia asked.

He peeked under the hand at his shoulder, then shrugged. "Not good, not bad," he said. "Jeanie, that's my youngest, she had her wisdom teeth pulled Wednesday, and now she sips her food through a straw and moans constantly. It's driving my wife crazy. And Billy, that's my second-oldest, he writes to me from school that he must have two hundred dollars to join a fraternity. My feeling is that for two hundred dollars he should forget fraternity and look for love, but I suppose that's what children are for. And you?"

"I don't know," Sylvia said. "This city—It's been doing something to me. To all of us, my husband, and my daughter, and me."

"This something—could you be a little more specific?"

"I don't know. I don't know."

"Yes," he said, nodding thoughtfully. "I recall that you made the same point just a moment ago."

"Everything is strange and unsettled," she said. "Everything has to do with uncertainty and—"

"And?"

"Change. I've been thinking a lot about change."

"I have fifteen cents," he told her.

A woman came out of the luncheonette across the street. "I've called an ambulance," she called to them. "They'll be here in a minute. Don't move. They'll be right here."

"I'll be leaving now," Sylvia told the workman. "I learned yesterday that I don't like ambulances."

"It's good to learn something new every day." He blinked, looked around as if seeing the ruined piano for the first time. "So much for wings of song."

"I like you," she said. "You're the first person I've found here that I like."

He shrugged. "You'll find everything in this city, sooner or later. Everything is here."

Richard called to say that he'd be late for dinner. "Incidentally," he said, "I forgot to mention it this morning. I like your hair blonde."

"I am blonde, Dick. I've always been blonde."

"Ah." There was a pause. "Well, I didn't say you weren't."

Maddy was playing with her dolls when Sylvia tiptoed to the door and looked in. It had become a habit with her to approach Maddy's room quietly, almost stealthily, hoping to surprise her daughter in surreptitious talk. Now, standing at the door, she felt ashamed. "Come on sweetheart," she said. "I'll read you a book."

Maddy paused, a doll in each hand, and frowned with the effort of deciding. She shook her head, no.

"Your new dinosaur book," Sylvia said. Maddy didn't bother to answer; she had already handed down her decision. "I'll be in the living room if you change your mind."

Sylvia sat on the sofa and read about the extinction of the dinosaurs. According to the book, it was a mystery that no one could adequately explain. At one moment of geologic time, they had covered the earth and filled the sky in all their grandiose reptilian glory, and the next moment they were gone, every one, almost before the rocks took notice. Sylvia became sad reading about it, and she turned back the pages to the earlier pictures, stegosaurs lumbering through the dense wet forests, pteranodons gliding through cloudless pink skies on wide membranous wings. She read until it was time to start dinner, and put the book reluctantly aside.

She thought about change while she chopped cabbage on a board laid over the kitchen sink, different kinds of changes: the shifting of colors beneath her eyelids at night, the changes of distance, of time. The long knife winked, rocking on its point. They were changing, Richard and Madeline, and she had to change as well, or she would die as the dinosaurs had died. She wondered what sort of fossils she would leave behind. She wondered if Richard would keep her in memory, with what color hair, and if the snapshot of her would remain taped to Maddy's wall.

She looked down. The cabbage was chopped past the point of coleslaw, past the point of any use that came to mind.

She left the knife on the cutting board and went into Maddy's room. "Want to play house?" Maddy smiled, nodded. She was always hungry for partners at house. Sylvia knelt beside her and stroked her hair. Maddy thrust a doll into her hands impatiently, as if to say that this was no time for petty affection. Sylvia walked the doll to the front of the ramshackle dollhouse that Dick had built in Eugene from scraps of lattice and dowel. "Is anybody home?" she said, falsetto. "I'm a blind person looking for the Clays' house. Is this it? Is anyone here?"

Maddy put her doll by the doorway and mimed opening a door.

"I heard something," Sylvia said, "but I'm blind. I can't see. Who is it?"

Maddy's doll paused as if considering; then it gently touched the shoulder of Sylvia's doll.

Sylvia's doll moved back. "Don't push. You're scaring me. Please tell me who you are."

Maddy left her doll on the floor of the dollhouse and sat hugging her knees. Sylvia touched her cheek. "Just one word. Your name. What you'd like for dinner tonight. Just to let me know you can." Maddy put her thumb in her mouth and closed her eyes. She looked to Sylvia like a three-year-old, like a two-year-old, like a newborn babe.

When Sylvia heard Dick's key in the lock, she went to stand in the hallway by the door. He looked tired when he came in, his shoulders hunched as if the weight of the briefcase was more than he could bear. She pictured how she must look to him, arms crossed, spatula in hand, hair awry, apron bloodied with tomato sauce. "We have to do something about Maddy," she said. He blinked and looked past her toward the living room, but she would not stand out of his way. "She doesn't talk. Do you understand? There's something wrong with her. It's more than just shyness or reticence; she doesn't use words at all."

He let the door swing shut behind him and dropped his briefcase on the floor. "Of course she does," he said. "Come out here for a minute, Maddy. Come on, pumpkin. Say something to your mom." Maddy came out of her bedroom, thumb in her mouth, Raggedy Ann doll dragging behind. "Tell your mom . . . oh, how school was today."

Maddy looked from him to Sylvia. She took her thumb from her mouth. "Yashut," she said quietly. "Fortung pith quasley fass. Feezee un mung."

"You see?" He peeled off his coat and hung it in the closet. "God, I'm tired." He eased himself into his customary chair and closed his eyes, his right hand groping for his pipe in the ashtray.

"Dick," Sylvia said in the careful, even voice that a parent might employ in explaining life to a child. "Maddy is not speaking English. She is not speaking any language known to any creature on this planet except herself. It was pretend. It wasn't real."

"Absolutely. She's more innovative than half the people in my department."

"Yes, but did you understand what she said?"

"Of course." He looked at her with surprise. "Didn't you?"

He woke up shouting again that night, his skin damp with sweat. Sylvia held his arm until it was over. "What was it?" she asked. "Please." He wouldn't reply, and a minute later he was asleep.

Sylvia found herself staring into the darkness. She moved the box of tissues on the night table, uncovering the face of the digital clock. It was 3:18. She closed her eyes and tried to sleep, counting seconds, minutes. Finally she climbed out of bed and left the room, guided by the cold blue glow of the numerals.

She went into the living room and sat in the easy chair, Dick's chair, in the dark. The seat was too wide for her, the armrests too far apart. She shifted uncomfortably, leaned against the armrest to her left. She tried to think about important matters, life, change, and found herself staring at the crisscross shadow on the ceiling, the window gates. Home, she told herself firmly, speaking to her loneliness, her confusion, her fear. This is home.

She left the apartment in the morning with no destination in mind, walking wherever the streets took her—south down Second Avenue, west on 66th, south again on Third Avenue, and so on, making her way diagonally across the city. The air was filled with the music of the city, the clicking, buzzing, shrieking jam of people and machines, the smells of cigarettes, and food, and gasoline fumes. Sylvia walked on, waiting for some sense of it all to reach her, hoping to discover her part, her place.

The day had started with clear skies, but as she walked, dark clouds blew over the horizon from the west. Watching them move in, she imagined a rain of pianos plummeting to the ground, fortissimo (and briefly considered a reign of pianos—"Ladies and gentlemen, our leader, the honorable and upright Baldwin."). The clouds spread across the sky, casting premature dusk through the streets. She wondered if time played tricks in the city, if time could be as desultory as weather here, Precambrian in the morning, Mesozoic in the afternoon, with patches of October in the west. Time was like a heartbeat in the city, she thought, an internal rhythm with only vague and half-felt connections to the sweep of time in the universe outside, the earth rotating through its days and revolving through its seasons, the oscillations of an atom of cesium-133. Instead of clouds, those could be hours or eons thickening in the sky.

She was strolling down a quiet residential street in the west 30s, daydreaming about time and the heartbeat of the city, when she first had the sense of being followed. She stopped and looked around; there were only a handful of pedestrians in sight, none familiar. She shook her head and went on, but something in her mood had changed, in her outlook on the day. She began to tire, to feel the cold, and the muscles in her legs were tight. She no longer had any clear idea of what she'd intended when she started out that morning. At the next corner she turned north, uptown, and started back to the apartment.

It came to her again as she walked down 36th, the sensation that someone was behind her. She stopped in the middle of the block and waited, watching, listening for sounds at the edge of her hearing. There was no one in sight at the moment. She looked at the windows of the houses. The row of brownstones across the street seemed slumped over in their places like tired old men with half-open eyes, long cracks in the stones like the creases in aged flesh. She wondered if that was where the feeling was coming from, all the windows, and she smiled at herself, her foolishness, a nervous smile. Steam rose like hot breath from an open manhole at the end of the block. There was nothing behind her but the city.

She began to walk again, but the feeling persisted that something was there, keeping its distance like the reflection of the moon on a lake. The feeling grew until she could no longer laugh at it, even nervously, and it became fear. On Sixth Avenue she found herself among people again, and she told herself that it was all right, there were people around her now, but her heart was leaping in her chest. It made no sense, but she was done with trying to make sense of the city. It was watching her with hungry eyes. She imagined it rising up around her, tongue of asphalt, jaws of stone. She imagined it opening beneath her feet. The sidewalk shivered as a subway car passed under her, and she started to run.

She ran until there was no more breath in her, knowing that the city was running behind her, ahead of her, knowing that there was nowhere to go. Finally all her air was gone, and she stopped, head down, hands on her knees, all her mind in her pulse. "Look," someone said. "Look at her. Look."

Sylvia was changing, slowly at first so that it seemed no more than a trick of light, and then faster and faster. Her skin grew grey and leathery. Her bones became hollow and light and changed in their proportions to each other so that she was forced to stoop over, to crouch. Her skull swept back, a plume of bone, and her mouth stretched into a long bill, hard and slender. She started to speak, but whatever the thought was, it was lost in the making. All thought was difficult for her now. Her arms withered while the small finger of each of her hands lengthened until they touched the sidewalk. A thick membrane grew between her arms and her body, hanging in folds from armpit to ankle. She began to stagger on her tiny feet, so unsuitable for the ground, and she looked around her in panic, looking past the bodies surrounding her, looking for the sky. Her great wings opened at her sides, rising high above her shoulders, and as she stepped forward she brought them down and they billowed as they caught the air and flung her toward the sky.

It was Dick's idea that they go to the Museum of Natural History that Saturday. They strolled past totem poles and insects, primates and meteorites. Dick stood beneath a life-sized model of a blue whale suspended from the ceiling in the Hall of Marine Life. "This is the sort of asset that you find only in a place like New York," he said. "This is the sort of benefit that makes it emotionally cost-effective to live here." He blew Sylvia a kiss, tousled Maddy's hair.

Maddy looked tired, worn out by running from room to room ahead of them, disappearing for minutes at a time. "Hambur," she said, her cheek resting against Sylvia's hip. "Amburg." She had been speaking in recognizable word fragments since waking that morning.

"There's a cafeteria in the basement," Sylvia said. "You two go ahead. I'll be along in a minute."

The dinosaurs were on the fourth floor in a room without windows. The walls were institutional green. Sylvia made her way through the crowd, passing by the bones of hadrosaurs and pteranodons laid out in beds of plaster. She looked at them coldly and moved on. She stopped by a glass case in which was sprawled the mummified body of a pterosaur, the brittle black skin flush against the bones, the limbs askew, twisted not by agony but by geological disorder and the desiccating years. She sniffed, but the only odor she smelled was a faint whiff of smoke from a fugitive cigar. She walked to the center of the room where two large skeletons stood erect on a concrete platform behind a wooden rail, Trachodon and Tyrannosaurus, the tops of their skulls inches from the eighteen-foot-high ceiling. Their bones were grey rather than white, etched with deep lines, empty of marrow. Sinuous metal poles embedded in the concrete rose to support the long spines and massive heads. The poles looked alive, curving around hips and ribs to find each strategic place of support. Sylvia imagined them suddenly gone, imagined the bones crashing to the floor, splintering like glass.

She found Dick and Maddy at a table in the cafeteria and sat across from them. Maddy was full of energy again. Dick, sitting beside her, looked overworked and tired, in need of a more substantial rest than he could find in a single weekend. "Something wrong?" he asked Sylvia.

She shook her head. "Nothing. Nothing at all. Let me have a bite." She reached for Maddy's hot dog, and Maddy yanked it away, laughing, flinging sauerkraut across the floor. Dick stood up.

"Let it stay," Sylvia said, making faces across the table at her daughter. "They'll clean it up. That's what we pay for."

Sylvia, walking home from the grocery store, noticed the little man nearly a block away. He was less than four feet tall, and his head was bald, pink, and astoundingly round. He fell into step beside her, the hem of his tattered shearling coat slapping at his ankles as he hurried to keep pace with her. "Please," he said in a breathless high voice. "Anything you can spare. A nickel, a penny. Anything at all. Please?"

Sylvia shifted the bag of groceries to her other arm and walked quickly on. A memory of him kept coming back to her that evening, a picture of his pie-pan face smiling up at her, beaming with hope while she ate her dinner, washed the dishes, sat before the TV.

Sylvia woke in the night to the sound of Dick's cries. She tried to calm him as she had the other times. When it was over, they lay in the darkness together, his skin damp with sweat, her head resting on his chest. She listened to the uneven sound of his breath for a minute. When he climbed out of bed, she followed him into the living room and sat on the sofa. She noticed how well he fit the easy chair, how exactly he filled that space.

"Perhaps," Dick said. He paused to clear his throat. "Perhaps we shouldn't have come here. Perhaps it was a negative . . . a mistake. A place like this is—I don't— Maybe you were right."

She tsked at him. "Don't be silly. Everything's fine now. It's only sleepiness that's making you sad." She went over and sat on his lap, curling up to rest her head on his chest as if they were still in bed.

"It isn't the way I thought it would be," he said. "Everything has changed. You've—" He hit the armrest with his fist. "Damn," he said. "Damn!"

She snuggled against his chest again, leaned her head up to kiss the crook of his neck. "You'll get used to it," she said.

The winds that sweep through Hollywood from Santa Ana are famed for their heat and ferocity, but perhaps they might carry more dangers than we know. The following story explores that possibility in a very eerie way.

J. Michael Reaves has written the novels *Dragonworld*, *I—Alien*, and *Darkworld Detective*.

WEREWIND

J. Michael Reaves

"WARNING EVERYONE TO STAY OFF THE STREETS if possible, particularly in the coastal canyon areas. The winds have been clocked at forty-five miles an hour, and the Tujunga and Beverly Glen fires are still out of control. Travelers' advisories are posted for all freeways, Angeles Crest and the Grapevine. I repeat, please do not drive unless absolutely necessary.

"In other news, the Hollywood Scalper's fifth victim has been identified as Karen Lacey, a twenty-two-year-old actress. The pattern of mutilation murders connected with show business thus continues. . . ."

Simon Drake turned the car radio's volume down when he heard a sudden grating sound in the old Chrysler's engine. Holding his breath, he turned off Hollywood Boulevard onto a side street, and a moment later the engine quit, and the car coasted to a stop near an empty parking lot.

"Oh, *Christ!*" Simon twisted the key several times, but the only result was the ominous grinding noise. He slumped back against the hot plastic seat cover and watched the palm trees near Sunset slowly shredding in the wind. "That's it," he muttered. "I've lost the part." He grimaced in disgust, then winced as his chapped lips cracked.

He was thirty-three years old and had ninety-one dollars in the bank. His rent was overdue, and his boss at the Cahuenga Liquor Store had told him not to bother coming back when he had left for his latest interview. And now he was going to miss that interview, and probably a role he wanted more than anything, because of engine trouble.

Simon slammed his hands against the steering wheel.

146

Sweat blurred his vision. The car's interior was stifling; he had the windows up despite the ninety-degree weather. It was impossible to drive otherwise during a Santa Ana windstorm; the hot dry gusts struck like solid blows. Simon looked about. There was no one on this street and only a few people crossing the intersection at Hollywood Boulevard. The wind kept most people indoors. A newspaper was slashed in half by his car's aerial. The wind howled. It hadn't stopped in six days; it wasn't going to stop now, just because he had to walk to a phone.

He sighed and opened the door, pushing with all of his hundred and fifty pounds against the wind. His eyes began to water behind his sunglasses. The gusts tore at the permanent his agent had suggested. The air smelled of smoke; sepia clouds from the canyon fires covered most of the sky. The baleful sunlight was appropriate lighting for his life, Simon thought as he walked toward the boulevard, leaning into the wind. He looked at his watch and realized he could not reach Marathon Studios on time now.

He stifled a yawn as he walked; he had gotten little sleep the night before, due to a neighbor's Doberman. The dog had barked all night at the wind. He watched the cars creeping cautiously along. A Dodge van cut in front of a Mercedes, and the little old lady driving the latter hit the horn and shouted a curse. Simon, watching her, stepped on a wad of chewing gum and kicked his foot free with the same curse. The wind fanned anger like it fanned the canyon fires. Even so, Simon felt that he had much to be angry about. He had come to LA from New York five years before, a graduate of a good actors' school, with several commercials and plays to his credit. His fascination was horror movies; his ambition, to be the next Boris Karloff. But so far he had barely been able to stay alive with a few bit parts on Saturday morning TV shows and a role in a low-budget vampire spoof. He had expected it to be hard. He had expected to struggle. But for five years?

Near a hot dog stand he saw a pay phone. As he reached for it, a spark he could see in the sunlight arced from his finger to the metal casing, painfully. He was too tired even to curse. He put his last dime in and dialed.

The greasy smell from the hot dog stand reminded him that he had had no breakfast or lunch. For the last month he had been living mostly on money from his part-time job, which was not nearly enough for the rent plus photographs and resumé xeroxes. So he had not bought groceries for two weeks.

During those same two weeks, however, Simon's agent had convinced Martin Knox, who was producing a horror picture, to consider Simon for the lead. Knox had been dubious, but after several tests Simon was still in the running. Or had been . . . Martin Knox's temper was legendary in the Industry, and he did not like to be kept waiting.

Simon wanted the part, and not only for economic reasons. He was sure that he could do things with the character that would win an Oscar, the first for a horror picture lead since Fredric March in the 1931 *Dr. Jekyll and Mr. Hyde*. He watched the tourists and locals as he waited for the studio switchboard to put him through. The Hollywood freaks would not be out in force until after dark, but some had already braved the heat and the wind. Krishna folk with tambourines and Jesus Freaks with tracts eyed each other warily. Aging hippies, long hair beginning to gray, shuffled by. And of course, there were the few too strange for any description. The Hollywood Scalper, Simon was sure, would look tame in a line-up with some of these. He saw Trapper Jake approaching: an old man, but still tall and burly, with long braided hair, a Bowie knife and pouch and hand-stitched buckskin clothes. Despite appearances, he was an amiable sort; once, while Simon and a date had waited in a movie line, he had regaled them with a story of being raised by bears in Yosemite. Simon turned and huddled against the phone stall. He wanted no tales from Trapper Jake today.

·Martin Knox answered the phone. "Hello, Simon." His voice was barely audible over the wind. "Why aren't you here?" He sounded annoyed.

"Car trouble, Mr. Knox. I was hoping we could reschedule—?"

"I see." Silence for a moment. Simon could picture Knox vividly, sitting owl-like behind his desk, eyes hooded. "Well, I'm afraid it won't be necessary, Simon. I think we'll be going with another actor. Your tests make you look too short for the part."

Simon tightened his fingers around the receiver. "I'm five-eleven," he said.

"You're also late." The phone clicked, and a dial tone began.

Simon hung up carefully, not allowing himself to slam

the receiver onto the hook, not allowing himself any feelings at all. Not thinking about how much he had wanted this part, about what he could have done with it. So you want to be in pictures, he said to himself.

He dug into his pocket and came up with a lone nickel. He stared at it, realizing that he couldn't even call a tow truck. He closed his hand over the nickel suddenly, digging fingernails into his palm.

A gust of wind hit the phone stall hard enough to shake the phone; it gurgled and dropped his dime into the return bin. Simon fished it out and looked at it, stifling a sudden strong urge to laugh. Christ, he thought. My SAG dues are coming up, too.

He called a tow truck, then stood staring across Hollywood Boulevard, wishing he knew someone he could call and talk to. In five years he had made few friends here. Usually he was too busy to feel the lack of companionship; hustling parts and working took up all of his time. But occasionally the loneliness would hit him hard.

The heat waves from the street, when not scattered by the wind, gave the scene a wavering, dreamlike appearance. Sometimes it seemed to him as if all Los Angeles was a mirage, populated by ghosts. The very ground was insubstantial, prone to earthquakes, and the city's main product was fantasy. Simon stood there, overwhelmed by loneliness and a sense of unreality. Then a sudden loud noise—an empty soft-drink can, propelled by the wind—made him jump nervously backward. He collided with someone and felt himself seized in a powerful grip and spun roughly about. "You watch who the *hell* you're knocking around!" a voice shouted, and he was pushed violently into the hot dog stand; the sharp edge of the counter dug into his back. Half-stunned by surprise and pain, Simon saw that it was amiable Trapper Jake who had pushed him. The giant old man, resembling in beard and buckskin the bear he claimed had raised him, came toward Simon. His face was choleric with rage and both fists were raised. Passersby stopped to watch with interest.

Simon ran past the phone stall toward the edge of the building. Jake changed course to intercept him, but at that moment a particularly strong burst of wind upset an overflowing wire trash bin, scattering garbage across the star-inlaid sidewalk. Jake slipped on a paper plate greased with chili and sprawled headlong through the trash, to the vast

amusement of the stand's patrons. Simon did not wait to
see what would happen next; he turned the corner and ran.
The wind seemed almost to help him, lifting him in great
lunar leaps down the deserted side street. He ran, full of
panic, elbows pumping, lungs sucking in the crackling air.
The fear combined with his hunger to exhaust him quickly.
He reached the empty parking lot by his car, stumbled
across the low chain at its edge and collapsed. The hot
blacktop, dusted with light ash from the fires, scorched his
cheek and arms. With a groan of pain he rolled into the
shade of a nearby brick building.

He lay there for a few minutes, sobbing with pain and
anger. He pounded both scraped hands painfully against
the rough asphalt. There had to be an end to this run of
bad luck—he would make an end to it, somehow! Some-
way, he promised himself, aware of the last-reel triteness
of it and not caring, he would make of this moment a turning point. He wanted to act, and to eat three times a day;
he wanted his name, eventually, on a sidewalk star. And he
wanted that role more than he wanted breath in his lungs.
He wanted it, and he intended to have it.

The wind was still blowing; harder now, it seemed.
Simon looked about him. There was no one in the lot's
kiosk. Against the adjoining wall was a large trash bin; a
department store mannequin with a broken head grinned,
one-eyed, at him. The sun, like a spotlight with a red gel,
cast crimson light over the scene. Simon felt again a dreamlike quality suffusing everything. He could hear the wind,
but it seemed somehow distant. The feeling was that of
loneliness and waiting.

The wind howled.

A dust devil blew into the parking lot, a skittering whirl
of hot dry air, picking up litter and dust and the fine white
ash from the fires and spinning it all about. But instead of
coming apart after a moment, it kept spinning, faster and
faster. It began to shrink. The debris that had defined it
before was flung from it. There was only dust and ash now,
and then not even that; just a silvery spinning of air, growing denser.

It was assuming a human shape.

The wind was still blowing, but it did not disturb the
whirling shape. There was a breathless tension to the air
around Simon. The shape coalesced, solidified. . . .

It became a woman.

She seemed younger than Simon, with silver hair and pale skin. She was naked. Though she looked solid, she seemed also insubstantial, as though she would blur or become transparent if viewed from another angle. Her face was beautiful, but somehow he could not make out her features clearly. Her eyes were wide and blank, like unminted silver coins.

She smiled at him. The smile would have been touching had it not been for the blank eyes; they made it hideous. It was a smile full of yearning, full of gratitude, of waiting at last fulfilled. Two steps toward Simon she took. He drew back against the wall, making a high, thin sound in his throat. She hesitated—and then a gust seized her, spun her around like a ballerina, faster and faster, until her hair was a thinning silver stain in the air, and the lines of her body ran like pale paint.

Then she was gone, and Simon was alone in the lot, save for the cry of the wind.

It had been a hallucination, of course. That was the only possible explanation. Considering the stress he had been under it was a wonder he had not seen the Beast from 20,000 Fathoms in that parking lot. So Simon told himself, starting as he stumbled out of the lot and continuing for the rest of the day. By evening, he had almost convinced himself of it.

Hallucination or not, he had made a promise to himself, lying there in the parking lot. He did not intend to let the part in Knox's picture escape him. He had been invited to a party the following evening, and he knew that Martin Knox would also be there. Perhaps Simon could persuade him to reconsider.

He arrived late at the small house deep in the maze of Laurel Canyon. He had almost changed his mind about coming; the thought of confronting Knox did unpleasant things to his stomach. But he had to make the effort. Also, he did not receive invitations to many parties.

Jon Shea, the host, handed him a drink at the door. He was also an actor, tall and well-built—he and Simon were members of the same gym. "How've you been, Simon?" Jon asked. "You're looking a bit wasted."

"Haven't been getting much sleep," Simon said. "Neighbor's dog keeps me up all night." He always felt slightly uncomfortable around Jon—any criticism, no matter how minor, from him always produced in Simon a need to explain and justify. Jon Shea was only a year older than Simon, but he had done much better as an immigrant New York actor: three movies and currently featured player in a TV series. Simon resented him for it, and disliked himself for feeling that way.

"This damn wind keeps me awake," Jon said. "My grandma says—she's from the old country, you know—" Simon recalled that Jon's name had been longer and full of consonants before his agency suggested a change—"anyway, she says a wind like this is a devil wind, an evil spirit—hey, are you okay?"

Simon had stopped in the hallway and leaned against the redwood wall. "Fine. Drink's a little strong . . . what did your grandmother say about the wind?"

"Oh, she's got a lot of old stories like that." He looked past Simon into the living room, where people circulated. "Gotta go play host. Lots of ladies around. Find yourself one." Then he was gone, before Simon could stop him.

Simon walked slowly through the small, cozy house, edging his way around groups of people, still feeling the coldness that had gripped his gut when Jon had mentioned his grandmother's theory about the wind. He thought about the apparition in the parking lot. Coincidence, he said to himself, sounding the word out syllable by syllable, chanting it as he might a mantra. Coincidence. A comforting word to know.

Disco accompanied his nervous heartbeat. The windows rattling in the wind sounded occasionally above the music. Simon rubbed the cool glass he held against one cheek as he paused in the doorway of the game room. An overhead light and ceiling fan hung over the pool table, where Knox was sinking the last ball. Several onlookers applauded as the cushion shot hit the pocket. The only one not watching was a woman with short dark hair, playing a Pachenko machine in a far corner.

Knox raised his glass to the applause and started out of the room. A large man in a dark suit followed him. Simon took a deep breath and stepped forward as Knox was about to pass him. "Mr. Knox," he said, smiling. That was as far as he got before a large hand encircled his arm, fingers meeting thumb easily. Simon looked up at the man accompanying Knox. He was very large; his face was battered and slightly bored. A pair of black, horn-rimmed glasses looked startlingly incongruous on him.

"It's all right, Daniel," Knox said. Simon's arm was released. He recalled that many people in the Industry had hired bodyguards in the past week, since the Scalper killings began. "Thank you," Simon said to Knox, somehow keeping the smile in place. "I just wanted to talk to you a bit more about the lead in your picture."

Knox's face was expressionless. "What exactly did you want to say?"

Simon dropped the smile for a serious look. The thought crossed his mind that he was acting harder now than he ever had in his life. "Frankly, I hope to talk you into reconsidering. I feel I'm right for the part."

Knox's face was as motionless as a freeze frame. "I'm afraid it's too late for that. Terrence Froseth is set for the part. I've already talked with his agent—"

Simon did not know who Terrence Froseth was, and did not care. Realizing that pressing the issue was bad form, he nevertheless plunged ahead. "It's never too late," he said intensely. "After all, Gable wasn't the first choice for *Gone With the Wind*. Karloff wasn't the first choice for the monster in *Frankenstein*."

"You put yourself in good company," Knox said dryly. "I must say your persistence is admirable, though you need to learn some manners . . . if Froseth cannot take the part for any reason, perhaps we shall talk further. That's all I'll say on the matter." He walked down the hallway. Daniel looked coolly at Simon and followed.

Someone in the room turned on a small television set, and a news anchorman's voice filled the air. "—as of this evening the latest fire in Topanga is under control. To repeat, the wind has increased slightly since yesterday, and driving is still hazardous.

"Police have not released the identity of the latest victim of the Hollywood Scalper, but they do confirm that he was a film director. This is the sixth Scalper victim in as many days. . . ."

The conversation had stopped, and the room's occupants were gathered intently around the set as Simon walked down the hall. He stood before a window and watched the trees, ghastly in orange and green lawn lights, thrashing in the wind. It had been blowing for a solid week. It suddenly occurred to him that the Hollywood Scalper's spree had

started the day after the Santa Anas had begun to blow.
The wind makes people crazy, he thought, remembering
Trapper Jake.

The Hollywood Scalper was yet another item of worry:
a psychotic who only killed show business people, knifing
them and then cutting a small scalplock from them, which
he presumably kept. But all the victims to date had been
people more advanced in their careers than Simon was.
Surely he was beneath the Scalper's notice.

He was still staring out the window when there suddenly
appeared before him a pale, transparent face, floating in
the night. He turned with a gasp—someone was standing
behind him. Simon sighed in relief. For an instant, the
shape of her face and the effect of the reflection had made
him think—

The dark-haired woman from the game room stepped
back a pace. "I didn't mean to startle you."

Simon smiled. "No problem. I—thought you were someone else."

She smiled as well. "My name's Molly Harren—and
you're Simon Drake. I saw you in that movie—"

"Oh God, no," he said, hiding his head in mock despair.
"Don't tell me you saw *Disco Dracula!*"

"You were good," she said, laughing, as did he. "The
movie was abysmal, of course, but you were good." Simon
grinned at her. Her black hair framed a fascinating face,
with large, dark liquid eyes. Though she was laughing at
the moment, he could see that her normal expression was
studious, almost intense. She wore a sleeveless evening
dress, and it showed her to be in very good shape—not
merely sleek and well-fed like most of the people there, but
lean, with graceful curves of musculature. She obviously
kept herself in shape with more than the obligatory morning jog. And her name sounded familiar. . . . "Are you an
actress?"

"No. A writer."

It hit him then, and his jaw dropped. "You wrote
Blackout!"

She nodded. "But that wasn't my title. I called it *The
Dark Side of Town.*"

He had been about to compliment her on the screenplay
—it had been one of his favorite recent suspense films,
about a psychotic terrorizing a town during a power failure.
Instead he said, "That's a much better title."

She nodded, pursing her lips in disgust. "The studios are all into monosyllabic titles now. 'Easier audience understanding.' They're talking a sequel, and of course they want to call it *Blackout II*. So imaginative." Then she shook her head and smiled. "Sorry. I—well, I overheard your conversation with Knox. I just wanted you to know that I understand how you feel. It isn't easy dealing with them sometimes."

Conversation came easily after that. They discussed her screenplay and his career, and the common interest they shared in horror and suspense films. Simon forgot about the disappointment of losing the Marathon part, at least momentarily. It had been quite some time since he had met a woman he could talk with so easily, one with whom he shared so many interests. He was aware once again of how lonely he had been, because now, for a time, he was not.

It was almost two a.m. when they noticed people leaving. "I'd better be going," Molly said. "It was very nice meeting you, Simon."

They were sitting on a rattan couch under a framed one-sheet poster of one of Jon Shea's three movies. Simon glanced at it as they stood and only realized later that he did not feel the usual pang of jealousy. He considered and discarded several clever come-on lines and instead said simply, "I'd like to follow you home, Molly."

She smiled slightly, almost wistfully. "I think I'd like for you to—but not tonight, I'm afraid. Why don't we get together for lunch—say, Wednesday?"

Wednesday was fine with him. He offered to walk her to her car. When they stepped outside, the wind struck at them savagely. Simon leaned into it, his shirt collar whipping at his neck, as he watched her drive away in a pale Fiat. The wind was strong enough to buffet the small car over the white line several times—he hoped she reached home safely.

His own car was still in the shop, and so he walked home, down Laurel Canyon to Hollywood, up Highland to Franklin. It was a long, nervous walk. Black and white patrol cars, spectral under the mercury lamps, cruised the streets. He was two blocks from his apartment when one stopped him and, after checking his ID, gave him a ride the rest of the way. It was after three when he wearily climbed the steps to his second-story apartment in the hills above Cahuenga. The building was one of the older, Spanish-style constructions, with pantiles and archways and a small open court filled with cactus and jacaranda. Simon could smell the heavy scent of the flowers, now strong, now faint, as the wind gusted. He could hear the power lines above the building humming, and he could also hear the Doberman in the yard next door barking. He saw it, a black shape restlessly prowling the driveway beyond the cyclone fence. It would be another sleepless night.

The street's acoustics made the wind sound sometimes like wolves howling, sometimes like babies screaming. Something flickered in the corner of Simon's vision as he stepped onto his porch; he heard a sharp *crack!* like a whip. He turned quickly and saw that a TV antenna line had come loose and was flapping against a wall across the street. All the way home he had felt like a character in a Val Lewton film, sure that someone or something had been following him, constantly looking behind him at the skirling leaves and clattering debris that the wind hurled about. He stared down at the deserted street, leached of color by the moon. The wind now sounded like the wailing of lost souls. He could not have felt more alone if he were the last man on Earth; he wished desperately that Molly had said yes.

Despite the night sounds, he managed to fall asleep, but not for long. He dreamed that someone was sinking in a black lake, calling to him, stretching long white arms out to him. He awoke with a start, still hearing his name being called.

The water bed rocked him gently as he rubbed his eyes. His body and shorts were damp with sweat. He looked at the luminous face of his watch: four-thirty. The wind still blew outside, but the dog had stopped barking. He felt more tired than ever. Understandable, with nightmares of someone drowning and calling his name. . . .

He heard the call again.

Simon lay quite still. Over the ceaseless rise and fall of the wind he had heard his name—a long, wailing cry, faint, breathless, like the cry of a woman drowning. He lay and listened with his entire body. And it came again: *Simonnn* . . . drawn out and whispered, almost as though the wind itself had cried to him. . . .

It *was* the wind! He heard it again, the rising whistle outside shaping itself into his name. He stared at the ceiling, not daring to turn his head, afraid to look at the silvered square of the window, knowing he would have to when the call came again.

Simonnn. . . .

He turned his head toward the window.

Limned in the moonlight, hair like streamers of fog, she stared at him with eyes cold as stars.

Simon rolled over and out of the bed with a cry and ran down the hall. The light of the full moon, coming through the living room window, spotlighted a large poster of Lon Chaney, Jr., as the Wolf Man. It seemed to be coming out of the poster toward him, jaws opening wide; Simon gasped, turned and stumbled into a hanging planter. The leaves scratched his face like spiders' legs. He clawed open the front door, lunging outside into the hot moving air, not thinking, simply running. He looked down from the porch at the street—shadows crawled in the wind. Then something—a blown leaf, his hair, or *her hand*—brushed his cheek. With a shriek he leaped down the tiled steps, tripped and fell, scrambled to his feet, turned—

She stood before him.

She was not more than three feet away. As before, she appeared corporeal and yet ghostly. Her hair floated behind her like a gossamer web. Her eyes were still silver wells, looking at him but not seeing him. Her expression was that of ineffable loneliness and longing.

She reached for him.

Simonnn. . . .

He did not see her lips move; the wind seemed to whisper his name. Frozen with fear, he saw the approaching hands very clearly: they were as pale and smooth as blown snow, no trace of fingerprints or veining. Her lips parted in a smiling rictus, and behind them was only darkness. . . .

Simon shut his eyes and flung himself backwards, hands flailing the air before him. He felt one pass through coldness, and then he had turned and was plunging through a flowerbed, not feeling the cactus rake his bare legs, fingers hooking into the links of the cyclone fence, the wind tearing, shrieking at him. He pulled himself up and over the fence, fell against cool concrete and heard a low growl nearby. He realized then where he had fled.

The Doberman leaped, a shadow with gleaming teeth. Simon lurched to his feet and ran, knowing it was useless. Then, above the wind's howling, he heard a crackling sound. He ran against a wall, knocking the breath from his lungs and falling. He turned over and saw that one of the high-tension lines from the power pole overhead had come loose. Like a sparkling whip it fell, lashing the charging dog squarely across the back. The dog's growl changed to an agonized yelp—the force of the shock hurled it across the driveway to land, quivering, against the fence. The broken power line danced and scattered sparks across the concrete.

Simon looked about him quickly, but there was no sign of her anywhere. The only sounds were the wind and the hissing of the power line. Oddly enough, all the noise had not aroused the neighbors. He looked at the dog—it had stopped quivering.

The wind brought the smell of burned flesh to him, and he turned away to be sick.

"Hey, Simon," Jon Shea said. "You're just in time to applaud. I'm going for two-seventy-five today."

Simon had just entered the workout area of the Golden West Health Spa. The large room, walled with mirrors, was filled with men working body-building equipment. An AM rock station played over the members' grunts and groans. Jon lay prone on a bench press, seized the bar and raised it over his chest, straining as he lifted a stack of weights six times. He rose slowly, skin shining with sweat, and looked at Simon. "You don't look good. Maybe you shouldn't work out."

"I—didn't get much sleep last night," Simon replied. He was pale, and he leaned against a rack of barbells. His legs still smarted from the cactus and the fall onto the driveway. "I just came in to ask you a question," he continued.

"Sure. Shoot."

Simon stared through the floor-to-ceiling window at the jogging track outside. No one was jogging, despite the rarity of a smog-free day. The wind vibrated the glass before him and he stepped back hastily.

"Your grandmother called this a demon wind, you said. What did she mean?"

Jon blinked in surprise. "Oh, it's just legends, you know. They had stories about werewinds, that were supposed to take human shape—you better sit down, you look awful."

Simon did so. "Go on, please," he said faintly.

Jon scratched his head. "I don't remember that much

about it . . . they're not evil so much as just lonely, sort of lost souls, I guess. You know how the wind is always described as sounding lonely? Well, the werewind is drawn to lonely people." He peered closely at Simon, who was staring out the window at the wind-shook spires of the Chinese Theatre. "Why the interest?"

"Oh . . . I had an idea it might make a good horror movie."

Jon snorted. "Everybody's a writer. But I think you're too late on that one. Molly Harren asked me about it days ago."

Simon asked, "How do you stop a werewind?"

"That's what Molly asked. I'll tell you what I told her— look in the library. I don't remember. It's all bullshit anyway."

"Yeah," Simon said, standing. "Right." He opened the door to leave, but at that moment the music piped into the spa stopped, and a voice said: "This is a news bulletin from KCCO. Yet another Hollywood Scalper victim has been found, this one in West Los Angeles. The body has been identified as that of Terrence Froseth, a young actor. This is the seventh Scalper victim in seven days. . . ."

Simon saw Jon go pale beneath his tan. Across the floor, another actor released his grip on a pulley and a stack of weights crashed down.

Simon leaned against the door, feeling quite weak. He felt a number of other emotions as well: horror and sympathy were among them. But the dominant feeling was a hideous sense of relief. And unbidden into his mind came a thought that disgusted him: I'm back in the running again.

Outside, the wind howled.

Simon left the gym and took a bus down to Mannie's Auto Repair on Melrose. He gave Mannie a check, wondering vaguely how he would cover it, then drove downtown to the main branch of the Los Angeles Library. There he spent several hours under the high, carved ceilings leafing through books of legends and superstitions.

He found several spells to make the wind blow, and a few references to various kinds of wind demons and manifestations both malign and benign. At last he discovered a passing reference to the legend of the werewind. According to the paragraph, the werewind could be bound by tying knots in a length of hair. The stronger the wind, the more knots were required, and it would not abate until the last knot had been tied. The passage cited an in-depth work on the subject in *The Omnibus of the Occult*, but when he looked for that book, he found that it had already been checked out.

Simon stood before the card catalogue files and pressed the heels of his hands against his eyes until green patterns spun in the darkness. He was not quite sure what to do next. He told himself that he should be out job-hunting, or looking through the trades and nagging his agent. But he did not move. He stood quietly, wishing he could stop the thoughts that whirled like dust devils through his head.

Such an apparition simply could not be—at least, not as he stood there with the sun streaming through the latticed windows. And so, Simon thought, I am probably having a nervous breakdown. He clasped his hands together to stop their trembling. Was any career worth this? But on the other hand, what else could he do? At thirty-three, with only odd jobs behind him, how could he hope to make a decent living even if he was interested in anything other than acting? He had been through worse times. He had lived in a Greenwich Village loft without heat during the winter while auditioning for plays. Things had gotten better since then. They would get better still, he told himself. Persistence, determination; those were the keys, even more than talent. Knox had indicated that he would reconsider if Froseth could not take the part. And Froseth certainly could not take the part now. He was dead.

And did the Hollywood Scalper or someone like him lie in wait for the next lead as well? Who knew—who could decipher the motivations of a sociopath? The wind seemed to encourage such psychotics—he had heard that there had already been one copycat killing similar to the Scalper's work. If Simon came into the limelight, might he not be the next victim?

He shook his head. He could not let fear rule him. Acting was his life—it had to be worth risking his life for. He wanted the lead in that picture more than he had ever wanted any role. He would wait a day or so, out of respect to the dead, and then call Knox again.

The library would be closing soon; he turned toward the exit. It was rush hour now. Usually he tried to avoid the bumper-to-bumper crawl of freeway traffic, but he knew that today he would feel safer driving in that sluggish flow, surrounded by cars and people. In the wind.

"—we repeat, Los Angeles police have taken into custody twenty-seven-year-old Greg Corey. He is charged with the Hollywood Scalper murders that have terrorized Los Angeles for the past eight days. . . ."

Simon heard the news while driving down La Cienega toward a health food restaurant where he was to meet Molly for lunch. He almost cheered out loud. Things at last seemed to be looking up! According to the report, it was a virtual certainty that the suspect was the Scalper—he had been caught in an attack on a producer and had admitted to the other slayings. Thank God, Simon thought. At least I don't have to worry about that any more.

He found Molly sitting at a corner table, all but hidden by a large potted fern. The corner was dark save for a candle's glow; after the merciless sunlight, Simon could see little except dazzle. "I hope you don't mind," she said. "I like seclusion when I eat." She looked different; he realized her hair was longer. She was wearing a fall.

They ordered. "Did you hear the news?" he asked. "The Hollywood Scalper's been caught."

She nodded and smiled. "But not before your competition was removed."

Simon blinked, somewhat nonplused and secretly uncomfortable because of his similar thoughts. "Well, of course, I don't look at it that way—"

"I understand," she said. "It is a terrible thing, but you mustn't let that stop you from taking advantage of it." She frowned at his expression. "Does that sound ruthless? I guess I am rather ruthless—you have to be in this town if you care about your art at all. If you have to work with people who think that having money gives them the right to dictate creativity."

Simon felt vaguely uncomfortable at her intensity. "Well, I haven't been in a position to argue with them too much. And I'm under no delusions about the artistic quality of my work so far."

"Everyone has to start somewhere. You were good in that cheap film; you don't have to worry. But the frustration applies more to me than to you, because I'm a writer. The film *starts* with me. No matter how good the actor, the director, the effects, *et cetera*, without a good script, the film is nothing. And so when a good script is written and they ruin it, it's a crime. More—it's a sin. You see?"

He saw that this was obviously her holy crusade, and so he merely nodded, though privately he felt that an actor's interpretation of a script was just as important as the script. Their lunch arrived and they spoke of other things. "I've raised the money to produce my latest script," she said. "That way, no idiot can ruin my work—if it fails it will be my fault. But this damned Santa Ana weather is delaying production. I'm losing money each day the wind blows. Not to mention nearly losing my house in Topanga to the fire."

Simon agreed with considerable feeling that the wind must stop soon. The subject changed, and he told her how much he wanted the lead in Knox's picture.

Molly nodded. "Martin Knox is one of the few good producers. Be careful of him, though; he has a temper, and money to back it up."

Simon looked stubborn. "I *know* I'm right for that part."

"Then you will probably get it, now that Froseth is dead. The show must go on—people have to have their fix of cinematic fantasy." She sounded slightly bitter. "The hell of it is, movies and TV are what's real to the rest of the world. Not us—not the ones responsible. We're just ghosts."

Her use of the word startled him. They split the check and left the cool interior for the wind and the sun.

The wind struck them both with a hard, dry gust as they descended the brick steps to the parking lot—Molly missed her footing and almost fell. Simon grabbed her arm, steadying her. "Thanks!" she shouted over the howling. "I really think this goddamn wind is out to get me."

Again her innocent words jarred him; he looked quickly, fearfully, around the parking lot, but there was no sign of the werewind. They walked over to her car and hesitated in the inevitable awkward moment of good-bye. Simon realized that he was very much afraid of her leaving him today—afraid to be alone again. "Molly," he said, "I'd like to invite you back to my place. I—it's not a come-on, really." The truth surprised him. He was not thinking of sex at all. He simply wanted to be with her; almost as big a fear as the werewind was the fear of his loneliness.

She looked away from him at the distant Hollywood Hills, clear and sharp in the dry air. The wind tore at her long dark fall; he wondered fleetingly why she wore it on such a day. At last she said, "I'm tempted." She chuckled as though surprised at herself. "You don't know what it takes to admit even that much; we Hollywood ghosts shy away from emotional commitments." She looked at him, then took his face in her hands and kissed him lightly on the mouth. The wind staggered them, almost ruined the moment. "I appreciate the offer very much, but . . . no. I have work that must be done."

"I understand, but—" the wind pushed them against the car. "Goddamn it!" Simon shouted, losing his temper and striking futilely at the air.

"Relax. You can't stop it that way," she said. "You've more important things to think about, like talking to Martin Knox. Let me know how that turns out, okay?"

He nodded. Then she was in the car and backing out of the lot. He saw a smile thrown his way, and then she was gone. The sound of the engine was quickly lost in the wind's roar.

Too late, he thought of asking her what she knew about the werewind. Jon had told him she was possibly thinking about a script based on it. Simon shuddered. He would not want to be in it.

The streets were almost deserted. The news station said that the wind in the canyons at times reached near-hurricane force. Simon drove carefully. He saw one lone pedestrian on his way back to his apartment—a tall woman with silver hair, standing on a corner of Santa Monica Boulevard. His heartbeat shook him for an instant before he realized that it was one of the few hookers still braving the wind. She looked at him with flat curiosity. He drove on.

At home the mail contained a notice from his answering service that he was being dropped for nonpayment. Simon hurled the notice at the wall. The fact that it was too light to strike with any degree of force and instead only drifted to the floor increased his anger. He seized the telephone, tempted to throw it; instead he sat down and pressed the number of Marathon Studios. He had intended to wait a day or so, but he had been waiting too long, he told himself.

There was a long wait after he gave the secretary his name, during which time Simon breathed deeply to relax. I will not sound eager or get angry, he told himself. I will offer my condolences and then ask about the part. After all, as Molly had said, the show must go on.

"Yes, Simon."

"I just wanted to say I was sorry to hear about Froseth, Mr. Knox."

"Yes, it is a tragedy." Knox's voice was emotionless.

"A pity they couldn't have caught the Scalper before this." Simon hesitated; Knox said nothing. "Have you given any thought to a replacement? I know this is rather quick, but . . ."

He trailed off. Knox said, "I'm sorry, Simon, but after further thought, I still don't think you'd be right for the part."

Simon heard someone say, "Am I still too short, Mr. Knox? I could wear stacked heels, you know."

"It's not exactly—"

"Or am I 'too' something else?" Simon realized that he was saying these words to Knox; he listened, faintly embarrassed, as if he were a bystander eavesdropping on a quarrel. "Am I too tall now? Too fat, maybe? Too thin?"

"We have your resumé on file," Knox said distantly. "Good-bye, Simon."

Simon sat listening numbly to the dial tone. It's over, he thought. I've done it now.

He hung up and stared out the window at the waving trees. He listened to the wind—the omnipresent, maddening wind. That was the cause of it all, he thought. He had been doing okay until the wind had started, so long ago. The future had not looked particularly bright, but he had been able to handle the pressure. Now he had ruined everything because of that damned wind. . . .

The dial tone gave way to a siren; he depressed the cradle button, then began to punch his agent's number. He stopped before hitting the last digit. What would he say? Well, Sid, I went a little crazy, started yelling at Martin Knox, so I'll be about as welcome at Marathon now as the Scalper would be at Disneyland. He hung up again, then looked at the clock. It was after six—Knox would have left the studio by now. If I could talk to him again, Simon thought, face to face. Apologize. Explain about the wind, how it had sawed away at his nerves . . . it was understandable, surely. . . .

It took several phone calls to learn Knox's home address; he finally got it from Jon Shea. Simon told Jon part of what had happened, and Jon tried to counsel a different course: "Let it lie for a while, Simon. Give him a call in a few days; maybe the wind'll die down by then, everybody'll be back to normal. We've all been under stress—he understands that. But don't push it now. He's got a temper, too. . . ."

He did not listen. That evening he drove west on Sunset, toward the ocean. As usual, there were few cars out; even on the Strip the lanes were clear. The wind hammered at the Chrysler. As the evening grew darker, Simon had to restrain himself from driving faster. Near Beverly Glen the boulevard was blocked off—he had to detour around UCLA. Ashes from the canyon fire fell like dirty snowflakes; at one point he had to turn on his wipers.

It was almost dark when he reached Knox's house in Pacific Palisades. The day's end washed the ocean in neon red and orange. Knox's house was on a cliff overlooking the Pacific Coast Highway. Simon parked at one end of the long, curved driveway, next to a lawn mower and a trash can full of shrubbery clippings left by a gardener.

He had given no thought to what he would say—he had not thought at all during the long drive. He pressed the doorbell and stood before the massive, carved door. It opened; Martin Knox stared at him in disbelief.

"What the hell do you want?"

"To apologize," Simon said.

"This is absurd." Knox began to close the door.

"Wait, please," Simon said; then, as the door continued to close, he suddenly shouted, "I said *wait!*" and grabbed it. The burst of anger had struck like a wind gust and vanished as quickly, but it had done its harm—it had aroused Knox's temper. "That does it," the producer said in a low voice. He turned and shouted, "Daniel!"

Simon stepped off the porch into the wind. "Mr. Knox, I only came to apologize . . . it's the wind, don't you see? It's making everyone crazy. . . ."

Knox opened the door again, and Daniel stood beside him. "Throw him off the property," Knox said. "Don't be too gentle."

Simon backed up as Daniel came toward him. The wind whirled about them. Daniel approached quickly, looking bored. Simon turned and ran toward his car, fumbling his keys from his pocket. He had parked near the edge of the bluff. He stabbed the keys at the door lock; living in Hollywood had habituated him to locking the car. Daniel came around the front of the car and reached for him.

As he did, a blast of wind knocked Simon off balance; he fell backward, away from the huge bodyguard. The same gust knocked the gardener's can over. The wind seized the leaves and grass trimmings and spun them in a green flurry across the lawn. As Daniel bent to seize Simon's shirt, the cloud of leaves and grass struck them like confetti, swirling around them, blinding them. Daniel waved his arms, staggered to one side—and slipped, falling over the bluff.

Simon screamed. He crawled to the edge, looking down. It was not a sheer drop to the highway below, but it was close enough. He saw Daniel's motionless dark form sprawled on the steep slope.

He stood carefully, holding onto the car. He looked back toward the house and saw Knox standing in the doorway, staring at him. He knew it appeared as if he had pushed Daniel over the cliff. Knox slammed the door. He's calling the police, Simon thought.

But another thought came to him, far more terrifying than that. There was a pattern to these events: when the wind struck, *she* appeared.

The Chrysler spun out of the driveway and down the winding road toward Sunset. Simon had no idea where he was going. He merely wanted to get away, to escape what he knew would surely come to him—the soulless, smiling werewind. He breathed raggedly, looking about frantically for any sign of her. There was none. He began to wonder where he could go.

Not back to his apartment, surely. He needed someone he could trust, someone he could tell what had happened. Molly. It had to be Molly.

She had said she lived in Topanga, in an A-frame on Grandview Drive. He did not have her number with him, did not know if she was home, but he started north on the Pacific Coast Highway nonetheless. She *had* to be home!

Soon he was driving recklessly up the winding road between sheer cliffs, toward Fernwood. Black skeletal trees, remnants of the recent fire, surrounded him. The wind between the close canyon walls was like a shotgun blast.

He found the street and the house, high on a hillside. Parked in the gravel driveway was her Fiat.

As he stepped out of his car, the wind knocked him off balance again; he sprawled in an untended bed of ivy beside the ramshackle porch. Scrambling to his feet, teeth clenched against screaming, he pounded on the door. Beyond the flimsy shelter of porch and bushes it seemed that demons shrieked and tore at the earth.

The yellow porch light went on above him and he saw her silhouette behind the door window. After a moment, the door opened a crack.

"Simon?" she sounded tired and confused. "What is it? What are you doing here?"

"Let me in, please, Molly," he pleaded. "Please. I'm in trouble."

"I can't, Simon." Half of her face was visible against the crack, sallow in the porch light. "I'm working on something very important—"

"Please!" The wind screamed about him, tugging at his hair like fingers, *her* fingers. . . .

Molly looked torn with indecision. At last she said, "All right, if you're in trouble. But it can only be a moment. Then you'll have to go." She opened the door and Simon entered quickly.

They stood in a small living room. A picture window in the far wall looked out on the lights of Topanga. Simon noticed distractedly that the place was a mess—dead plants in pots, clothing strewn everywhere, books and records stacked haphazardly on old, worn furniture. Far in the back of his mind he was surprised and slightly disappointed—he had thought she would be neater.

A television was on in one corner, inaudible due to the wind outside.

Molly faced him, wearing jeans and a dark T-shirt. He noticed she was not wearing her fall this time. "Well?" she said. "What's wrong?"

"I don't know where to start," he said wearily. Even inside, the wind forced him to speak loudly. The whole house shook with its force. The lights dimmed, then returned. Molly looked at them in concern.

"Simon, I don't want to turn you out if you're in trouble, but you have to hurry! The wind is getting worse!"

"I know!" he said. "Jon Shea was right! It's a werewind —I've seen it!"

Her eyes went wide and her face paled. She seized his arms in a surprisingly strong grip. *"What?"*

"We've got to try the hair," he said, aware that he was babbling and not caring. "The spell, tying knots in the hair—"

"How did you know about that?" She was shaking him, her gaze burning with sudden rage. For an instant, Simon was more afraid of her than the werewind.

And then a blast of air hit the house and the picture window exploded into the room. Simon saw it but had no time to dodge. He felt flying splinters of glass sting his cheeks, miraculously missing his eyes. And he saw the rage in Molly's face turn to shock as a score of cuts and lacerations stitched the length of her back. She sagged into his arms and he felt blood running over his hands. He looked at her back, pulled strips of her shirt, cut by the glass, away from the wounds. None appeared to be serious. He looked about for something to serve as bandages—

—and saw who stood in the shattered window, framed by the night and the jagged glass.

Simon backed up, letting Molly fall to her knees. The gales still boomed and battered outside, but did not enter the house. The werewind approached him as he retreated in terror. Behind him a narrow flight of stairs led up to darkness; Simon turned and fled up them. They opened onto a narrow loft lit by a single dim bulb. A door at the far end led out onto a porch. On the walls hung several varying lengths of dark, knotted rope; on the table was an open book. The title at the top of the page was *The Omnibus of the Occult.* Also on the table was another length of rope— then he realized it was hair, Molly's dark fall, with knots tied in half its length.

Simonnn. . . .

Simon grabbed the fall, hands sweaty with terror. Simultaneously the wind struck the house again, shaking it to its foundations with a sound like thunder as she appeared at the head of the stairs, facing him.

Sobbing, Simon tied another knot in the fall. Her mouth opened in a silent scream, revealing darkness; arms extended, she came toward him. Simon backed up, whimpering, somehow managing to fumble yet another knot together. Then he turned and flung himself against the porch door as she came around the table.

He stumbled out onto the porch, into the wind.

It struck him like a giant fist, hurling him, half-stunned, against the railing. It tore at the length of hair in his hand, but somehow he managed to retain it. She followed him onto the porch, unaffected by the wind. Simon hooked one arm around the railing as the wind buffeted him, and she came closer, closer. . . .

Hanging there over darkness, half-paralyzed with fear, he managed to twist the final knot in the length of hair as the werewind touched him with her cold hands.

The howling rose to a scream. A final blast struck him, almost hurling him from the porch—and seized her as well, tearing at her, streaming her away like mist. Simon thought he heard a single, long drawn-out cry . . .

And the wind stopped.

Suddenly there was silence, louder than the wind, and stillness. Simon sagged to his knees, hearing his blood pounding. Hardly daring to believe it, he pulled himself to his feet. The air was motionless. For the first time in over a week, the wind had stopped.

He began to laugh as he looked out at the night and the still trees. He did not laugh long—his throat was too dry. Welcome tears moistened his eyes and cheeks. It was over. He had won! He and Molly were safe!

Then he turned toward the house with a gasp. "Jesus. Molly!" he shouted, running back into the loft. He staggered down the stairs into the living room.

She was not there.

The TV set droned quietly in the corner, broadcasting the news.

"—I repeat, the winds seem to have stopped everywhere.

"Recapping our top story, police have admitted that Greg Corey, arrested earlier today, is not the Hollywood Scalper. New evidence shows him to be a copycat killer who imitated the Scalper's crimes. The real Scalper is still at large. . . ."

"Molly?"

He looked closely for the first time at the fall he still held. It was not a fall. He could see very clearly the knot of flesh on one end of it, dark with dried blood. He remembered the other knotted lengths he had thought were ropes, hanging on the loft wall. He knew now that they were not ropes.

It occurred to him then that the werewind had never harmed him, had in fact saved him from Trapper Jake and the Doberman and Daniel.

Simon heard a noise behind him and turned.

Light glinted on a knife blade.

"I'm sorry, Simon," Molly said. "I did like you. . . ."

The neighborhood bar has always been a good place to meet new people and old friends. Somewhere, though, in some strange bar, they might be new and old at the same time: people you've never met who seem oddly familiar. They're the Regulars of this quiet story.

Robert Silverberg's many fine novels are well known to readers of science fiction and fantasy; his most recent book is *Majipoor Chronicles*.

THE REGULARS

Robert Silverberg

IT WAS THE PROVERBIAL NIGHT NOT FIT FOR man nor beast, black and grim and howling, with the rain coming on in sidewise sheets. But in Charley Sullivan's place everything was as cozy as an old boot, the lights dim, the heat turned up, the neon beer signs sputtering pleasantly, Charley behind the bar filling them beyond the Plimsoll line, and all the regulars in their regular places. What a comfort a tavern like Charley Sullivan's can be on a night that's black and grim and howling!

"It was a night like this," said The Pope to Karl Marx, "that you changed your mind about blowing up the stock exchange, as I recall. Eh?"

Karl Marx nodded moodily. "It was the beginning of the end for me as a true revolutionary, it was." He isn't Irish, but in Charley Sullivan's everybody picks up the rhythm of it soon enough. "When you get too fond of your comforts to be willing to go out into a foul gale to attack the enemies of the proletariat, it's the end of your vocation, sure enough." He sighed and peered into his glass. It held nothing but suds, and he sighed again.

"Can I buy you another?" asked The Pope. "In memory of your vocation."

"You may indeed," said Karl Marx.

The Pope looked around. "And who else is needy? My turn to set them up!"

The Leading Man tapped the rim of his glass. So did Ms. Bewley and Mors Longa. I smiled and shook my head, and The Ingenue passed also, but Toulouse-Lautrec, down at the end of the bar, looked away from the television set

172

long enough to give the signal. Charley efficiently handed
out the refills—beer for the apostle of the class struggle,
Jack Daniels for Mors Longa, Valpolicella for The Pope,
Scotch-and-water for The Leading Man, white wine for Ms.
Bewley, Perrier with slice of lemon for Toulouse-Lautrec,
since he had had the cognac the last time and claimed to
be tapering off. And for me, Myers on the rocks. Charley
never needs to ask. Of course, he knows us all very well.

"Cheers," said The Leading Man, and we drank up, and
then an angel passed by, and the long silence ended only
when a nasty rumble of thunder went through the place at
about 6.3 on the Richter scale.

"Nasty night," The Ingenue said. "Imagine trying to
elope in a downpour like this! I can see it now, Harry and
myself at the boathouse, and the car—"

"Harry and *I*," said Mors Longa. " 'Myself' is reflexive.
As you well know, sweet."

The Ingenue blinked sweetly. "I always forget. Anyway,
there was Harry and I at the boathouse, and the car was
waiting, my cousin's old Pierce-Arrow with the—"

*—bar in the back seat that was always stocked with the
best imported liqueurs,* I went on silently just a fraction of
a second ahead of her clear high voice, *and all we had to
do was drive 90 miles across the state line to the place
where the justice of the peace was waiting—*

I worked on my rum. The Leading Man, moving a little
closer to The Ingenue, tenderly took her hand as the nasty
parts of the story began to unfold. The Pope wheezed sym-
pathetically into his wine, and Karl Marx scowled and
pounded one fist against the other, and even Ms. Bewley,
who had very little tolerance for The Ingenue's silliness,
managed a bright smile in the name of sisterhood.

"—the rain, you see, had done something awful to the
car's wiring, and there we were, Harry on his knees in the
mud trying to fix it, and me half crazy with excitement and
impatience, and the night getting worse and worse, when
we heard dogs barking and—"

*—my guardian and two of his men appeared out of the
night—*

We had heard it all fifty times before. She tells it every
horrid rainy night. From no one else do we tolerate any
such repetition—we have our sensibilities, and it would be
cruel and unusual to be forced to listen to the same fol-
de-rol over and over and over—but The Ingenue is a dear

sweet young thing, and her special foible it is to repeat herself, and she and she alone gets away with it among the regulars at Charley Sullivan's. We followed along, nodding and sighing and shaking our heads at all the appropriate places, the way you do when you're hearing Beethoven's Fifth or Schubert's Unfinished, and she was just getting around to the tempestuous climax, her fiance and her guardian in a fight to the death illuminated by baleful flashes of lightning, when there was a crack of real lightning outside, followed almost instantly by a blast of thunder that made the last one seem like the sniffle of a mosquito. The vibrations shook three glasses off the bar and stood Charley Sullivan's framed photos of President Kennedy and Pope John XXIII on their corners.

The next thing that happened was the door opened and a new customer walked in. And you can imagine that we all sat to attention at that, because you would expect only the regulars to be populating Charley's place in such weather, and it was a genuine novelty to have a stranger materialize. Well timed, too, because without him we'd have had fifteen minutes more of the tale of The Ingenue's bungled elopement.

He was maybe 32 or a little less, roughly dressed in heavy-duty Levi's, a thick black cardigan, and a ragged pea-jacket. His dark unruly hair was soaked and matted. On no particular evidence I decided he was a merchant sailor who had just jumped ship. For a moment he stood a little way within the door, eyeing us all with that cautious look a bar-going man has when he comes to a new place where everyone else is obviously a long-time regular; and then he smiled, a little shyly at first, more warmly as he saw some of us smiling back. He took off his jacket, hung it on the rack above the jukebox, shook himself like a drenched dog, and seated himself at the bar between The Pope and Mors Longa. "Jesus," he said, "what a stinking night! I can't tell you how glad I was to see a light burning at the end of the block."

"You'll like it here, brother," said The Pope. "Charley, let me buy this young man his first."

"You took the last round," Mors Longa pointed out. "May I, Your Holiness?"

The Pope shrugged. "Why not?"

"My pleasure," said Mors Longa to the newcomer. "What will it be?"

"Do they have Old Bushmill here?"

"They have everything here," said Mors Longa. *"Charley* has everything. Our host. Bushmill for the lad, Charley, and a double, I think. And is anyone else ready?"

"A sweetener here," said The Leading Man. Toulouse-Lautrec opted for his next cognac. The Ingenue, who seemed to have forgotten that she hadn't finished telling her story, waved for her customary rye-and-ginger. The rest of us stood pat.

"What's your ship?" I asked.

The stranger gave me a startled look. *"Pequod Maru,* Liberian flag. How'd you know?"

"Good guesser. Where bound? D'ye mind?"

He took a long pull of his whiskey. "Maracaibo, they said. Not a tanker. Coffee and cacao. But I'm not going. I —ah—resigned my commission. This afternoon, very suddenly. Jesus, this tastes good. What a fine warm place this is!"

"And glad we are to see you," said Charley Sullivan. "We'll call you Ishmael, eh?"

"Ishmael?"

"We all need names here," said Mors Longa. "This gentleman we call Karl Marx, for example. He's socially conscious. That's Toulouse-Lautrec down there by the tube. And you can think of me as Mors Longa."

Ishmael frowned. "Is that an Italian name?"

"Latin, actually. Not a name, a sort of a phrase. *Mors longa, vita brevis.* My motto. And that's The Ingenue, who needs a lot of love and protection, and this is Ms. Bewley, who can look after herself, and—"

He went all around the room. Ishmael appeared to be working hard at remembering the names. He repeated them until he had them straight, but he still looked a little puzzled. "Bars I've been in," he said, "it isn't the custom to make introductions like this. Makes it seem more like a private party than a bar."

"A family gathering, more like," said Ms. Bewley.

Karl Marx said, "We constitute a society here. It is not the consciousness of men that determines their existence, but on the contrary their social existence determines their consciousness. We look after one another in this place."

"You'll like it here," said The Pope.

"I do. I'm amazed how much I like it." The sailor

grinned. "This may be the bar I've been looking for all my life."

"No doubt but that it is," said Charley Sullivan. "And a Bushmill's on me, lad?"

Shyly Ishmael pushed his glass forward, and Charley topped it off.

"So friendly here," Ishmael said. "Almost like—home."

"Like one's club, perhaps," said The Leading Man.

"A club, a home, yes," said Mors Longa, signalling Charley for another bourbon. "Karl Marx tells it truly: we care for each other here. We are friends, and we strive constantly to amuse one another and protect one another, which are the two chief duties of friends. We buy each other drinks, we talk, we tell stories to while away the darkness."

"Do you come here every night?"

"We never miss a one," Mors Longa said.

"You must know each other very well by this time."

"Very well. Very very well."

"The kind of place I've always dreamed of," Ishmael said wonderingly. "The kind of place I'd never want to leave." He let his eyes pan in a slow arc around the whole room, past the jukebox, the pool table, the dart board, the television screen, the tattered 1934 calendar that had never been changed, the fireplace, the piano. He was glowing, and not just from the whiskey. "Why would anyone ever want to leave a place like this?"

"It is a very good place," said Karl Marx.

Mors Longa said, "And when you find a very good place, it's the place where you want to remain. Of course. It becomes your club, as our friend says. Your home away from home. But that reminds me of a story, young man. Have you ever heard about the bar that nobody actually ever does leave? The bar where everyone stays forever, because they couldn't leave even if they wanted to? Do you know that one?"

"Never heard it," said Ishmael.

But the rest of us had. In Charley Sullivan's place we try never to tell the same story twice, in order to spare each other's sensibilities, for boredom is the deadliest of afflictions here. Only The Ingenue is exempt from that rule, because it is her nature to tell her stories again and again, and we love her all the same. Nevertheless it sometimes happens that one of us must tell an old and familiar story

to a newcomer; but though at other times we give each
other full attention, it is not required at a time such as that.
So The Leading Man and The Ingenue wandered off for a
tête-à-tête by the fireplace; and Karl Marx challenged The
Pope to a round of darts; and the others drifted off to this
corner or that, until only Mors Longa and the sailor and I
were still at the bar, I drowsing over my rum and Mors
Longa getting that far-away look and Ishmael, leaning intently forward, saying, "A bar where nobody can ever
leave? What a strange sort of place!"

"Yes," said Mors Longa.

"Where is there such a place?"

"In no particular part of the Universe. By which I mean
it lies somewhere outside of space and time as we understand those concepts, everywhere and nowhere at once,
although it looks not at all alien or strange apart from its
timelessness and its spacelessness. In fact, it looks, I'm told,
like every bar you've ever been in in your life, only more
so. The proprietor's a big man with black Irish in him, a lot
like Charley Sullivan here; and he doesn't mind setting one
up for the regulars now and then on the house; and he
always gives good measure and keeps the heat turned up
nicely. And the wood is dark and mellow and well polished,
and the railing is the familiar brass, and there are the usual
two hanging ferns and the usual aspidistra in the corner
next to the spittoon, and there's a dart board and a pool
table and all those other things that you find in bars of the
kind that this one is. You understand me? This is *a perfectly standard sort of bar,* but it doesn't happen to be in New
York City or San Francisco or Hamburg or Rangoon, or
in any other city you're likely to have visited, though the
moment you walk into this place you feel right at home
in it."

"Just like here."

"Very much like here," said Mors Longa.

"But people never leave?" Ishmael's brows furrowed.
"Never?"

"Well, actually, some of them do," Mors Longa said.
"But let me talk about the other ones first, all right? The
regulars, the ones who are there *all the time.* You know,
there are certain people who absolutely never go into bars,
the ones who prefer to do their drinking at home, or in
restaurants before dinner, or not at all. But then there are
the bar-going sorts. Some of them are folks who just like

to drink, you know, and find a bar a convenient place to get their whistles wetted when they're en route from somewhere to somewhere else. And there are some who think drinking's a social act, eh? But you also find people in bars, a lot of them, who go to the place because there's an emptiness in them that needs to be filled, a dark cold hollow space, to be filled not just with good warm bourbon, you understand, but a mystic and invisible substance that emanates from others who are in the same way, people who somehow have had a bit of their souls leak away from them by accident, and need the comfort of being among their own kind. Say, a priest who's lost his calling, or a writer who's forgotten the joy of putting stories down on paper, or a painter to whom all colors have become shades of gray, or a surgeon whose scalpel hand has picked up a bit of a tremor, or a photographer whose eyes don't quite focus right any more. You know the sort, don't you? You find a lot of that sort in bars. Something in their eyes tells you what they are. But in this particular bar that I'm talking about, you find *only* that sort, good people, decent people, but people with that empty zone inside them. Which makes it even more like all the other bars there are, in fact the Platonic ideal of a bar, if you follow me, a kind of three-dimensional stereotype populated by flesh-and-blood clichés, a sort of perpetual stage set, do you see? Hearing about a place like that where everybody's a little tragic, everybody's a bit on the broken side, everyone is a perfect bar type, you'd laugh, you'd say it's unreal, it's too much like everybody's idea of what such a place ought to be like to be convincing. Eh? But all stereotypes are rooted firmly in reality, you know. That's what makes them stereotypes, because they're exactly like reality, only more so. And to the people who do their drinking in the bar I'm talking about, it isn't any stereotype and they aren't clichés. It's the only reality they have, the realest reality there is, for them, and it's no good sneering at it, because it's their own little world, the world of the archetypical saloon, the world of the bar regulars."

"Who never leave the place," said Ishmael.

"How can they? Where would they go? What would they do on a day off? They have no identity except inside the bar. The bar is their life. The bar is their universe. They have no business going elsewhere. They simply stay where they are. They tell each other stories and they work hard to keep each other happy, *and for them there is no world outside.* That's what it means to be a regular, to be a Platonic ideal. Every night the bar and everything in it vanishes into a kind of inchoate gray mist at closing time, and every morning when it's legal to open, the bar comes back, and meanwhile the regulars don't go anywhere except into the mist, because that's all there is, mist and then bar, bar and then mist. Platonic ideals don't have daytime jobs and they don't go to Atlantic City on the weekend and they don't decide to go bowling one night instead of to their bar. Do you follow me? They stay there the way the dummies in a store window stay in the store window. Only they can walk and talk and feel and drink and do everything else that window dummies can't do. And that's their whole life, night after night, month after month, year after year, century after century—maybe till the end of time."

"Spooky place," said Ishmael with a little shudder.

"The people who are in that bar are happier than they could possibly be anywhere else."

"But they never leave it. Except you said some of them do, and you'd be telling me about those people later."

Mors Longa finished his bourbon and, unbidden, Charley Sullivan gave him one more, and set another rum in front of me, and an Irish for the sailor. For a long while Mors Longa studied his drink. Then he said, "I can't really tell you much about the ones who leave, because I don't know much about them. I intuit their existence logically, is all. You see, from time to time there's a newcomer in this bar that's outside of space and time. Somebody comes wandering in out of the night the way you did here tonight, and sits down and joins the regular crowd, and bit by bit fits right in. Now, obviously, if every once in a while somebody new drops in, and nobody ever leaves, then it wouldn't take more than a little while for the whole place to get terribly crowded, like Grand Central at commuter time, and what kind of a happy scene would that make? So I conclude that sooner or later each of the regulars very quietly must disappear, must just vanish without anybody's knowing it, maybe go into the john and never come out, something like that. And not only does no one ever notice that someone's missing, but *no one remembers that that person was ever there.* Do you follow? That way the place never gets too full."

"But where do they go, once they disappear from the bar

that nobody ever leaves, the bar that's outside of space and time?"

"I don't know," said Mors Longa quietly. "I don't have the foggiest idea." After a moment he added, "There's a theory, though. Mind you, only a theory. It's that the people in the bar are really doing time in a kind of halfway house, a sort of purgatory, you understand, between one world and another. And they stay there a long, long time, however long a time it is until their time is up, and then they leave, but they can only leave when their replacement arrives. And immediately they're forgotten. The fabric of the place closes around them, and nobody among the regulars remembers that once there used to be a doctor with the d.t.'s here, say, or a politician who got caught on the take, or a little guy who sat in front of the piano for hours and never played a note. But everybody has a hunch that that's how the system works. And so it's a big thing when somebody new comes in. Every regular starts secretly wondering, Is it I who's going to go? And wondering too, Where am I going to go, if I'm the one?"

Ishmael worked on his drink in a meditative way. "Are they afraid to go, or afraid that they won't?"

"What do you think?"

"I'm not sure. But I guess most of them would be afraid to go. The bar's such a warm and cozy and comforting place. It's their whole world and has been for a million years. And now maybe they're going to go somewhere horrible—who knows?—but for certain they're going to go somewhere *different*. I'd be afraid of that. Of course, maybe if I'd been stuck in the same place for a million years, no matter how cozy, I'd be ready to move along when the chance came. Which would you want?"

"I don't have the foggiest," said Mors Longa. "But that's the story of the bar where nobody leaves."

"Spooky," said Ishmael.

He finished his drink, pushed the glass away, shook his head to Charley Sullivan, and sat in silence. We all sat in silence. The rain drummed miserably against the side of the building. I looked over at The Leading Man and the Ingenue. He was holding her hand and staring meaningfully into her eyes. The Pope, hefting a dart, was toeing the line and licking his lips to sharpen his aim. Ms. Bewley and Toulouse-Lautrec were playing chess. It was the quiet part of the evening, suddenly.

Slowly the sailor rose, and took his jacket from the hook. He turned, smiled uncertainly, and said, "Getting late. I better be going." He nodded to the three of us at the bar and said, "Thanks for the drinks. I needed those. And thanks for the story, Mr. Longa. That was one strange story, you know?"

We said nothing. The sailor opened the door, wincing as cold sheets of rain lashed at him. He pulled his jacket tight around him and, shivering a little, stepped out in the darkness. But he was gone only a moment. Hardly had the door closed behind him but it opened again and he stumbled back in, drenched.

"Jesus," he said, "it's raining worse than ever. What a stinking night! I'm not going out into that!"

"No," I said. "Not fit for man nor beast."

"You don't mind if I stay here until it slackens off some, then?"

"Mind? Mind?" I laughed. "This is a public house, my friend. You've got as much right as anyone. Here. Sit down. Make yourself to home."

"Plenty of Bushmill's left in the bottle, lad," said Charley Sullivan.

"I'm a little low on cash," Ishmael muttered.

Mors Longa said, "That's all right. Money's not the only coin of the realm around here. We can use some stories we haven't heard before. Let's hear the strangest story you can tell us, for openers, and I'll undertake to keep you in Irish while you talk. Eh?"

"Fair enough," said Ishmael. He thought a moment. "All right. I have a good one for you. I have a really good one, if you don't mind them weird. It's about my uncle Timothy and his tiny twin brother, that he carried around under his arm all his life. Does that interest you?"

"Most assuredly it does," I said.

"Seconded," said Mors Longa. He grinned with a warmth I had not seen on his face for a long time. "Set them up," he said to Charley Sullivan. "On me. For the house."

Now we move to Mexico, on the southeast coast of Yucatán, where Mayan ruins tell of a mysterious past . . . where Americans today vacation or go to retire . . . where strangeness can still invade the most quiet of lives.

James Tiptree, Jr., is the author of *Up the Walls of the World* and a number of award-winning shorter stories. Tiptree reports that this story is the first of several to be set in the Quintana Roo, and that its original title was "What Came Ashore at Lirios."

LIRIOS: A TALE OF THE QUINTANA ROO

~~~~~~~~~~~~~~~~~~~~~~~~~~~~~~~~~~~~~~

James Tiptree, Jr.

> *The tourists throw spent Polaroid*
> *Where Spaniards threw spent slaves:*
> *And now and then a tourist joins*
> *Four thousand years of graves;*
> *For loves it's wiser to avoid*
> *Smiles from those brilliant waves.*

THE OLD COCO-RANCH FOREMAN SAW HIM FIRST.
It was a day of roaring hot south wind. The beach smoked under the thrashing coco-palms, and the Caribbean raved by like a billion white devils headed for Cuba, four hundred miles north. When I went down to see what *Don* Pa'o Camool was peering at, I could barely hold one eye open against the glaring, flying sand.

The beach stretched empty to the hazed horizon: dazzling white coral marked only by faint hieroglyphs of tar and wrack.

"*¿Qué?*" I howled above the wind-shriek.

"*Caminante.*"

Interested, I peered harder. I'd heard of the *caminantes*, the Walking Men of old days, who passed their lives drifting up and down this long, wild shore. One of the dark streaks was, perhaps, moving.

"*¿Maya caminante?*"

The old man—he was a decade younger than I—spat down hard at a ghost-crab blowing by. "*Gringo.*" He took

184

a hard sideways squint up at me, as he always did when he used that word.

Then he screwed his face into one of his wilder Maya grimaces, which might mean anything or nothing, and stumped back up the bluff to his lunch, slapping his big old-fashioned *machete* as he went.

My eyes were caked with salt and sand. I too retired up to my wind-eroded patio to wait.

What finally came plodding into view along the tide-line was a black skeleton, a stick figure with fuzz blowing around the head. When he halted by the compass-palm and turned to look up at the *rancho* I half-expected the sea-glare to shine through his ribs.

The *rancho* was a straggling line of five small pole-and-thatch huts, three smoky copra-drying racks, and a well with a winch-bucket. At the end was a two-room owner's *casita,* on whose rented patio I sat.

The apparition started straight up toward me.

Nearer, I saw he was indeed a *gringo:* the hair and beard whipping his sun-blackened face was a crusted pinkish grey. His emaciated body was charred black, with a few white scar-lines on his legs, and he was naked save for a pair of frayed shorts and his heavy leather sandals. A meagre roll of *serape* and a canteen were slung on his shoulders. He could have been sixty or thirty.

"Can I have some water, please?"

The English came out a bit rusty, but it was the voice that startled me: —a clear young voice right out of Midwest suburbia."

"Of course."

The sun glittered on a shark-knife hanging from the stranger's belt, showing its well-honed edge. I gestured to a shady spot on the patio curb and saw him slumped down where I could keep an eye on him before I went in. Incongruous young voices like his aren't unknown even here; they come from the scraps of human flotsam that drifts down the tropic latitudes hoping that tomorrow, or next year, they will get their heads in order. Some are heart-breaking; a few are dangerous, while they last. I knew that slant eyes were watching from the *rancho*—but no one could see into the *casa* and only a fool would rely on a Maya to protect one old *gringo* from another.

But when I came out he was sitting where I'd left him, gazing out at the blazing mill-race of the sea.

"Thank you . . . very much."

He took one slow, shaky sip, and then two more, and sat up straighter. Then he uncapped his canteen, rinsed, and filled it carefully from my pitcher before drinking more. The rinse-water he poured on my struggling casuarina seedling. I saw that the canteen under its cooler-rag was a sturdy anodised Sealite. The knife was a first-rate old Puma. His worn sandals were in repair, too; and wearing them was a mark both of status and sense. When he lifted the glass again, the eyes that glanced at me out of his sun-ravaged face shone a steady, clear, light hazel.

I picked up my own mug of cold tea and leaned back.

"Buut ka'an," the young stranger said, giving it the Maya click. "The Stuffer." He jerked his wild beard at the brilliant gale around us, and explained, between slow sips, "They call it that . . . because it blows until it stuffs the north full, see . . . and then it all comes blasting back in a Northeaster."

A scrap of my typing paper from the local dump came flittering by. He slapped a sandal on it, smoothed it, and folded it into his pack. As he moved, a nearby palm-root suddenly reared up and became a big iguana. The creature stared at us over its wattles with the pompous wariness which had carried it from the Jurassic, gave two ludicrous intention-bobs, and streaked off at a flying waddle, tail high.

We both grinned.

"More water?"

"Please. You have good water here." He stated it as a known fact, which it was.

"Where did you fill your canteen?"

"Pajaros. *Punta* Pajaros. Ffah!"

I refilled the pitcher, more than a little appalled. All ground-water quits at the lagoon-mouth a kilometer south. Even considering that he was walking north, with the wind, had this man, or boy, really come the thirty miles of burning, bone-dry sandbar between here and the Pajaros lighthouse on that canteen? Moreover, Pajaros itself has no water; the fishermen who camp there occasionally bring in an oil-drum full, but were otherwise believed to subsist on beer, tequila, and other liquids not usually considered potable. No wonder he had rinsed the canteen, I thought, hunting out my pack of sodium-K tabs. Even without the Stuffer blowing, people can desiccate to congestive heart failure without feeling it, on this windy shore.

But he refused them, rather absently, still staring at the sea.

"All the electrolyte you need, right there. If you're careful. Our blood is really modified sea-water . . . isn't that right?"

He roused and turned round to look at me directly, almost appraisingly. I saw his gaze take in the corner of the room behind us, where my driftwood bookshelves were dimly visible through the glass sliding doors that had long ceased to slide. He nodded. "I heard you had a lot of books. *Muy pesados*—heavy books. *Libros sicológicos.* Right?"

"Um."

This chance visitation was changing character unwelcomely. It wasn't odd that he should have known much about me—gossip has flowed ceaselessly up and down this coast for three thousand years. Now I had the impression that something about those "heavy psychological books" had drawn him here, and it made me uneasy. Like many experimental psychologists, I have had harrowing difficulties trying to explain to some distressed stranger that an extensive knowledge of, say, the cognitive behavior of rats, has no clinical applications.

But his own radar was in excellent shape. He was already wrapping his canteen and slinging on his roll.

"Look, I don't mean to interrupt you. The breeze is easing off. It'll be nice later on. If you don't mind, I'll just go down by that big driftlog there and rest awhile before I move on. Thanks for the water."

The "breeze" was doing a roaring 30 knots, and the huge mahogany timber down on the beach could hardly be seen for flying sand. If this was a ploy, it was ridiculous.

"No. You're not interrupting anything. If you want to wait, stay here in the shade."

"I've snoozed by that log before." He grinned down at me from his skeletal height. His tone wasn't brash, just gentle and resolute; and his teeth were very white and clean.

"At least let me pass you a couple of spare grapefruit; I've more than I can eat."

"Oh, well, great . . ."

Looking back, it's hard to say when and why it began to seem important that he stop and not go on. Certainly my sense of him had changed radically about that time. I now saw him as competent to this country, and to his

strange life, whatever it might be; doubtless more competent than I. Not flotsam. And not in need of any ordinary
help. But as time went on, something—maybe a projection
of my own, maybe the unrelenting wind-scream that day
—perhaps merely the oddness of the sea-light reflected in
his pale eyes—made me sense him as being, well, *marked*.
Not at all "doomed"—which isn't uncommon in this land,
particularly if one neglects to contribute to the proper
officials. And not "scarred" as by some trauma. Or watched
by an enemy. I had merely an unquieting sense that my
visitor was at this time in some special relation to a force
obscure and powerful, that he was significantly vulnerable
to—I knew not what, only that it waited ahead of him,
along the lonely sand.

But his talk, at first, couldn't have been less ominous.
Stowing the wizened grapefruit, he told me that he came
down every year to walk this coast. "Sometimes I get as
far as Bélizé, before I have to start back. You weren't here
when I passed going south."

"So you're on your way home now. Did you make
Bélizé?"

"No. The business went on too late." He jerked his beard
in the general direction of Yankeedom.

"May I ask what the business is?"

He grinned, a whimsical black skeleton. "I design swimming pools in Des Moines. My partner does most of the
installation, but he needs my designs for the custom jobs.
We started in college, five years back. It really took off; it
got so heavy I had to get away. So I found this place."

I poured myself some more stale tea to let that sink in.
Would my scrap of paper end as a sketch for some good
citizen's Iowa patio?

"Do you ever run into any of the old *caminantes?*"

"Only a few left, old men now. Hidden Star Smith—
Estrella Escondida Camal. Camol, Camool, it's like Smith
here, you know. He stays pretty close to Pajaros these days.
And Don't Point at Rainbows."

"I beg your pardon?"

"Another old *caminante*, I don't know his name. We were
watching this storm pass at sunset, see? Maybe you've
noticed—they can throw this fantastic double, triple *arc iris*.
Rainbows. First one I'd seen. I pointed at it and he got
excited and clouted my arm down." He rubbed his elbow
reminiscently. "He doesn't speak much Spanish, but he got

it to me that something bad would jump out of the rainbow and run down my arm right into my ear. So whenever I meet him I tell him *'No puncto,'* and we have a laugh."

My visitor seemed to be enjoying talking to someone who knew a little of this shore, as his Des Moines clients would not. But his gaze still roved to the gale-torn sea, and he had not unslung his blanket-roll.

"How do you get across those two monster bays between here and Bélizé? Surely you can't hike around? Or have they finally cut back there too?"

"Not yet. No way. What isn't under water is tribal treaty land. I saw an air photo with three unnamed villages on it. I know where a couple of *sac bés* come out though—you know, the old Maya roads. They're nothing but limestone ridges now. There was this man on one of them one night, he wasn't wearing pants. He disappeared like—whht! . . . I wanted to walk back in a ways this trip, but—" His gaze turned away again, he frowned at the wind. "I hated to get so far . . . inland."

"So, how do you cross?"

"Oh, I work my way on a fishing boat, fixing stuff. It's unreal, what this climate does to engines. They keep them going on string and beer. I have a couple of guys who watch for me every year. If I could only leave a set of tools, but—"

We both knew the answer to that one.

"Sometimes they take me all the way, or they drop me at Punta Rosa and I walk down and catch another ride over Espiritu Sanctu."

I asked him about the rather mysterious stretch of coast between the two huge bays.

"The beach is mostly rocks; you have to watch the tide. But there's an old jeep track up on the bluff. Five, no, let's see—six coco plantings. And the Pickle Palace, you know about that?"

"You mean it really exists?"

"Oh yes. This incredible *rico-rico* politico from Mexico. The pickles were just a sideline. I guess he wanted a private paradise. Turrets, stained glass windows, at least a dozen guest-houses, everything tiled. An airstrip. And every damn bit brought in by lighter, through the reef. They say he went down a couple of times but his mistresses didn't like it. Of course it's all overgrown now. There's an old care-taker who chops it out and grows corn by the fountain. The thing is, the whole place is in exquisite taste. I mean really lovely. Nineteen-thirties art deco, top grade."

The incongruous words from this wild naked stranger—like the Pickle Palace itself—were eroding my sense of reality. This is not unusual in the Quintana Roo.

"And nobody seems to have looted the inside. I went in the kitchens, he had what has to be the first microwave oven in the world. Didn't stay long—there was a live tiger asleep in the living-room."

"You mean a jaguar?"

"No. A real tiger-tiger from India, with stripes. And huge. He must have had a zoo, see—there's birds that don't belong here, too. This tiger was on a white velvet couch, fast asleep on his back with his paws crossed on his chest, the most beautiful sight I ever saw. . . ." He blinked and then added quietly, "Almost."

"What happened?"

"He woke up and took off right over my head out the door." My guest grinned up, as if still seeing the great beast sail over. "Of course I was down, crawling like a madman out the other way. I never told anybody. But when I came by a couple years later there was his skull speared up on the wall. Pity."

"That's a lovely story."

"It's true."

His tone made me say quickly, "I know it is. That's why it's good; made-up yarns don't count. . . . Look, this wind isn't going to quit soon. Maybe you'd like to come in and wash up or whatever while I scare us up a snack. Tea suit you, or would a Coke or some *cerveza* go better?"

"That's really good of you. Tea's fine."

As he followed me in he caught sight of his reflection in the sandy glass, and gave a whistle. Then I heard a clank: he had quickly unstrapped the knife and laid it down inside the sill.

"You really are *bueno gentes,* you know?"

I pointed out the old gravity-feed shower. "Don't get too clean, it'll draw the *chiquistas.*"

He laughed—the first carefree young sound I'd heard from him—and started turning out his pockets, clearly intending to walk straight under, shorts and all.

I put the kettle on my gas one-burner and started loading a tray with cheeses and ham. He came out just as I was pouring, and I nearly dropped the kettle on us both.

His skin was still burnt black, showing several more scars where he had apparently tangled with a coral-reef. The wet shorts were still basically khaki, but now visibly enlivened by sturdy Mexican floral-print patches, and edged top and bottom by pink lines of less-burnt skin. The effect was literally and figuratively topped off by his damp, slicked-down hair and beard: relieved of its crust, it shone and flamed bright strawberry red, such as I've seldom seen in nature—or anywhere else.

He seemed totally unconscious of the change in his appearance, and was looking carefully around the kitchen corner and my wall of books.

"You like stories?" he inquired.

"Yes."

"For a taste of that real maple syrup up there I'll swap you a good one. I mean, true. I want to ask you a question about it."

I was too occupied reassembling the tray and my perceptions to indulge in any more suspicions, and answered simply, "With pleasure."

He watched appreciatively as I poured a generous dollop into a baggie and secured it in a sea-scoured *detergente* jar. "You scrounge the beach, too. . . ."

"My *supermercado*," I told him.

"That's right." His gravity was returning. "Everything you need . . . it sends."

When we'd got ourselves settled I saw that the Stuffer really was subsiding slightly. The coco-palms swept the sand in a wind which had lost a decibel or two; and the sea beyond was regaining some of its wondrous Carib turquoise, shot with piercing lime-green in the coral shallows. The white lemmings of the bay raced northward still; but the far reef was now visible as a great seething tumbling snow-bank, lit with the diamonds of the afternoon sun. It might be a nice night.

"It began right out there by your north point, as a matter of fact," my guest pointed left with his piece of cheese, and took a small bite. "This particular evening was fantastic—dead calm, full moon. You could see colors. It was like looking at a sunny day through a dark cloth, if you know what I mean."

I nodded; it was a perfect description.

"I was going along, watching the sea like I always do. You know there's an old pass through the reef out there?

You can't see it now." He peered out to our left, absently
laying down the cheese. "Well, yes, you can if you know.
Anyway, that's where I noticed this pole sticking up. I
mean, first I saw it, and then I didn't, and then it bobbed
up again, shining in the moonlight. I figured some idiot had
tried to stick a channel-marker there. And then I saw it
was loose, and wobbling along in the current. I guess you
know there's about a three-knot current to the north all
along here."

"I do. But look, eat first, story later. That cheese will die
of old age."

I passed him some ham on a tortilla. He thanked me,
took one big bite and laid it on his knee, his eyes still
frowning at the reef, as though to recapture every detail.

"I slowed down to keep pace with it. Every big swell
would wash it in closer. It kept almost disappearing, and
then it'd come up again, bigger than before. For awhile I
thought it might be some huge fluorescent tube—you know
how they come in, waving—but when it got inside the reef
I saw no bulb could possibly be that big, and it had some
sort of—something—on it. By this time it was free of the
reef, and going along north at a pretty good clip. Just this
big pole in the sea, swaying vertically along getting shorter
and taller—maybe two metres at times. I stayed with it,
puzzled as hell. By this time I figured it might be the spar
of some buoy, maybe dragging a chain that kept it upright."

He broke off and said in a different tone, "That lad in
the blue hat. He your boy?"

I peered. A familiar battered bright-blue captain's hat
was disappearing over the dune beside the *rancho*.

"That's Ek. Our local *niño*." I tapped my temple in the
universal gesture that means here, child of God. "He's
somebody's wife's sister's son by somebody's cousin. Sort of
a self-appointed guard."

"He chased me off your well with a *machete* when I
came by last year."

"I think he's harmless really. But strong."

"Yeah . . . Well, anyway, this thing, whatever it was,
had me sort of fascinated. When it got hung up I'd sit
down and wait until it went on again. I wanted it, see. If it
was an instrumented buoy maybe there'd be valuable stuff
on it. I've heard of people getting return rewards— Aaah,
no. That's just what I told myself. The truth is, I just *wanted*

it. I had a feeling—maybe this sounds crazy—like it was meant for me. I don't tell this well. You know, something coming in from the sea all by itself, and you're all alone—"

"I know exactly what you mean. This tea-tray came in like that. I spent half a morning getting it, in a Noreaster."

He nodded his amazing-colored head and gently touched the fine wood of the tray, as if I had passed some test.

"Yeah. Anything you need . . . Well, by this time what tide there was was going out, and I saw that the thing wasn't coming any closer for awhile. But we were about half-way to that point where there's a back-flow. What they call a point around here is about as flat as your hand, but this one really does shift the current. About ten miles down. Some crazy Yank tried to build a resort there. *Lirios.*"

"Yes. The Lilies. I came here the year the government had chased him out. Misuse of agricultural land, they called it. He seems to have left owing everybody. I imagine they cleaned him out pretty well first; he had great plans. Is anything left?"

"Just some foundations with nice tiling, and part of a construction trailer. Fellow called Pedro Angel from Tres Cenotes has his family there; he runs a one-bottle *cantina*. Among other things. The *poso* is still fairly good. I was going to get my water there if you weren't here."

I shook my head, thinking of those extra miles. "Ek shouldn't have done that to you. I'll talk to Don Pa'o."

He glanced at me, Maya-wise. "Don't bother. I mean, it won't help. Thanks anyway. Look—are you sure you want to hear all this?"

"Very sure. But I wish you'd put that ham out of its misery; you've picked it up six times. Is there anything you'd rather eat?"

"Oh no, this is great." Obediently, he took two small bites and drank some tea, looking for the moment like a much younger man, a boy. His eyes were still on the calming reef, where even I could now see the zig-zag of darker water that was the old pass. The tide was running out. A solitary cloud cast a rosy reflection on the glittering horizon, and the palms were quieting. It would be a beautiful night indeed—with, I now recalled, a fine full moon. I had long since planned to bed my visitor down on a hammock in my "study." Maya hospitality is no problem; every corner has its hammock-hooks, and most commercial travellers even carry their own nets.

"Anyway, there I was, with this thing making long, slow bounces getting taller and shorter, and me following right along. This beach in the moonlight . . ." His voice softened; the face in its flaming frame was still a boy's—but shadowed now by deeper feeling.

"The moon had started down inshore, so that it really lit up the pole, and just about the time we got to Lirios I saw that the markings were something wrapped around it. When it came up high I could see sort of white bulges, and then some dark stuff started to drift loose and blow. At first I thought it was seaweed, and then I decided it was an old flag. And I hadn't seen it before because the chain, or whatever was weighting it, held it down in deep water. But now it was dragging on the shallows, riding much higher out. And then it stuck on the Lirios sandbar; and I saw it was a long thin bundle, wrapped or tied on the pole. It stuck there until a swell turned it around and carried it right toward me."

"And I saw the face."

His own face had turned seaward now, so that I had to lean toward him to catch the blowing words.

"It was a person, see, or a—a body. Tied to that spar, with long black hair floating and a sort of white dress flapping out between the ropes, starting to dry whenever it stayed out of the sea. . . . The person had to be dead, of course. But I didn't stop to think much, after I saw the face. . . . It . . . the . . ." He swallowed. "Anyway, there's a rotten back-flow there. Even if they say there's no such thing as an undertow, it feels like one. A sea-puss. I was wading and stumbling out, see. It's steep, and rough gravel. Not like here. But I swim a lot."

I repressed a protest. The Yank who built Lirios lost four customers before he would believe the locals: the surf there is no place to swim, even on the calmest days.

"The first wave that lifted me up, I saw the thing wasn't a buoy at all; there was more stuff surfacing beside the spar. Next time I got a look, I saw gunwales, and the top of a cabin astern. A fancy long-boat, see, maybe eight or ten metres. And polished—I could see the moon on wood and brass. The—the person was tied on the broken-off mast."

He took another mouthful of cold tea, his eyes on an inner vision. He seemed to be making an effort to recount this very carefully and undramatically.

"Polished . . ." He nodded to himself, yes. "Wet wood might look shiny, but not those oarlock things. Hell, I *felt* it, too! I'd got there, see, not even thinking. I mean, I'd never touched any dead people. Not really *dead*-dead. Just my grandfather's funeral, and his casket had glass. This was a lot different. I thought about what really dead fish were like, and I almost turned back. And then the next wave showed me the face close, and the eyes—her eyes were open. By then I was sure it was a woman. Her eyes seemed to be looking right at me in the bright moonlight. Shining—not dead. So huge . . . and her arm moved, or floated, like it was pulling at the ropes. So I kept on."

His hand instinctively moved to touch the knife he'd laid beside him.

"My leg hit something on the side of the boat beside her —that's where I got that one." He indicated a long grey scar. "And I started cutting ropes, all in among this silky stuff. The boat rolled as under water. I remember thinking, 'Oh God, I'm cutting into dead meat; maybe she'll come all apart.' And the boat rolled worse; it was hung up on its keel, trying to go turtle." He drew a long breath. "But then her arm hit me and it felt firm. So I got a good grip on it and took another lungful of air, and cut the footropes way down under, and kicked us both out of there just before the whole thing rolled." He sucked in another lungful, remembering.

"After that it was just a battle. All that damn silk, and I can still see the moon going round and round through it; and I couldn't get any decent air at all, until a lucky wave rolled us up on that sliding gravel stuff. It isn't like here. I knew I had to get us farther up fast before the backwash. I caught one good look at this face, with the dark hair streaming over it. Her eyes were closed then. I sort of passed out for a minute; but I couldn't quite, because I knew I had to do something about the water in her. But all I could do was grab her waist—it was tiny, I could almost touch both hands around and kind of jolt her face-down as I crawled up the shingle on my knees. A gush of water came out. And then we both fell into the trash-line, and there was my canteen. So I managed to pour some fresh water more or less into her mouth through the hair, and I thought her eyes were opening again just as I passed out for good. . . . Funny," he added in a different tone, and frowned.

"What?" I was frowning too, wondering how strong those skeleton tendons could be. A formidable feat, if true. But he was not, after all, much thinner than Cousteau, and a lot younger. And the Quintana Roo is peopled with survivors of harrowing ordeals.

"The trash-line was different," he said slowly. "No *basura,* no kipple at all—just a little natural tar, and weed and sea-fans, you know. I can see it." He screwed up his eyes, remembering hard for a moment.

"Anyway," he went on, "I was out cold, I don't know how long. The next thing I remember is hearing that voice." His lips twitched in a dreamy grin.

"It was a perfectly beautiful voice, soft and rough-low —contralto, d'you call it?—going on and on. I just lay still awhile, listening. She was standing up somewhere behind my head. This incredible emotion! And complicated too. Controlled. I couldn't make out the language, although I heard '*Dios*' a few times. And then I caught the lisp: *ththth. Thetheo,* what they call Castilian. I'd heard it once on a tape, but never like this. At first I thought she was thanking God for saving her." His grin flickered again.

"She was cursing. Swearing. Not like a *puta,* no simple stuff, but this long-cadence, complex, hissing fury. So intense—I tell you it was so savage it could scorch you if you didn't know a word. Among everything else, she was letting God know what she thought of Him, too.

"You know they say down here the Spanish is five hundred words, and four hundred are curses. She used up the ones I knew in a minute or so and went on from there. I began to understand better—a lot about *oro, poso dorado,* fountain of gold; and about her crew. She was pacing then, every so often I could hear her stamp. I pieced together that they'd found something, gold or treasure maybe —and her crew had deserted and left her tied on the boat. Or maybe they'd hit a rock in a storm—it was all pretty confusing. There was a lot about fighting, very violent. Maybe she'd tied herself on when she was alone in the storm. It sounded unreal, but real, too—I mean, I'd cut those ropes. And now she was asking—no, she was *telling* God exactly how to punish everybody. I think she was partly talking to the Devil, too. All in the most graphic detail, you couldn't imagine—talk about bloody-minded—"

His lips still smiled, but his eyes were wide and sober, staring north up the beach.

"I lay listening to her, and picturing her in my mind. Like a woman out of Goya, you know?—Someone I'd never believed existed. Then I got my eyes open—it was bright, blazing moonlight, everything glittered—and I rolled over to see. Oh, God.

"I was looking up straight into this beautiful furious face —big black eyes actually flashing; scornful, utterly sensuous curled lips and nostrils—talk about aristocratic. She'd pulled her hair back and tied it. But then I saw the rest of her. It was all wrong. My woman was gone. The person was a man."

He shook his head slowly from side to side, eyes closed as if to shut out some intolerable sight, and went on in a flat, controlled tone.

"Yeah. He was younger than me, no beard. What I'd thought was a dress was this great white silk shirt, he was stuffing it back in his pants while he cursed and paced. Shiny tight black britches, with this horrible great fly, codpiece, whatever, right in my face. He had loose soft black boots, with heels, and tiny feet. Ah, Christ, if I had the strength I'd have dragged him right back into the Caribbean and left him on that boat, I wanted my woman back so bad. . . .

"Then he noticed I was awake. His only response was to wind up one terrifying curse, and say 'Vino' at me. Not Hello or what—just 'Vino,' without hardly looking at me. Like I was some kind of a wine-machine. And paced off again. When he turned back and saw I hadn't moved he glanced at me sharper and repeated 'Vino!' quite loud. I still wasn't moving. So he came a step nearer and said, 'Entonces. Agua.'

"I just stared up at him. So he snapped his fingers, like he was talking to a dog or an idiot, and said very clearly, '¡A-gua! Agua para tomar.'

"You never saw arrogance like that. To get his point over, he flipped the empty canteen over in the sand toward me with the toe of his boot. That really pissed me off, getting sand on the screw-threads. I had him figured for some zillionaire general's spoiled brat, playing games. I started getting up, not really sure whether I was going to murder him or just walk away. But I found I was so weak that standing up was about it for me then. So I remembered this thing a lady had put me down with, and wrestled it into my best Spanish.

" 'The word you're groping for, man, is thank you.'

"It must have sounded like some weird dialect to him, but he got the point of that 'hombre.' Oh, wow! Did you actually ever see anyone's nostrils flare with rage? And the mad eyes—you wouldn't believe. His right hand whipped around and hit a scabbard I hadn't noticed—lucky for me it was empty. I could see the gold jewel-work on it glitter in the moonlight. That gave him a minute to look me over hard.

"I guess I puzzled him a little, when he came to look. I was a lot huskier then, too, and my gear was in better shape. Anyway, he stayed real still in a sort of cat-crouch, and said abruptly, 'Ingles.'

" 'No,' I told him. 'Estados Unidos del Norteamerica.'

"He just shrugged, but the edge was off his rage. He repeated more calmly, extra-clear, 'I desire more water. Water to drink.'

"I was still mad enough to say, 'More water—please.'

"Man, that nearly sent him off again; but he was still studying me. I was bigger than him, see, and he didn't know I was about to fall down if he pushed. I saw his eyes flicking from my hair to my knife to this big flashy diver's watch I wore. By luck the thing did one of its beeps just then, and his fantastic eyebrows curled up and met, in the moonlight. Next second he gave a chuckle that'd curl your hair, and suddenly bent and swept me an elaborate bow, rattling off the most flowery sarcastic speech you ever heard —I could only get parts, like 'Your most gracious excellency, lord of the exalted land of hell-haired lunatics,' and so on, ending with a rococo request for water. The word 'please' was of course nowhere in it. No way.

"Would you believe, I started to like the little son-of-a-bitch?"

My visitor turned to look straight at me for a moment. The blaze of the calming sea behind him made a curly fire of that beard and hair, and there was a different look in his hazel eyes. I recognised it. It's the look you see in the eyes of men from Crooked Tree, Montana, or Tulsa, or Duluth, when you meet them sailing the Tasman sea, or scrambling up some nameless mountain at the world's end. The dream—faintly self-mocking, deadly serious dream of the world. *Farther*, it says. *Somewhere farther on is a place beyond all you know, and I shall find it*. It had car-

ried this boy from Iowa to the wild shore of Yucatán, and
it would carry him farther if he could find the way.

"—maybe it was just his *macho*," my visitor was saying.
"I mean, the little bastard had to be half-dead. And his
crazy get-up, and the *poso dorado* business. For some reason I figured he might be from Peru; there's some pretty
exotic super-rich types down there. But it was more than
that. More like he'd found a key to some life way out, free
—something neat. I mean really far off, far away, *lejos . . .*"

His own voice had become far-off too, and his eyes had
gone back to the sea. Then he blinked a couple of times
and went on in his normal tone.

"He misunderstood my standing there, I guess. 'I will
pay you,' he told me. *'Pagaré.* Gift. *Te regalaré. ¡Mira!'*

"And before I could find words he had reached down and
slapped one boot-heel, and his hand came up with this
wicked little three-inch stiletto on his thumb. His other
hand was yanking up his shirt. The next thing, he was
sticking this blade right in by his lowest rib.

" 'Hey, man—No!' I sort of lurched to get his arm, but
then I saw he was just slicing skin. Two big gouts came
welling out. They fell on the sand, with only a little blood
—and they rolled! One of them flashed deep green in the
moonlight, deep green like the sea. He picked them up,
with that thumb-sticker pointed straight at me, and looked
them over critically. The green one he dropped into his
boot somewhere, and the other one he held out to me. It
was dark, about as big as a small marble, lying on this
slender, pointy-fingered hand.

" 'A token of my estimation for your timely assistance.'
"When I didn't move, the palm began gracefully to tilt,
to spill the stone on the ground. So I took it. Anybody
would. Not meaning to keep it, you know, just out of
curiosity, to see it close.

"It wasn't gem-cut, only polished-off cabochon, but when
I held it up the moonlight showed through dark blood-red,
like there was a fire inside. It had to be a ruby. If it wasn't
too badly flawed, it must have been worth God knows
what. I figured it was good, too; obviously he had chosen
his best stuff to sew into his hide.

"My Spanish was drying up. I was trying to make up a
suitably polite refusal and get the thing back into his hand,
when I saw his eyelids sliding down, and his whole body
sagged. He got himself straightened up again, but I could

see him swaying, fighting to stay on his feet. Jesus, I got scared he was going to die in front of my face after what he'd been through.

" 'Rest. I will bring water.'

"I had the sense not to touch him, even then. I just picked up the canteen, nearly falling over myself, and smoothed off a clean spot for him to settle onto. He sank down gracefully, resting his chin and arms on one knee, the knife still in his hand. The moon was starting down behind us, into the inland jungle, and its pitch-black shadow was spreading from the bluff to the beach where we were. I couldn't spot the trail up to Lirios. It's all low there, though, and I knew it had to be close, so I just started straight up the nearest gully.

"I needed both hands to haul myself up, so I stuck the ruby in my pocket." My visitor's hand went to his shorts. "The left back one, with the button." He nodded his head. Again I had the impression he was trying to recall every detail. "I remember I had a hell of a time securing it, but I knew I shouldn't lose *that*. And then I went on up to the top of the rise. Wait—" He clenched his eyes, saying almost to himself, "Coco-palms. Did I see cocos there? . . . I don't know. But there aren't very many; it's never been farmed. Just wild ones.

"When I hit the top, I found I'd made it wrong. There wasn't any clearing, just a trail. But Lirios's damn radio goes twenty-four hours a day; I knew I'd hear it soon. The night was dead calm now, see; every so often I could hear a wave flop on the beach below. So I staggered along north, stopping every few steps to listen. I was feeling pretty low. If Pedro's radio was off, there was no use looking for a light—he shuts up tight. All I heard was a couple of owl hoots, and the moon getting lower all the time. And dry—I tried to chew a palm-leaf, but it only made me worse.

"I'd just about decided that I should have gone south— this was only my second trip in there, see—when I saw a clearing right ahead and there was this funny slurping sound. The moon was shining on a kind of *ruina* by one side. I wondered if maybe this was a secret *poso*—people don't tell you everything, you know. When I got about ten steps into the moonlight a peccary exploded out and tore off like a pint-size buffalo. It about scared the pants off me, but I knew that slurping had to mean water. So I went

over to the stone blocks and stepped in a wet place. This
struck me odd at the time, because it was a dry year; the
lagoons even were low; but I didn't stop to worry about it.
I just crawled through till I found the hole, and stuck
my head in and guzzled. Then I filled the canteen and a
plastic bag I had, and got everything on me soppy wet, for
that poor lad down below. I remember thinking this would
be a nice spot to camp out for a couple days till we got our
strength back, so I stood up to orient myself. The moon
was still on the *laguna* right down below me and I sighted
on an islet with a big strangler fig. The lagoon was high
here, but that didn't bother me—you know how this
weather varies; one place can get soaked while the rest of
the coast dries up. Then I cut straight up over the dune
and more or less fell down to the beach, and went back
south on the last edge of moonlight to where I'd left him.

"I found him easy; he'd had the sense to crawl to a patch
of light before he collapsed. Now he was lying face-up,
asleep or unconscious. I was scared for a minute, but his
head was thrown back and I could actually see the pulse
going by his long, full throat. The jaw-line was delicate,
like a child's or a girl's, and those great soft black lashes on
his cheeks made him look more than ever like a beautiful
woman. I knelt down by him, wondering if it could possibly be. I'd only seen the bottom of his ribs, you know.
And those stuffed pants could be a fake—people do crazy
things. And I'd felt that tiny waist. I was just getting my
nerve to pull the shirt up, when the lashes lifted and the
huge dark eyes met mine.

" '*Agua pura.*' I held the canteen by his mouth. 'Drink—
tome.'

"The hands made a feeble movement, but they were too
weak to hold the canteen. I could see the fight was gone
too; the eyes looked like a bewildered child's.

" '*Perdón,*' I said, just in case, and slid one hand carefully through that glossy mass of hair to join canteen and
mouth.

" 'Slowly. Drink slowly, *despacio.*'

"Obediently, my patient took long, slow sips, breathing
deeply and stopping now and then to stare up at me.
Presently an innocent, beautiful smile came on the lips. I
smiled back, realizing that this stranger had in all probabil-
ity decided that I had taken his gem and left him there to
die. But just as my hand went to my pocket to give it back

to him, his head fell back again across my arm. It was so heavy that I had to lie down alongside to support it, and the canteen was finished that way. I bathed the forehead and face with my wet bandanna, too.

"When I produced my plastic water-bag the smile changed to pure wonder, and the eyes grew wider still. Despite thirst, that transparent plastic had to be felt and poked at before my patient would drink . . . I can remember how oval and shiny the nails were. Not polished, you know, but buffed in some way. And very clean; I could even see their white half-moons.

"The real moon was going down fast behind us. In the last light on the shore, I noticed that the long-boat had washed close in. She was riding heeled over, dousing that broken mast in and out with every quiet swell. It would have been a torturing end for someone tied there. I guess I shuddered.

"The person in my arms raised up enough to follow my gaze, and for a second I saw again the furious aristocrat. Saw and *felt*—it was like a jolt of voltage through my arms and chest. I didn't like the idea of what so much rage could do in a person so weak. By luck I had just located an old piece of health-bar in my shirt. It was sodden but okay, so I broke it and touched it to the stranger's lips.

" *'Es bueno. Come.'*

"A tongue-tip came out to explore the lips, dainty as a cat.

" *'¡Chocolate!'* My patient stared at me open-mouthed, the boat forgotten.

" *'Sí*, it's good. Eat some.'

" *'¡Chocolate!'* And the next thing I knew the stranger had stuffed the whole thing in his or her mouth, like a kid, with me trying to say 'Take it easy' and both of us grinning like mad.

"I recall thinking that chocolate couldn't be all that rare in Peru or wherever. Was it possible the person I was holding in my arms was simply a refugee from some expensive nut-house?

"But there was one thing I was determined to find out, if I could just hold out until my companion went to sleep. It wouldn't be long now; another sip or two of water, and the furry lashes were sweeping low with fatigue. The only trouble was, I was almost asleep myself. And the darkness coming over us didn't help. Even the occasional muffled clanking from the boat was starting to sound like music. I wedged a sharp rock under my shoulder, and that helped a bit. The person in my arms was drifting off; I could feel the body softening and fitting against mine in a way that made me absolutely convinced it had to be a woman, or the damnedest gay earth ever created. But that rock was getting to feel soft. I was desperate enough to actually try pinching myself as hard as I could, with fingers that felt like Jello.

"The second time I did that, I hit the lump in my back pocket and remembered the ruby. That woke me a little; it seemed unbearable that this aristocrat might think the stone had bought that water. So I wriggled enough to unbutton and carefully pull it out. Or rather, I tried to. My fingers have never felt so clumsy. It was almost like the stone was hiding, it didn't want to come.

"But I finally managed to get hold of it and ease it across my body toward where one of her hands was lying on the sand beside her head. A star shone right through as I raised it. I guess a poet could find the right words, but the truth is that the only red flash I've ever seen like that was on a police squad-car.

"The hand was lying palm-up, with the fingers slightly curled, and I went to put the ruby in it. Again I had trouble. The hand moved but without moving, if I can describe it—maybe I was just too dead to focus right. And her body was half under mine now, and it moved in a way that— well, you wouldn't have thought mine could respond, in the state I was in, but I did. That made me more than ever eager to get rid of that damned stone. I made three grabs at that little hand and caught the wrist, and forced the thing in her palm and curled her fingers over it, so I could get my own hand back where it wanted to be.

"But by then her body had slackened and fallen away from me, and before I could stop myself my nose went down in her cool dark hair and I was dead to the world.

"I didn't remember until next day that just at the very end, as I was folding her warm fingers, they seemed to change too, and turn kind of cold and stiff. And there was a strange faint sound from away on the sea, I guess it might have been a kind of wail from the boat's scraping, or like a bird's voice . . ."

His own voice had grown cool and quiet.

"That's it, really."

He showed his teeth in a comfortless grin.

"I woke up in a blazing sunrise, all alone. There wasn't one mark on the beach, not even my own footprints. But lots of plastic trash now—there was a Clorox bottle by my head. It hadn't been there before. Maybe the tide sent up a little wavelet, enough to smooth everything out without waking me. It was far out again by then, farther than I've ever seen it. No sign of a boat, of course. I guess if this was a good ghost story, there'd have been *something*"—he gave that joyless grin—"but there wasn't a single trace. Not even one long black hair. I looked, you see. I looked. The only tiny thing was, my hip pocket was unbuttoned. Oh how I searched. And all the while hearing Lirios's damn radio yattering from over the bluff."

He made a sound somewhere between a cough and a sigh.

"After . . . after awhile I climbed up; the path was right behind me. When I looked back I noticed three or four dark knobs of wood sticking out of the water 'way far out, like in a line . . . I bought some tacos off Pedro, and filled up the canteen on his skunk-water, with the radio banging out mariachis and tire ads. The thing is, Pedro's *poso,* his well, was right where the old *cenote,* the water hole, had been. I checked—it was the same view, but the water was low, like everywhere else that year. So I went back on the beach and walked on north. It was like a dream—I mean, not the other; the dream was Lirios and Pedro's *chistas*—joking. Or no, it was more like two dreams at once . . . ever since."

He was eyeing me intently, Maya-style, out of the corners of his clear *gringo* eyes. I got very busy discouraging some sugar-ants that were after his pack-roll.

"When I came by next year, you weren't around."

"No. I was late."

"Yeah. And I was earlier. . . . Nobody was around but some kids and that lad with the *machete.*"

He nodded his beard at Ek, who had resumed surveillance at extreme range.

"When I got by Lirios there were five *borrachos* from the *Gardia Nacional* roaring up and down the beach on their new Hondas and firing handguns at the moon. So I went on by. About sunrise I met an old *ranchero* walking down from Tuloom. We talked awhile. A fine old guy, I gave him my plastic water-bag. Turned out he knew all about me—you know how it goes around here."

"*De vero.* I've never yet gone anywhere I wasn't expected."

"Yeah." He wasn't listening. "Anyway, he wanted to make sure I'd passed by Lirios at full moon the year before. When I told him 'Yes,' he said, 'Good. In *la noche negra,* the moon-dark, the very bad ones come. Not often, you understand—but they *can.*' Then he asked me if anybody had given me anything there.

"I told him, 'No, at least, I didn't keep it.' He looked at me real hard and serious. '*Bueno,*' he said. 'If you had kept it, you would be *perdido*—lost. So long as you touch or hold anything. And are you free now? It is much the best that you go by day. Do you know the name of that place?'

" 'No.'

" '*El Paso del Muertes.* The pass or place of the dead, their *querencia.* Because all things come to the shore there. From Ascensión, Morales, Jamaica even. Sometimes quite big *lanchas,* shrimp-boats even from the Gulf. The rocks turn the current under water, you see, very far out. People used to make *mucho dinero* from what came there. But only by day, you understand. Only in the light of the sun. But that's all finished now. The *Gardia Aereo* finds them first from their planes.' He pointed out east. 'Where the sea turns by the *rifé de Cozumel.* Only wood and *basura,* worthless things come now.'

" 'I think I saw the ribs of one old wreck. The tide was very far out.'

" 'Ah?' He gave me that penetrating stare again. 'It must have been indeed very low water,' he said. 'Only once, in my youth, have I seen such a thing. I waded out to see it —in the day. It had been a sailing-boat. You know the metal *grimpas* used to hold the mast-ropes?' He did a little sketch in the sand, showing the stays. 'These were not fitted in, my friend, the way they do today. They were made of hot metal, poured right into the side of the ship. Which has not been done for two, three hundred years.' "

My visitor gave a deep sigh, or shudder, and tried the grin again.

"Anyway, we said goodbye and went our ways, and when I got to Tulum I heard that something had happened to one of the drunk *soldarero* kids the night before. I found out later that Pedro's brother dragged the Honda out of the drink and filed off all the numbers. He's trying to fix it up."

Abruptly, the light eyes locked on mine. I couldn't dodge.

"Look. *Is it* possible?" He nodded at the shelves behind the glass. "You're supposed to know things. Aren't you? Could I have, well, *dreamed* all that? I mean, it went on so long—it started right over there, you know. I must have walked after that thing for ten miles."

His voice got low and slow, the words almost forced out.

"Could I have—made it up? Believe me, I'm not a day-dreamer, I don't even dream much at night. And I don't drink, only a few beers. No grass for years now. And the other shit they have down here, I learnt not to mess with that the first week I was here. And fiction, movies, mystic stuff—forget it. Here, look—" He bent and fished a thick pamphlet out of his pack. It was titled *Hydraulic Properties of Natural Soil Aggregates*. He put it back and looked straight up at me.

"Am I—crazy? How could I have made up all that? Was I in a different time? *Am I crazy?* . . . What do you think?"

He was really asking.

I was thinking that I knew many people who would be delighted to take charge, to enlighten him on the ultimate nature and limits of reality, or the effects of dehydration and solitude on cerebral function. But some minutes earlier I had discovered I wasn't one of them. What in hell *did* I think, what had I been doing all during that long account, except believing him? . . . I knew what I *should* think, of course. All too well I knew. But, well—maybe one can dwell too long on the sands of the Quintana Roo.

I started a tentative mumble when he interrupted me, almost whispering: "How could I have made up that song?"

"Song?"

"I—I guess I didn't tell you about that." His face had turned back toward the sea, so that all I could catch from the fading gusts of the Stuffer was something about "at the end, see . . . and even this year."

He coughed again, and began to hum tunelessly, and finally sang a phrase or two, still watching the far reefs. His voice was clear and pleasing, but totally off any conceivable key.

"You see?" He glanced briefly at me. "I can't sing *at* all. So how could I . . . ? I can hear it, though."

The tune he had produced could have been any of a hundred Spanish wails—*amorado, corazon de oro, amor dorados lejos, lejos por la mar—Quisierra viajar;* that sort of thing: love, golden love far over the sea, who would not journey to the golden heart of the sea? . . . If there was anything extraordinary there, my Spanish could not detect it. Yet it seemed to have significance for him, as sometimes the most ordinary phrases do, in our dreams. Could I salvage my own sanity by hinting at this?

But whatever I might have said, I had delayed too long. His gaze was on the sea again, and he spoke in a whisper, not to me.

"No. I didn't make up that song."

Our moment had passed. Abruptly, he was on his feet, picking up his pack and canteen. The sea was almost calm now, a burnished splendor of green-gold and salmon, flushed with unearthly lavender and rose, reflections of the tropic sunset behind us. My dismayed protests blended with his farewell.

"Please wait. I'd assumed you'd spend the night here. I have a good spare *amaca.*"

He shook his flaming head, smiling politely.

"No. But thanks for the stuff and everything, I mean, really."

"Can't you wait a moment?—I meant to give you some—"

But he was already moving away, turning to stride down the beach. My last view of his expression was a mingled eagerness and sadness, a young face shadowed by a resolution I couldn't hope to break. The sunset behind us was now filling the air with golden haze, the palms were still.

After a moment I followed him down to the beach, irresolute. His easy stride was deceptive; by the time I reached the tide-line his thin figure was already filmed by the soft twilight air between us. Even to catch him now I would have to run. The mad notion of accompanying him on his walk through the night died before the reality of the old heart jittering in my ribs.

I could only stand and watch him dwindle, fade into the stick-figure I had seen at first. Tropic dusks come fast. By the time he was rounding the point I could barely make him out, had it not been for an occasional glint of red hair.

Just as he turned the corner of the mangroves a new light came from sea-ward and lit up his head with rosy fire. Then he was gone.

I turned and saw that the full moon was rising through the cloud-castles on the sea, a great misshapen ball of cold, gaseous light. For a moment it shone clear, at the apex of its luminous sea-path; and the beach became a snow-scape in silver and black. Then the high clouds took it again, in racing patterns of lemon and smoky bronze; and I turned to make my way up to the dark *casa*. Automatically I registered the high cirrus from the east—tomorrow would be fine. As I neared the patio, Ek's hat scuttled behind a dune on the road. He too had been watching the stranger go.

And that's it, really, as the strange boy said.

The night turned greasy-hot, so that about midnight I went down to cool myself in the placid sea. Mayas do not do this; they say that the brown sharks come close in on calm nights, to bear their young in the shallows. I waded out hip-deep to my sand-bar, wondering where my visitor was now. Great Canopus had risen, and in the far south I could just see Alpha Centauri, magnificent even in the horizon veils. The sheer beauty of the scene was calming. No wonder my young friend wanted to make his way by night. Doubtless he was already near Tuloom, perhaps curled up in one of his wayside nets, savoring a grapefruit, fighting off the *chiquitistas*.

The thought of the grapefruits had reassured me some time back. Surely a man does not set out to meet God knows what, to follow delusions or invoke spirits or yield to succubi—armed with two mediocre grapefruits and a baggie of maple-syrup?

But as I stood there in the quicksilver Caribbean, a triangular shadow with something large and dark below it caught my attention. Only a sea-fan, no doubt. But I decided it would be prudent to return to land before it came into the channel I had to cross. And as I splashed ashore another memory came back; my young friend claimed to have fed chocolate to his particular apparition. Was my maple-syrup possibly destined for the same?

This troubling notion combined with the extraordinary heat and heavy calm—effects not often met on this shore—and with an overactive conscience to give me a very bad hour on the patio that night. What had I done, letting him go on? Hallucinated or sane, it was equally bad. Several times I came within a gull-feather of rousing out Don Pa'o's son to ride me to Lirios on his bike. But what then? Either we would find nothing, or ignominiously come upon my young man eating Pedro's tacos. And either way, my hard-won reputation of being fairly sensible, for a *gringo,* would be gone for good. . . . I fear that selfishness, rather than good sense, drove me finally to my hammock and uneasy sleep. And in the fresh morning breeze, what passes for sanity prevailed.

The tale has no real ending, but only one more detail which may have no bearing at all.

The next week of fine weather saw me plunged back into some long-overdue paperwork, during which no gossip came by. And then the advent of the *rancho's* first real live school-teacher threw everyone into a great bustle. She was a resolute and long-suffering Maya maiden, sent by the *Goberniente* to see that the *rancho's* grandchildren did not grow up as wild as their parents had. I found myself involved in making peace between her and the owner, who paid one of his rare visits expressly to get her out. My task was almost hopeless, until the generator conveniently —and expensively—broke down, and I was able to convince him that it might be useful if someone could read the manual. Thus, with one thing and another, I found no occasion to query Don Pa'o about the *gringo caminante* before it was time for me to go.

The next year I came early, and found myself keeping one eye on the beach. Nothing came by, until there was a little excitement at Lirios: a body did wash ashore. But I quickly discovered it was the corpse of a small dark man with the name OLGA tattooed on his arm.

That evening was another windless one, and I strolled over to where Don Pa'o and his lady were dining alone in their outdoor kitchen. The last of their resident sons was staying in Cozumel that year, learning to lay bricks.

After the ritual greetings, I remarked that one was reminded of the red-haired *gringo* walker, who did not seem to have come by this year. As I spoke, the old man's mouth drew down, until he looked exactly like the petty Maya chieftain his grandfather had been.

"Do you think he will come this year?"

Don Pa'o shrugged, and the globular brown matron who had borne his ten children gave the all-purpose Maya matron's cackle, intended to convey nothing except possibly a low opinion of her conversant.

"Perhaps he has gone back to Norte America?" I persisted.

Don Pa'o squinted at me hard for an instant, and then his slant eyes drooped, and his chin swung slowly from shoulder to shoulder.

"*No,*" he said with finality.

At the same moment his wife made an extraordinary complex criss-cross of one hand across her abdomen. It puzzled me, until I recalled that some of the high-status older ladies here profess a brand of Catholicism whose rites and dogmas would doubtless astonish the Roman church. Then she got up to take the plates.

I did not need another look at the old man's archaic face to know that the subject was closed—and to sense too that I would not be seeing the strange red-haired boy again.

But why? I thought, as I made my farewells. What do they, what can they know? I have enough casual informants along this coast to ensure that nothing really disastrous or sensational could have occurred without my catching at least an echo of it, after this long. Mayas love morbidity; the actual fact was probably that my young friend was minting money in the swimming pool business, or had decided to explore someplace else.

Yet as I sat on my moonlit patio, listening to the quiet splash of the wavelets on the beach below, they seemed to be sighing out the odd little tuneless tune my visitor had tried to sing. *Amor dorado, lejos, lejos por la mar.* I realized I'd been half-hearing it now and again, particularly when I swam on quiet days, but I had put it down to the murmur in my bad ear. Now it was plainer. And the stranger's whole tale came back to me, as I had not let it do before. A year had passed and cooled; I could reflect.

I found I did not believe it—or rather, I did not believe in its outward detail and aspect. It could, I suppose, be some unquiet spirit who came to my young friend, some long-dead Spaniard or revenant Conquistador, some androgynous adventurer proffering ghostly gold; a life-hungry succubus from the shadows between the living and the dead. Or he could have been, very simply, out of his head. Yet I didn't quite believe that either.

What haunts me is the idea that something . . . did come to him there, something deeper than all these, which took on those manifestations to lure and seek him out. Something to which he was peculiarly vulnerable; and which, I fear, took him to itself on the night he left me. (For it has been five years now that he has not been seen here, and there is word that his partner in Des Moines has never seen him back.) What could it be?

I gazed out long at the impersonal beauty before me, scarcely daring to name it: the last great wonder of the world . . . "Anything you need," the boy had said. Whimsical as a tea-tray, seductive as a ruby, more terrible than all the petty armies of man. Who could say what was not in it, despite all our tiny encroachments and sorties? Perhaps we will kill it. And with it, ourselves. But it is far from dead yet—and its life is ours. As the boy had said too, our blood is its very substance, moving in our veins.

As I prepared to cease gazing and go to my human sleep, I recalled a trivial detail which carried an odd conviction. The Spanish word *mar* has one extraordinary aspect: *El mar, la mar*—the sea is the only word in Spanish, or any other tongue known to me, which is both female and male indifferently and alike. If it was indeed the sea itself which came for my friend, is it any wonder that it came in double guise?

> Quintana Roo, maps call it,
> That blazing, blood-soaked shore;
> Which brown men called Zama, the Dawn,
> And other men called names long gone
> Four centuries years before.
> Still songs of Gold that dead men sought,
> And lures of Love whom Death forgot,
> And hungry Life by Death begot,
> Murmur from ocean's floor.
> For those who myth from fact would know
> Dwell not in the Quintana Roo.

Here is an Oriental fantasy about a young girl who dies and embarks on a strange death-journey. Rich with authentic details of Oriental beliefs, it's a story that will move you in unfamiliar ways.

Jessica Amanda Salmonson is the author of the Tomoe Gozen novels, and edited the World Fantasy Award—winning anthology *Amazons!*

LINCOY'S JOURNEY

Jessica Amanda Salmonson

LINCOY WITH ALMOND EYES AND HAIR LIKE A midnight fountain was in her seventh year when first she tasted death. Some of it was sweet, but most of it was fearful, and it was most assuredly a long and perilous journey for one so tiny and young.

It was not purposely that Lincoy had wandered so far from school. The wild grapes had just come to ripeness along the vine-grown banks of the canal, and she quickly learned that the biggest and the bluest grapes amid the clusters were sweet and succulent. She began to force her way through the underbrush, working her way further and further from the school, with always the grapes ahead seeming bigger and bluer than the ones growing where she was picking. So on she went along the canal, losing all track of time and distance, foraging for the fruit, stuffing all she could into her mouth and the rest into the large front pocket of her long, drab dress.

So far had she ventured that she did not hear the school bell ring or see all the other children run back to class. She was enthralled with the nectar-rich marble-sized prizes at her fingertips. Never in young Lincoy's recollection had she beheld manna in such abundance simply hanging on vines along the canal. Soon both her cheeks and her pocket were bulging; both her hands and her face were stained a vivid purple.

It was as though the fruit were scattered along the right places especially to lead Lincoy to her death.

When finally there were no more grapes to be had, except little sour ones, Lincoy sat amid the vines and greenery feeling disheartened that there was nothing left to pick. She sat there in the sun-spattered shade, lower lip protruding, head turning back and forth, searching for just one more ripe, blue treat. Her pocket was filled to overflowing, yet it somehow seemed important to find just one more.

Greed, however minor, is seldom worth a man's undoing. This is equally true for a young child; and often lessons are not kindly taught. There were no more grapes worth having, but there was another fruit nearly identical in coloration, smaller in size, which grew near the ground rather than on vines. It was not a berry common to the country, but sometimes the gentle current of the canal brought seeds from distant and strange lands and deposited them where they did not belong. The sight of these berries delighted Lincoy, for they were even bluer than the grapes. She picked all there were—one small handful—and having no more room in her pocket, she ate them. Then she was well satisfied and decided to head back.

Being so small and inexperienced, she became lost with great rapidity. Had she stayed in sight of the canal and followed it back the way she came, she could not have ended up anywhere but at the school. But with no grapes to make threading through the undergrowth worth the effort, Lincoy forged away from the canal, out of the heavy growth, and severed herself from the only landmark recognizable to her. It is a fact that Lincoy was a child with little fear and much trust, especially in Buddha, and she never considered the possibility that she was going the wrong way. She just walked on and on, confident that eventually she would end up either home or at school.

Not long after, she grew irresistibly sleepy, so she looked around for a quiet spot. The ground was everywhere hard, stony, or covered wtih coarse weeds, so she fought her tiredness a short while.

For a spell she walked on with eyelids more often closed than open. She fell various times and squashed her grapes in the process so that the front of her dress was all stained as with purple ink. She eventually stumbled onto a path which led up a hill, and though her tired legs would rather have gone down a hill than up one, there was no turning the path around, so she headed up, directly finding a rustic bench constructed of a split log. Upon this bench she lay down to sleep.

When the sun was low, Lincoy still lay there, unmoving

except to shake with a chill. Her face was wet with fevered
perspiration. Once she opened her eyes and saw a man
dressed in yellow, but it was much pleasanter to sleep
than to ask who are you.

It was a Buddhist monk who had come down the hillside
and found the girl lying there ill. He picked her up in his
arms and took her on up through the forest and into the
temple where he and other monks cared for her and tried
to awaken her enough to get her to take curative herbs. She
was delirious that night and would not take food or water,
much less the herbs which were bitter.

Lincoy's death was not sudden, and for a while the next
morning it seemed as though she would be all right. She
awoke having no idea where she was. But she was not a
child easily made afraid. She found herself in a large room
where she had never been before, and she was alone, but
that was not in itself cause for alarm.

She rose from the wooden pallet and went exploring
through the temple, searching for something to play with.
The temple was of goodly size, much of it underground,
and though it was occupied by many Buddhists, Lincoy
passed no one in the halls and found no one in the rooms
she inspected. In one room were shelves stacked with many
books and scrolls. In another room were many beautiful
vases and carvings of jade and silkstone. In several rooms
there were coffins and urns, and in one of these rooms
Lincoy spied a skeleton lying in its entirety on a wooden
pallet very similar to the one she had slept upon. The bones
were very dusty, and Lincoy took this to mean nobody
cared about them. So in her innocence and lack of fear,
Lincoy took away the grinning skull to play with. She found
her way back to the room she had been asleep in and sat
down upon the floor to play with her new found possession.

In a few minutes the same shaven-headed man in yellow
who had found her the day before, and who Lincoy remembered only as a vague and not unpleasant dream, came
in and saw her with her small arm shoved up inside the
hollow of the skull. He was instantly horrified, but properly
composed himself before approaching her.

He told her in a gentle but grave tone that she must give
him the skull.

To Lincoy's reasoning, this seemed an unfair request.
This was her only plaything, one that she had searched

hard for and hauled back herself, and it was a much more interesting toy than she had ever had before, with all its white teeth and funny holes for nose and eyes and its hinged jaw; and whoever had it before didn't even bother to clean it so they must not have wanted it. She did not wish to part with it and held it near.

"No," she told him bluntly. "It is mine."

"It is not yours," the monk corrected. "It belongs to another."

They argued a while in quiet tones until the monk decided simply to take it away. But her arm was still half inside the skull, which gave Lincoy an edge in keeping it, and the monk stepped away for fear their struggling over it would cause the skull to be broken.

"Very well," he finally agreed, changing his strategy. "It is yours. But right now is not the time to play. It is the time to eat. So you must put your toy away."

Lincoy, though obstinate about parting with something she honestly believed was hers, was not a disrespectful or disobedient child. So when she was told it was not the time to play, she asked where she was supposed to put the skull. The monk had a shoulder pouch hanging at his side and he opened it saying, "You may keep it here."

Immediately suspicious, Lincoy hesitated and asked, "Are you going to throw it away?"

"I promise I won't throw it away."

And so Lincoy put the skull into the monk's pouch. She never knew what a terrible deed it was to upset the bones of the dead priests who were kept in the temple, and it was not in the monk's heart to reprimand her. But he was very much afraid for her after that, and since he did not know what Lincoy had eaten the day before, he blamed all that happened to her afterward upon the skull.

All morning long she seemed healthy. She told the monks her name, and they sent a messenger to seek her parents. But she would not eat or drink, and all the monks thought this strange for always people should be very hungry after a night of fever. But one monk did not find it strange. He knew that spirits did not take nourishment, and he believed the girl was possessed by the spirit of the priest whose bones she had unsettled.

By the time the sun approached its zenith, Lincoy once again fell weak and drowsy, and she lay down on the floor to fall fast asleep. When her father came, neither he nor the monks could arouse her, and this greatly disturbed her father.

The monk who had found her on the path and later with the skull took Lincoy's father aside and whispered so none else could hear how his daughter was now possessed and he must take her away from the temple and tell no one where she had been. This Lincoy's father did.

Lincoy lay in sickness all the rest of the day and most of the next, never once stirring during that period. Her family, from oldest grandfather to youngest brother, spent all the lighted hours working among the ripening crops, so Lincoy was alone when finally she woke.

She was so weak she could not raise her arms, and only with greatest effort did she turn her head to see out the open door. Her throat was so painfully dry she could not call out.

The only one to look in on her was her wild-haired brother of three years. When she saw him enter, she managed with much difficulty to rasp out a small request. "Give me something."

"Give you what?" the little boy inquired, moving near the bed.

She tried to say specifically that she wanted water, but she could make no other sound. The boy ran quickly into another room and returned with a piece of fruit which he put into her mouth. Lincoy could not swallow it, and it had a terrible taste to her. She tried to move her tongue to get the thing out of her mouth, but that simple task seemed inordinately toilsome. Having the fruit thus clogging her mouth became the center of her attention, and it seemed insidious having it stuck there. She despaired over it; but she was too dehydrated even to cry.

It was at that precise moment that she died. Her little brother returned to his chores and only when the entire family returned to the house to eat did they find Lincoy dead. Her brother admitted it was he who had put the food into her mouth, but he thought she had only gone back to sleep afterward. It was good, Lincoy's mother had said, that she had taken at least a small portion of nourishment before death, for it would give her ghost strength for the journey into the next life. Then all wept, and messengers were sent to those of the family who had moved away from the farm, telling them that a funeral was to be prepared.

To Lincoy it did not seem that she had died. It seemed

instead that she had awakened all alone and, no longer
feeling weak and tired, left the house to search for her
father and mother. Outside, they were nowhere to be
found, so she started down the cart-rutted, dusty road. The
world looked as it had always looked, except there were no
people tending the farms, no crickets calling from the
brown grasses, no colorful birds singing and flitting in the
trees and bamboo.

The road brought her to the canal. Usually it was busy
with fishermen, houseboats, and occasionally a ship or two
from lands near and far. But today there was only a single
junk adrift in the quiet mirror waters, and what a junk it
was!

It sported a huge, square sail of rice paper more color-
fully printed than the grandest kite ever flown. And, in
truth, that junk sailed so smoothly that it seemed more to
fly as would a kite than to float. The hull was carved with
dragons and lesser animals, and standing in the prow was
a woman of unsurpassed beauty.

As the junk approached the bank, Lincoy stood in awe
of that lady's beauty. She was tall, shapely slender, dressed
in an Ao Dai gown of shimmering gold, and upon her
head she wore a tall, pointed adornment. Her small, perfect
hands were held in prayer between her breasts and she
stood like a perfect statue, her wide slanted eyes staring
straight into those of Lincoy.

There was not the slightest ripple upon the still waters,
nor gentlest breeze in the air. With neither current nor
wind, Lincoy was at a loss to guess what powered the junk.
As though of its own accord, the junk stopped just short of
the bank and brought one side around to make boarding
easy. Lincoy knew she was welcome to ride in the vessel,
but for some reason she hesitated.

"Are you not ready to come with me?" asked the pretty
golden lady, her eyes like black suns, her face the loathing
of jealous empresses.

Lincoy could not think what to answer, so she silently
climbed into the junk, and it began to sail down the canal
toward the setting sun. She wondered where the golden
lady might take her, for it was Lincoy's childhood belief
that the canal led everywhere in all the world. On and on
the boat sailed, and finally Lincoy broke the silence to ask
about the destination.

The golden lady answered mysteriously, "To a land very near yet very far."

Hours seemed to have gone by, but always the sun remained at the same point at the end of the waterway, as if the junk were following it around and around the world, giving it no chance to set. Or could it be that time had stood still in the strange little ship? Were these hours or eons that were going by?

They passed through lands Lincoy had never heard tell of from parents or teachers. Unfamiliar plants grew along the shores, and unrecognized mountain peaks were visible far away. Later the shores turned into endless barren desert. And still later the canal took them between two stone-faced cliffs that rose into infinity.

When wonders came so close together, they soon ceased to amaze Lincoy, and she remembered that she had not eaten since the day she found the grapes. "I am hungry," she said.

"Soon you will never have to be hungry again."

After a short term of silent thought, Lincoy stated, "I am thirsty."

"Soon you will have no need of water."

Lastly Lincoy proclaimed, "I need a toilet."

Against this the beautiful lady could not argue, so the junk neared the shore and Lincoy climbed out. But she did not need a toilet at all. She was thinking only of her father and mother, and she began to run back along the way the junk had brought her.

At this time, Lincoy awoke in her coffin. She had never been in one before and did not recognize it, else she might have been more afraid. As it was, she was only confused. The preparation for burial consisted of the binding of the ankles, of the knees, the waist. The upper arms were bound to the sides and the forearms were bent above the chest with the wrists tied together and the hands in prayer. Inside her praying hands was placed a yellow lotus.

Lincoy could not move her jaw to cry out, for her whole mouth was stiff and immobile. She could not open her eyes, for they were encrusted and stuck shut. Being properly bound for burial, she could not have kicked even had she the strength. She did manage to rock from side to side, banging her elbows on the coffin floor, but it did not make much of a sound.

All around the outside of the coffin had been placed

large guavas, for guavas have the power to absorb terrible
smells and were always kept around the unburied dead.
The only reason Lincoy was not yet placed below the
ground was that her oldest sister in another village was ill,
and the family wanted to wait for her before they began
the ritual bathing; for each among the family should help
purify the body before setting it into the land.

Lincoy's grandfather came into the room with fresh
guavas, for they had to be changed every day in such a
warm climate. He picked up all the fruit of the day before
and replaced them with new. His old age had robbed him
of much of his ability to hear, so the dull thudding from
within the small coffin went unheard. But he was not left
without clues. On his way across the farmland with his
bundle of old guavas to throw away, he dropped one and
it burst open.

As all know, when a guava is used to absorb the smell of
the dead, to burst one open is to release all that odor, and
it is a scent many times worse than rotten pheasant eggs.

So the old man cursed his clumsiness and bent to pick
up the dropped fruit. To his surprise, it did not smell at all,
and he thought this very odd indeed.

In the meanwhile, Lincoy had been captured by the beautiful lady in gold and taken back to the junk. "You
mustn't do that again!" Lincoy was scolded. She cried the
longest while, but eventually forgot her tears and looked
out at the wonders unfolding before and below her.

First the waters of the canal turned a rich sky blue, then
a warm sun yellow, and as they drifted along, the waters
turned a beautiful grassy green, and then bright red, and
then orange, and every other color imaginable. It was a
grand sight unlike any other in Lincoy's experience, and
she could not lift her eyes from the intensity of the colors
as the spectrum flashed back and forth in its indescribable
splendor.

All the while the sun led the way.

When Lincoy managed to raise her eyes from the
painted waters, she discovered that the shore was not so
friendly. Bamboo had grown dense, and she could see that
if she tried to escape again, she would never survive that
forest. Many of the bamboo limbs and shoots were broken,
beveled, and sharp. A person would quickly be impaled if
an attempt were made to run through there.

And it became worse. The bamboo knives grew more

and more plentiful and began to reach out over the canal to form a tunnel. Lincoy was forced to lay flat on her back in the bottom of the junk to escape being poked and scratched. But the sharp spikes and stalks turned aside from the golden lady who still stood straight and tall at the prow, and even the paper sail was not torn.

It had been decided that if Lincoy's sister had not arrived on the morrow, they would proceed with the burial without her. But they did not have to delay that one extra day because the older sister was nearly home even as that decision was being made.

Several shaven-headed monks in yellow were in attendance for the ceremonial bathing, as well as a Buddhist priest and a great gathering of friends and relatives, plus a few mild acquaintances who had nothing better to do that day. Lincoy's father removed his daughter from the casket, and the casket was taken away to be used by others in the family when they died, for poor people could scarcely afford to bury caskets with bodies.

Many tears were being shed and many people wore solemn faces while the priest spoke over the dead girl. But the old grandfather was not paying attention. He slipped to where the casket had been sitting and plucked up one of the guavas. He purposely broke it open and sniffed of it.

"She is not dead!" he cried out, interrupting the priest's words.

"What do you say, old one?" the priest asked.

"That she is not dead! She has lain here for seven days but her flesh does not melt. And smell this fruit! It is still good enough to eat!" And when he said this, he took a big bite out of the casket guava, letting the pulp and juice drip down his chin. This made the gathering gasp, for it would seem no less vile to bite into a dead buffalo crawling with maggots than eat a guava which had been used to absorb the scent of death.

While the priest smelled the pulp in some surprise, Lincoy's father returned to his little daughter's side. He listened at her chest, felt for a heartbeat at her temple, then behind her ear. Her body was cold and there was no life in it to be found.

"Get me string and cotton!" he commanded, and Lincoy's mother quickly obeyed. With everyone standing around in silent expectation, Lincoy's father held a string with a cotton ball tied to it before Lincoy's lips and nose. If she breathed but slightly, the ball would swing. Her father held his arm steady half an hour, an hour, one hour and a half, two hours. They were a patient people who stood around, and they did not lose interest in the silent ordeal. Every eye remained riveted to the cotton ball, and all were careful not to breathe in that direction.

At long, long last the father took his aching arm away and, shoulders sagging, he turned and assured the rest, "She is dead."

Then was Lincoy filled with a feeling of despondency. The golden lady would not talk to her as they passed through the Dark Land, and this increased Lincoy's inner loneliness. She felt more sure than ever that she would see her family never again.

Despite her fearlessness, this part of the journey was particularly terrorizing. The sun still glowed at the mouth of the canal, but its light seemed not to shine on this shadowed land. The canal had become more like a narrow channel through a misty swamp, and on either side of the channel red eyes could be seen blinking in the black shadows of giant bog trees. Hisses, slitherings, splashes, muted groans, and even sinister chuckling were the sounds that filled her ears.

Lincoy looked with moist eyes at the tall woman and admitted, "I am afraid."

"This is the last land we must pass through," the golden lady answered in her usual mystical manner. "Then you will never again be afraid."

When she heard it said that this was the last land they would pass through, Lincoy knew with full certainty that she was never going home, and her depression increased tenfold with this knowing. She cried hardest then, but without whimpering or even a slight sniffle, for she did not want the golden lady to hear her.

She forgot all about the monsters in the dark. All she could think about was how greatly she missed her father and mother. All other fears were overcome, and Lincoy feared only that this was her last and only chance to return to her home. In a burst of blind courage, she leapt over the side of the junk, scrabbled for the mucky shore, and climbed out of the dirty waters. Her legs sank knee deep in the mud, making running next to impossible. Still, Lincoy ran.

The golden lady could only watch in sadness and pity and call out twice for Lincoy to come back. She could not run and bring the girl back this time, for this was a land even the golden lady feared to enter.

Behind her, Lincoy heard the sound of cruel laughter and when she looked over her shoulder, she saw two hairy men with buffalo tails and horns chasing after her with forked spears.

She tried to run faster, but it seemed as though a spell slowed her pace. Like a magic rope: the harder one struggles to escape it, the tighter the rope becomes. The faster she tried to go, the heavier her feet became.

Her heart felt as though it might pound out of her chest. She feared to look back again, for she knew without checking that the devil men were about to grab her. Her legs sank further and further into the stinking swamp filth until she could not raise them up one more time. So she closed her eyes and took a hold of a bog tree's trunk and with tears flowing she cried out, "Buddha, Buddha, Buddha! Help me! Help me!"

Then she felt a strong, powerful arm sweep around her and snatch her out of the mud. The hideous laughter suddenly ceased and when she opened her eyes, Lincoy was sitting in Buddha's lap as he sat in lotus, smiling down at her and washing away all her fears.

As one by one, the family of Lincoy purified her body. A bowl of water was set by her prone form, and each person wetted his or her hands and cleansed the dead girl's legs or thighs or belly or breast or neck or face.

Many wet hands ran over her flesh, one after the other, so that badly needed moisture was being absorbed into her dehydrated body. The friction warmed her cold skin. The massaging renewed the circulation of her stilled blood.

Yellow-clad monks stood behind her with bald heads bowed. Incense trailed through the room. And those who had not yet helped wash the body awaited their turn. When Lincoy's grandfather began to gently wet her face with water, he saw her eyes open a trifle. He froze, looking down at her, his hands still on her cheeks. Maybe, he thought, his hands had caused her eyes to open. He had already made a fool of himself once during the ceremony, and he wondered if there was any wisdom in alarming the gathering all over again.

He concluded in that instant of thought he could only be

twice the fool he had already proven himself, so he cried out again, "She is alive!"

Of course nobody gave much credence to what by now could be considered the senile ravings of a mournful old man, but no one dared show disrespect to one of such years. Besides, Lincoy's father wanted very much to believe that the impossible was the fact, and once again he moved into activity.

He gently moved his old father aside and whispered, "Get me a cup of water," and when it was delivered, he poured it down his daughter's throat until it came up her nose.

Then he began to remove the funeral bindings from her ankles, knees, thighs, and arms. The dry brittle lotus in her bound hands fell and crumbled on the floor. There was minor protest, but when even the priest shushed them, Lincoy's father continued to untie her. He sat her up and she was limp as a rag doll, all the water spilling out from between her teeth and from her nostrils.

The gathering watched with varying secret thoughts, but said nothing. Her father rubbed her arms and legs all over, and was as persistent in this maneuver as he had been with the cotton ball.

From Lincoy's dry throat came three words, spoken so softly and with lips so unmoving that only her father, grandfather, mother and three monks who stood directly behind her heard what she said.

"Give me water," was her whispered request.

When these words were spoken by the presumed dead girl, two of the monks ran out of the house and did not stop until they were safe in their temple. The remaining monk was the one who had found her the first day of her illness, and he only smiled as though with knowing relief. Lincoy's mother stood gawking with mouth open while her husband rubbed Lincoy's flesh more vigorously. The grandfather began to jump and halloo and grab and hug the other people who were either amazed beyond reaction or as yet uncertain what was going on.

It was many days before Lincoy regained the strength to stand alone, but she could speak within the hour, and she wanted to know: "What were you doing with me?"

"You were dead," her father told her. "We were going to bury you. And we would have, too, if your sister had not arrived so late."

"Who told you I died?" the little girl demanded in protest. "I did not die! I only went to sleep!"

"No one goes to sleep for seven days," her father disagreed.

Lincoy persisted, "I did not sleep for seven days! I got up and went to the canal. A golden lady took me on a river of many colors. Buddha—he brought me back."

Her father could only smile at such childhood fancy and hug her tightly as he did. But there was one thing he could not dispute: Buddha had brought her back.

We live our lives largely on momentum, continuing to do and say the things we've learned are "right" in our own cultures, nations, cities or villages. But what if, one day, everyone woke up somewhere else in the world? What if, for instance, you woke to find yourself in Spain, in a city full of people from Africa, Tibet, Canada, Afghanistan, Australia . . . ?

This novelette has, as I write, just won the Nebula Award, and is nominated for the Hugo Award. Its author, Michael Bishop, has written such novels as *Stolen Faces*, *Catacomb Years*, and *No Enemy but Time*.

THE QUICKENING

Michael Bishop

I.

LAWSON CAME OUT OF HIS SLEEP FEELING drugged and disoriented. Instead of the susurrus of traffic on Rivermont and the early-morning barking of dogs, he heard running feet and an unsettling orchestration of moans and cries. No curtains screened or softened the sun that beat down on his face, and an incandescent blueness had replaced their ceiling. "Marlena," Lawson said doubtfully. He wondered if one of the children was sick and told himself that he ought to get up to help.

But when he tried to rise, scraping the back of his hand on a stone set firmly in mortar, he found that his bed had become a parapet beside a river flowing through an unfamiliar city. He was wearing, instead of the green Chinese-peasant pajamas that Marlena had given him for Christmas, a suit of khaki 1505s from his days in the Air Force and a pair of ragged Converse sneakers. Clumsily, as if deserting a mortuary slab, Lawson leapt away from the wall. In his sleep, the world had turned over. The forms of a bewildered anarchy had begun to assert themselves.

The city—and Lawson knew that it sure as hell wasn't Lynchburg, that the river running through it wasn't the James—was full of people. A few, their expressions terrified and their postures defensive, were padding past Lawson on the boulevard beside the parapet. Many shrieked or babbled as they ran. Other human shapes, dressed not even remotely alike, were lifting themselves bemusedly from paving stones, or riverside benches, or the gutter beyond the sidewalk. Their grogginess and their swiftly congealing fear, Lawson realized, mirrored his own: like him, these people were awakening to nightmare.

Because the terrible fact of his displacement seemed more important than the myriad physical details confronting him, it was hard to take in everything at once—but Lawson tried to balance and integrate what he saw.

The city was foreign. Its architecture was a clash of the Gothic and the sterile, pseudoadobe Modern, one style to each side of the river. On this side, palm trees waved their dreamy fronds at precise intervals along the boulevard, and toward the city's interior an intricate cathedral tower defined by its great height nearly everything beneath it. Already the sun crackled off the rose-colored tower with an arid fierceness that struck Lawson, who had never been abroad, as Mediterranean. . . . Off to his left was a bridge leading into a more modern quarter of the city, where beige and brick-red highrises clustered like tombstones. On both sides of the bridge buses, taxicabs, and other sorts of motorized vehicles were stalled or abandoned in the thoroughfares.

Unfamiliar, Lawson reflected, but not unearthly—he recognized things, saw the imprint of a culture somewhat akin to his own. And, for a moment, he let the inanimate bulk of the city and the languor of its palms and bougainvillea crowd out of his vision the human horror show taking place in the streets.

A dark woman in a sari hurried past. Lawson lifted his hand to her. Dredging up a remnant of a high-school language course, he shouted, "¿Habla Español?" The woman quickened her pace, crossed the street, recrossed it, crossed it again; her movements were random, motivated, it seemed, by panic and the complicated need to *do* something.

At a black man in a loincloth farther down the parapet, Lawson shouted, "This is Spain! We're somewhere in Spain! That's all I know! Do you speak English? Spanish? Do you know what's happened to us?"

The black man, grimacing so that his skin went taut across his cheekbones, flattened himself atop the wall like a lizard. His elbows jutted, his eyes narrowed to slits. Watching him, Lawson perceived that the man was listening intently to a sound that had been steadily rising in volume ever since Lawson had opened his eyes: the city was wailing. From courtyards, apartment buildings, taverns, and plazas, an eerie and discordant wail was rising into the bland blue indifference of the day. It consisted of many strains. The Negro in the loincloth seemed determined to separate these and pick out the ones that spoke most directly to him. He tilted his head.

"Spain!" Lawson yelled against the uproar. "*¡España!*"

The black man looked at Lawson, but the hieroglyph of recognition was not among those that glinted in his eyes. As if to dislodge the wailing of the city, he shook his head. Then, still crouching lizard-fashion on the wall, he began methodically banging his head against its stones. Lawson, helplessly aghast, watched him until he had knocked himself insensible in a sickening, repetitive spattering of blood.

But Lawson was the only one who watched. When he approached the man to see if he had killed himself, Lawson's eyes were seduced away from the African by a movement in the river. A bundle of some sort was floating in the greasy waters below the wall—an infant, clad only in a shirt. The tie-strings on the shirt trailed out behind the child like the severed, wavering legs of a water-walker. Lawson wondered if, in Spain, they even had water-walkers. . . .

Meanwhile, still growing in volume, there crooned above the highrises and Moorish gardens the impotent air-raid siren of 400,000 human voices. Lawson cursed the sound. Then he covered his face and wept.

II.

The city was Seville. The river was the Guadalquivir. Lynchburg and the James River, around which Lawson had grown up as the eldest child of an itinerant fundamentalist preacher, were several thousand miles and one helluva big ocean away. You couldn't get there by swimming, and if you imagined that your loved ones would be waiting for you when you got back, you were probably fantasizing the nature of the world's changed reality. No one was where he or she belonged anymore, and Lawson knew himself lucky even to realize where he was. Most of the dis-possessed, displaced people inhabiting Seville today *didn't* know that much; all they knew was the intolerable cruelty of their uprooting, the pain of separation from husbands, wives, children, lovers, friends. These things, and fear.

The bodies of infants floated in the Guadalquivir; and Lawson, from his early reconnoiterings of the city on a motor scooter that he had found near the Jardines de Cristina park, knew that thousands of adults already lay dead on streets and in apartment buildings—victims of panic-inspired beatings or their own traumatized hearts. Who knew exactly what was going on in the morning's chaos? Babel had come again and with it, as part of the package, the utter dissolution of all family and societal ties. You couldn't go around a corner without encountering a child of some exotic ethnic caste, her face snot-glazed, sobbing loudly or maybe running through a crush of bodies calling out names in an alien tongue.

What were you supposed to do? Wheeling by on his motor scooter, Lawson either ignored these children or searched their faces to see how much they resembled his daughters.

Where was Marlena now? Where were Karen and Hannah? Just as he played deaf to the cries of the children in the boulevards, Lawson had to harden himself against the implications of these questions. As dialects of German, Chinese, Bantu, Russian, Celtic, and a hundred other languages rattled in his ears, his scooter rattled past a host of cars and buses with uncertain-seeming drivers at their wheels. Probably he too should have chosen an enclosed vehicle. If these frustrated and angry drivers, raging in polyglot defiance, decided to run over him, they could do so with impunity. Who would stop them?

Maybe—in Istanbul, or La Paz, or Mangalore, or Jönköping, or Boise City, or Kaesŏng—his own wife and children had already lost their lives to people made murderous by fear or the absence of helmeted men with pistols and billy sticks. Maybe Marlena and his children were dead. . . .

I'm in Seville, Lawson told himself, cruising. He had determined the name of the city soon after mounting the motor scooter and going by a sign that said *Plaza de Toros de Sevilla.* A circular stadium of considerable size near the river. The bullring. Lawson's Spanish was just good enough to decipher the signs and posters plastered on its walls. *Corrida a las cinco de la tarde.* (Garcia Lorca, he thought,

unsure of where the name had come from.) *Sombra y sol.*
That morning, then, he took the scooter around the stadium three or four times and then shot off toward the
center of the city.

Lawson wanted nothing to do with the nondescript highrises across the Guadalquivir, but had no real idea what he
was going to do on the Moorish and Gothic side of the
river, either. All he knew was that the empty bullring, with
its dormant potential for death, frightened him. On the
other hand, how did you go about establishing order in a
city whose population had not willingly chosen to be there?

Seville's population, Lawson felt sure, had been redistrib-
uted across the face of the globe, like chess pieces flung
from a height. The population of every other human com-
munity on Earth had undergone similar displacements.
The result, as if by malevolent design, was chaos and suffering. Your ears eventually tried to shut out the audible
manifestations of this pain, but your eyes held you ac-
countable and you hated yourself for ignoring the wailing
Arab child, the assaulted Polynesian woman, the blue-eyed
old man bleeding from the palms as he prayed in the
shadow of a department-store awning. Very nearly, you
hated yourself for surviving.

Early in the afternoon, at the entrance to the Calle de
las Sierpes, Lawson got off his scooter and propped it
against a wall. Then he waded into the crowd and lifted
his right arm above his head.

"I speak English!" he called. "*¡Y hablo un poco Español!*
Any who speak English or Spanish please come to me!"

A man who might have been Vietnamese or Kampu-
chean, or even Malaysian, stole Lawson's motor scooter
and rode it in a wobbling zigzag down the Street of the
Serpents. A heavyset blond woman with red cheeks glared
at Lawson from a doorway, and a twelve- or thirteen-year-
old boy who appeared to be Italian clutched hungrily at
Lawson's belt, seeking purchase on an adult, hoping for
commiseration. Although he did not try to brush the boy's
hand away, Lawson avoided his eyes.

"English! English here! *¡Un poco Español también!*"

Farther down Sierpes, Lawson saw another man with
his hand in the air; he was calling aloud in a crisp but
melodic Slavic dialect, and already he had succeeded in
attracting two or three other people to him. In fact, pockets

of like-speaking people seemed to be forming in the crowded commercial avenue, causing Lawson to fear that he had put up his hand too late to end his own isolation. What if those who spoke either English or Spanish had already gathered into survival-conscious groups? What if they had already made their way into the countryside, where the competition for food and drink might be a little less predatory? If they had, he would be a lost, solitary Virginian in this Babel. Reduced to sign language and guttural noises to make his wants known, he would die a cipher. . . .

"*Signore,*" the boy hanging on his belt cried. "*Signore.*"

Lawson let his eyes drift to the boy's face. "*Ciao,*" he said. It was the only word of Italian he knew, or the only word that came immediately to mind, and he spoke it much louder than he meant.

The boy shook his head vehemently, pulled harder on Lawson's belt. His words tumbled out like the contents of an unburdened closet into a darkened room, not a single one of them distinct or recognizable.

"English!" Lawson shouted. "English here!"

"English here, too, man!" a voice responded from the milling crush of people at the mouth of Sierpes. "Hang on a minute, I'm coming to you!"

A small muscular man with a large head and not much chin stepped daintily through an opening in the crowd and put out his hand to Lawson. His grip was firm. As he shook hands, he placed his left arm over the shoulder of the Italian boy hanging on to Lawson's belt. The boy stopped talking and gaped at the newcomer.

"Dai Secombe," the man said. "I went to bed in Aberystwyth, where I teach philosophy, and I wake up in Spain. Pleased to meet you, Mr.——"

"Lawson," Lawson said.

The boy began babbling again, his hand shifting from Lawson's belt to the Welshman's flannel shirt facing. Secombe took the boy's hands in his own. "I've got you, lad. There's a ragged crew of your compatriots in a pool-hall pub right down this lane. Come on, then, I'll take you." He glanced at Lawson. "Wait for me, sir. I'll be right back."

Secombe and the boy disappeared, but in less than five minutes the Welshman had returned. He introduced himself all over again. "To go to bed in Aberystwyth and to

wake up in Seville," he said, "is pretty damn harrowing.
I'm glad to be alive, sir."

"Do you have a family?"

"Only my father. He's eighty-four."

"You're lucky. Not to have anyone else to worry about,
I mean."

"Perhaps," Dai Secombe said, a sudden trace of sharp-
ness in his voice. "Yesterday I would not've thought so."

The two men stared at each other as the wail of the city
modulated into a less hysterical but still inhuman drone.
People surged around them, scrutinized them from foyers
and balconies, took their measure. Out of the corner of his
eye Lawson was aware of a moonfaced woman in summer
deerskins slumping abruptly and probably painfully to the
street. An Eskimo woman—the conceit was almost comic,
but the woman herself was dying and a child with a
Swedish-steel switchblade was already freeing a necklace
of teeth and shells from her throat.

Lawson turned away from Secombe to watch the plun-
dering of the Eskimo woman's body. Enraged, he took off
his wristwatch and threw it at the boy's head, scoring a
glancing sort of hit on his ear.

"You little jackal, get away from there!"

The red-cheeked woman who had been glaring at Lawson applied her foot to the rump of the boy with the
switchblade and pushed him over. Then she retrieved the
thrown watch, hoisted her skirts, and retreated into the
dim interior of the café whose door she had been haunting.

"In this climate, in this environment," Dai Secombe told
Lawson, "an Eskimo is doomed. It's as much psychological
and emotional as it is physical. There may be a few others
who've already died for similar reasons. Not much we can
do, sir."

Lawson turned back to the Welshman with a mixture of
awe and disdain. How had this curly-haired lump of a man,
in the space of no more than three or four hours, come to
respond so lackadaisically to the deaths of his fellows? Was
it merely because the sky was still blue and the edifices of
another age still stood?

Pointedly, Secombe said, "That was a needless forfeiture
of your watch, Lawson."

"How the hell did that poor woman get here?" Lawson
demanded, his gesture taking in the entire city. "How the
hell did any of us get here?" The stench of open wounds

and the first sweet hints of decomposition mocked the luxury of his ardor.

"Good questions," the Welshman responded, taking Lawson's arm and leading him out of the Calle de las Sierpes. "It's a pity I can't answer 'em."

III.

That night they ate fried fish and drank beer together in a dirty little apartment over a shop whose glass display cases were filled with a variety of latex contraceptives. They had obtained the fish from a *pescadería* voluntarily tended by men and women of Greek and Yugoslavian citizenship, people who had run similar shops in their own countries. The beer they had taken from one of the classier bars on the Street of the Serpents. Both the fish and the beer were at room temperature, but tasted none the worse for that.

With the fall of evening, however, the wail that during the day had subsided into a whine began to reverberate again with its first full burden of grief. If the noise was not quite so loud as it had been that morning, Lawson thought, it was probably because the city contained fewer people. Many had died, and a great many more, unmindful of the distances involved, had set out to return to their homelands.

Lawson chewed a piece of *adobo* and washed this down with a swig of the vaguely bitter *Cruz del Campo* beer.

"Isn't this fine?" Secombe said, his butt on the tiles of the room's one windowsill. "Dinner over a rubber shop. And this a Catholic country, too."

"I was raised a Baptist," Lawson said, realizing at once that his confession was a non sequitur.

"Oh," Secombe put in immediately. "Then I imagine you could get all the rubbers you wanted."

"Sure. For a quarter. In almost any gas-station restroom."

"Sorry," Secombe said.

They ate for a while in silence. Lawson's back was to a cool plaster wall; he leaned his head against it, too, and released a sharp moan from his chest. Then, sustaining the sound, he moaned again, adding his own strand of grief to the cacophonous harmonies already afloat over the city. He was no different from all the bereaved others who shared his pain by concentrating on their own.

"What did you do in . . . in Lynchburg?" Secombe suddenly asked.

"Campus liaison for the Veterans Administration. I traveled to four different colleges in the area straightening out people's problems with the GI Bill. I tried to see to it that— Sweet Jesus, Secombe, who cares? I miss my wife. I'm afraid my girls are dead."

"Karen and Hannah?"

"They're three and five. I've taught them to play chess. Karen's good enough to beat me occasionally if I spot her my queen. Hannah knows the moves, but she hasn't got her sister's patience—she's only three, you know. Yeah. Sometimes she sweeps the pieces off the board and folds her arms, and we play hell trying to find them all. There'll be pawns under the sofa, horsemen upside down in the shag—" Lawson stopped.

"She levels them," Secombe said. "As we've all been leveled. The knight's no more than the pawn, the king no more than the bishop."

Lawson could tell that the Welshman was trying to turn aside the ruinous thrust of his grief. But he brushed the metaphor aside: "I don't think we've been 'leveled,' Secombe."

"Certainly we have. Guess who I saw this morning near the cathedral when I first woke up."

"God only knows."

"God and Dai Secombe, sir. I saw the Marxist dictator of . . . oh, you know, that little African country where there's just been a coup. I recognized the bastard from the telly broadcasts during the purge trials there. There he was, though, in white ducks and a ribbed T-shirt—terrified, Lawson, and as powerless as you or I. He'd been quite decidedly leveled; you'd better believe he had."

"I'll bet he's alive tonight, Secombe."

The Welshman's eyes flickered with a sudden insight. He extended the greasy cone of newspaper from the *pescadería*. "Another piece of fish, Lawson? Come on, then, there's only one more."

"To be leveled, Secombe, is to be put on a par with everyone else. Your dictator, even deprived of office, is a grown man. What about infant children? Toddlers and preadolescents? And what about people like that Eskimo

woman who haven't got a chance in an unfamiliar environment, even if its inhabitants don't happen to be hostile? ...
I saw a man knock his brains out on a stone wall this morning because he took a look around and knew he couldn't make it here. Maybe he thought he was in Hell, Secombe. I don't know. But his chance certainly wasn't ours."

"He knew he couldn't adjust."

"Of course he couldn't adjust. Don't give me that bullshit about leveling!"

Secombe turned the cone of newspaper around and withdrew the last piece of fish. "I'm going to eat this myself, if you don't mind." He ate. As he was chewing, he said, "I didn't think that Virginia Baptists were so free with their tongues, Lawson. Tsk, tsk. Undercuts my preconceptions."

"I've fallen away."

"Haven't we all."

Lawson took a final swig of warm beer. Then he hurled the bottle across the room. Fragments of amber glass went everywhere. "God!" he cried. "God, God, God!" Weeping, he was no different from three quarters of Seville's new citizens-by-chance. Why, then, as he sobbed, did he shoot such guilty and threatening glances at the Welshman?

"Go ahead," Secombe advised him, waving the empty cone of newspaper. "I feel a little that way myself."

IV.

In the morning an oddly blithe woman of forty-five or so accosted them in the alley outside the contraceptive shop. A military pistol in a patent-leather holster was strapped about her skirt. Her seeming airiness, Lawson quickly realized, was a function of her appearance and her movements; her eyes were as grim and frightened as everyone else's. But, as soon as they came out of the shop onto the cobblestones, she approached them fearlessly, hailing Secombe almost as if he were an old friend.

"You left us yesterday, Mr. Secombe. Why?"

"I saw everything dissolving into cliques."

"Dissolving? Coming together, don't you mean?"

Secombe smiled noncommittally, then introduced the woman to Lawson as Mrs. Alexander. "She's one of your own, Lawson. She's from Wyoming or some such place. I

met her outside the cathedral yesterday morning when the
first self-appointed muezzins started calling their language-
mates together. She didn't have a pistol then."

"I got it from one of the Guardia Civil stations," Mrs.
Alexander said. "And I feel lots better just having it, let me
tell you." She looked at Lawson. "Are you in the Air
Force?"

"Not anymore. These are the clothes I woke up in."

"My husband's in the Air Force. Or was. We were stationed at Warren in Cheyenne. I'm originally from upstate
New York. And these are the clothes *I* woke up in." A
riding skirt, a blouse, low-cut rubber-soled shoes. "I think
they tried to give us the most serviceable clothes we had
in our wardrobes—but they succeeded better in some cases
than others."

" 'They'?" Secombe asked.

"Whoever's done this. It's just a manner of speaking."

"What do you want?" Secombe asked Mrs. Alexander.
His brusqueness of tone surprised Lawson.

Smiling, she replied, "The word for today is Exportadora.
We're trying to get as many English-speaking people as we
can to Exportadora. That's where the commercial center
for American servicemen and their families in Seville is
located, and it's just off one of the major boulevards to the
south of here."

On a piece of paper sack Mrs. Alexander drew them a
crude map and explained that her husband had once been
stationed in Zaragoza in the north of Spain. Yesterday she
had recalled that Seville was one of the four Spanish cities
supporting the American military presence, and with persistence and a little luck a pair of carefully briefed English-
speaking DPs (the abbreviation was Mrs. Alexander's) had
discovered the site of the American PX and commissary
just before nightfall. Looting the place when they arrived
had been an impossibly mixed crew of foreigners, busily
hauling American merchandise out of the ancient buildings.
But Mrs. Alexander's DPs had run off the looters by the
simple expedient of revving the engine of their comman-
deered taxicab and blowing its horn as if to announce
Armageddon. In ten minutes the little American enclave
had emptied of all human beings but the two men in the
cab. After that, as English-speaking DPs all over the city
learned of Exportadora's existence and sought to reach it,
the place had begun to fill up again.

"Is there an air base in Seville?" Lawson asked the woman.

"No, not really. The base itself is near Morón de la Frontera, about thirty miles away, but Seville is where the real action is." After a brief pause, lifting her eyebrows, she corrected herself: "Was."

She thrust her map into Secombe's hands. "Here. Go on out to Exportadora. I'm going to look around for more of us. You're the first people I've found this morning. Others are looking, too, though. Maybe things'll soon start making some sense."

Secombe shook his head. "Us. Them. There isn't anybody now who isn't a 'DP,' you know. This regrouping on the basis of tired cultural affiliations is probably a mistake. I don't like it."

"You took up with Mr. Lawson, didn't you?"

"Out of pity only, I assure you. He looked lost. Moreover, you've got to have companionship of *some* sort—especially when you're in a strange place."

"Sure. That's why the word for today is Exportadora."

"It's a mistake, Mrs. Alexander."

"Why?"

"For the same reason your mysterious 'they' saw fit to displace us to begin with, I'd venture. It's a feeling I have."

"Old cultural affiliations are a source of stability," Mrs. Alexander said earnestly. As she talked, Lawson took the rumpled map out of Secombe's fingers. "This chaos around us won't go away until people have settled themselves into units—it's a natural process, it's beginning already. Why, walking along the river this morning, I saw several groups of like-speaking people burying yesterday's dead. The city's churches and chapels have begun to fill up, too. You can still hear the frightened and the heartbroken keening in solitary rooms, of course—but it can't go on forever. They'll either make connection or die. I'm not one of those who wish to die, Mr. Secombe."

"Who wishes that?" Lawson put in, annoyed by the shallow metaphysical drift of this exchange and by Secombe's irrationality. Although Mrs. Alexander was right, she didn't have to defend her position at such length. The map was her most important contribution to the return of order in their lives, and Lawson wanted her to let them use that map.

"Come on, Secombe," he said. "Let's get out to this

Exportadora. It's probably the only chance we have of making it home."

"I don't think there's any chance of our making it home again, Lawson. Ever."

Perceiving that Mrs. Alexander was about to ask the Welshman why, Lawson turned on his heel and took several steps down the alley. "Come on, Secombe. We have to try. What the hell are you going to do in this flip-flopped city all by yourself?"

"Look for somebody else to talk to, I suppose."

But in a moment Secombe was at Lawson's side helping him decipher the smudged geometries of Mrs. Alexander's map, and the woman herself, before heading back to Sierpes to look for more of her own kind, called out, "It'll only take you twenty or so minutes, walking. Good luck. See you later."

Walking, they passed a white-skinned child lying in an alley doorway opening onto a courtyard festooned with two-day-old washing and populated by a pack of orphaned dogs. The child's head was covered by a coat, but she did appear to be breathing. Lawson was not even tempted to examine her more closely, however. He kept his eyes resolutely on the map.

V.

The newsstand in the small American enclave had not been looted. On Lawson's second day at Exportadora it still contained quality paperbacks, the most recent American news and entertainment magazines, and a variety of tabloids, including the military paper *The Stars and Stripes*. No one knew how old these publications were because no one knew over what length of time the redistribution of the world's population had taken place. How long had everyone slept? And what about the discrepancies among time zones and the differences among people's waking hours within the same time zones? These questions were academic now, it seemed to Lawson, because the agency of transfer had apparently encompassed every single human being alive on Earth.

Thumbing desultorily through a copy of *Stars and Stripes*, he encountered an article on the problems of military hospitals and wondered how many of the world's sick had awakened in the open, doomed to immediate death because the care they required was nowhere at hand. The smell of spilled tobacco and melted Life Savers made the newsstand a pleasant place to contemplate these horrors; and, even as his conscience nagged and a contingent of impatient DPs awaited him, Lawson perversely continued to flip through the newspaper.

Secombe's squat form appeared in the doorway. "I thought you were looking for a local roadmap."

"Found it already, just skimmin' the news."

"Come on, if you would. The folks're ready to be off."

Reluctantly, Lawson followed Secombe outside, where the raw Andalusian sunlight broke like invisible surf against the pavement and the fragile-seeming shell of the Air Force bus. It was of the Bluebird shuttle variety, and Lawson remembered summer camp at Eglin Air Force Base in Florida and bus rides from his squadron's minimum-maintenance ROTC barracks to the survival-training camps near the swamp. That had been a long time ago, but this Bluebird might have hailed from an even more distant era. It was as boxy and sheepish-looking as if it had come off a 1954 assembly line, and it appeared to be made out of warped tin rather than steel. The people inside the bus had opened all its windows, and many of those on the driver's side were watching Secombe and Lawson approach.

"Move your asses!" a man shouted at them. "Let's get some wind blowing through this thing before we all suffo-damn-cate."

"Just keep talking," Secombe advised him. "That should do fine."

Aboard the bus was a motley lot of Americans, Britishers, and Australians, with two or three English-speaking Europeans and an Oxford-educated native of India to lend the group ballast. Lawson took up a window seat over the hump of one of the bus's rear tires, and Secombe squeezed in beside him. A few people introduced themselves; others, lost in fitful reveries, ignored them altogether. The most unsettling thing about the contingent to Lawson was the absence of children. Although about equally divided between men and women, the group contained no boys or girls any younger than their early teens.

Lawson opened the map of southern Spain he had found in the newsstand and traced his finger along a highway route leading out of Seville to two small American enclaves outside the city, Santa Clara and San Pablo. Farther to the south were Jerez and the port city of Cádiz. Lawson's heart misgave him; the names were all so foreign, so formidable in what they evoked, and he felt this entire enterprise to be hopeless. . . .

About midway along the right-hand side of the bus a black woman was sobbing into the hem of her blouse, and a man perched on the Bluebird's long rear seat had his hands clasped to his ears and his head canted forward to touch his knees. Lawson folded up the map and stuck it into the crevice between the seat and the side of the bus.

"The bottom-line common denominator here isn't our all speaking English," Secombe whispered. "It's what we're suffering."

Driven by one of Mrs. Alexander's original explorers, a doctor from Ivanhoe, New South Wales, the Bluebird shuddered and lurched forward. In a moment it had left Exportadora and begun banging along one of the wide avenues that would lead it out of town.

"And our suffering," Secombe went on, still whispering, "unites us with all those poor souls raving in the streets and sleeping facedown in their own vomit. You felt that the other night above the condom shop, Lawson. I know you did, talking of your daughters. So why are you so quick to go looking for what you aren't likely to find? Why are you so ready to unite yourself with this artificial family born out of catastrophe? Do you really think you're going to catch a flight home to Lynchburg? Do you really think the bird driving this sardine can—who ought to be out in the streets plying his trade instead of running a shuttle service—d'you really think he's ever going to get back to Australia?"

"Secombe—"

"Do you, Lawson?"

Lawson clapped a hand over the Welshman's knee and wobbled it back and forth. "You wouldn't be badgering me like this if you had a family of your own. What the hell do you want us to do? Stay here forever?"

"I don't know, exactly." He removed Lawson's hand from his knee. "But I do have a father, sir, and I happen to be fond of him. . . . All I know for certain is that things are *supposed* to be different now. We shouldn't be rushing to restore what we already had."

"Shit," Lawson murmured. He leaned his head against the bottom edge of the open window beside him.

From deep within the city came the brittle noise of gunshots. The Bluebird's driver, in response to this sound and to the vegetable carts and automobiles that had been moved into the streets as obstacles, began wheeling and cornering like a stock-car jockey. The bus clanked and stuttered alarmingly. It growled through an intersection below a stone bridge, leapt over that bridge like something living, and roared down into a semi-industrial suburb of Seville where a Coca-Cola bottling factory and a local brewery lifted huge competing signs.

On top of one of these buildings Lawson saw a man with a rifle taking unhurried potshots at anyone who came into his sights. Several people already lay dead.

And a moment later the Bluebird's front window shattered, another bullet ricocheted off its flank, and everyone in the bus was either shouting or weeping. The next time Lawson looked, the bus's front window appeared to have woven inside it a large and exceedingly intricate spider's web.

The Bluebird careened madly, but the doctor from Ivanhoe kept it upright and turned it with considerable skill onto the highway to San Pablo. Here the bus eased into a quiet and rhythmic cruising that made this final incident in Seville—except for the evidence of the front window—seem only the cottony aftertaste of nightmare. At last they were on their way. Maybe.

"Another good reason for trying to get home," Lawson said.

"What makes you think it's going to be different there?"

Irritably Lawson turned on the Welshman. "I thought your idea was that this change was some kind of *improvement*."

"Perhaps it will be. Eventually."

Lawson made a dismissive noise and looked at the olive orchard spinning by on his left. Who would harvest the crop? Who would set the aircraft factories, the distilleries, the chemical and textile plants running again? Who would see to it that seed was sown in the empty fields?

Maybe Secombe had something. Maybe, when you ran for home, you ran from the new reality at hand. The effects of this new reality's advent were not going to go away very soon, no matter what you did—but seeking to reestablish

yesterday's order would probably create an even nastier
entropic pattern than would accepting the present chaos
and working to rein it in. How, though, did you best rein
it in? Maybe by trying to get back home . . .

Lawson shook his head and thought of Marlena, Karen,
Hannah; of the distant, mist-softened cradle of the Blue
Ridge. Lord. That was country much easier to get in tune
with than the harsh, white-sky bleakness of this Andalusian
valley. If you stay here, Lawson told himself, the pain will
never go away.

They passed Santa Clara, which was a housing area for
the officers and senior NCOs who had been stationed at
Morón. With its neatly trimmed hedgerows, tall aluminum
streetlamps, and low-roofed houses with carports and picture windows, Santa Clara resembled a middle-class ex-
urbia in New Jersey or Ohio. Black smoke was curling over
the area, however, and the people on the streets and lawns
were definitely not Americans—they were transplanted
Dutch South Africans, Amazonian tribesmen, Poles, Ethio-
pians, God-only-knew-what. All Lawson could accurately
deduce was that a few of these people had moved into the
vacant houses—maybe they had awakened in them—and
that others had aimlessly set bonfires about the area's
neighborhoods. These fires, because there was no wind,
burned with a maddening slowness and lack of urgency.

"Little America," Secombe said aloud.

"That's in Antarctica," Lawson responded sarcastically.

"Right. No matter where it happens to be."

"Up yours."

Their destination was now San Pablo, where the Americans had hospital facilities, a library, a movie theater, a
snackbar, a commissary, and, in conjunction with the
Spaniards, a small commercial and military airfield. San
Pablo lay only a few more miles down the road, and Lawson contemplated the idea of a flight to Portugal. What
would be the chances, supposing you actually reached
Lisbon, of crossing the Atlantic, either by sea or air, and
reaching one of the United States's coastal cities? One in a
hundred? One in a thousand? Less than that?

A couple of seats behind the driver, an Englishman with
a crisp-looking moustache and an American woman with a
distinct Southwestern accent were arguing the merits of
bypassing San Pablo and heading on to Gibraltar, a British
possession. The Englishman seemed to feel that Gibraltar

would have escaped the upheaval to which the remainder of the world had fallen victim, whereas the American woman thought he was crazy. A shouting match involving five or six other passengers ensued. Finally, his patience at an end, the Bluebird's driver put his elbow on the horn and held it there until everyone had shut up.

"It's San Pablo," he announced. "Not Gibraltar or anywhere else. There'll be a plane waitin' for us when we get there."

VI.

Two aircraft were waiting, a pair of patched-up DC-7s that had once belonged to the Spanish airline known as Iberia. Mrs. Alexander had recruited one of her pilots from the DPs who had shown up at Exportadora; the other, a retired TWA veteran from Riverside, California, had made it by himself to the airfield by virtue of a prior acquaintance with Seville and its American military installations. Both men were eager to carry passengers home, one via a stopover in Lisbon and the other by using Madrid as a stepping-stone to the British Isles. The hope was that they could transfer their passengers to jet aircraft at these cities' more cosmopolitan airports, but no one spoke very much about the real obstacles to success that had already begun stalking them: civil chaos, delay, inadequate communications, fuel shortages, mechanical hangups, doubt and ignorance, a thousand other things.

At twilight, then, Lawson stood next to Dai Secombe at the chain link fence fronting San Pablo's pothole-riven runway and watched the evening light glimmer off the wings of the DC-7s. Bathed in a muted dazzle, the two old airplanes were almost beautiful. Even though Mrs. Alexander had informed the DPs that they must spend the night in the installation's movie theater, so that the Bluebird could make several more shuttle runs to Exportadora, Lawson truly believed that he was bound for home.

"Good-bye," Secombe told him.

"Good-bye? . . . Oh, because you'll be on the other flight?"

"No, I'm telling you good-bye, Lawson, because I'm leaving. Right now, you see. This very minute."

"Where are you going?"

"Back into the city."

"How? What for?"

"I'll walk, I suppose. As for why, it has something to do with wanting to appease Mrs. Alexander's 'they,' also with finding out what's to become of us all. Seville's the place for that, I think."

"Then why'd you even come out here?"

"To say good-bye, you bloody imbecile." Secombe laughed, grabbed Lawson's hand, shook it heartily. "Since I couldn't manage to change your mind."

With that, he turned and walked along the chain link fence until he had found the roadway past the installation's commissary. Lawson watched him disappear behind that building's complicated system of loading ramps. After a time the Welshman reappeared on the other side, but, against the vast Spanish sky, his compact striding form rapidly dwindled to an imperceptible smudge. A smudge on the darkness.

"Good-bye," Lawson said.

That night, slumped in a lumpy theater chair, he slept with nearly sixty other people in San Pablo's movie house. A teenage boy, over only a few objections, insisted on showing all the old movies still in tins in the projection room. As a result, Lawson awoke once in the middle of *Apocalypse Now* and another time near the end of Kubrick's *The Left Hand of Darkness*. The ice on the screen, dunelike *sastrugi* ranged from horizon to horizon, chilled him, touching a sensitive spot in his memory. "Little America," he murmured. Then he went back to sleep.

VII.

With the passengers bound for Lisbon, Lawson stood at the fence where he had stood with Secombe, and watched the silver pinwheeling of propellers as the aircraft's engines engaged. The DC-7 flying to Madrid would not leave until much later that day, primarily because it still had several vacant seats and Mrs. Alexander felt sure that more English-speaking DPs could still be found in the city.

The people at the gate with Lawson shifted uneasily and whispered among themselves. The engines of their savior airplane whined deafeningly, and the runway seemed to tremble. What woebegone eyes the women had, Lawson thought, and the men were as scraggly as railroad hoboes. Feeling his jaw, he understood that he was no more handsome or well-groomed than any of those he waited with. And, like them, he was impatient for the signal to board, for the thumbs-up sign indicating that their airplane had passed its latest rudimentary ground tests.

At least, he consoled himself, you're not eating potato chips at ten-thirty in the morning. Disgustedly, he turned aside from a jut-eared man who was doing just that.

"There're more people here than our plane's supposed to carry," the potato-chip cruncher said. "That could be dangerous."

"But it isn't really that far to Lisbon, is it?" a woman replied. "And none of us has any luggage."

"Yeah, but—" The man gagged on a chip, coughed, tried to speak again. Facing deliberately away, Lawson felt that the man's words would acquire eloquence only if he suddenly volunteered to ride in the DC-7's unpressurized baggage compartment.

As it was, the signal came to board and the jut-eared man had no chance to finish his remarks. He threw his cellophane sack to the ground, and Lawson heard it crackling underfoot as people crowded through the gate onto the grassy verge of the runway.

In order to fix the anomaly of San Pablo in his memory, Lawson turned around and walked backward across the field. He saw that bringing up the rear were four men with automatic weapons—weapons procured, most likely, from the installation's Air Police station. These men, like Lawson, were walking backward, but with their guns as well as their eyes trained on the weirdly constituted band of people who had just appeared, seemingly out of nowhere, along the airfield's fence.

One of these people wore nothing but a ragged pair of shorts, another an ankle-length burnoose, another a pair of trousers belted with a rope. One of their number was a doe-eyed young woman with an exposed torso and a circlet of bright coral on her wrist. But there were others, too, and they all seemed to have been drawn to the runway by the airplane's engine whine; they moved along the fence like desperate ghosts. As the first members of Lawson's group mounted into the plane, even more of these people appeared—an assembly of nomads, hunters, hodcarriers, fishers, herdspeople. Apparently they all understood what an airplane was for, and one of the swarthiest men among them ventured out onto the runway with his arms thrown out imploringly.

"Where you go?" he shouted. "Where you go?"

"There's no more room!" responded a blue-jean-clad man with a machine gun. "Get back! You'll have to wait for another flight!"

Oh, sure, Lawson thought, the one to Madrid. He was at the base of the airplane's mobile stairway. The jut-eared man who had been eating potato chips nodded brusquely at him.

"You'd better get on up there," he shouted over the robust hiccoughing of the airplane's engines, "before we have unwanted company breathing down our necks!"

"After you." Lawson stepped aside.

Behind the swarthy man importuning the armed guards for a seat on the airplane, there clamored thirty or more insistent people, their only real resemblance to one another their longing for a way out. "Where you go? Where you go?" the bravest and most desperate among them yelled, but they all wanted to board the airplane that Mrs. Alexander's charges had already laid claim to; and most of them could see that it was too late to accomplish their purpose without some kind of risk-taking. The man who had been shouting in English, along with four or five others, broke into an assertive dogtrot toward the plane. Although their cries continued to be modestly beseeching, Lawson could tell that the passengers' guards now believed themselves under direct attack.

A burst of machine-gun fire sounded above the field and echoed away like rain drumming on a tin roof. The man who had been asking, "Where you go?," pitched forward on his face. Others fell beside him, including the woman with the coral bracelet. Panicked or prodded by this evidence of their assailants' mortality, one of the guards raked the chain link fence with his weapon, bringing down some of those who had already begun to retreat and summoning forth both screams and the distressingly incongruous sound of popping wire. Then, eerily, it was quiet again.

"Get on that airplane!" a guard shouted at Lawson. He was the only passenger still left on the ground, and everyone wanted him inside the plane so that the mobile stairway could be rolled away.

"I don't think so," Lawson said to himself.

Hunching forward like a man under fire, he ran toward the gate and the crude mandala of bodies partially blocking it. The slaughter he had just witnessed struck him as abysmally repetitive of a great deal of recent history, and he did not wish to belong to that history anymore. Further, the airplane behind him was a gross iron-plated emblem of the burden he no longer cared to bear—even if it also seemed to represent the promise of passage home.

"Hey, where the hell you think you're goin'?"

Lawson did not answer. He stepped gingerly through the corpses on the runway's margin, halted on the other side of the fence, and, his eyes misted with glare and poignant bewilderment, turned to watch the DC-7 taxi down the scrub-lined length of concrete to the very end of the field. There the airplane negotiated a turn and started back the way it had come. Soon it was hurtling along like a colossal metal dragonfly, building speed. When it lifted from the ground, its tires screaming shrilly with the last series of bumps before take-off, Lawson held his breath.

Then the airplane's right wing dipped, dipped again, struck the ground, and broke off like a piece of balsa wood, splintering brilliantly. After that, the airplane went flipping, cartwheeling, across the end of the tarmac and into the desolate open field beyond, where its shell and remaining wing were suddenly engulfed in flames. You could hear people frying in that inferno; you could smell gasoline and burnt flesh.

"Jesus," Lawson said.

He loped away from the airfield's fence, hurried through the short grass behind the San Pablo library, and joined a group of those who had just fled the English-speaking guards' automatic-weapon fire. He met them on the highway going back to Seville and walked among them as merely another of their number. Although several people viewed his 1505 trousers with suspicion, no one argued that he did not belong, and no one threatened to cut his throat for him.

As hangdog and exotically nondescript as most of his companions, Lawson watched his tennis shoes track the pavement like the feet of a mechanical toy. He wondered what he was going to do back in Seville. Successfully dodge bullets and eat fried fish, if he was lucky. Talk with Secombe again, if he could find the man. And, if he had any sense, try to organize his life around some purpose other than the insane and hopeless one of returning to Lynchburg. What purpose, though? What purpose beyond the basic, animal purpose of staying alive?

"Are any of you hungry?" Lawson asked.

He was regarded with suspicious curiosity.

"Hungry," he repeated. *"¿Tiene hambre?"*

English? Spanish? Neither worked. What languages did they have, these refugees from an enigma? It looked as if they had all tried to speak together before and found the task impossible—because, moving along the asphalt under the hot Andalusian sun, they now relied on gestures and easily interpretable noises to express themselves.

Perceiving this, Lawson brought the fingers of his right hand to his mouth and clacked his teeth to indicate chewing.

He was understood. A thin barefoot man in a capacious linen shirt and trousers led Lawson off the highway into an orchard of orange trees. The fruit was not yet completely ripe, and was sour because of its greenness, but all twelve or thirteen of Lawson's crew ate, letting the juice run down their arms. When they again took up the trek to Seville, Lawson's mind was almost absolutely blank with satiety. The only thing rattling about in it now was the fear that he would not know what to do once they arrived. He never did find out if the day's other scheduled flight, the one to Madrid, made it safely to its destination, but the matter struck him now as of little import. He wiped his sticky mouth and trudged along numbly.

VIII.

He lived above the contraceptive shop. In the mornings he walked through the alley to a bakery that a woman with calm Mongolian features had taken over. In return for a daily allotment of bread and a percentage of the goods brought in for barter, Lawson swept the bakery's floor, washed the utensils that were dirtied each day, and kept the shop's front counter. His most rewarding skill, in fact, was communicating with those who entered to buy something. He had an uncanny grasp of several varieties of sign language, and, on occasion, he found himself speaking a monosyllabic patois whose derivation was a complete mystery to him. Sometimes he thought that he had invented it himself; sometimes he believed that he had learned it from the transplanted Sevillanos among whom he now lived.

English, on the other hand, seemed to leak slowly out of his mind, a thick, unrecoverable fluid.

The first three or four weeks of chaos following The Change had, by this time, run their course, a circumstance that surprised Lawson. Still, it was true. Now you could lie down at night on your pallet without hearing pistol reports or fearing that some benighted freak was going to set fire to your staircase. Most of the city's essential services—electricity, water, and sewerage—were working again, albeit uncertainly, and agricultural goods were coming in from the countryside. People had gone back to doing what they knew best, while those whose previous jobs had had little to do with the basics of day-to-day survival were now apprenticing as bricklayers, carpenters, bakers, fishers, water and power technicians. That men and women chose to live separately and that children were as rare as sapphires, no one seemed to find disturbing or unnatural. A new pattern was evolving. You lived among your fellows without tension or quarrel, and you formed no dangerously intimate relationships.

One night, standing at his window, Lawson's knee struck a loose tile below the casement. He removed the tile and set it on the floor. Every night for nearly two months he pried away at least one tile and, careful not to chip or break it, stacked it near an inner wall with those he had already removed.

After completing this task, as he lay on his pallet, he would often hear a man or a woman somewhere in the city singing a high, sweet song whose words had no significance for him. Sometimes a pair of voices would answer each other, always in different languages. Then, near the end of the summer, as Lawson stood staring at the lathing and the wall beams he had methodically exposed, he was moved to sing a melancholy song of his own. And he sang it without knowing what it meant.

The days grew cooler. Lawson took to leaving the bakery during its midafternoon closing and proceeding by way of the Calle de las Sierpes to a bodega across from the bullring. A crew of silent laborers, who worked very purposively in spite of their seeming to have no single boss, was dismantling the Plaza de Toros, and Lawson liked to watch as he drank his wine and ate the breadsticks he had brought with him.

Other crews about the city were carefully taking down the government buildings, banks, and barrio chapels that no one frequented anymore, preserving the bricks, tiles, and beams as if in the hope of some still unspecified future construction. By this time Lawson himself had knocked out the rear wall of his room over the contraceptive shop, and he felt a strong sense of identification with the laborers craftily gutting the bullring of its railings and barricades. Eventually, of course, everything would have to come down. Everything.

The rainy season began. The wind and the cold. Lawson continued to visit the sidewalk café near the ruins of the stadium; and because the bullring's destruction went forward even in wet weather, he wore an overcoat he had recently acquired and staked out a nicely sheltered table under the bodega's awning. This was where he customarily sat.

One particularly gusty day, rain pouring down, he shook out his umbrella and sat down at this table only to find another man sitting across from him. Upon the table was a wooden game board of some kind, divided into squares.

"Hello, Lawson," the interloper said.

Lawson blinked and licked his lips thoughtfully. Although he had not called his family to mind in some time, and wondered now if he had ever really married and fathered children, Dai Secombe's face had occasionally floated up before him in the dark of his room. But now Lawson could not remember the Welshman's name, or his nationality, and he had no notion of what to say to him. The first words he spoke, therefore, came out sounding like dream babble, or a voice played backward on the phonograph. In order to say hello he was forced to the indignity, almost comic, of making a childlike motion with his hand.

Secombe, pointing to the game board, indicated that they should play. From a carved wooden box with a velvet lining he emptied the pieces onto the table, then arranged them on both sides of the board. Chess, Lawson thought vaguely, but he really did not recognize the pieces—they seemed changed from what he believed they should look like. And when it came his turn to move, Secombe had to demonstrate the capabilities of all the major pieces before he, Lawson, could essay even the most timid advance. The piece that most reminded him of a knight had to be moved according to two distinct sets of criteria, depending on whether it started from a black square or a white one; the "rooks," on the other hand, were able, at certain times, to *jump* an opponent's intervening pieces. The game boggled Lawson's understanding. After ten or twelve moves he pushed his chair back and took a long, bittersweet taste of wine. The rain continued to pour down like an endless curtain of deliquescent beads.

"That's all right," Secombe said. "I haven't got it all down yet myself, quite. A Bhutanese fellow near where I live made the pieces, you see, and just recently taught me how to play."

With difficulty Lawson managed to frame a question: "What work have you been doing?"

"I'm in demolition. As we all will be soon. It's the only really constructive occupation going." The Welshman chuckled mildly, finished his own wine, and rose. Lifting his umbrella, he bid Lawson farewell with a word that, when Lawson later tried to repeat and intellectually encompass it, had no meaning at all.

Every afternoon of that dismal, rainy winter Lawson came back to the same table, but Secombe never showed up there again. Nor did Lawson miss him terribly. He had grown accustomed to the strange richness of his own company. Besides, if he wanted people to talk to, all he needed to do was remain behind the counter at the bakery.

IX.

Spring came again. All of his room's interior walls were down, and it amused him to be able to see the porcelain chalice of the commode as he came up the stairs from the contraceptive shop.

The plaster that he had sledgehammered down would never be of use to anybody again, of course, but he had saved from the debris whatever was worth the salvage. With the return of good weather, men driving oxcarts were coming through the city's backstreets and alleys to collect these items. You never saw anyone trying to drive a motorized vehicle nowadays, probably because, over the winter, most of them had been hauled away. The scarcity of gasoline and replacement parts might well have been a factor, too—but, in truth, people seemed no longer to want to mess with internal-combustion engines. Ending pollution and noise had nothing to do with it, either. A person with dung on his shoes or front stoop was not very likely to be convinced of a vast improvement in the environment, and the clattering of wooden carts—the ringing of metal-rimmed wheels on cobblestone—could be as ear-wrenching as the hum and blare of motorized traffic. Still, Lawson liked to hear the oxcarts turn into his alley. More than once, called out by the noise, he had helped their drivers load them with masonry, doors, window sashes, even ornate carven mantles.

At the bakery the Mongolian woman with whom Lawson worked, and had worked for almost a year, caught the handle of his broom one day and told him her name. Speaking the odd, quicksilver monosyllables of the dialect that nearly everyone in Seville had by now mastered, she asked him to call her Tij. Lawson did not know whether this was her name from before The Change or one she had recently invented for herself. Pleased in either case, he responded by telling her his own Christian name. He stumbled saying it, and when Tij also had trouble pronouncing the name, they laughed together about its uncommon awkwardness on their tongues.

A week later he had moved into the tenement building where Tij lived. They slept in the same "room" three flights up from a courtyard filled wtih clambering wisteria. Because all but the supporting walls on this floor had been knocked out, Lawson often felt that he was living in an open-bay barracks. People stepped over his pallet to get to the stairwell and dressed in front of him as if he were not even there. Always a quick study, he emulated their casual behavior.

And when the ice in his loins finally began to thaw, he turned in the darkness to Tij—without in the least worrying about propriety. Their coupling was invariably silent, and the release Lawson experienced was always a serene rather than a shuddering one. Afterward, in the wisteria fragrance pervading their building, Tij and he lay beside each other like a pair of larval bumblebees as the moon rolled shadows over their naked, sweat-gleaming bodies.

Each day after they had finished making and trading

away their bread, Tij and Lawson closed the bakery and
took long walks. Often they strolled among the hedge-
enclosed pathways and the small wrought-iron fences at the
base of the city's cathedral. From these paths, so overwhelmed were they by buttresses of stones and arcaded
balconies, they could not even see the bronze weathervane
of Faith atop the Giralda. But, evening after evening, Lawson insisted on returning to that place, and at last his
persistence and his sense of expectation were rewarded by
the sound of jackhammers biting into marble in each one
of the cathedral's five tremendous naves. He and Tij, holding hands, entered.

Inside, men and women were at work removing the altar
screens, the metalwork grilles, the oil paintings, sections of
stained-glass windows, religious relics. Twelve or more oxcarts were parked beneath the vault of the cathedral, and
the noise of the jackhammers echoed shatteringly from
nave to nave, from floor to cavernous ceiling. The oxen
stood so complacently in their traces that Lawson wondered if the drivers of the carts had somehow contrived to
deafen the animals. Tij released Lawson's hand to cover
her ears. He covered his own ears. It did no good. You
could remain in the cathedral only if you accepted the
noise and resolved to be a participant in the building's destruction. Many people had already made that decision.
They were swarming through its chambered stone belly like
a spectacularly efficient variety of stone-eating termite.

An albino man of indeterminate race—a man as pale as
a termite—thrust his pickax at Lawson. Lawson uncovered
his ears and took the pickax by its handle. Tij, a moment
later, found a crowbar hanging precariously from the side
of one of the oxcarts. With these tools the pair of them
crossed the nave they had entered and halted in front of
an imposing mausoleum. Straining against the cathedral's
poor light and the strange linguistic static in his head, Lawson painstakingly deciphered the plaque near the tomb.

"Christopher Columbus is buried here," he said.

Tij did not hear him. He made a motion indicating that
this was the place where they should start. Tij nodded her
understanding. Together, Lawson thought, they would dis-
mantle the mausoleum of the discoverer of the New World
and bring his corrupt remains out into the street. After all
these centuries they would free the man.

Then the bronze statue of Faith atop the belltower would come down, followed by the lovely belltower itself. After that, the flying buttresses, the balconies, the walls; every beautiful, tainted stone.

It would hurt like hell to destroy the cathedral, and it would take a long, long time—but, considering everything, it was the only meaningful option they had. Lawson raised his pickax.

THE YEAR IN FANTASY

Jeff Frane

IF 1981 MAKES NO OTHER MARK ON THE HIS-
tory of fantasy literature, it *ought* to be known as the year
we gave up trying to define the term "fantasy." A great
many books and stories were published that could be
recognized subjectively as fantasy, but the startling diver-
sity in the field would doom any attempt to define them all
by a set of objective standards. The "high fantasy" of
Fairyland, from unimaginative Tolkien derivatives to highly
creative variants, sits side by side on the shelf with tradi-
tional horror. "Modern" fantasy, with its juxtaposition of
real and imaginary worlds, is read by some of the same
folk who can lose themselves in tales of sword-wielding
barbarians. A taste for the imaginative can lead to a
strange diet, and 1981 provided a tempting and highly
varied menu.

Two fantasy novels in particular illustrate the variety of
fantasy available last year. John Crowley's superb *Little,
Big* (Bantam) is an intricate, vaguely mad fairy tale about
a young man who falls in love and comes to live in a very
strange house—a world in itself, and an exceedingly odd
world at that. In vivid contrast is *The War Hound and the
World's Pain* (Timescape), a rich allegory of the Age of
Reason by Michael Moorcock. It's about a man seeking to
save himself, and the world, by helping to liberate the
Devil from his own error, during one of the most hellish
periods in European history.

Kate Wilhelm's psychological ghost story, *A Sense of
Shadow* (Houghton Mifflin), is as frightening as any tra-
ditional horror novel, yet gets there without any creaking

257

doors or bogeymen in the basement. F. Paul Wilson's *The Keep* (Morrow), on the other hand, uses familiar symbols —a castle in eastern Europe with an apparently predictable inhabitant—in a most effective manner to achieve a genuinely scary result. A completely different sort of vampire appears in Chelsea Quinn Yarbro's *Path of the Eclipse* (St. Martin's), the fourth installment in her series about Count Saint-Germain; this novel follows his travels through thirteenth-century China and India. Les Daniels' *Citizen Vampire* (Scribner's) presents yet another sort of vampire. Like Yarbro's character, Don Sebastian appears at different times throughout history (in this, the third novel, he's brought back to life during the French Revolution), but he's far more sinister and demonic than Saint-Germain.

Even more than in science fiction, the norm in fantasy has become the series novel. Ever since *The Lord of the Rings* was published in three separate volumes, fantasy readers seem to have come to expect trilogies, tetralogies, and open-ended sagas. In the face of acclaim from writers, publishers, and readers, objections to the series syndrome seem a little foolish, but there is something to be said for books that begin and end within their pages. Some creations, however, refuse to be bound by the limits of a single volume, and many of the fantasy novels published in 1981 were the beginning, middle, or (rarely) final installments in a group of related books.

Gillian Bradshaw's *Kingdom of Summer* (Simon & Schuster) is the second in an excellent series derived from the legend of King Arthur and focusing on Gwalchmai (more familiarly known as Gawain). *The Claw of the Conciliator* (Timescape) is the sequel to Gene Wolfe's award-winning *The Shadow of the Torturer*, part of the five books to be known as The Book of the New Sun, and has already won the Nebula Award as best novel of the year. Another fine book is Robert Stallman's *The Captive* (Timescape), sequel to *The Orphan;* the books comprise two-thirds of what is probably the best lycanthropy story since *The Werewolf of Paris.*

Camber the Heretic (Del Rey) is the latest installment in Katherine Kurtz's highly popular series. Avram Davidson offers the second volume in a series begun ten years ago, *Peregrine: Secundus* (Berkley). Nancy Springer's *The Sable Moon* (Pocket) is the third book in a series that began with *The White Hart*. Shirley Rousseau Murphy's

The Joining of the Stone (Atheneum) and Patricia Wright-son's *Journey Behind the Wind* (Atheneum) are both parts of extended series.

Tanith Lee's *Delusion's Master* (DAW) and Andre Norton's *Gryphon in Glory* are series books. Roger Zelazny's *The Changing Land* (Del Rey/Underwood-Miller) isn't really a series novel, per se, but does concern a continuing character of his, Dilvish the Damned.

Adam Corby's *The Former King* (Timescape) is a first novel in two senses. It's the author's first book, and the first volume in a trilogy, a brooding sort of "heroic fantasy" (which is the term that seems to be used to distinguish between the "good stuff" and the bad—"sword and sorcery"). Other first novels of promise include Kenneth C. Flint's *Storm Upon Ulster* (Bantam), based on Cuchulain and the Red Branch of Irish legend, and *The Prince of Morning Bells* (Timescape) by Nancy Kress. Jessica Amanda Salmonson, whose anthology *Amazons!* won the World Fantasy Award for 1980, began her fantasy series with *Tomoe Gozen* (Ace), a novel set in a mythical Japan.

Although the novel has become the dominant form in fantasy, the short story and novelette have yet to die out. At the risk of charges of nepotism, I would recommend Terry Carr and Martin Harry Greenberg's *A Treasury of Modern Fantasy* (Avon) as unquestionably the best reprint collection of 1981, and a highly useful anthology to have around the house at any time. Terri Windling and Mark Arnold have edited a massive anthology, *Elsewhere* (Ace), which includes both original and reprinted fantasies.

There are even series anthologies in fantasy. *Shadows of Sanctuary* (Ace) is the third "Thieves' World" volume, a sort of round-robin of tales written by various authors but set in the same world with recurring characters. *Flashing Swords!* was a series of anthologies begun by Lin Carter years ago, featuring the members of the Swordsmen and Sorcerers Guild of America (SAGA), mostly old-time writers. The fifth volume, *Demons and Daggers* (Dell), features relatively newer writers, including C. J. Cherryh, Tanith Lee and Diane Duane. *Dragons of Darkness* (Ace), edited by Orson Scott Card, is the sequel to last year's *Dragons of Light*, and features the same format, with a different illustrator for each story. Both *Shadows 4* (Doubleday), edited by Charles L. Grant, and *Whispers III* (Doubleday), edited by Stuart David Schiff, focus primarily on horror fiction. Larry Niven, best known for his science fiction, edited a fantasy anthology titled *The Magic May Return* (Ace).

Single-author collections that are primarily fantasy are in short supply, but C. J. Cherryh's *Sunfall* (DAW) has a strong fantastic element. The title story of Elizabeth A. Lynn's *The Woman Who Loved the Moon* (Berkley) tied for the World Fantasy Award for 1980.

Short fantasy fiction also appeared in the magazines. In fact, a brand-new fantasy magazine with the rather ponderous title *Rod Serling's The Twilight Zone Magazine* was launched under the editorship of horror writer T. E. D. Klein. Ostensibly publishing stories "in the *Twilight Zone* tradition," the monthly periodical offers a good variety of fantasy fiction, and a column on fantasy films by Gahan Wilson which by itself is worth the price of the magazine. *The Magazine of Fantasy & Science Fiction* continues after more than 30 years, now under the editorship of Ed Ferman.

A couple of semi-professional (a term which means the magazines generally pay, but not much, and usually don't get newsstand distribution) magazines are available, with fantasy fiction and articles. *Shayol*, edited by Pat Cadigan and Arnie Fenner, published one issue last year, with their trademark high-quality production and attention to detail. *Fantasy Book* was launched last year by some Los Angeles area fans. Although planned as a quarterly, only two issues appeared in 1981. The quality of the fiction isn't very high as yet, but they could provide a useful outlet for beginning fantasy writers. They can be reached at P.O. Box 4193, Pasadena, CA 91106.

Very little of the non-fiction published last year touched on fantasy fiction. Marshall B. Tymn's *Horror Literature* (Bowker) collects a number of dry essays and bibliographies in the genre. Far more entertaining is Stephen King's *Danse Macabre* (Everest House), a highly idiosyncratic and extremely readable look at horror, both in fiction and on film.

If 1981 was a good year for fantasy literature, it was a bonus year, at least commercially, for fantasy films. Many, if not most, of the top-grossing movies had strong fantasy elements. Lucas and Spielberg's tribute to the serials, *Raiders of the Lost Ark*, qualifies by virtue of its magical ending. *Dragonslayer*, which featured special effects courtesy of Walt Disney studios, will probably trigger a spate of dragon films. The second half of the Superman movie, *Superman II* (*such* a clever title), appeared, and no doubt there will be more to come.

The critics varied considerably on what exactly *Excalibur* was. The best comment I saw likened it to a Taoist myth. Whatever it was, it wasn't Malory, and many had their doubts it was King Arthur, but it was certainly fantasy of a particularly baroque sort. Nicol Williamson's histrionic Merlin was the high point. Critical *and* popular opinion was also mixed on Terry Gilliam's child-like *Time Bandits,* about a little boy and a pack of rather crazed dwarves hopping about through all the holes God left in the time-space continuum. With Ralph Richardson as God, David Warner as the Devil, and Sean Connery as Agamemnon, the dad every boy could want, certain flaws in the film can be overlooked.

Less easy to forgive are the problems with *Heavy Metal,* an animated version of the magazine of the same name. It has its moments, but they're too far between. *Clash of the Titans* is Ray Harryhausen's magnum opus, concentrating as usual on the special effects of monsters. *Ghost Story,* based on Peter Straub's brilliant novel, was released at the end of the year and has apparently disappeared from view almost before it could be seen.

1981 was a particularly big year for werewolf movies, for some reason. *The Howling* is sympathetic to werewolves, and features spectacular shape-changing special effects. Some of the same effects are used in *An American Werewolf in London,* which struggles mightily to blend horror and humor. *Wolfen* pits Albert Finney, as an American cop, against a super race of werewolves in the ruins of the South Bronx.

Several of fantasy's talents were lost last year. H. Warner Munn began his career as a writer for *Weird Tales* magazine in the 1920s, and then drifted away from it until his retirement in the '60s. His published work includes *The Werewolf of Ponkert, The King of the World's Edge, Merlin's Ring,* and *The Lost Legion,* a historical novel. His book of poetry, *The Banner of Joan,* was issued in conjunction with the first World Fantasy Convention.

Nicholas Stuart Gray was a British author and playwright. His more popular books, which were generally classified as juveniles, included *Grimbold's Other World* and *Mainly in Moonlight*. Another British author, Robert Aickman, won the World Fantasy Award in 1975 for "Pages from a Young Girl's Journal." He died in February at the age of 66. Known primarily for his innovative approach to the ghost story, his books include *Cold Hand in Mine, The Late Breakfasters,* and *Painted Devils*.

Lee Brown Coye, best known in the fantasy field for his eccentric and grotesque illustrations for *Weird Tales* magazine and Arkham House books, died in September at age 74. Coye, whose work in a wide variety of media was displayed in the Whitney and Metropolitan museums of art, was twice awarded the World Fantasy Award for Best Artist. Another well-known fantasy artist, Wallace Wood, committed suicide in November, at the age of 54. Wood's distinctive style influenced a generation of comic artists brought up on his contributions to the science fiction comics, *Mad* magazine, and his own breakthrough magazine, *Witzend*.

Fantasy awards are beginning to proliferate much as the science fiction awards have. Each is associated with an annual convention, beginning in April with the Balrog Awards, presented at Fool-Con, held in 1981 in Overland Park, Kansas. Most of the awards are voted on by the convention's members, with an additional award given for lifetime contribution chosen by a panel of writers and artists. This year's awards included Best Novel: *The Wounded Land* by Stephen Donaldson; Best Collection/Anthology: *Unfinished Tales* by J. R. R. Tolkien, edited by Christopher Tolkien; Best Short Fiction: "The Web of the Magi" by Richard Cowper; and Best Poet: H. Warner Munn. The special award was presented jointly to Fritz Leiber and Jorge Luis Borges.

In July, Fantasycon VII was held in Birmingham, England. Guest of Honor at the convention was author Peter Tremayne; Special Artist Guest was Alan Hunter; and Karl Edward Wagner was Master of Ceremonies. The convention, described as "low-key and friendly," drew a good cross-section of British writers and fans. The British Fantasy Awards were presented for Best Novel: *To Wake the Dead* by Ramsey Campbell; Best Short Fiction: "Stains" by Robert Aickman; Best Small Press: *Airgedlamh,* edited by McFerran, Jones, and Sutton; Best Film: *The Empire*

Strikes Back; Best Artist: Dave Carson; and a Special Award to Stephen King for an outstanding contribution to the genre.

The World Fantasy Convention is held over Halloween weekend in a different location each year. Held in 1981 at the lovely Claremont Hotel in Berkeley, California, the convention drew its limit of 750 members, with a good showing from professional writers, editors, and artists, as well as plenty of fantasy fans. The tone of the convention was changed somewhat from previous years, with Guests of Honor Brian Froud and Peter S. Beagle contributing to a stronger emphasis on "high fantasy," in contrast to earlier years' focus on horror. Appearances from England by Michael Moorcock and M. John Harrison were pleasant surprises.

The 1981 World Fantasy Awards, chosen by a jury which changes annually, were presented by Toastmaster Karl Edward Wagner for Life Achievement: C. L. Moore; Best Novel: *The Shadow of the Torturer* by Gene Wolfe; Best Short Fiction: "The Ugly Chickens" by Howard Waldrop; Best Anthology: *Dark Forces,* edited by Kirby McCauley; Best Artist: Michael Whelan; Special Award (Professional): Donald A. Wollheim; Special Award (Nonprofessional): Pat Cadigan & Arnie Fenner, for *Shayol;* and a Special Convention Award was given to Gahan Wilson for his contributions to fantasy.

The 1982 World Fantasy Convention will be held October 29–31 at the Park Plaza in New Haven, Connecticut. Guests of Honor are Peter Straub, Joseph Payne Brennan, and Don Maitz. Inquiries should be sent to: P.O. Box 8262, East Hartford, CT 06018.

JEFF FRANE is a Contributing Editor to *Locus: The Newspaper of the Science Fiction Field,* and was co-chairman (with Jack Rems) of the 1981 World Fantasy Convention. Frane and Rems coedited *A Fantasy Reader.*

RECOMMENDED READING—1981

Terry Carr

Jim Aikin: "The Princess, the Fencing Master and the Unicorn." *Pandora 8.*

Ramsey Campbell: "Again." *The Twilight Zone*, November 1981.

John Cheever: "The Island." *The New Yorker*, April 27, 1981.

C. J. Cherryh: "A Thief in Korianth." *Flashing Swords! #5.*

Ronald Anthony Cross: "The Dolls: A Tragic Romance." *Berkley Showcase, Vol. 3.*

Jack Dann: "Fairy Tale." *Berkley Showcase, Vol. 4.*

Gardner Dozois, Jack Dann, and Michael Swanwick: "Touring." *Penthouse*, April 1981.

David Drake: "King Crocodile." *Whispers III.*

Diane Duane: "Parting Gift." *Flashing Swords! #5.*

Phyllis Eisenstein: "Point of Departure." *Whispers III.*

Parke Godwin: "Stroke of Mercy." *The Twilight Zone*, September 1981

Stephen King: "The Man Who Would Not Shake Hands." *Shadows 4.*

Ellen Kushner: "The Unicorn Masque." *Elsewhere.*

Thomas G. Lyman: "The Prayer Machine." *Weirdbook 15.*

Michael Moorcock: "Elric at the End of Time." *Elsewhere.*

Keith Roberts: "Kaeti's Nights." *Fantasy and Science Fiction*, October 1981.

Karl Edward Wagner: "The River of Night's Dreaming." *Whispers III.*

Evangeline Walton: "The Chinese Woman." *Weird Tales #3.*

Manly Wade Wellman: "Can These Bones Live?" *Sorcerer's Apprentice*, Summer 1981.

Kate Wilhelm: "With Thimbles, with Forks and Hope." *Isaac Asimov's Science Fiction Magazine*, November 23, 1981.

Chelsea Quinn Yarbro: "Art Songs." *A Fantasy Reader.*

Roger Zelazny: "Unicorn Variation." *Isaac Asimov's Science Fiction Magazine*, April 13, 1981.